THE
SHANGHAI FACTOR

CHARLES McCARRY served under deep cover as a
CIA operations officer in Europe, Asia and Africa.
He is the author of twelve previous novels, as well
as numerous works of non-fiction.

D0184056

THE
SHANGHAI
FACTOR

'Charles McCarry is better than John le Carré. Which makes him perhaps the best ever. And this is his first long-form fiction in years. Excited yet? You should be. *The Shanghai Factor* is hypnotic, engaging, subtle, and deeply, deeply satisfying.'

—*Lee Child*

'Charles McCarry has been compared to John le Carré – but maybe le Carré should be compared to McCarry. *The Shanghai Factor* is certainly the best-written spy thriller you will read this year. A perfect blend of sex, intrigue, exotic locales, and deadly danger.'

—*Nelson DeMille*

'Charles McCarry is a master of intelligent, literate spy fiction. And that is why I believe you will like, really like, *The Shanghai Factor*.'

—*Alan Furst*

'*The Shanghai Factor* is a brilliant espionage novel by the master of the form. It is also terrifying and astonishingly timely, dealing with the ominous threat of an undeclared – and victorious – Chinese cyberwar with the U.S.'

–Joseph Finder

'Only someone who has been a player can write about the Great Game of Espionage the way Charles McCarry does. In *The Shanghai Factor*, we are lured, page by page, paragraph by paragraph, into a fictional Heart of Darkness populated by a succubus straight out of the Gehenna of our nightmares. A great read by a master of the art and craft of espionage novels.'

–Robert Littell

'Charles McCarry, the reigning grand master of American spy thriller writers, delivers one of his best novels in years with *The Shanghai Factor*, a compelling page turner that propels its characters through McCarry's complex plot and reveals our real world of shadow powers better than most "factual" reporting. McCarry captures the hearts and minds of the mere mortals we call spies.'

–James Grady

THE
SHANGHAI
FACTOR
CHARLES McCARRY

A Mysterious Press Book
for Head of Zeus

First published in 2013 by Mysterious Press,
an imprint of Grove/Atlantic, New York

First published in hardback in the UK in 2013 by Head of Zeus Ltd.
The paperback edition published in the UK in 2014 by Head of Zeus Ltd.

9 7 5 3 1 2 4 6 8

A CIP catalogue record for this book is available
from the British Library.

Papeback ISBN: 9781781855119
eBook ISBN: 9781781855089

Printed and bound by CPI Group (UK) Ltd., Croydon CR0 4YY.

Head of Zeus Ltd
Clerkenwell House
45-47 Clerkenwell Green
London EC1R 0HT

www.headofzeus.com

For David Laux

How do I know this is true?
I look inside myself and see.

—Laozi

ONE

1

Those who keep an eye on me think I have a weakness for Chinese women. This is true as far as it goes, but it goes both ways. I am a hairy man, and certain East Asian women like that. My first Chinese girl called sex with me "sleeping with the chimpanzee." Her name was Mei, easy for a chimp to pronounce and remember. We met cute. One day, as I pedaled along Zhongshan Road, she crashed her bicycle into mine. In those days I was new to the life of a spy, so my paranoia wasn't yet fully developed, but I immediately suspected that this was no accident. My first thought was that Chinese counterintelligence had sniffed me out and sent this temptress to entrap me. Then I took a look at the temptress and wondered why I should mind. She was lying facedown, miniskirt awry, next to the wreckage of our two bikes—curtain of blue-black hair, slender legs the color of honey, snow-white virginal panties covering her round bottom. She was in pain—writhing, moaning, sucking in air through her teeth. I crouched beside her and in my stumbling Mandarin asked the usual stupid question. She turned her head and looked at me—starlet's face, unblinking dark eyes filled with tears. I asked the same question again, "Are you all right?" First she heard me, now she saw me. And smelled me. It was a hot, muggy day. I needed a haircut. I hadn't shaved. Chest hair tufted from the open neck of a shirt I had been wearing for three days. Her lips twisted, her eyes blazed. All expression drained from her face. She said nothing. I might as well have been attempting to communicate in American Sign Language. Then she sat up. Her face, her whole person radiating anger, as if I had pinched her in her sleep. Her eyes went cold. She shouted at me. At length. In Shanghai dialect. I understood almost nothing she said, but had no difficulty grasping her meaning. A little crowd gathered. They understood every word, and it made them laugh. When she stopped talking, the crowd drifted away.

The girl got to her feet. Her knees were scraped. She bled from an elbow. She cradled the wounded arm in her other arm, as if in a sling.

Taking great care with the tones, I attempted to say, "Please speak Mandarin so I can understand the insults."

Daggers. She kicked her bike—the front wheel was as bent out of shape as she was—and said, "Your fault."

I said, "You hit me."

"My machine is ruined. Look at the front wheel."

"That proves you hit me. If I had hit you, my bike would be the one with the broken wheel."

"You speak this language like you ride a bicycle. Ugly Chengdu accent. Was that clear enough for you to understand?"

"I think so."

"It thinks!" she said. "I think it had better give me some money for a new bike before I call the police. They'll be here any minute anyway, so hurry up."

"Good. The police will see who was at fault."

"Ha."

In the middle distance I saw a knot of witnesses leading a policeman to the scene of the crime. The girl saw them, too.

"Now you will find out about China," she said.

I didn't doubt that she was right. Getting mixed up with the police was the last thing I was supposed to let happen to me. I was in Shanghai to speak Chinese, not to get the cops interested in me.

I said, "I'll go with you to a bicycle shop and pay for the repairs. But no money."

"*New* bike."

The cop and the witnesses were getting closer. I said, "Let's talk about it on the way."

She smiled triumphantly, lips pressed together. "I ride. You carry my bike."

I picked up the wreckage. She vaulted onto the saddle of my machine, a four-thousand-dollar one bought on the expense account, as if she were leaving Lourdes after being cured by the patron saint of lady bicyclists. I watched her go—her legs and the rest of her, in motion now. She was even better to look at. Dutiful to my vocation, I wondered why would she wear a miniskirt and that skimpy top instead of jeans and long sleeves if she had planned this collision or had it planned for her? Paranoia 101, as taught to novices in a secret installation in Virginia, answered the question: precisely because her handlers knew that her tiny wounds, her lovely face, her shining hair, her sweet body, her sharp tongue, her crackling intelligence, would cause me to think with some other organ than my brain. It was obvious that this girl had been born knowing this.

Oh, she was wily. So were her handlers. Nevertheless—couldn't help it—I thought *poor kid* as she weaved her way through the river of bicycles. Her figure grew smaller and smaller as she pedaled faster and faster. She turned recklessly across traffic into a side street, leaning the bicycle within centimeters of the horizontal, sprocket, pedals and feet a blur. I kissed my bike good-bye. I thought I'd never see it or her again.

I was wrong. A short way down the side street, she waited in front of a bicycle shop. Band-Aids now covered her wounds. She must have had

5

them in her backpack just in case. Inside the shop, bicycles hung from the ceiling.

She pointed. "That one."

The proprietor got it down. It was the very best bicycle available in China, therefore in the world, he said, the only one of its kind in the store, and perhaps in all of Shanghai, since this model flew out of the shops and the manufacturer was in despair because he could not keep up with demand. He named the price. I flinched.

I still held her wrecked machine in my arms. I said, "Wait a minute. What we want is to have this one repaired."

"New bike," she said.

To the proprietor, I said, "How much to fix this bike?" He looked at me blankly but did not answer.

She said, "This man does not do repairs."

"Then we'll find someone who does."

The girl said something to the proprietor in Shanghainese. He went to the door of his shop and shouted. In seconds a very stern policeman appeared.

In English the girl said, "Shall I tell him you assaulted me?"

"And if you do?"

"Investigation."

I didn't reply. She studied my face and apparently saw what she had been hoping to see—profound anxiety. In Mandarin she said to the policeman, "This man is new to our country. He wants to know if this is a good bike."

"The best," the policeman said. "Very expensive. Worth the price."

He left without even asking for my passport. Another little thrill of suspicion ran through my mind. How did this policeman happen to be nearby? Why did he turn himself into a sales assistant? Where was his officiousness? The girl did not trouble to read my mind. She was bargaining with the proprietor. Or seemed to be. They were speaking

Shanghainese, a language I didn't understand. Long minutes passed. The volume rose. At last they stopped talking. Proudly the girl told me the staggering price she had negotiated—a month's pay for a rookie spook. Fortunately, I had just been to the money changer, so I had enough yuan in my pocket to pay the bill. I got out my wallet. She smiled happily, but at the bicycle, not me.

Outside, she said in Bostonian English, "What made you hire a teacher from Chengdu?"

"It was all Chinese to me. Where in the States did you go to school?"

"Concord-Carlisle High School, in Massachusetts."

"Exchange student?"

She nodded.

"Cheerleader?"

"Volleyball."

"College?"

"I came home for that."

"To which college?"

"Questions, questions. What are you, an American spy?"

She was watching my face. I asked her name. "Mei," she said, and in Mandarin asked if I could remember that. She asked my name. I provided an alias. It was a difficult name, Polish with many syllables and odd diphthongs, that belonged to a Hessian running back who played my position for my school while I sat out my senior year on the bench.

She said, "I'm supposed to take that seriously?"

"Why not? Are you some kind of racist?"

"Of course I am—I'm Han. We look down on everybody. I'll call you Dude. It suits you."

"We're going to be friends?"

"Up to you, Dude."

"Fine," I said. "Let's give it a try. One thing I insist upon. Never speak English to me again. You can have your way in everything else."

Apparently this was okay by her. She called me Dude for the next two years. I called her by the only name I knew, Mei. I never asked—never—what her real name might be. Who cared?

On the day of the bicycle wreck, I took her to lunch, then showed her where I lived. Later I took her dancing and, at her suggestion, to a rave where I was the only foreigner. We went for rides on our new bikes, picnicked in parks, found a group to join for morning calisthenics. Soon we were making love three times a night, twenty-six times a month, and sometimes, when the coast was clear, in the daytime. I was twenty-nine. She was five or six years younger, so we were both indefatigable. It was not part of her assignment, or in her nature, to love me. In that we were alike. In bed she was a comic. Everything about copulation, my simian body especially, struck her as funny, and laughter excited her almost as much as fur. She giggled during foreplay, guffawed with joy after her orgasms and made funny noises during them. When we were not going at it, she loved to talk about books and movies and television shows. So did I, so we had a lot to talk about. We watched television and went to the movies, sitting in different rows. She read to me in Mandarin and required me to do the same and get it right before we got into bed. She insisted that I make phone calls to numbers she provided—friends of hers, she said—on the theory that no one really understands a foreign language unless he can understand it over the telephone. For the same reason she taught me songs in Mandarin, and we sang them to each other. Many laughs about my mistakes at first, but my Mandarin improved as my ear quickened in a hopeless attempt to keep up with her. I even learned to flounder around in Shanghainese, a Wu language that is incomprehensible to speakers of most other Chinese tongues.

I was sure from the start that she was on duty, that she reported everything, that she had bugged my room. The funny thing was, she never asked for information, never probed. She showed no curiosity about my family, my education, my politics, my first love, or the girls I had slept with in high school and college and afterward. Probably this was because she had been briefed about these matters by the folks at Guoanbu, the Chinese intelligence service (within Headquarters called "MSS," short for Ministry of State Security) and had no reason to ask. I never questioned her, either. She dressed well, she glowed with health, she had money, she disappeared in the daylight hours, so presumably she had a job or another lover. She explained nothing, never mentioned her primary life, not a single detail, though I did learn that she had gone to Shanghai University, where I was auditing a couple of courses, when I ran into someone who knew her and this person seemed to know about us. Just another inscrutable encounter. I didn't bother to be suspicious. Either Mei was an agent or she was a lunatic. If the former, we were both on duty. If the latter, the benefits were terrific. Besides, I was fulfilling my mission. I had been sent to China to learn to talk like a native, and I was certainly making progress with that. Mei insisted on living entirely in the here and now. That was okay by me. In time we got to know each other very well indeed.

The learning process was wonderful. Liberating. I had never before lived in the total absence of emotional clutter, let alone complete sexual gratification. Nor had I ever imagined it was possible to know a woman this well while knowing next to nothing about her, or that the key to such hidden knowledge was to know nothing about her except what the five senses told you. I wondered if any other American boy, living or dead, had ever been so fortunate. If I did not love Mei, I liked the hell out of her, and I was as mesmerized by her smooth, perfect body as she seemed to be by my Paleolithic one. I certainly did not even want to think about saying good-bye to her and going back to the land of the crazy women.

2

While in Shanghai I was, in the jargon, a sleeper, meaning that I was supposed to wait for instructions, lead a transparent, predictable life, and do nothing that would call attention to myself—such as messing around with a girl like Mei, or buying her a bicycle with a thousand dollars of the taxpayers' money, or getting hammered with strangers at parties where everyone except me was Chinese. I had no contact with anyone in the local base of U.S. intelligence and didn't even know for sure if such an office existed. I hardly ever talked to a Caucasian, though I was accosted by many. I was under orders to avoid Americans, but they were everywhere, and could never discipline themselves to just walk on by when they saw what they thought was a fellow countryman. "You *American*?" Then came the standard student center quiz. It was no different in this exotic place than it had been back home—where was I from, where had I gone to college, how liberal was I? What was my major, did I hate my parents ("You *don't*? Wow!"), was I, um, straight or gay, where did I live, what was my phone number, my favorite band, movie, song, author, microbrew? As Mei and my training had taught me, I provided no answers, asked no questions in return. At first

I pretended to be a Canadian, anti-American to the bone and proud of it. This worked too well. Most American expatriates detested the U.S.A., too, so my progressive gibberish made them want to strike up a friendship. I learned to say I had to run—that cheap Chinese food!

My only American friend was a fellow who went by the fictitious name of Tom Simpson, a nobody like me who worked in Headquarters. Once a month he and I exchanged e-mails. Simpson seemed to have nothing better to do than keep up our correspondence, and it was easy to see he put a lot of work into his messages. Probably he wanted to be a writer when he retired thirty years down the line. Many spies are aspiring novelists, and Headquarters values a way with words above almost everything else. Partly because he was so eager to do well at something that did not matter, I supposed Simpson was low man on the China desk. As time went by, we developed an old drinking buddy joviality, and the correspondence was a pleasure in its way. More important, it told me I had not been forgotten, though someone smarter than me might have hoped for the opposite. The idea—I should say the hope—at Headquarters was that Guoanbu's hackers would read my mail and conclude that I was just another American clod they could safely ignore, maybe for the rest of my life. This is called building cover. In fact it is giddy optimism. Like much else in the practice of espionage, it is built on hope, denial of reality, wishful thinking, ignorance, the tendency to look upon insignificant results as important outcomes, and the Panglossian belief that those who spy by the rules don't get caught.

Needless to say I told Simpson only the barest details where Mei was concerned—the accident, the new bike as an expense account item, that was it. Even to a babe in the woods like me, it was obvious that discovery of my indiscretions would not be good for my career. Yet somehow, the folks back home got wind of Mei. Maybe one of those Budweiser guys I met at the wild Chinese parties Mei dragged me to knew someone I didn't know—such as a case officer from the local Headquarters outpost. It was

Simpson who clued me in. He and I seeded our e-mails with code phrases we called wild cards. "Horny as hell," for example, meant that everything was just fine. "Pain in the ass" meant get me out of here fast. In theory I had committed all these phrases and their real meanings to memory, but even when you're not trying to learn Mandarin, the brain in its infinite playfulness will, as we all know, move memories from one part of the frontal lobe to another. Therefore when I read the words "It's raining possums and rednecks in the Old Dominion" in a message from Tom, I drew a blank. I knew it was a wild card because such phrases were always signaled by a semicolon in the preceding sentence. That archaic punctuation mark was never otherwise used in our correspondence. Of course that made the code easier to spot if you were a snoop, but if you didn't know what the following wild card meant, you couldn't figure it out. It was undecipherable because it wasn't a cipher. Or so the catechism insisted.

Mei arrived moments after I received Simpson's e-mail—a happy coincidence, since what followed for the next two or three hours cleared my mind like nothing and nobody else could do. Mei liked foreplay games. Usually these consisted of a feat of Mandarin recitation performed by myself (with my eyes closed) while Mei messed around. No penetration allowed until my feat of memory was perfectly executed, though unlimited cock teasing was okay under the rules, and that's what Mei liked about the game. A couple of days earlier, she had given me these lines, composed around 200 B.C. by the poet and statesman Qu Yuan:

廣開兮天門　紛吾乘兮玄雲
令飄風兮先驅　使涷雨兮灑塵

In English, the poem, called "Da Si Ming," reads something like this:

Open wide the door of heaven!
On a black cloud I ride in splendor

Bidding the whirlwind drive before me,
Causing the rainstorm to lay dust.

It reads better in the original language. I had memorized these lines as ordered, suffering the usual flashes of agony, and now, while Mei rubbed her unclothed body and fingertips against my Esau-like pelt, I recited it in Mandarin. "Flawless!" Mei said. "You're getting too good. Make mistakes so we can go slower!" I said that rules were rules. Midway through the third act of our daily scenario, my mind awakened and I remembered that "raining possums and rednecks" meant that I was summoned to a meeting with someone from inside the apparatus, and "Old Dominion" meant that Headquarters had reason to believe that I was under surveillance. Of course it did. I had reported this to Tom Simpson weeks before. Instructions would follow.

"Shit," I said.

Between outcries, Mei said, "Speak Mandarin."

Tom's e-mail had told me nothing I didn't already know. I had noticed that I was being watched months before, or soon after the surveillance began. I assumed it was routine, not worth reporting, because I had been forewarned that Chinese eyes would be watching me as a matter of course. I had been told to keep my tradecraft sharp by exercising its rules at all times, so I did what I could to be the Mr. Goodspy I was being paid to be. I studied faces in the crowd in case I ever saw one of them again. This might seem like a hopeless undertaking in China, but in fact the Chinese look no more alike—and no more unalike—than any other people with the exception of Americans, whose five centuries of interbreeding has produced an almost infinite number of countenances. The French, for example, have eight or nine faces to go around, the Germans, the Italians, the Indians, and the Arabs roughly the same number. The Han have only a few more than that. There are subtle variations, of course, but in order to remember a face you have only to recognize its category and remember a variation or two in order to know whether you are looking at a person you have seen before.

It was soon after Mei and I got together that I noticed men and women whose faces I soon began to recognize had taken up positions outside my apartment building. There were twelve of them who worked two-hour shifts as three-person teams. The group watching me was composed of professionals. Seldom did I see the same three faces on the same team, and when they followed me, or followed Mei and me when we were together, the faces changed as they were replaced every block or two by folks from the other two teams. Like almost everyone else in Shanghai, they talked nonstop on cell phones, presumably to each other or a controller. As I was not engaged in espionage and had nothing to hide except a Han girlfriend who had little interest in hiding, I did not mention the surveillance to Mei and she did not remark on it, though it's hard to believe that anyone as wide-awake as she was could have failed to notice. If she wasn't worried, I supposed I had nothing to fear. It was fun in its way.

Headquarters took it more seriously. I heard from Tom again within the week. He told me that the Cardinals were burning up the National League central division, and were in first place with a 7.5-game lead. This hand of wild cards decoded as an instruction to meet a Headquarters man ("first place") who wore a red necktie ("burning") at noon (7 + 5 = 12) on Wednesday next ("central division") at the bar of the Marriott Hotel ("National League") and to use a certain recognition phrase ("game.")

I was followed to the rendezvous as usual, but as far as I could see, no one followed me inside the hotel. At 12:17 P.M. on Wednesday, seventeen minutes after the meeting time dictated by the wild card, a man in a wrinkled blue blazer and a red necktie approached me in the bar of the designated hotel. He was fortyish, tall, skinny, balding, bespectacled, unsmiling. He wore a Joe Stalin mustache.

He said, "Ever been to Katmandu?"

"Not yet," I said. "But I'm hoping to get there someday."

That nonsensical exchange was the recognition code I had been told to use in case of a clandestine meeting with one of our people. The stranger shook hands with me, pressing a fingernail into my wrist. If this too was part of the ritual, nobody had forewarned me, but I responded by squeezing his hand until I saw pain in his eyes. He let go. Dead eyes. The bartender approached. I had already drunk my Coke. The stranger waved him away and said, "Follow me. Don't walk with me. *Follow* me."

He was a fast walker, so I did follow him as he led me through jammed back streets that smelled of sweat and bad breath and rang with shouts to get out of the way. At last we came to a restaurant and went inside. It was almost as noisy and crowded as the streets. He was well known to the host and the waiters, who greeted him with happy grins and bursts of Shanghainese. I was a little shocked by this reception because in my newborn way, I had the idea that seasoned operatives kept themselves to themselves and faithfully practiced tradecraft at all times. For all I knew, that was exactly what this guy thought he was doing.

When we were alone, I said, "What do I call you?"

"Try Steve."

"I'm—"

"Nameless."

The host showed us to a table. He hovered for quite a long time while a smiling Steve bantered with him, ordering lunch for both of us. His mood changed as soon as the fellow departed. He looked me over with his unwavering lifeless eyes, which were slightly magnified by the lenses of his glasses. Beer was brought, then an appetizer. The food was very good. Figuring that Steve didn't care whether I was enjoying my lunch, I didn't bother to comment. Nor did I ask any questions or otherwise say a word. It was obvious that Steve was not happy to be wasting his time on an *Üntermensch* like me. Skinny or not, he was an industrious eater, and when the host came by after each course to ask how he had liked it, Steve reverted to his jollier self, smiling through his mustache. He spoke not a word to me.

At last we came to the end of the meal. I expected that we would now retire to a soundproof room hidden inside a safe house and have a serious talk, but instead, Steve decided to have the discussion right where we were. He had a really loud voice, the ear-splitting kind you hear bellowing at the umpire at baseball games. He talked freely, as if we were indeed in an unbuggable bubble in the basement of an American embassy. The adjoining tables were inches away. This didn't really matter, since everyone else was shouting, too, and maybe because the adage that no one eavesdrops on a loudmouth but strains to hear a whisperer applied in this place. The restaurant was ostentatiously humble but in truth it was upscale, full of sleek, expensively dressed Han who almost certainly went to college in the United States and spoke excellent English.

He said, "So you think you're being watched."

"You could say that."

"It's your job to say it, kid. Yes or no?"

"Yes."

"Why?" He spoke with his mouth full.

"Because I see the same twelve faces every time I go out."

"*Twelve?*"

"Four rotating teams of three."

"Wow. You can remember twelve Chinese faces? Describe them."

I did as he asked. He went back to his fish, all the while staring at me out of that mask. Flecks of carp had lodged in his mustache.

This man was an ass, or for some reason wanted me to think that he was an ass. His behavior, I knew, was meant to discomfit, to intimidate, to gain the upper hand. I had learned about the technique at training camp from a teacher of interrogation and agent-handling methods who took these tricks as seriously as Steve seemed to do. The instructor believed it was a good idea on first contact to let the agent think he was smarter than his case officer. This made it easier to manipulate the agent. I wanted to get out of there, to get myself fired, to go back to Mei. I could teach English like the other Americans did. I was tempted to throw some money disdainfully on the table as my share of the bill and leave with dignity. But even then, green as I was, I had more sense than that. Why would Mei be interested in an English teacher? And even if she was interested, she would be lost to me because her handlers would certainly assign her to another, more productive case.

Finally Steve spoke. "I am instructed to ask you a question and give you a message," he said. "The question is, Why do you think your dirty dozen are watching *you*?"

"Who else would they be watching?"

"Very good question," he said. "You should think about it, turn it over in your mind, see if there's anyone in your life who's more interesting than you."

I said, "I'll work on that."

Steve ignored me. I took this as permission to speak. I said, "If that's the question, what's the message?"

"Good news," he said. "CI is interested in you."

He waited—intent, almost smiling—for my reaction. I probably blanched. *CI?* Counterintelligence was interested in me? My bravado wavered. CI was Headquarters's bad dream. Its job was to know everything about everybody. However, nobody was allowed to know anything about it, including its methods and its success rate. Night and day, in peace and war, the men and women of the counterintelligence division were on the lookout not only for enemy spies, but also for traitors, for sleepers, for the inexplicably nervous, for spendthrifts who couldn't explain where their money came from. They tailed guys who chase women, women who sleep around, homosexuals, neurotic virgins. Their job was to finger the bad guy inside every good guy and banish the sinner to outer darkness. For CI, no holds were barred, no one was above suspicion except themselves, and nobody had the power to do unto them as they did unto others.

Now Steve was letting me know these demons were after me. Was it because I had committed fornication? Or was it something I had omitted to do? I was unlikely to find out tonight. Steve continued to hold me in his contemptuous gaze.

I said, "Gee, that's interesting. Did they tell you why they're interested in some Insignificant McNobody like me?"

"Interested in some what?" Steve said.

"A joke. Forget it."

"You think this is a joke?"

"No, but you're making me nervous. When I'm nervous I make jokes." I thought I owed him that much obsequiousness.

"You should try to overcome that," Steve said. "Answer the original question. Why do you think it's you who's being surveilled?"

"I thought I'd already explained that. Because these people follow me wherever I go."

"You haven't gotten beyond that simple explanation?"

"I guess not. What's the complex explanation?"

"You've got a girl, right?"

"Yes."

"Name?"

"Mei."

"Mei what, or I guess I should say What Mei. I want her full name, or the name she said was her name."

"I don't know."

"You don't know. Have you asked?"

"That's not the way we work. We ask each other no questions."

"She doesn't know your name either?"

"Unless she's a Guoanbu asset on assignment, no."

"How did you meet?"

"She crashed her bike into mine."

"How long ago?"

"Months."

"You saw no need to report this?"

"I reported the accident to my pen pal and submitted an expense account item for the new bike I bought her."

"How much?"

"About a thousand, U.S."

Steve whistled. "But not a word since?"

"No."

"You really are something, kid. No wonder CI is interested in you."

He was sneering. The temptation to make things worse was great, but I resisted it. No response from Steve, but I was used to that by now. The silence was heavy, Steve's manner was disdainful, and Steve such a shit that summary dismissal from the service did not seem to be an unlikely next move.

I said, "So what now?"

"Carry on," Steve said. "Change nothing. Be your usual harmless self. But be careful, my friend. You've got yourself into something you may not be able to get yourself out of."

"And let me guess. I'll get no help."

He pointed a forefinger. "You got it. Lucky you."

He called for the check, paid it with a big tip, kidded around with the host. Then he stood up as if to go. I stood up too. I was taller than Steve, and angrier.

I said, "Is that the message you said you were instructed to give me?"

"No, that was just me taking pity," Steve said. "The message is, you may be traveling soon. Your pen pal will provide the details."

And then he walked out.

3

I had cycled to my meeting with Steve and when I emerged from the hotel garage, wheeling my bike, there they were, well back in the crowd, two men and a woman, ready to leap into the saddle. It was five or six kilometers from the hotel to my place, so they switched riders every click or so. In their clockwork way they always did this just as I turned a corner and they were out of sight for the moment. Then they would pop up again in my mirrors. The bikes were always the same, so a keen-eyed operative like myself was able to keep track of the familiar faces in my wake. Taking advantage of Steve's expert advice to just be my dim-witted fictitious self, I made no attempt to shake them.

It was almost dark when I reached my building. I was warmed by the thought that Mei would soon be home. It had been a hot day. I was sweaty but Mei liked me that way, or so she said—every once in a while she took one of my smelly T-shirts home with her as a nightgown—so I decided not take a shower. She usually arrived at about seven for my Mandarin lesson, and then we would have supper and a couple of beers, and then Mei would test my Mandarin again, and tonight we would watch a DVD of *Destry Rides Again* I had bought on the street because, as I planned to tell her, no one can understand U.S. English properly unless she can unscramble the lyrics when Marlene Dietrich sings "See What the Boys in the Backroom Will Have." That was the routine. I liked everything about it. I liked everything about the life that Mei and I were living—even the tiny pre-Mao apartment I had rented as an element of my cover as a poor, feckless if somewhat overage student. The walls bulged, the concrete floor had waves in it so that the furniture tipped, the sputtering plumbing had air pockets, the electricity came and went.

Waiting for Mei, listening to Ella Fitzgerald sing the blues, I fell asleep. I woke at nine. No Mei. This was a disappointment, but I felt no stab of panic. Sometimes, as when her period started or she had an impulse to skip me for a night, she just didn't show up. I had no phone number for her, no address, no true name, no hope of finding her in a city of twenty-three million in which maybe a million of the females were named Mei and the Mei I knew was almost certainly not named Mei. I waited another hour, spent repeating my memorization for the day (a passage from Laozi's *Daodejing*) into a recorder. By now I was hungry. Because I had no refrigerator, Mei always brought supper with her, collecting exactly my half of the cost before we ate, and since I had eaten the leftovers for breakfast, there was no food in the house. I decided to go out. It would serve Mei right if she arrived and found me gone, though I fervently hoped she'd hang around until I got back.

The night was almost as suffocating as the day had been. Chemical odors, so strong that you could almost see their colors, wafted on a sluggish breeze. The endless waves of humanity rolled by more slowly than usual. On this night they looked a little different, smelled a little different, as if wilted after a day in the glare of the sun. Something else was different—there were no familiar faces. I searched the crowd to make sure I had not missed them. They just weren't there. Why? My watchers had been with me earlier in the day. They had never before deserted me. Had they decided I wasn't going anywhere tonight, and gone home? Had they been replaced by a new bunch whose faces I would have to learn? Were they shadowing Steve? I felt a certain unease. Breath gathered in my lungs. Life as a spook under cover in a hostile country is nagged by the fear that the other side knows something you don't know and cannot possibly know no matter how well you speak the language or how much at home you tell yourself you feel. You are an intruder. You can never be a fish swimming in their sea, you are always the pasty-white legs and arms thrashing on the surface with a tiny unheeded cut on your finger. Meanwhile the shark swims toward the scent of blood from miles away. At any moment you can be pulled under, eaten, digested, excreted, eaten by something else and then something else again until there is nothing left of the original you except a single cell suspended in the heaving darkness.

Oh so melancholy, and no Mei to laugh at me. However, the fact remained that I was hungry, so I set off into the night and walked, only half conscious of where I was going, until I found myself in front of a noodle place Mei and I liked. She called it the Dirty Shirt after the proprietor's soup-stained singlet. I ordered a bowl of noodles and slurped them down. One doesn't savor fast food in China, where everyone except the Westernized elite, seldom seen in this neighborhood, takes care of bodily needs as unceremoniously as possible and gets right back to business. I paid and left and went into another place a few blocks away and gulped a tepid beer. Still no sign of my watchers. When I emerged I saw a face or two I might or might not have seen earlier. I memorized these possibles and decided to take a longer walk to see if they were still with me when I got to where I was going. My plan was to travel in a circle that would bring me back to my building in about an hour. Because there was little elbow room on the street, I had to travel at the same speed as the shouting, spitting multitude in which I was embedded. Nor was there much chance of using shop windows as rear-view mirrors because there were few shop windows and most of them were dark. Now and then I crossed the street so I could look behind me, and sometimes I thought, though I did not really trust my eyes, that I spotted one of the suspects passing through the glow spilling out the door of the open door of an all-night shop. The street lighting on main arteries in this part of Shanghai was dim, and even dimmer in the side streets, which appeared as mere slits of darkness between the gimcrack buildings. I gave them a wide berth. The Chinese plunged into them as if they were wearing miner's caps.

I was almost home when they—whoever they were—made the move. Two men in front of me slowed their pace, the two on either side moved in and seized my arms. They were big fellows for Chinese, not as tall as me but solid meat. There were four of them until suddenly, as I stepped back, thinking to make a break for it, I realized they were six as the two behind me moved heavily against me. I felt a mild sting in the vicinity of my right kidney, then the heat of an injection. I lurched as if trying to break free. The phalanx squeezed in tighter. I might as well have been nailed in a box and there was as little point in shouting for help as if I really were in a coffin. I began to feel faint as the injection took effect. Would it kill me? It seemed possible. I was losing my senses one by one—first to go was touch, then hearing, then sight, and finally taste as my tongue and lips went numb. I could still smell. *How odd,* I thought in the instant before I lost contact with my brain. In Afghanistan, *the last time I thought I was dead, everything stopped at once.* I had never imagined that there might be more than one way to cease to exist.

I smelled cigarette smoke. But I was still in darkness, still in silence, still blind. I felt motion, bumps, mild pain as my kidneys jounced. I began to hear—a whining motor, the sound of the bumps coming quickly one after the other, as if water were slapping the bottom of a boat. I was lying on my back. I was conscious but not really awake.

Opening my eyes I saw darkness, spotted with moving green lights and red lights, and the stronger glow of small white lights. Finally I smelled water—foul water. I *was* on a boat, the boat was moving, I saw stronger lights sprinkled along the shore, heard tinny faraway music and knew the boat was on the Yangtze. Otherwise my mind slept on. I tried to look at my watch and discovered that my hands were bound. Also my feet. If I was taking inventory in this way I must be alive. I wasn't sure.

In Shanghainese someone with a tenor voice said, "He's awake." The tone, somewhere between *la* and *ti* on the diatonic scale, surprised me—a deeper, gruffer timbre would have suited the situation better. Somebody kicked me in the ribs, not really hard but hard enough to make me grunt. This person bent over me and opened my eyes with his fingers. I smelled his breath, cabbage and tofu. My clothes were wet. They smelled of filth. I wanted to urinate—proof positive that I lived.

In American English the tenor said, "Are you awake?"

I wasn't sure I could speak, so I didn't try to answer. My eyes remained open. He said, "*Wide*-awake?"

He and another man stood me on my feet. I fought to keep my knees from buckling but did not succeed. The tenor said, "Oops-a-daisy," and tightened his grip. I staggered toward the gunwale. They understood I wasn't trying to escape and helped me. I vomited over the side. Now that I was fully conscious the water smelled even worse. In the thin light of the stern lantern I saw or hallucinated drowned rats and other nasty things churned up by the prop. The Yangtze smelled like something that had been dead for a long time.

The tenor held a bottle of *maotai* to my lips. I took a sip, then spit it out. He said, "Better now?" His voice was pleasant, his manner easy. There was just enough light to identify him by race (Han), but not enough to make out his features. He sounded like he had grown up in Southern California. His family must have been in Orange County a long time if nineteenth-century baby talk like oops-a-daisy came to him so naturally. The boat bucked. I staggered. The tenor grabbed my arm and steadied me. No special effort was made to restrain me. There was no need. The only move possible for me was to topple overboard into this running sewer with my wrists and ankles chained together.

The tenor put the cork back in the *maotai* bottle and handed it to the other man. Then he said, "You're pretty relaxed. That speaks well for you, given the circumstances."

"Thanks." My voice stuck in my throat.

"No problem."

I gagged, turned my head, hawked, spat. The tenor waited politely for me to finish.

He said, "Can you swim?"

"Yes."

"Good," the tenor said. "Before we go any farther, I want to give you a heads-up. In a few minutes something is going to happen. It will not be enjoyable. However, nobody is going to shoot you or stab you or strangle you or hit you on the head with an ax. You will be given an opportunity to save your own life. That's it. The idea is to teach you a lesson, nothing more."

The tenor's tone was reasonable, sympathetic even, like a friendly hand laid on the shoulder of someone less fortunate than he. He seemed to want me to understand that he was not personally responsible for whatever he was going to do to me next. I wondered what I had done to deserve Steve and this guy in a single twenty-four-hour period, but here I was.

I said, "May I ask a question?"

"I probably won't know the answer. But go ahead."

"Are you sure you've got the right man?"

He spelled my full name and recited my Social Security number. "Is that you?"

I didn't say no. I did say, "Another question—two, actually. What have I done and who have I done it to?"

"I have no idea. Everyone says you're smart, so it shouldn't be hard for you to figure it out."

"Who's 'everyone'?"

"I have no idea."

I said, "Where are we?"

"On the river."

"Yes, but where on the river?"

"Upstream."

"How far upstream?"

"We've been under way for maybe an hour," the tenor said. "Time to get you out of that rig."

He knelt and swiftly unlocked the shackles on my ankles. "Now the wrists," he said. "Please don't do anything foolish."

Doing something foolish was exactly what I had in mind. There were only two of them, and by now I had most of my strength back. I thought I had a chance to fight my way out of this situation. Then the tenor raised his voice and said something in a dialect I did not understand. The other four fellows suddenly appeared. Apparently they had been relaxing belowdecks. That explained the cigarette smoke. Two of them grasped my arms, two more my legs, and the fifth grabbed me around the waist.

Then, as if they were one creature with ten arms and a single brain, they lifted me above their heads, grunted in unison like the acrobats they were, and threw me overboard.

4

The Yangtze was the temperature of body fluids. It was full of dead things and other foul matter. It moved swiftly, it seized me and pulled me under. If, as the tenor had said, this was an opportunity to save my own life, I was in trouble. I am a good swimmer for a man with heavy bones, but as I sank I realized that swimming had little to do with what was happening to me. I kicked, I clawed the soup of turds and piss and the hundreds of condoms that fluttered in the current like schools of albino worms. I willed myself to rise to the surface as I had done hundreds of times before, but I was being pulled down, as if something alive had hold of my foot. I was drowning. I knew this, my eyes stung, I saw nothing but darkness. The acrobats had taken me so completely by surprise that I hadn't had time to take a full breath before I hit the water, and I knew that I would not be able to hold that tiny gulp of oxygen in my lungs long enough to find my way to air. I was dying. Again. Clearly it was my destiny to do that over and over, but there had to be a last time and surely this must be it. I was not frightened. I took this notion as a good sign. Crazily I thought, *Fright is part of the survival instinct. It means you still think you can live, that at the last minute some immortal hand or eye will get you out of this.* But I was damned if I would die just because some nameless son of a bitch had decided I should. I swam harder, counting the strokes like I used to count the steps when I ran the football. Breath leaked from my nose, I could not see the bubbles but I felt them leave my body and knew I could not stop the rest from escaping, too.

My head broke surface. Something hard and heavy struck me on the skull. Seeing stars, I reached for it and grabbed hold and hugged it. In the darkness I could tell it was a metal sphere about the size of a medicine ball. I knocked on it. It was hollow, it rang. A container, a mine, a clever Oriental safe full of money or ancient texts? I wondered if my scalp was bleeding, but I was too wet and slimy to tell. I considered the consequences of an open wound in this world of microbes. My sight cleared. There was no moon, there was never a moon over Shanghai. All around me I saw feeble green and red and yellowish white boat lights. It was too dark to see the boats. On one of them the tenor and the acrobats were looking for a man overboard. I tried to put the sphere between me and everything upstream but the sphere was spinning, so I knew I was popping into view every few seconds like a mechanical figure on a steeple clock. There were more lights along the riverbanks now and more switched on in the windows of a wilderness of identical slablike apartment buildings. Using the second hand of the Rolex skin diver's wristwatch I inherited from my father after he shot himself, I estimated that the Yangtze was flowing at about twelve miles an hour. It was five-twenty. I should be in Shanghai proper around six. A splinter of light appeared along the eastern horizon. A slice of the sun followed it, coloring the blanket of smoke and poisonous fumes that overhung the city. A dead baby, white and bloated and wide-eyed, floated by, then something that might have been another. The sun, a misshapen parody of itself, strengthened. Its cantaloupe rays crept across the river. The water shone dully like the rainbow in an oil slick.

In the distance I could see the glittering towers of downtown. A little wind came up. My sphere had been floating in midstream, but now it drifted closer to shore. Up ahead I saw the great Yangtze Bridge. I was as close to dry land as I was likely to get. I let go of the sphere and trod water. I started to swim. Three strokes facedown in this cesspool were all I could manage, so I turned over and backstroked to shore. Several men were fishing near my landing point. Like time travelers from the coolie past they wore big straw pancake hats. Half a dozen plump fish quivered on the mud, slapping their tails as they suffocated. The fishermen gave me barely a glance as I staggered by, vomiting as I went: just another crazy foreigner.

When I got home, I found Mei in bed. She lay on her back, covered to her waist by a sheet, pretty breasts visible, childlike feet with red toe-nails sticking out below. She seemed to be sound asleep but as I tiptoed toward the bathroom she said, "Why do you smell like that?"

I said, "I fell into the river."

Her face was sleepy. "Ah," she said. "Better take a bath." Catching my full scent, she made a throaty sound of disgust. "Take *two* baths."

In the tiny bathroom I emptied my pockets of money and passport and keys, took off my clothes and shoes, rolled them into a ball, and threw them out the window. The hot water, all ten liters of it, lasted long enough to rinse away some of the oily filth that clung to my skin. Then, shivering, I soaped and rinsed, soaped and rinsed again and again and again, washed between my toes and inside every orifice just as many times, and kept on until the pipes shuddered and the water lessened to a rusty trickle. When I went back into the bedroom Mei awaited me, a bottle of alcohol in her hands.

"Lie down," she said. She rubbed every square centimeter of my body except the male parts, which I protected with cupped hands. As she worked she asked no questions, made no jokes. There was no accusative female "Where have you really been all night?", no jocular "Did you enjoy your swim?" She asked for no explanations whatsoever. She did ask if I had memorized today's material, 春日醉起言志 ("Waking from Drunkenness on a Spring Day"), by the Tang dynasty poet Li Bai, who drowned when he tried to kiss his own image in a moonlit river. I told her I had not got around to it. "Then we can't have our lesson," said Mei. "Go to sleep."

She got dressed and left. No word, no kiss, no smile, no scent except for the alcohol fumes that filled the room. Perhaps I am inventing memories, but it seems to me now that I sensed at that moment that something was unfixably wrong, that things were no longer as they had been, that the Mei I knew was going to change into another Mei, perhaps even the real Mei whom I had never known, that she had a new secret, that she was going to put an end to something, perhaps to everything, that she was wrapped in melancholy. So was I.

Why then, you may wonder, did I not ask her a single question, if only a simple "what's wrong?" or "what's going on?" Why didn't we fight, scream, threaten, accuse, demand explanations? Why didn't we do something instead of pretending that nothing was happening?

Well, Mei was Mei, whoever Mei really was or whoever she was about to become. And my mind was elsewhere. As soon as she was out the door I e-mailed Tom Simpson, no easy matter because there were no wild cards that described my night on the Yangtze. Evidently I came close enough, because Tom told me by return e-mail to get out of China the next day on a certain Delta flight, and to take nothing with me but my passport and the clothes I stood up in.

That evening, to my surprise, Mei arrived on time and brought a better dinner than usual and a bottle of cheap truly awful Chinese chardonnay that we drank warm. I recited Li Bai's poem—I had had all day to memorize it—and the foreplay went as usual. Afterward as she lay on top of me I told her I was going away for a while. That I was leaving the next day. Her body clenched. She rolled off me. I saw something in her eyes I had not seen before. To my surprise, she asked questions— peppered me with them. All of a sudden she burned with curiosity. I had never seen her like this, never known she could be like this.

Where was I going? why was I going? when would I return?

I answered with the truth—America, business, I didn't know.

What kind of business?

Family business.

Was I meeting someone I knew?

Yes, but it was a business trip. No doubt I'd be introduced to strangers.

She turned over on her face, covered herself scalp to toes with the sheet. I went into the bathroom to get a glass of water.

"One more question," Mei called out from the other room. "Exactly how much does this person you're going to meet weigh?"

In my delight on hearing Mei, who never asked questions, ask such a question, I wanted to laugh. Instead I pretended not to hear her. I sensed, rather than saw, that she was putting on her clothes. Because she wore only three garments—skirt, T-shirt, underpants, plus sandals, this took only seconds. When I came back, she was gone.

5

At Dulles International Airport I was met by a pale freckled young redhead. She wore a wedding band on the wrong finger of her left hand. Pointing to herself with that hand, she said, "Me friend. Welcome home. Good flight?" I said, "Dehydrating. A little bumpy over Alaska."

Sotto voce, as if we were down the rabbit hole, the redhead said, "I'm Sally. Follow me."

In the parking lot we piled into a cluttered old Mazda. The load of soda cans and coffee containers and McDonald's and Popeye's boxes and CDs and old newspapers in back shifted and tumbled every time Sally turned a corner or stepped on the brakes. She dropped me off in front of a brick row house on a cul-de-sac just off Spout Run, in Arlington. "Same recognition phrase," she said.

I climbed the steep stairs and rang the bell. The door, gleaming with brass and varnish, opened before the chimes stopped ringing and I was greeted by a rotund, bespectacled Chinese who wore the regulation meritocrat chinos, tennis shirt, blazer, and Docksiders. No socks. He was a little guy, a foot or so shorter than me, and he had to lean back to get a look at my face. I waited for the magic words Sally had told me to expect, but instead of speaking them he let loose a torrent of Mandarin. I answered, briefly, in the same tongue. In the flat English of the Ohio-born he said, "Please repeat in Mandarin what I just said to you." I did so as best I could remember. He said, "That takes care of that. But we've got to go through the motions. Come on in and we'll talk some more. Then you'll meet Mr. Polly."

Apparently this fellow did not bother with cover names, because he neither offered me one nor asked me to supply one. We sat down at the tiny kitchen table. I had the impression that we were alone. The house smelled like a safe house—dusty, untended, empty. Quiet. You could hear the whoosh of traffic on Spout Run, but little else. It was one o'clock in the afternoon. The doorbell rang again. He went to the door and came back with a pizza box. He opened the box. Peppers, mushrooms, black olives. "You hungry?" I nodded. For the next couple of hours, we conversed in Mandarin, the level of difficulty rising as the minutes passed. He spoke the language beautifully. At last he looked at his watch and said, "Almost time for Mr. Polly. Let's knock it off." Obviously this chat had been some sort of test. I asked him how it had gone. "You get an A," he said. "Heavy Shanghai accent, though. But you have an ear, so it'll go away if you hang out with a different crowd." He picked up the pizza box and took it and its fingerprints and traces of DNA with him as he left without saying good-bye.

"Mr. Polly" turned out to be a homophone, a polygraph operator carrying his magic machine, an Apple laptop. He went through the whole rigmarole of recognition phrase, phony name ("Ed"), all the while sema-phoring that he knew things I could never know. He wore a necktie on a Saturday, along with a glen plaid suit that didn't fit around the neck or shoulders and was too tight across the stomach. He sent me into the next room while he set up his apparatus. When I came back, the window shades had been drawn, the lights extinguished. He sat behind me, so I couldn't see his face or his gear.

Being polygraphed ("boxed," in the jargon) is a mixed experience—part Frankenstinian medical exam, part simulated torture, part mesmerism, part fraternity initiation. It bothers most people, which may reflect the truth in the cliché that everybody has something to hide. This was certainly true of me, since I was sure this whole exercise was about Mei, my chief guilty secret. Otherwise, to the best of my knowledge, I was clean. I had never stolen anything or cheated on a wife or sold out to the enemies of my country or felt sexual guilt or believed in God, so they could ask me about anything but my Chinese lover without making the needles jump. I thought that the best thing to do was to think of something besides Mei. I thought about combat—not a good choice, apparently. The polygraph examination went on somewhat longer than usual while Mr. Polly asked his mindless questions.

When the ritual was over, I didn't remember a single thing he had asked me. After he packed up his equipment—it seemed to be okay for me to look at the forbidden object now that it knew my secrets—he handed me a manila envelope, sealed with a two-inch strip of Scotch tape that an enemy agent could have peeled and then resealed without leaving a trace. "Memorize, burn, and flush," he said. "You leave first. I'll lock up."

I walked for a while through the unpeopled neighborhood, then sat down on a bus-stop bench and opened the envelope. It contained a typed note that gave me a phone number to call at precisely 0743 EDT the next morning, a confirmed reservation in a cover name at a motel in Rosslyn, a Visa card in a name that matched the one on the reservation, a cell phone, and twenty crisp new fifty-dollar bills.

6

At **0743 the next morning** I dialed the number. A man answered on the first ring and instead of saying hello, recited the number back to me in regulation style. I knew this was the routine, but wondered, *Now what?* He then gave me the same recognition phrase Sally had used. I supplied the response. He said, "Be out front at eight-thirty reading the *Wall Street Journal*." Click.

The driver of the mud-splashed Chevy that picked me up took me to Headquarters. The destination surprised me. I was not asked for ID at the gate, a good thing because I had none—no plastic card with photo and hieroglyphics to hang around my neck, no nothing. Undocs— undocumented agents like me—never carry official ID. This absence of proof that they're up to no good is their protection. Otherwise, they are warned, they're on their own. If they get themselves into trouble, they'll get no help. If they do well, they'll get no thanks. That formula is, of course, catnip to romantics.

I was dropped at a side entrance where Sally the redhead awaited. Unsmiling, wordless, not quite frowning but by no means aglow, she led me to an elevator. There were no numbers on the buttons. She pressed one of them—no wedding band today—and up we went. We debouched into a brightly lit corridor and then turned left, walking past color-coded doors, Sally in the lead. No one had ever told me what the colors indicated. I still don't know. Sally walked rapidly, heels drumming. I checked her out as a matter of course. She was whippet-thin as was the American style, but after eighteen months of ogling Chinese bottoms, hers seemed broad. She knocked on an unmarked door, opened it, and stepped aside. I walked in and found myself in a space the size of the inside of a small house with the interior walls removed. This vast room was windowless but brightly lighted by buzzing fluorescent ceiling fixtures. Government gray file-cabinet safes lined the walls. Other safes were piled on top of them, smaller ones on top of those. Rolling ladders of the kind used in libraries stood in the narrow aisles. I tried to calculate the collective weight of the safes and failed, but wondered why they had not long since plunged through the concrete floor and onto the heads of the bureaucrats in the offices below. I saw no sign, smelled no odor of human occupancy. The possibility that Sally had locked the door behind me passed through my mind.

Then, as if from very far away, a deep resonant actorish voice—you could imagine it singing "Old Man River" at a class reunion in the old frat house—called out, "This way."

I stepped farther into the room and saw at its far end a desk at which a man was seated. He was gray of hair and skin. He was bony, even skeletal. His skull was unusually large, with a sloping forehead. He wore horn-rimmed reading glasses with round lenses. He was in his shirt-sleeves: red-striped shirt with a white collar and cuffs, bow tie. He wore a steel watch and on his right hand, a class ring. A single thick file folder rested at the exact center of his desk blotter. I assumed that this was my own file, plucked for the occasion from among thousands stored in the safes. Otherwise the desk was bare except for a very bright halogen lamp. No pictures of the wife and kids, no cup of pencils and pens, no appointments pad, no coffee cup—not even the smell of coffee, the signature aroma of American offices. Behind him, on the only segment of wall that was clear of safes, hung portraits in oils of old men I recognized as former directors of the organization.

A single chair stood in front of his desk. In the vestiges of a southern accent, he said, "Please. Sit down."

I did as commanded and almost slid out of the chair. Gripping the seat, I leaned over and looked at the chair legs. The front legs had been sawed off so they were a couple of inches shorter than the back legs.

The man at the desk noted my scrutiny and said, "You are a student of details, I see. Good."

I held my tongue. I was finding it surprisingly difficult not to slide out of the chair. The seat seemed to be waxed. You had to think every minute about keeping your backside in place. This made full concentration on anything else difficult. It was petty, a schoolboy prank, ridiculous. But effective. I realized who this man was. He could only be Luther R. Burbank, Headquarters's head of counterintelligence.

He opened the file, a surprisingly thick one for a small fish like me, and studied it for a long moment, as if absorbed in a novel. At length he looked up—or rather, looked over my left shoulder, and said, "We don't know much about you—yet." His voice, so like a tuba, fell strangely on the ear.

After Steve, after Sally, after Mr. Polly, after all the others except the plump, apparently sane Chinese gentleman I met at the safe house, I really had had enough of this nonsense. I said, "Then tell me please what else you want to know. That might save you some time."

As if a joystick had been manipulated, his eyes swiveled from his mountain of safes to the view over my other shoulder. He said, "I think you misunderstand the situation."

"In that case I'm eager to be enlightened, sir."

"No need to call me sir," Burbank said. "A simple 'you' will do. Relax. I'm interested in you, not suspicious of you."

He lifted his eyes as if to catch my reaction.

Burbank riffled the pages of my file. I expected him to ask me about my swim in the Yangtze, to be hungry for details about this bizarre happening. Instead, he said, "You're not exactly a stranger to me. I knew your father at school. Fine mind, excellent athlete. Great quarterback. All everything in track, scratch golfer, did you know?"

"I don't remember him mentioning it."

A smile. "He wouldn't, of course. Modesty was his style. Must have kept him busy. Handsome devil, gift of gab. Handy with the girls. His death must have been difficult for you. You were how old?"

"Eight and a half. I hardly knew him."

"Meaning?"

"I seldom saw him. He worked at the office all day and well into the night and played golf on weekends."

"You resented that?"

"No. He was the same as everybody else's father, he took the train before I got up, came home after I was asleep. His death was just another absence. My mother wasn't broken up about it. She remarried a year and a day afterward."

"What did you think of that?"

"I was fine with it. My stepfather was a nice guy."

"You look like your father. Taller."

"So I'm told. You knew him well?"

"From a distance. We were classmates, but we were in different categories at school—captain of the team, member of the poetry club. There were no Hessians in those days, and even if there had been they'd have been no competition for him."

Ah, so he knew about my downfall as a starter on the prep school eleven. This was inside dope indeed. He was letting me know he knew a lot more about me than I thought. His school was my school, too, and he was listed as a trustee on the masthead of their begging letters, so he would have been privy to the gossip. My file contained a lot of details. Knowing only the little that I already knew about files, I wondered how much of it was true. By the time our interview was over, I had a better idea. Maybe half of his data were more or less accurate—a surprisingly large proportion, as these rough drafts of reality go. At bottom, a full field investigation is a compendium of gossip, a way of seeing some hapless person as many unnamed others see him. Having heard what they have to say, what to believe? What to doubt? Burbank's snoops had covered the waterfront—my marks in school and college, eight or nine of the girls I had known as Adam knew Eve and one I had impregnated at sixteen in one of the many scrapes my stepfather got me out of with a last-minute five hundred in cash; my male friends, teachers both hostile and fond (mostly hostile), military service, what I read, what my politics were assumed to be, where I hung out, who I hung out with, what I drank, what I smoked, what I tended to say in the candor of intoxication. This had been a far broader and deeper investigation than the standard background check, which hardly ever turns up anything that is worth spit on the sidewalk. Evidently Burbank *was* interested in me, probably because he was so interested in my dead father. I assumed he had flown me back from Shanghai with the intention of telling me something that would knock my socks off. But what? Fire me, hire me, see what I had to spill? I picked up no hints. He played his cards close to his vest—the effect would have been comical had he been somebody else—under the pretence that he was not Torquemada and all this Q & A was just a conversation between two guys who had everything in common except age and wisdom.

"You went to college on a ROTC scholarship," Burbank said at one point. "Why was that? How did you do it? There was no ROTC program at your university."

"I got up early on certain days and put on my uniform and drove to the state university for class and drill."

"Why go to all that trouble?"

"There was no reason my stepfather should have to pay my tuition."

"You didn't really want to be an army officer?"

"Actually, I wanted to go to West Point. Didn't make it."

"Interesting. Not many Old Blues go in for the military life. How did your stepfather take your decision?"

"Stoically. It saved him a lot of money, and he had no reason to care where I went to college, so why would he be disappointed?"

"Well, in its way it was a rejection. He'd raised you. He liked you. He had plenty of money. He expected to pay."

Really? How would Burbank know? He had not asked me a question, so again I did not reply even though clearly he expected a rejoinder. When he didn't get one, he went on as if nothing had happened. He kept up the pretense that we were two preppy old boys chewing the fat—but in fact this was an interrogation. I wished he'd stop demonstrating his omniscience and come to the point. All my life I have hated to be questioned, hated to confide, hated even more to be euchred into pretending to confide.

Burbank said, "Bad luck, your reserve outfit shipping out so soon after you graduated."

"That was the understanding. You took the money and if you were deployed you shut up and went where they sent you."

"Afghanistan in your case."

Again I sat silent in my trick chair. I was getting a little tired of being told what I was and where and what I had been. At this point in our chat Burbank had assigned any number of admirable qualities to me. Few of them applied. It was like listening to an old queen trying to ingratiate himself with the straight kid sitting next to him at the bar.

He said, "You were wounded."

"Yes."

"What were the circumstances?"

"Forgive me," I said, "but what possible bearing can that have on this discussion?"

Burbank sighed. He was not used to having his patience tried. He said, "I am trying to know you."

To what purpose? In fact, he was assessing me and we both understood that.

"Then this line of questioning won't get you home," I said. "I remember almost nothing about it."

"I'd be interested in what you do remember."

"I saw the explosion but didn't hear it. It was so close I lost consciousness halfway through the first second. My identity dissolved. I went under believing I had been killed. When you wake up in a hospital after a bomb goes off in your face, you think you're coming back from the dead."

"You were in the hospital for how long?"

"Seven months."

"You survived and kept your arms and legs," Burbank said. "Do you ever wonder why and for what purpose?"

"Blind luck. Zero purpose."

Burbank looked like he was going to say something, maybe about God's purposes. He looked the type, and he certainly had the voice for it. He was said to know the Bible by heart. Behind me I heard china rattling. Burbank's eyes lifted. Sally appeared, carrying a tray on which she balanced two small bowls, a pottery teapot, and a plate covered with a paper napkin. Apparently it was coffee-break time. It was plain that this was not the part of Sally's job that she enjoyed most, but I didn't think there was anything sexist about it. No doubt you had to have a top secret code word clearance to enter this room and she was junior, so she was it. She put down the tray and went away.

"Have some green tea," Burbank said, pouring the acrid stuff into the bowls. "It's a good pick-me-up." He lifted the white napkin. "We have carrots and celery. And what's this? Tangerine segments."

Was he a vegetarian? For me, this was breakfast. The bitter tea did in fact shock the nervous system and clear the mind. Burbank ate the crunchy tasteless food with real appetite. For some reason, this was sort of touching. To my surprise, I realized that I was beginning to like him. We chewed and drank in silence, a great blessing. After the repast, Burbank—how can I put it?—withdrew into himself. I don't want to fancify. He didn't exactly go into a trance, but he was no longer fully present. His eyes were open but unseeing. I thought he might be meditating—it fitted in with the vegetarianism. He remained in this suspended state for several minutes. I didn't want to stare at him, so I looked at the pictures on the wall, and thinking hard, remembered the names of three or four of the ex-directors in the portraits. I counted the safes. There were 216 of them—three triple-deck rows of 72 each. Did they all have the same combination? Unlikely. But how could even Burbank remember all the different ones, and why didn't he just store his data on thumb drives, and lock them all up in a single safe?

Burbank opened his eyes and closed my file with a thump and came to the point. He said, "Tell me exactly what happened on your night on the Yangtze. No detail is too small."

I complied, leaving nothing out.

When I was done, he said, "Have you asked yourself the reason why?"

"Of course I have."

"And?"

"I haven't a clue."

"But you do. They said they were teaching you a lesson."

"Yes."

"On somebody's else's behalf, yes?"

"That was the implication."

"Does this not suggest that you have offended someone?"

"That's one of the possibilities."

"What are the other possibilities?"

"That the guys who did this don't like foreigners, especially Americans. That they're crazy or under discipline. That they were just having fun on their day off. That they had made a bet. That they were high. That it was a case of mistaken identity. That all of the above apply. Shall I go on?"

Burbank, gazing into space, considered my words for a long moment. Then he said, "In other words, the whole thing makes no sense."

I shrugged.

"You shrug," Burbank said. "Shrugs are the sign language of defeat. They get you nowhere."

True enough. I said, "So what's the alternative?"

He tapped on his desk with a forefinger. "In this work there's only one requirement, and it always applies. Take everything seriously. There is always a reason."

"Always?"

"Always. Our job is to look for the reason, discover the reason, overcome the threat."

"To what purpose?"

"Usually the issue is tiny," Burbank said. "But in certain cases it is an acorn that contains an oak. I don't know how these acrobats, as you call them, could have made that any plainer, or how they could have had any purpose apart from making you understand that this was your last chance, and the next time they come for you, you'll die. Don't you want to know why before it's too late?"

The answer was, Not really. What I wanted to do was go back to Shanghai, find the tenor, and throw *him* in the river. This did not seem to be the right answer, so I said nothing. Neither, for the moment, did

Burbank. He looked beyond me, apparently lost in thought. I guessed that this was part of the technique. The stillness accumulated. Certainly this man had no need to gather his thoughts or choose his words. Even on short, uncomfortable acquaintance I thought his mind was quicker than his behavior suggested, and far more capacious. I was quite sure that mental copies of everything stored in the 216 safes were filed away in the appropriate pigeonholes in his brain. I waited. This interview had already gone on for more than an hour. The strain of keeping myself in the tilted chair was taking its toll. My legs quivered. Abruptly I stood up, staggered a little.

Burbank registered no surprise. He said, "Why don't you take a little walk to the end of the room and back?" Limping slightly at first, I did as he suggested. When I was back in front of his desk, he said, "Do you need a break?" I shook my head, turned the chair around and straddled it, my arms folded across the back. This made it much easier to keep from sliding off. Burbank's expression did not change. He made no comment.

As if the conversation had never been interrupted, he said, "You haven't answered my question."

"I'm not sure there is an answer."

Burbank said, "You don't like questions. This has shown up in your polygraphs."

"And what does that suggest to you?"

"It suggests, among other possibilities, that you aren't easily intimidated. That you're your own man. That you see no need to impress others."

Was he *trying* to be clumsy?

Burbank smiled as though he read the thought. "That seems to be your most noticeable characteristic," he said, pouring it on. "Nearly everyone we interviewed remarked on it." He pointed at the chair. "For example, no one else has ever turned that stupid chair around as you just did, even though it's the obvious thing to do."

I was surprised no one had ever hit him over the head with it, but again I was discreet enough to keep what I hoped was a poker face. Burbank was doing the same, of course, because his masklike mien seemed to be pretty much the only facial expression he had.

"Now I want you to put cynicism aside for the moment," he said, "and listen to what I have to say to you."

I lifted a hand an inch or so: be my guest. It was a disrespectful gesture. Burbank ignored the lèse-majesté and went on.

"I want to put an idea into your head," he said. "What happened to you in Shanghai is significant whether you think so or not or will admit it or not. This is just a proposal for you to consider, no need to say yes or no right now. I have something in mind for you. If you decide to do it, you alone will be the agent of your fate. You will have to be smart enough to get the job done and strong enough, callous enough to live with it. People might die, I will not lie to you. And in a sense you would have to give your life to it also. I don't mean that it's likely you'd die like the others, just that this project would take years, almost certainly many years."

"May I ask who the ones who are going to die might be?"

"Enemies of mankind. You may think what happened the other night is trivial, but believe me when I tell you it is the seed of something that can be large indeed."

"Like what, exactly?"

"You'll know more when you need to know it. Nobody but you and me—nobody—will have knowledge of this operation. Ever. You will work for no one but me, report to no one but me, answer to no one but me."

I didn't know what to say to all that, so for once I wasn't tempted to say anything.

For a long moment, neither did Burbank. Then he said, "Do you know what a dangle is?"

"You bait a hook and hope the adversary takes the lure."

"Exactly."

"And I'm the lure?"

"I've been looking for a long time for someone I thought could handle this, waiting for the opening," Burbank said. "I believe you can handle it, and I also think no one else can."

He did? Talk about the chance of a lifetime. I said, "Why?"

"Because you're a good fit," Burbank said. "Because you keep interesting company. Because mainly you tell the truth if you know it, you're brave even if you choose to deny it, you have a good ear for difficult languages, you're arrogant but you try not to let it show. People trust you—especially a certain kind of woman. Most importantly, if I understand what you've half-told me, you seem to have died at least twice, or thought you did, and you didn't care. That's a rare thing. There's one more reason, out of your past."

"Namely?"

"You want to be the starting running back, as you deserve to be."

7

I was out of Burbank's office in seconds, out of the building in minutes. It was a Friday. Sally had told me as she took me down in the elevator that Burbank had mentioned that I might want to spend the weekend with my mother in Connecticut, then on Tuesday call a different number at a different hour. I called Mother on the way to the airport. Her voice rose by a tone or two when she heard my voice. For her this was the equivalent of a shriek of delight. She collected me at the train station. I was glad of the chance to be back in the country. Summer was coming in, everything was in leaf and color. I breathed more deeply than usual, as if inhaling my native air awakened some earlier self. Mother seemed glad enough to see me. She smiled at me, rose on tiptoes and kissed me on the cheek. She smelled, as always, of expensive perfume and makeup. In the car she behaved as if I were home from school, asking no questions about where I had been or what I had seen in the last year and a half. She drove her coughing twenty-year-old Mercedes with competence. She talked about her forgetful sister, about the wretched political slough America had become with everyone, even the children, turning into bloody-minded bigots, about a grocery store ("It couldn't be nicer!") she had discovered across the state line in Massachusetts that had wonderful produce and excellent fish and very nice cheeses. She was still pretty and slim and dressed by Bergdorf. She had no news. She knew only six people in town by first and last name. Nearly everyone she had known had died or been locked up in a nursing home. She had lived alone since my stepfather died. His name did not arise. Nor did my natural father's name, but he had been absent from her conversation for many years. It had taken her about three days after the funerals to forget her late husbands—probably even less time in my father's case. Men died and ceased to be useful, women lived on. Once a protector could no longer protect, though he was still expected to provide, what was the use of thinking about him? As far as I knew she did not have lovers, but how would I know? Remembering the sounds of frolic that issued from the master bedroom when she and my stepfather were together, I reserved judgment.

I soon fell in with Mother's routine. By day I went for walks so as to breathe as much of the crystalline air as possible. In the evening we read a lot—companionably, each of us in a favorite chair under a good lamp, Mother with her Kindle, me with a thriller from long ago I found in my room. Since my stepfather's departure, Mother had had no television set or radio. She disliked the news, abominated sitcoms and cop shows, thought that pop music was noise. The food was excellent. We made our own breakfasts, always the rule in this house, and a taciturn young woman, a recovering crack addict who had been a chef before she crashed, came in and made the other two meals and put the dishes in the dishwasher. A second woman, a cheerful Latina, came in daily, even on Sunday, and did the housework. On Monday, when Mother and I said good-bye, she patted my cheek. Her eyes were misty. This was not exactly a surprise. Though she had never said so, I knew she had affection for me in spite of the fact that I was my father's child.

Late Tuesday afternoon, from Reagan National Airport, I made the call I had been instructed to make at the minute I was supposed to make it. Same routine at the other end, but this time in Sally's voice. She told me exactly where to wait for my ride. The car that came for me was a gleaming black Hyundai, the luxury model. Remembering the battered motorpool Chevy and Sally's motorized garbage can, I didn't think this could be my ride, but it was and it was as shipshape inside as out. The driver was Burbank himself, who maneuvered through rush-hour traffic to Arlington National Cemetery without speaking a word and parked in an isolated lot. It was too hot to walk among the headstones on this day in early June. Leaving the engine running so that the air-conditioning would go on working, he cleared his throat and in his rumbling basso asked the question.

"Yes or no?"

I said, "Yes."

Burbank said, "You understand what you're getting yourself into?"

"I know what you told me."

He handed me an envelope. I didn't open it.

He said, "Go back to Shanghai. Finish your language immersion. Will a year be enough?"

"A lifetime probably wouldn't be enough, but my Mandarin should get better if I can keep the teacher I have."

"On the basis of the benefits so far, why would you do anything else?"

From another, larger envelope he handed me a blue-backed contract. "This changes your status from staff agent to contract agent," he said. "From now on you'll be working outside, under cover, on your own except for your case officer, me. The contract provides for a one-grade promotion, so you'll be making a little more money. You'll still receive overseas pay and the same allowances, so you should be rolling in dough. If you continue to do well, more promotions will follow. You can also be summarily dismissed, but that's always been so. Read before signing."

The contract was addressed to me in my funny name, the one I had been assigned for internal use only after my swearing-in. I asked about retirement and medical benefits.

"Nothing changes except the title. Contract agents cannot mingle with the people inside. In theory they cannot *go* inside. It will be as I told you. No one but me even has a need to know who you are or what you're up to. You'll be alone in the world."

Just what I always wanted. I said, "One small question. What about the tenor and his friends?"

"Next time you'll see them coming."

"And?"

"Evade or kill."

"Are you serious?"

"Everyone has a right to defend himself."

"I am unarmed and outnumbered."

"That may not always be the case. Buy what you need and expense it as taxi fares."

I read the contract twice and signed it. We talked a bit more. Burbank told me to stop e-mailing Tom Simpson and write to him, Burbank, instead, on the seventeenth day of every month. His name for this purpose was Bob Baxter—impromptu cover names like this one, don't ask me why, almost always began with the same first letter of the owner's true surname. In the envelope I found a list of new wild cards. Also my e-ticket and ATM and credit cards on a bank different from the one I had been using. I was to go back to Shanghai tonight and go on as before, living the life I had lived, playing the amiable dumb shit, hanging out with the Chinese, absorbing as much Mandarin as possible, staying away from other Americans and Europeans, especially Russians and Ukrainians and people like that.

"Speaking Mandarin as well as you do, with your war experiences and the resentments they'll assume those experiences generated, you'll be a natural target, so somebody, even an American, may try to recruit you. Just laugh and tell them to get lost. And let me know in the next e-mail if this happens, with full wild card description of the spotter and his friend who makes the pitch."

"Any exceptions?"

"Listen with an open mind to any Chinese who approaches you."

"And?"

"Let me know immediately. The person who hired the tenor and the acrobats may try to befriend you. Will try, probably."

"And I'm supposed to welcome the overture?"

"'Tis a consummation devoutly to be wished," said Burbank.

With that Burbank gave me a searching look, our first prolonged eye contact, and backed out of the parking space. It was a silent ride to the nearest Metro station, a silent parting. No wasted handshake, no "Good luck!"

It wasn't until Burbank had dropped me off and driven away that I realized I had neglected to ask what happened, what I was supposed to do, if he died before I did. He had transformed himself, I realized, into my only friend.

8

When I got back to Shanghai, I found no sign or scent of Mei. A ripple—come on, a tsunami of anxiety passed through me. I could tell she had been in my room after I left. The bed was made and all signs of bachelor disorder had vanished. She had sprayed the room with air freshener, a new touch. Did that mean she'd soon be back or that she had gone a step beyond wiping off her fingerprints and was erasing her own scent and that of the two of us, and this was good-bye forever? The second possibility seemed the more likely. Mei had a talent for exits. After six days without her I was very horny. But maybe she simply had had enough of the hairy ape. These thoughts were uppermost, but also I longed to speak Mandarin and had no one to talk to. My instincts told me she was gone. I'd never see her again. I had always expected this to happen—all those unasked questions, and maybe too much lust, had broken the back of our relationship. There would be no second bicycle crash. We could live in this teeming city for the rest of our lives and never bump into each other again. There was nothing to do but go out for a bowl of noodles and get on with my life. After eating the noodles and passing the time of day with the woman who sold them to me, I went home, read as much of the stoutly Communist *Jiefang Daily* as a political agnostic could bear, and fell asleep. About an hour after I drifted off, Mei—her old merry wet naked self—woke me up in the friendliest fashion imaginable. It was possible, even probable now that I had begun to see the world as Burbank saw it, that she was just carrying out her assignment as a Guoanbu operative, but if this was the case, 'twas a consummation, etc.

I spent the next twelve months in Shanghai unmolested by the tenor or anyone like him, exploring Mei's body and as much of her mind as she chose to reveal. We still arrived separately at parties, almost never dined in a restaurant or showed ourselves together in public, never sat together at the movies. We saw the local company of the Peking Opera—same performance as usual. I met more of her friends. Always, I was the only American at the party. Only one category of Chinese attended, *taizidang* as they were called—"princelings," the children of the most powerful of China's new rich. Strictly speaking, the title applied to the descendants of a handful of Mao's closest comrades in China's civil war, but Mei's friends, the B-list, children of the new rich, qualified for the honorific, though in quotes.

It took me a while to figure this out. Most of these people were smart in all senses of the word, brainy and absolutely up-to-the-minute when it came to fashion of any kind—clothes, movies, slang, books, ideas, dangerous opinions, music, dances. They behaved as if freedom of speech was revered and encouraged by the Communist Party of China. How could they feel so invulnerable? Easy—they were the children of the high leadership of the Party who were the new capitalists. As long as their fathers were in favor, they were immune from the police, from informers, even apparently from the most powerful components of Guoanbu, since they were openly living la dolce vita and denouncing the stupidity of the Party instead of building communism in a labor camp. Since Mei was one of them, she too must have a power dad. Like Mei, they had all done well at good schools and universities, in China and abroad. At least half of them were Ivy Leaguers. They all spoke English, often very rapidly, to one another, as if it were a kind of pig Latin that only they could understand. They never spoke English to me—Mei's rules, I guessed. In their cultishness they reminded me of American elitists, but less narcissistic and romantically paranoid. Unlike their Western counterparts, they did not have to pretend that they lived in a bogey-man, crypto-fascist, totalitarian state whose ruthless apparatus could mercilessly crush them the moment their fathers fell out of favor, or for no apparent reason at all. They understood that the absolute power and the absolute corruption of their rulers was their reality, knew as a birthright that the worst could happen tomorrow or an hour from now. So they ate, drank, and were merry.

Not that they didn't have serious moments or hidden agendas. The princelings didn't address one another by true name in the usual Chinese way, but instead used nicknames. I was called Old Dude, in English. Mei's nickname was Meimei, or "little sister." That nickname can also mean "pretty young thing," but in the next lower stratum of slang it translates as "pussy," so I didn't really get the joke or the insult. Just before my last year of living Chinese came to an end, a member of the cohort who was called Da Ge, or "big brother" took me aside. Mei was particularly friendly with Da Ge. He was as handsome as she was beautiful—in fact they looked a little alike. Naturally they paired off. They spent hours together in corners, giggling and confiding and holding hands. This looked a lot like flirtation, though they never danced together or made eyes at each other or nuzzled. In the back of my mind I thought he might be her case officer. Or the lover I suspected she saw when she wasn't with me.

One night, out of the blue, Da Ge asked me, while everybody else was dancing to the din of Metallica, if I would like to meet his father, who was CEO of a Chinese corporation that did a lot of business with American and European multinationals.

I was taken by surprise. I asked Da Ge why his father wanted to meet me. He said, "He is interested in you." Where had I heard those exact words before? Was Burbank at work here? Was this the first phrase of a recognition code to which I had not been told the response? Not likely. There was only one way to find out what was going on. With as much nonchalance as I could summon, I said, "Sure, why not?"

After all, I was following orders, because Burbank had told me what to do in a situation like this. Da Ge named a date and time and said a car would come for me. He didn't have to ask for my address. Next day I ordered a good suit and a couple of white shirts from a one-day tailor and bought a necktie and new shoes. I told Mei nothing about this.

The car turned out to be a stretch Mercedes shined to mirror brightness, Da Ge in the backseat. We were driven through traffic at a snail's pace to a grand private house in a posh neighborhood I had never before visited. Da Ge made the introduction—"My father, Chen Qi."—and disappeared. Chen Qi's appearance took me aback. I saw in him, to the life, the father who had died a quarter of a century ago. Ethnic characteristics were erased. I did not know how a Chinese could so strongly bring to mind a dead WASP whom I barely remembered, but the resemblance was startling. Chen Qi was the same physical type as my late parent— tall, muscular, handsome as an aging leading man, possessed of a smile that pleased but gave away nothing, abundant dark hair with streaks of gray, skeptical brown eyes projecting wary intelligence, perfect manners, bespoke clothes, an almost theatrical air of being to the manor born. Of course both men were the recent descendants of peasants, so maybe that was the key to their patrician manner. Before dinner Chen Qi and I drank four-ounce martinis—three apiece. These, in larger quantity, had been my father's favorite cocktail. The gin quickly made me drunk. The dinner itself, served by a drill squad of servants in tuxedos, was not the endless parade of Chinese banquet dishes I had anticipated, but instead the sort of twentieth-century faux French meal one gets, if one is rich enough, in a three-star restaurant in Paris or London or New York— four courses artfully presented, small portions, terrific wines. My host led a conversation that in its good-natured triviality mimicked banter. Again like my departed father, Chen Qi smiled his concocted smile seldom, but to great effect.

Over espresso and brandy in what I think he called the drawing room—a Matisse on one wall, a Miró on another—he came to the point. "My son speaks highly of you," he said.

"That's kind of him."

"Kindness has nothing to do with it. He has been brought up to be truthful and to keep me informed about his friends. Through him and others I have been aware of you for some time."

I said, "Really?"

"Yes, almost since you first came to Shanghai," Chen Qi said. "Not many foreigners get on in China as well as you do, let alone penetrate our life as you have done." He inserted a barely perceptible pause before the word *penetrate*.

"I've been fortunate in my friends."

"Indeed. And you had the right introductions. That's very important. Also you speak Mandarin very well—almost too well, some might say. Do you get on as easily with Americans and other Westerners as you do with the Chinese?"

"Mostly," I said. "But I've also met people everywhere who didn't exactly fall in love with me."

The smile. Chen Qi switched to English. "So have we all," he said. "Now I would like to come to the point."

Thereupon he offered me a job in his company. He explained that he did a lot of business in America, which, even though he was speaking English, he called by its Chinese name, *Meiguo,* the beautiful country.

I was startled by the offer. Chen Qi saw this and said he had long been in search of a young but experienced American who knew both China and the United States and could move comfortably between the two and help him and his corporation to avoid unnecessary misunderstandings with its U.S. partners and other Westerners. He understood I spoke good French and fair German and thanks to the army, a certain amount of Dari, was this correct? I would work directly for Chen Qi, taking orders from no one but him, and if I succeeded, as he fully expected I would, the rewards would be appropriate. My starting salary would be $100,000 a year before bonuses and stock options, with a substantial raise after a six-month period of probation. I would have free occupancy of an apartment in Shanghai owned by the corporation and an expense account. The corporation would cover the full cost of medical care for any illnesses or injuries that might occur anywhere in the world. I would have six weeks of vacation a year but no Chinese or American holidays except October 1, National Day, which celebrates the Foundation of the People's Republic of China, Christmas, and lunar New Year's. This job, Chen Qi said, was a position of trust, and he would expect my full professional loyalty.

9

"**So what was your response?**" Burbank asked.

"I told Chen Qi I needed a week to think his offer over and I'd give him my answer when I got back from the States."

"How did he react to that?"

"He seemed to be okay with it," I said. "He asked why I was going home."

"And?"

"I told him I was going to visit my aged mother."

"Then you'd better make sure you visit her," Burbank said. "The eyes of China are upon you."

I had gotten off an airplane less than an hour earlier and had spent every moment of that time giving Burbank a detailed report of my conversation with Chen Qi. Burbank and I were seated in a Starbucks in Tysons Corner, Virginia. The place was almost empty at this time of day.

Burbank sipped his milky coffee and made a face. It must have seemed insipid after green tea. Disdainfully he slid the paper cup across the tabletop until it was out of reach. My news had had a visible effect on him. This was something new. Clearly this bolt from the blue gave him something to think about, and I supposed that thinking was what he was doing now. He had fallen into one of his mini-meditations. I waited for him to come back to this world.

After a minute or two, a shorter interval than usual, Burbank revived and said, "What was your reply to the bit about full professional loyalty?"

"I asked if my loyalty to him was supposed to supersede my loyalty to the United States."

"And he said?"

"That that particular issue would never arise."

"Even though it has already arisen. You are no longer a dangle. You are a penetration agent. He's taken the bait."

Or maybe *we* had. I left this thought unspoken.

Burbank said, "What questions did he ask you about your background, your qualifications?"

"None. I assumed he must already know everything he needed to know."

"A reasonable assumption. They've been assessing you for two and a half years—maybe longer, seeing that you majored in Chinese and your teachers were Chinese, no?"

"Some of them were," I said. "Neither they nor anyone I met in Shanghai ever asked me a personal question."

"Of course they didn't," Burbank said. "Chen Qi, or whoever in the background put him onto you, probably had some New York law firm run a background investigation on you. Perfectly legal, forever confidential under American law—attorney-client relationship."

"Why would they be interested?"

"Because you're a catch. You've got potential. Especially for them."

"A multibillion-dollar Chinese corporation wants to pay a hundred thousand a year for potential?"

"They do it every day. To them, if in fact it's them paying the bill instead of some shadowy third party, a hundred grand is chicken feed."

"You think Chen Qi is a puppet?"

"I think Chen Qi is a loyal Party man who has done extremely well for himself and would roast his own mother on a spit to keep what he has."

"In short, we're dealing, in your opinion, with Guoanbu."

"If we're lucky," Burbank said.

I was lost. Burbank was going to order me to take this job. He was going to order me to go to work—actually, pretend to go to work—for Chinese intelligence. I knew this before the sound of his voice died. I needed a moment to get myself together. I could tell by the look of him that Burbank wanted to get out of Starbucks, wanted to go to some bleak location, park the car, and condemn me to my fate. I had long since drunk my double espresso. After the flight, after forty minutes of Burbank, I needed more caffeine. I said, "I'm going to get another coffee. Want anything?"

He said, "God, no. Order the coffee to go. We can't continue this conversation here."

At least he was predictable. While I was at the counter, Burbank made a phone call. It lasted maybe five seconds. Inside the immaculate Hyundai he said nothing. Now he seemed to be meditating and driving at the same time. I slept, waking up when he braked or made a sharp turn, then going under again. We took country roads, one after the other, and somewhere west of Leesburg, he pulled up to an isolated barn that had been converted into a house. It had a keyboard lock. Burbank entered the combination and we went inside. It was cool, nicely furnished, the walls hung with large hyperrealistic paintings that looked like the next stage of photography. All were depressing—mournful swollen pregnant girls whose fetuses were visible as in sonograms, curly-haired, beautiful brown children wearing prostheses, ruddy workers in hard hats, faces frozen in terror as if watching a mushroom cloud in the last nanosecond of their lives.

"Not very cheerful," Burbank said. "The caretaker is the painter. Believe it or not, she sells this stuff for good money."

By now it was early evening. To my surprise he poured drinks—single malt scotch—and shook unsalted nuts from a can into a bowl. Like the methodical spy he was, he turned on the stereo to defeat listening devices that one really would not expect to be present in a safe house. All the more reason, according to the unwritten manual, to take precautions. Believe nothing. Trust no one. Every lock can be picked, every flap unglued, every seal counterfeited, every friend suborned.

Burbank crossed his leg, thin ankle resting on bony kneecap. He said, "Can you stay awake?"

"Possibly."

"Try. This meeting may go on for a while. We have a lot to talk about. Let me know if you get to the point where you can't concentrate."

"If I fall sleep, that's the signal."

Burbank did not acknowledge the pleasantry. "For starters," he said, "let me ask you what you think of Chen Qi's offer."

"I think it's genuine in its way," I said. "He has some reason for hiring me. His offer was bizarre. I think he knew that I saw what he was up to, or wondered what he was up to, and that he wanted me to draw certain conclusions from it."

"Like what?"

"Like the offer actually came from Guoanbu, that he *was* Guoanbu, that I was caught in the flypaper."

"He was threatening in manner?"

"Far from it. He was as civilized as they come, on the surface. He reminded me of my father."

Burbank lifted a palm. "Explain."

"There are physical and other resemblances."

Burbank gave me a quizzical look but asked for no details. I wondered if I had been wise to feed him this psychic clue. Burbank seemed to be wondering the same thing, using his own unique terms of reference. I was too tired to regret my words or worry about their effect on him.

At 6:00 P.M. exactly Burbank stopped asking questions, turned off the stereo, and tuned into the evening news. Drinking scotch and chomping on nuts, he was absorbed by today's recycling of yesterday's stories. I hadn't watched American television for a long time, and almost never the news, so I recognized neither the anchorperson nor the hot topics. In minutes I went to sleep. An hour later, when Burbank switched off the set, I woke up and stumbled into the bathroom. When I came back I saw no sign of him. Was he in another bathroom? A long time passed. I looked in the master bath. He wasn't there. I called hello. No response. I turned on the outside lights. The Hyundai was gone. It was raining, sheets of it. Well, if he didn't come back, I could always go back to sleep. I was hungry. I looked in the refrigerator. Lettuce, celery, carrots, low-fat yogurt, red and yellow Jell-O, a lemon with a strip of peel removed, an unripe melon, two minibottles of water. In the freezer, two frozen organic dinners (vegetarian). I was looking at the demented paintings again when Burbank came back, a six-pack of microbrew lager in one hand and a bag from a sandwich shop in another. I smelled hot tomatoey American food. He put his packages on the kitchen table and said, "One tofu with sprouts, arugula and roasted red pepper, one meatball with provolone, red onions, hot peppers, and black olives. Which do you want?"

"The meatballs."

"Sit ye down," said Burbank.

To the prodigal home from China, the meal was at least as delicious as the mixture of canned pork and beans and canned spaghetti that Nick Adams, just back from epicurean Paris, mixed together, as I remembered it, over a campfire in Hemingway's "Big Two-Hearted River." Fearful that the beer would put me back to sleep, I drank the water, stealing the second tiny bottle for good measure.

When we finished, Burbank tidied up, putting the debris back into the sandwich bag, washing his beer bottle and my water bottles with soap, presumably to erase our fingerprints, brushing the crumbs into his hand, then into the bag, wiping the tabletop with a sponge, then with a paper towel. He looked happy. Apparently the indoor picnic had been as much of a treat for him as for me.

He brewed some green tea for himself. I drank instant espresso. We remained at the kitchen table. I was glad not to be in the same room with the caretaker's paintings. Burbank waited for his tea to cool, then drank it in a single thirsty gulp.

He said, "What really do you make of this offer of Chen Qi's?"

We had already discussed this in mind-numbing detail, but I went along, as I was paid to do. I said, "As you said, Guoanbu comes to mind."

"Why? Do you suspect that girl who's teaching you Mandarin?"

The answer, of course, was yes, but I didn't want to betray Mei to the likes of Burbank. If *betray* was the word. More than once the thought had crossed my mind that she was being run not by Guoanbu but by Burbank. Her objectives were his objectives: be my crammer in Mandarin, put me in touch with young Chinese who might someday be useful, fuck me cross-eyed to keep me away from sexual technicians from Guoanbu. Just as often, I told myself she could not be working for anyone but Guoanbu. If the usual rules applied, she had been setting me up all along for Chen Qi's recruitment pitch. Only at certain moments did I think she was nothing more than a lusty woman who just happened to have a thing about hairy Americans.

To Burbank I said, "What do *you* think?"

"I think it's a golden opportunity," Burbank said.

"For whom? To do what?"

"For us. To do what we do."

"You don't think it's a trap?"

He snorted in amusement. "Of course it is, in the opposition's calculations," he said. "But that can be an advantage for our side. Some of the best operations we've ever run involved walking into a trap—or, to be more exact, by pretending to be stupid enough to do so. The idea is to demonstrate your low IQ, move the trap, change the bait so the trapper goes looking for his missing trap and steps on it himself and has to chew off his own leg to escape."

Burbank's face positively glowed as he imparted this wisdom. As the animal for whom the trap was being baited and set, I found it hard to join in his enthusiasm. And yet I was learning something. He was showing me his mind, or more likely the fictitious mind he had invented for the purposes of this conversation.

Burbank said, "What do you think the opposition's purpose might be?"

The answer that sprang to mind was, *Same as yours—to own me, to ruin my life.* What I said was, "To recruit me, to compromise me, to double me, to expose me, to pump me out for the utterly trivial things a nobody like me knows. To embarrass the United States, and if I'm lucky, to swap me in due course for some Chinese agent of greater value."

"To surround us, in short. Do you play *weiqi*?"

He meant the Chinese game called Go in Japan and in the West. In Mandarin *weiqi* means "the game of surrounding." I had often played it with Mei, who always skunked me. I said, "After a fashion."

"Work on it. You can't understand them if you don't understand *weiqi*."

"Do you know the game?" I asked.

"No one does unless he's Chinese. I play it. It's hard to find partners. Chen Qi is a *weiqi* man. The game is a passion with this guy. We know that about him. Work on it. Get a teacher, get good enough to play him. Beat him if you can. He'll think all the more of you if you do."

These were orders? What next? Who knew but what *weiqi* was the basis of Burbank's technique as a counterspy. Certainly I felt surrounded. It was time to change the subject.

I said, "I'm curious about something."

Burbank lifted his eyebrows. I took this for permission to go ahead.

I said, "Why do you have all those safes in your office?"

He thought this over. He saw what I was trying to do and decided to humor me.

"You think I should digitize all that information and store it in a computer?"

"Why not?"

"Because safes are safe," he said. "Because they contain things I need to know, need to keep in secure storage, one copy only." He was spacing his words as if teaching me some arcane truth in a language I did not fully understand. He continued, "Think about the origins of the word *safe,* the meaning of that term to the collective subconscious, think of what the concept of being safe has meant to mankind over millennia. We are weaker than the other carnivores. We fear other tribes of our own kind with all our hearts and souls. Our existence depends on our being safe from the Others, capital *O*. We are obsessed by it. The lust for safety is the reason why clubs and spears and gunpowder and nuclear weapons were invented. If experience has taught us anything in recent times, it is that computers are *not* safe. Computers are gossips, they are compulsive talkers. Touch them in the right place, with the right combination of digits, and they swoon and spread their legs. That's what they're designed to do—disgorge, not safeguard. That's what they do. Safes have no brains, no means of communication, therefore no such vulnerability."

I said, "They can't be cracked?"

Burbank ignored the question. He said, "You have reservations about this opportunity." No question mark.

66

"Serious ones," I said. "Don't you?"

"Of course I do. There are always reservations. Think about landing on the moon in that LEM. It might as well have been made of papier-mâché and it was built to fly in a vacuum, but Armstrong and Aldrin showed that it could be done."

Excellent analogy for the equipment for this mission, I thought. I said, "I have no wish to be an Armstrong or an Aldrin."

"You won't be. Others have gone before."

Yes, and never came back. I said, "Suppose we go ahead with this, whatever it is. What would it accomplish?"

"Nothing, maybe. But maybe a lot more than we imagine." Burbank said. "There are no certainties. There never are. But you'd be on the inside, and. . . ."

"Inside what? A corporation."

Burbank said, "A corporation, please remember, that is a wholly owned subsidiary of Guoanbu."

Burbank sounded as if he had taken it for granted that I would be as enthusiastic about this operation as he seemed to be, that I would be as unconcerned as he was about the risks that I, not he, was going to take. To myself, I was one of a kind, new to the world, never to be born again or otherwise duplicated. To Burbank, I knew, I was just one stone, black or white, it didn't matter which, waiting on one of the 361 squares on his *weiqi* board for his finger and thumb to move me.

"Penetrate the corporation and we penetrate Guoanbu?" I said.

"Mighty oaks from little acorns grow."

"And I would do what to make that happen? Please tell me."

"Build a network. Let them discover it."

"Who would be crazy enough to sign up?"

"The friends of your girlfriend." His voice was calm, his manner urbane, and he showed other signs of madness.

I said, "You're serious?"

"It doesn't have to be a real network. The Chinese just have to think it's real and eliminate it."

Yes, he was serious. I said, "And how do you propose I create this thing that does not actually exist?"

"The usual methods," Burbank said. "Befriend, befuddle, betray."

We studied each other's faces for a time. Finally I said, "Guoanbu will kill those people."

"Very likely," said my new chief. "I told you that from the start. But Guoanbu will never know if they killed everybody. Think about it. They'll lose face on a catastrophic scale. They'll be looking over their shoulders till the end of communism, which may be quicker in coming if we pull this off."

I said, "May I ask what gave you the idea I would go along with something like this?"

"Well, for one thing, it's what you're trained to do and paid to do," Burbank said. "Besides that, you have a chance, a reasonable chance, to slay the dragon. That would be a great service to your country. To China and all its people. To mankind. You will be remembered."

Remember by whom, I wondered, if only Burbank knew what I had done? I said, "I am at a loss for words."

After a long pause he said, "So?"

I know, I knew then what I should have said. But a new Faust is born every minute, so what I did say was, "I'll sleep on it."

10

I slept for two days in my old bedroom in my mother's apartment on the East Side of Manhattan. On her sixty-fifth birthday, a summery night, I took her to dinner at the Four Seasons. She had been to the hairdresser that day. She looked lovely. She wore a new dress, her large but not too showy diamond rings, her jewel-encrusted Cartier watch, her ruby and sapphire necklace, her sable coat. My late stepfather had been a generous expense-account tipper, so the maître d' remembered her and gave us a good table. The waiters fussed over her. She had a lovely time. Oysters, lobster bisque, grilled sea bass, Roederer Cristal throughout, dessert that made the liver thump, not a serious word spoken.

Mother was thinner, much thinner, than she had been the year before—pancreatic cancer, she told me the next morning with her usual absence of affect. The oncologist couldn't be nicer. I wasn't to bother about the situation. Her executor, my stepfather's old partner, would handle arrangements—cremation, no clergy, no eulogy, "just a simple brief sniffle at graveside," she told me. I needn't come all the way from

China to be present, if that was where I was when it happened. I wept, dumbstruck that she was mortal. Mother watched tears roll down my unshaven cheeks with a faint sympathetic smile, but did not touch me or speak to me. Just like old times.

For a couple more days I walked the streets or wandered through the Metropolitan Museum—thinking of Mother, yes, but mostly grappling with the Chen Qi/Burbank dilemma. It was almost impossible to believe that I was dealing with reality, but the fact is, I was in the grip of temptation, with all the fears and hesitations that go with it. I had felt this way before when, for example, I contemplated seducing the hot new wife of a clueless friend. She had married what she could get, not what she wanted, and reading her signals I knew she wouldn't say no if I made the move. But what about afterward? What about the tricks of fate, the unpredictability of women? What about remorse? What about death—my death, final and real for a change, at the hands of the man I had betrayed? Then as now, I had no one to talk to. Mother was not a candidate for confessor and wouldn't have been even if she had been in the best of health. The urge to confide in someone, to spill everything, to make this chimera go away by drawing a picture of it, was very strong. Standing before a Titian in the Met, I felt a compulsion to turn to the stranger beside me, confess my dark secret, and ask for advice. I restrained myself—this poor guy from Iowa, in the city for the weekend, would think, more rightly than he knew, that I was a nut case. A bartender would do—in one ear, out the other, another wacko on his fifth scotch. Nobody could possibly believe the grotesque truth. Passing a Catholic church on Saturday evening, I decided to go inside. People, mostly women, were lined up for confession. I joined the queue. I had seen confessional boxes in the movies but, not being a Catholic, had never entered one. Except for weddings and funerals, I had seldom before been inside any church or even heard prayers spoken aloud, let alone whispered them to the Almighty. As a child I was given no religious instruction. The name of Jesus was unfamiliar to me until I went to school. When I asked questions, Mother advised me to make up my own mind about God. She herself didn't think there was one. The fairy tales in the Old and New Testaments couldn't possibly explain the grandeur of the enterprise—just look at the stars, just imagine the infinite and eternal universe rushing across time and space to who knew what destination. (Her exact words: she talked to me like that when I was seven years old.) She hadn't baptized me, a fact that created misgivings years later in Headquarters when I was being cleared for employment by friends of the Savior. Did this guy have a comsymp for a mother, or what?

Outside the confessional, my turn came. In the dimness on the other side of the box (is that where the nickname of the polygraph came from?) sat a priest with bushy black eyebrows. I cleared my throat, but I didn't know the drill, so I said nothing. Sounding like a gruff cop near the end of his shift, the priest said, "Speak!" I just couldn't do it. The safe was locked, there was no key. I said, "Sorry." The priest said, "No doubt you should be. What have you done?" I said, "I can't do this. I took an oath." In a weary voice the priest said, "Then hell is your destination. Beat it."

On my way out I remembered something helpful. Mother, thinking no doubt of my father's peccadilloes and maybe of her own, liked to say that people did what they wanted to do. Always. They might say they did what they had to do, or that they had no choice, or that they were helpless in the grip of circumstance. They might even struggle against the inevitable. But the truth was, *they did what they wanted to do* even knowing that it would end in self-destruction. It was as simple as that. It was in the DNA.

In my case, at least, she was right. On the steps of the church, I called Burbank on my cell phone and said, "The answer is yes." The next morning, early, I said good-bye to Mother and received the two air kisses I knew would be the last she would ever give me. Smelling her Chanel No. 5 and noting the threadlike wrinkles beside her eyes that she probably would have had fixed by a plastic surgeon if terminal cancer had not intervened, I felt the fond amusement that was her idea of love instead of the pointless grief she would not have forgiven.

11

I went back to Shanghai. No Mei was there to greet me, there was no sign or scent of her in my room. This time her absence was permanent, but I had expected that. Her work was done.

Chen Qi, now the boss, no longer the genial host, welcomed me to my new job with a hard handshake but no smile. When I accepted his offer, his eyes were cold. He had bought me. From now on, like everyone who worked for him, I would address him and speak of him as Chen Zong, or when speaking English, "CEO Chen." There was no longer any need for him to be charming. I was given an office with glass walls on the same floor as his, a great honor. Thereafter, on the first day of every month, the sum of $8,333.33 was deposited to my account in the Bank of China. As Chen Qi had promised, I moved into a fully furnished apartment a dozen floors below the corporate offices, and commuted by elevator. It was a nifty but sterile place, something like a suite in the Hilton, with maid service and a fine view of the boundless city floating in its pall of smog. Of course the apartment was wired just as my office was wired, and probably equipped with cameras. I didn't incriminate myself by looking for bugs and lenses. Anyone who wished to do so could observe me to his heart's content. Why should I mind? It was nice, in a way, to be of interest, to be present in someone else's imagination, as Mei was in mine. I caught glimpses of her ghost every day.

At first I was given trivial work to do. Pointless though they might have been, these assignments were heavy with importance because they came directly from Chen Qi's office by hand of messenger. I hardly ever saw Chen Qi himself, and almost never saw him alone. Sometimes when he was receiving an American visitor, he summoned me. The other American was usually disconcerted to see the likes of me working in a place like this for a man like Chen Qi. Though they all smiled and shook hands and repeated my name in hearty tones, few such visitors were friendly. What was an American *doing* here? It was okay to do business with these greedy Communists, money was money, but *work* for them? Be their *underling*? Once or twice a week in the elevator or the corridors I ran into a princeling Mei had introduced me to. It was the same with them, and there were quite a few of them. They averted their eyes. They didn't speak, nor did I. Needless to say I was no longer invited to their parties. I never had been invited by them, of course, Mei had just brought me along as a curiosity. Without her, I was isolated, of no interest, and besides that, a potential menace because I saw Chen Zong, heard his voice, and if I did not actually touch him, I touched papers that he had touched. Did this bode well or ill for the fictitious network of agents and assets that Burbank imagined? Who knew?

I had expected to be used as an interpreter, but there was no need for my services because Chen Qi spoke serviceable English. Besides, he had a whole corps of interpreters. One of them, a jolie laide named Zhang Jia, worked in the office next to mine. At first she ignored me, then she was indifferent, then sometimes she nodded when we passed in the corridor. Gradually this mock foreplay escalated. Meaningful looks were exchanged through the glass wall that separated us. When I asked her to dinner she accepted without hesitation and spent the evening with me in a restaurant on a lower floor of the tower. Judging by the stares, interracial couples were uncommon in the restaurant. This did not seem to bother Zhang Jia. We spoke English to each other. Hers was flawless and ladylike, something like Mother's Miss Porter's elocution with a faint Chinese counterpoint. Unlike Mei, Zhang Jia talked about herself, providing her entire curriculum vitae as if reading from a script. This was regarded in CI circles as the likely sign of an agent regurgitating a cover story. No surprise there. Zhang Jia said she was from Beijing, the daughter of workers who had wanted a son but being kindhearted, refrained from drowning her when she was a baby. When she was twelve and a star pupil, the revolution discovered her and took her to its bosom. She went away to a boarding school in another part of China, where she learned English. She was an alumna of Wellesley College and Beijing Foreign Studies University. We dined alone in her apartment. She was an excellent cook, a pleasant companion. We played tennis on the courts in the basement. She was a fine player. I was out of practice and out of shape. She sometimes beat me and probably could have beaten me more often than she did. She had been good enough to play on the Wellesley varsity. We went to the movies in the tower's theaters and sat together. We played *weiqi*. She was unbeatable. Through all this chaste fraternization we mostly spoke English. One night, in her apartment, we got into bed, Jia leading me by the hand, and switched to Mandarin. She was a more decorous lover than Mei, but skilled.

After that first night together, we never spoke English again. As time went by, my Mandarin got better and better. Zhang Jia taught me etiquette, a subject Mei had neglected. For a long time I learned very little besides that and Mandarin and *weiqi*, but millimeter by millimeter, second by second, that changed. Zhang Jia was like a wife. She dominated, or thought she did, by submitting. Her job, apparently, was to manage me. She was diligent. We began to see Chinese couples socially—encouraging news for Burbank. They all lived in the tower and worked for the corporation. They were different from Mei and her friends—more real, more serious, more sober. Nicer. Clean as whistles politically. Children of the proletariat. They seemed to like me, but they could not possibly have trusted me. In accepting me, or making believe they accepted me, they were almost certainly doing what they were told. How could such behavior be otherwise explained?

Except for Zhang Jia, I was never alone with any of them. But in its way my friendship with her was almost beautiful. So was she, I realized, as her face gradually became as familiar as my own.

TWO

12

Sluggishly, time passed. Burbank had reminded me more than once that truly great operations took a long time to come to fruition. Espionage was a molasses waterfall, he said, it was brain surgery performed while wearing boxing gloves, it was like really having to urinate while following a subject who was walking on the roofs of cars in a traffic jam. "They'll watch you for a long time, years probably, they'll place temptations in your way," he had warned me. "If you make no false moves, the inevitable will happen."

At the office, things went well enough. Gradually, CEO Chen gave me more significant work. I saw signs, tiny signs, that he was pleased by the way I did it. At the end of the six-month probation period, my pay increased by 20 percent. I was given a larger office, even nearer to his. I welcomed this perk because it meant that the wifelike Zhang Jia would no longer be next door, watching me day and night. My affection for her was considerable, but it owed something to the Stockholm syndrome, and there were days and nights when I longed for Mei, who used to drop in for noodles, Mandarin, sex that was always new, and movies and chatter, and then vanish for the next twenty-four hours. My sex life with Zhang Jia was adequate—she was nothing if not dutiful and expert—but it was a routine that never varied, first the clever hand, then the clever tongue, then the slippery prize. Her idea of conversation was close interrogation, another sharp change from life with Mei. I fought exasperation and often lost. Zhang Jia throbbed with curiosity. Although our transparent offices no longer adjoined, she found ways to keep me under observation. Who was that on the telephone when I was so animated? Why was I so often away from my desk, and when I was out of sight for ten minutes, what had I been doing at the mystery destination or destinations? I wondered if she had an earpiece concealed beneath her thick gleaming hair so that a hidden interrogator could feed her questions, as a television producer feeds them to the perky blonde with the microphone. Even though there was no such thing as an empty space in Shanghai, I fantasized running into Mei in an elevator where we were alone. She would hit the red emergency STOP button, ignore the cameras, and say hello as only Mei could. The weight would lift from my chest. Empty dreams.

Chen Qi began taking me with him on trips abroad. He traveled in the company jet, I flew commercial, leaving a couple of days earlier to make sure all was as it should be on his arrival and he would not waste a minute. In private he was still distant, chilly, curt. However, in the company of American customers he treated me as an honorary equal. As the money rolled in from Sino-American joint enterprises, I was better accepted by the doubters among my countrymen, who seemed to conclude that I was in it for the bucks, too, and therefore an okay guy. At meetings, Chen Qi would sometimes let me make the presentation. This happened more often if the people we were meeting were new to him. His English was good but not perfect, and he was wary of embarrassment. He understood almost everything the Americans said, of course, but often he would interrupt a conversation and speak to me in Mandarin, as if asking for a clarification. We were always on the up-and-up about what we said in Mandarin in the presence of Americans. Who knew but one of those smart young people sitting against the wall understood the language? Cunning, these ever-smiling Yanks. Half of the along-the-wall crowd were women, and some of them were babes. I had been away from American females for so long that I had become as sexually curious about them as I used to be about Chinese women. I remembered the sulks and the accusations, but couldn't quite remember how they smelled, how they looked and behaved with their clothes off. The urge to ask one of them to go dancing was strong, but like the asset under discipline that I was, I resisted. My American date would almost certainly be mistaken by Guoanbu for a Headquarters asset, and because the whole world believes that American spies are everywhere, there was no possibility whatsoever of evading observation. Unlike others from the tower who could only go outside in groups of two or more when on foreign soil, I was allowed to walk alone wherever I was. But I was under instructions always to carry a mobile phone so that Chen Qi could always get in touch. The real reason for this protocol, of course, was that the GPS in the phone told CEO Chen's security people exactly where I was at all times. I was under no illusion that I was ever alone.

American businessmen, I discovered, were just as paranoid as spies. I learned a lot of secrets while traveling with Chen Qi, but they were business secrets, which accounted for the Americans' suspicions. How did they know that I hadn't been planted on Chen Qi by some rival U.S. company that was paying me to conduct industrial espionage? They would pour me drinks and interrogate me—all the standard questions, always getting around to how come I spoke such good Chinese. Where had I learned it? "In bed," I would reply. They would laugh as if they actually believed the lucky dog.

It never occurred to me to report what I learned to Burbank. For one thing, though neither Chen Qi nor the American executives would have believed it, Headquarters was prohibited by law from spying on American citizens, and it took this taboo seriously. For another, reporting anything to Burbank meant being in contact with Burbank—the last thing he or I wanted.

I had last seen him a year before, at Mother's graveside service. Somehow she managed to live almost a year after our dinner at the Four Seasons. Because she didn't want anyone who knew her to watch her die, or to look at her wasted body after she died, I never saw her again. Twelve people attended the obsequies, as she called her burial rites—my dotty Aunt Penny, the anorexic recovering addict who had been Mother's cook and gardener, the Guatemalan cleaning lady, three women Mother played bridge with, an assistant undertaker, my stepfather's former law partner, me—and, lurking behind the monuments, Burbank. Naturally no clergyman was present. Aunt Penny, in good though quavering voice despite the November cold and the wind and the graveside mud on her shoes, read an Emily Dickinson poem—the one about Death driving his passenger in a carriage to the next world. The law partner spoke about the beauty and grace and unfailing kindness of the deceased, and about her brilliant, almost Olympian horsemanship as a young woman. The gravediggers waited some distance away, hidden, except when they peeked around a corner, by a marble crypt the size of a delivery van. As Mother's coffin, the urn of ashes inside, was lowered into the grave, Aunt Penny said in a loud voice, "I hope Sis didn't insist on being buried with her jewels. Those fellows just steal them. Strip them off the corpse's fingers after the family has left."

When it was over, everyone except me drifted away. I stayed beside the grave for a while, giving Burbank time to saunter among the headstones and take himself out of sight. I followed and saw a car—not the Hyundai—parked with the motor running, Burbank at the wheel. I got in.

Burbank said, "Do you have a cell phone on you?"

"No," I said. "Do you?"

"No," Burbank said. "No GPS in this car, either."

Dusk was upon us. Until nightfall we drove aimlessly on country roads, going nowhere, saying nothing, spotting no surveillance. Back in the village, we parked three blocks from Mother's house and walked the rest of the way by separate routes. Tradecraft to the max was the rule of the day—everything but chalk marks on utility poles. Because these techniques were a dead giveaway, I hadn't used them for more than two years except when I was in the United States. Burbank got lost, of course, as spies sometimes do because they're concentrating on what's behind them instead of where they're going, but eventually he found his way to the door. I let him in, threw the dead bolts, and led him past furniture covered by sheets to the windowless basement, where on weekends my stepfather used to watch ball games on television. The room was soundproof, so as not to bruise Mother's eardrums with the roar of the crowd and the babble of the announcers. It had a well-stocked bar and a microwave and a cabinet filled with canned chili and other guy food. Burbank sat at the bar. I went behind it, unplugged the telephone, and poured two glasses of Laphroaig. I drank mine at a swallow, poured myself another, and handed him his.

Burbank lifted his glass and said, "I'm sorry for your loss."

Was he now? As usual when I was with Burbank, words it would be wiser not to speak came to mind. However, I lifted my glass in thanks, and this time sipped rather than gulped the sublime, peaty varnish.

"So," Burbank said. "How's it going?"

"Imperceptibly."

He nodded as though that was precisely the word he had been hoping to hear. He smiled with his lips together. He commiserated. He understood. He had often been bored himself when operational. It was part of the game. It made the good moments better when they came, as they always did. He said, "Some guy wrote that the craft is like being in love—long periods of frustration, suspicion and loneliness, punctuated by brief moments of intense gratification, or words to that effect." He changed the subject. There were housekeeping details to discuss. I had been promoted to GS-13 ("It's a bit early in the game, but you're a special case"), not that it mattered, aside from the honor of the thing. Because Chen Qi was paying me more than twice as much as my government salary, and I was being allowed for cover purposes to keep that money for the time being, Headquarters's bookkeepers had offset my official salary against my cover earnings, so I was being paid nothing by the government. So far the bookkeepers had not come up with a way to compute the dollar value of my benefits, which admin regarded as part of my compensation.

I said, "You mean I'm going to owe you money when all this is over?"

"Of course not," Burbank said. "It will be written off, but admin wanted you to be up to speed on the technicalities, as they put it. They have no idea who you are or what you're doing. They just go by the book."

Burbank pointed to his glass. I poured him another whisky. He was unflustered. He was supposed to be. Agents got upset. The drill was to radiate calm and assurance, to reassure them, to set their minds at ease, to suggest but never say that a vast, powerful, invisible force was looking out for them every minute of the day and night, and you were personally making sure that the force would keep them from harm no matter what.

"Enough trivia," Burbank said. "What exactly have you been up to since the last time we met?"

With some omissions and some additions, I told him what I have already told you. As usual, he paid rapt attention. You could almost see the 1s and 0s, or whatever binary code the human brain employs, combining into data and speeding to their various destinations inside the vault of Burbank's bony skull.

"It sounds like things are working out pretty much as we hoped," he said. "Do you agree?"

"I see no sign of progress, but maybe I'm too close to it. It's not easy to know what Chen Qi and friends are up to. It's tricky enough, keeping a grip on your sanity, locked up in a tower with a bunch of people to whom you look and smell like an ape."

"You believe that's really the way they feel?"

"The Chinese are racists like everyone else, only more so," I said. "They see nothing wrong with it. I overhear remarks. I see the looks on faces. I know how I smell to them because they let me know."

Burbank was examining me with a new look on his face "Beware paranoia," he said.

He was telling *me*? Burbank was director of paranoia for the most hated intelligence service in the world. He lived and breathed paranoia. He was Headquarters's therapist, never dismissing the possibility, nursing the hope that his worst suspicions might turn out to be justified. The reality was, Burbank would have been a pretty poor chief of counterintelligence if he wasn't paranoid.

He refused a third whisky. I didn't ask if he was hungry. It was early still, and remembering the tofu sandwich, I guessed he wouldn't be much interested in what my stepfather's ghost had to offer. For long moments, he seemed lost in thought. Then he said, "You didn't mention getting laid."

"Should I?" I asked.

"Everything is relevant. For example, are you still screwing that wild woman you met on the Bund?"

I said, "No, but I miss her. She was good for the mission. She taught me Mandarin. Also *weiqi*. You advised me to concentrate on both."

"Then you and I have reason to be grateful to her. Her name again?"

"Mei."

"Surname?"

"I have no idea."

"Why not?"

"As you know, we exchanged no personal information."

"Just secretions."

I said, "That's disgusting."

Burbank said, "What word would you choose to describe an agent under discipline and deep cover who slept with a foreign woman for two and a half years and never officially reported that fact to Headquarters?"

"Discreet. I thought you must be running her. Now I'm even more suspicious."

"You are?"

With a smile (*"I'm joking!"*) I said, "If I never mentioned her, how would you know about her?"

"Many matters come to my attention." Burbank waved a hand—weakness noted, subject closed, sin locked in the appropriate safe. Let's move on.

"So what are you doing for poontang now?" he asked.

"For what?"

"Pussy—pardon the twentieth-century slang. This wild woman is not welcome in the tower, I assume."

"I have never seen her there. Or anywhere else since I got back to Shanghai. As you know, because I have reported it, I now sleep with a somewhat more conventional female."

"The Wellesley girl? The one who works for Chen Qi?"

"Yes."

"Was provided by Chen Qi?"

"That's my assumption, unless you know otherwise."

"Have you chosen the next bedfellow?" Burbank asked.

"I didn't choose the other two," I said. "I'm hoping for yet another nice surprise."

Suddenly Burbank laughed, a bark followed by a snort. It was startling to hear such sounds issuing from this mirthless being. Then, in his sudden way, he shut up and got lost in thought. For a moment I thought the conversation was over.

But it wasn't. Burbank's eyes refocused and he said, "About the Chinese ladies, enjoy yourself. I think your dingus may lead us in an interesting direction."

We talked a little more, pleasantly enough for a change, just passing the time of day. Before Burbank left by the cellar door, he wiped the fingerprints from his whisky glass, then dropped it into his coat pocket. Mother would not have been pleased. The glass was crystal with the Dartmouth coat of arms engraved upon it, a present from her, and my stepfather had been very fond of it and the eleven others—now ten—just like it.

13

On my return to Shanghai, Zhang Jia, sitting in a straight chair with her knees primly together, told me that she had met a prospective husband, a civil servant who was a fellow graduate of her university in Beijing, and that our friendship must come to an end. She wanted to have a child. For the sake of its future, its father could not be an ape. Her prospective husband was intelligent, upstanding, the son of workers, a loyal Party member. Wifely to the last moment, she cautioned me against being too much alone after she left. Until I found another woman, I should have lunch and dinner in the cafeteria. The food was nourishing and there were plenty of nice, educated people to talk to. Her friends would welcome my company. Perhaps I would meet another girl while shoveling noodles. At the very least, communal dining would be good for my Mandarin. I was speaking so much English while traveling with Chen Qi that I was beginning to make small but unfortunate mistakes in syntax. I needed to converse with people who would correct my errors in a friendly way. If the overwhelming relief that consumed me on hearing the news of her imminent departure showed in my face, Zhang Jia gave no sign that she noticed. When she finished her presentation she stood up, bowed ever so slightly in my direction, as if animated by some genetic memory of female submissiveness, and walked out. We did not hug or kiss. We had never kissed. Zhang Jia just left, closing the door quietly behind her. It was the most civilized breakup I'd ever had.

Not long after that, CEO Chen called me in and told me that he had decided that he needed a personal representative in Washington, and I was his choice for the job. My assignment was to keep in touch with his American customers. I should travel around the United States as much as necessary, keeping an eye out for new business opportunities, new American ideas, and the tides of American politics. Sometimes he would ask me to join him in the States or in other countries. The corporation had an office in Washington, and I would have a desk there but would not belong to that office. I would continue to report directly to him. I should avoid fraternization with the other people in the office. Chen Qi would keep in touch by telephone and e-mail. I would be provided with a new smart phone to be used for communicating with him and for no other purpose. I should carry the phone on my person at all times. After Chen Qi told me this news, he dropped his eyes and went back to what he was doing. To him, I was now invisible. Minutes later, when I was back in my office, a man I had never seen before brought me the new phone and an Internet confirmation for an Air China flight two days hence to New York. No one in the tower said good-bye to me.

A car took me to the airport. Another met me at Dulles. In the corporation's offices on Connecticut Avenue, a stocky, plain young woman with china-doll bangs and buttonhole eyes who introduced herself as Sun Huan, my assistant, showed me to my office. No one else made an appearance. All other doors were closed. The made-in-China Scandinavian-style furniture in my corner office was handsome in its way. The room was a most desirable space, filled with light. Someone— my first in-house enemy, no doubt—must have been moved out to make room for me. Sun Huan gave me the keys to my apartment, located a mile up the avenue, and told me the doorman's name. Very convenient, Sun Huan said. She lived in the same building and walked to work every day with her roommates.

Now that I was back in my own country, where only the FBI, the NSA, and various agencies of the Department of Homeland Security read other people's mail, I sent Burbank a handwritten letter, using an accommodation address I had memorized at our last meeting. I received no reply. No pay phones that worked remained in Washington, a serious loss to spies, whose three essential qualities when on the sidewalk were said, in pre–cell phone days, to be an accurate watch, a strong bladder, and a pocketful of change for coin telephones. One evening I took a chance, rode the Metro to Bethesda, and paid cash for a cheap throwaway, no-GPS cell phone in a shopping mall. On another day I took the Red Line to the zoo, and from the men's room called Burbank's old contact number. It rang twelve times. Nobody answered. I tried again a couple of hours later. Again, no reply. I flushed the phone's memory card down the toilet at the zoo and dropped the rest of it, wiped as clean as if Burbank had done the job himself, into a trash can in a movie theater miles away. Very wasteful, the clandestine life.

There was nothing to do but wait. Burbank knew where I was. When the situation began to explain itself, as in his philosophy it must, he would make contact. Or maybe not.

Evenings and weekends, I worked on re-Americanizing myself. I had half-forgotten how to live in my own country while I spent one-fourth of my life blundering around Afghanistan or lying in army hospitals or living a lie as every honest secret agent must do, or reducing my mind to rubble by speaking nothing but Mandarin and screwing Chinese women whom I could not permit myself to love without breaking my solemn oath of loyalty to my country and my craft. In my absence, everything had changed just slightly—the slang, the food, the music, the clothes, the drugs, the etiquette or such potsherds as remained of it, the conscience of the nation and its hopes and fears, the president, the Constitution. The educated class, always less happy than it deserved to be, was deeply, maybe incurably peeved. Many who died on 9/11 were people like themselves, who were not supposed to die in American wars. Now that the taboo was shattered, something worse could happen with even more disconcerting results. No one was safe, no matter how many diplomas he or she had, no matter how special he or she might be. Suicide bombers could not be far in the future—in fact, they should have started blowing themselves up in America long ago. This loss of immunity, this end of specialness, was somebody's fault, probably a hidden somebody or more likely a vast conspiracy of hidden somebodies. Mother had been right, America was askew. Anger was the fuel of politics. In her opinion, the atmosphere was worse than the sixties. Now as then, the nonconformists only succeeded in being all alike—same thoughts, same vocabulary, same costumes, same delusions, same cookie-cutter behavior masquerading as rebellion. Coming home to this country on the brink of a nervous breakdown was like waking from a coma and seeing two moons in the sky.

CEO Chen kept me busy running around the country to talk to harried executives who made time for me with the greatest reluctance. These were tough customers. They listened to my presentations with wandering minds. A deep recession was in progress. Business was slow. They had no interest in spending more money than they were already spending. Still, the work was not without interest. These entrepreneurs explained that they were biding their time until a new business cycle began. I had no MBA, it was true, but surely even I could understand that. Creative destruction was taking place. It happened at intervals in a free enterprise system. After the wrecking ball had done its work, something more profitable always resulted. Like Chinese philosophers of old, they believed in constants. The capitalists had their own scriptures, just like the Communists had had Marx and Lenin in their blood-drenched heyday. One irascible executive in Texas, his store of politeness exhausted and three drinks under his belt, reminded me that multinational capitalism had accomplished in a decade that which blundering international communism had failed to do in almost a century of effort—it had unified the world in the service of a single idea without murdering a single soul. The motivating force for this great revolution, he said, tapping on the gleaming conference table to emphasize each word, was the God-given love of money. That, he added, was the difference between an idea that harnesses human nature and one that denies it. "It woke up a billion-plus Chinese to their true nature," he said. "They're a nation of compulsive capitalists, always have been, and if they had channeled the energy they put into the Cultural Revolution and the rest of that Maoist bullshit into good old-fashioned business, they'd be running the world." I was sorry Chen Qi was not present to hear this, but then again, if he had been, the words I heard would probably never have been spoken.

Right after this meeting, I flew back to Washington. An American Chinese gentleman was seated beside me on the airplane. After an hour or so of silence, I dropped something on the floor. As I bent over to retrieve it, so did the Chinese gentleman. Our heads bumped. I wasn't much affected, but he was a small man, and he had a lump on his bald skull. He seemed so dizzy and out of it that I rang for the flight attendant and asked for ice. She brought it and told him, as if she were a trained nurse, not to go to sleep in case he was concussed. "*Concussed?*" the gentleman said. "Is that a word?" He held the plastic bag full of ice to his skull and soon recovered, though he must have had a bad headache. We began to talk about nothing. He spoke rapid colloquial English with a deep southern accent. He told me all about himself. I knew what that might mean, in terms of the craft. He was a third-generation American, born in Tuscaloosa, Alabama. He had served a hitch in the U.S. Navy as a gunnery officer on a destroyer. His children were all going to good colleges—Brown, William and Mary, Stanford. He him-self had gone to Auburn.

He gave me his card. I told him I didn't have one of my own on me—I'd given them all away on my trip. This didn't worry him. Business comes first, he said. He said, "Do you like Chinese food?" He got out a pen and on the back of his card scribbled the name of a restaurant on Connecticut Avenue. "Excellent," he said. "The chef is from China. So is everybody else. Nobody but the owner speaks English, so you have to point at the menu. If you like Peking duck, his is the best in town. Very prettily served, too. I advise you to order it even if you don't like it, to enjoy the show."

14

The next day Chen Qi summoned me to London. He was accompanied by two Chinese in Italian suits. They were about my age. I had never seen either one of them before, but there were sealed floors in the tower, so there was nothing to wonder about except that they were now being revealed to me. Chen Qi always traveled with a couple of bodyguards, but these new types, comfortable in their suits and ties and quick to demonstrate how smart they were, were not members of the bodyguard class. They spoke good English, and to me, nothing but English. For a week, in meetings, they did the talking and the interpreting while I sat by, silent but tempted to raise my hand when something was garbled in translation. Chen Qi would not have noticed had I done so. Not once during the days we were together did he rest his eyes on me for as much as a second. I wondered why I was there.

After the final meeting, Chen Qi satisfied my curiosity. He drew me aside in the lobby of the office building and told me in Mandarin that this was my last day as an employee of the corporation. My return fare to the United States had already been paid. I would receive six months' severance pay. I could remain in my Washington apartment for one month. He had no criticism to make of me. I had performed my duties in an entirely satisfactory manner, but unfortunately I was a speck in the eye of the corporation. My presence made others uncomfortable. I spoke Mandarin too well. I copulated with a Chinese woman on company property. My ways were not China's ways. The authorities had noticed me and my unfortunate habits. I should go back to America, work in America, be an American. With my language skills and my experience of China, I should have no trouble finding a job even in these difficult times. He handed me an envelope. Then we were done. He turned on his heel without a word or a change in expression, and walked away. The hotshots followed. They would never give me another thought, and why should they?

There went Burbank's fictitious network—or so in my innocence I supposed. I felt a rush of relief but also, I confess, a certain sour disappointment. I may have loathed the mission, but I also wanted to accomplish it. All my life I had been given Everests to climb—beat up the bully, make the team, make the girl, get into a college I could mention with nonchalance at a cocktail party, and in the army, take that hill, kill that stranger, hold that position, recover from those wounds. Something was up. Something worse would come next.

Half a day later my flight landed in New York. I took the shuttle to Reagan National Airport, the Metro to Dupont Circle. Walking home, dragging my carry-on suitcase behind me, I passed the restaurant the Chinese American gentleman with whom I bumped heads on a different airplane had recommended. For months I had walked by the place every day without giving it a second glance. It was still open at 11:00 P.M. I stopped, read the menu, and went inside. The host, who spoke monosyllabic English, led me to a booth. I ordered a beer. I wanted noodles. Like my friend on the airplane, the host looked pained and recommended Peking duck. "You will like it," he said. "Trust me."

The duck was a long time in coming but finally it appeared, borne on a tray by an almost unbelievably beautiful Chinese girl. Smiling shyly, she showed me the glazed bird. It was whole and nicely displayed. She donned transparent plastic gloves, showed her perfect teeth again, picked up a razor-sharp Chinese knife, and carved the duck. She had a knack for it and she disjointed the bird and sliced its breast in minutes, arranging the pieces on a platter as she went. There was three times as much duck as I could eat, plus the usual mountain of rice.

When she set this feast before me, I spoke to her in Mandarin—a compliment on her deftness. Up to this point she had not looked at me. Now she did, with wide, startled eyes. Then she fled into the kitchen, heels clattering, raven hair flying.

A Chinese man, lean and saturnine, wearing jeans, Nikes, and a plain black T-shirt had just been seated in the opposite booth. He watched the girl go and caught my eye. No smile, but he had an intelligent face. He was unmistakably a native Chinese.

In English I said, "What was all that about?"

He said, "You speak very good Mandarin. Possibly she's an illegal. She probably thought you were an immigration agent."

"If I were, I'd certainly never deport her."

"You've lost your chance," he said. "By now she's in a car on her way out of town. Bad luck for the restaurant. She was an attraction."

He ordered a bowl of noodles. He switched to Mandarin. We had a polite conversation about Laozi. We quoted the sage's famous sayings back and forth. I asked my new friend what his favorite lines were. He said, "The one about a small fish being spoiled by too much handling." I said I liked the one about water, a soft thing, always overcoming iron, a hard thing. "Laozi is always relevant," he said. He quoted another passage:

"Why are people starving?
Because the rulers eat up the money in taxes.
Therefore the people are starving.
Why are the people rebellious?
Because the rulers interfere too much."

I said, "You sound like a Republican running for president."

"No. Laozi sounds like Laozi."

His noodles were delivered. He stopped talking. I left first. My friend, eating with his bowl under his chin, paid no attention. He had not divulged a single detail about himself except that he seemed to have memorized the whole of Laozi. This told me something—perhaps. Maybe he was a follower of the Dao. Or someone like me.

Trudging up the hill toward bed, I was too tired to care what he was or what that meant. *To be worn out is to be renewed,* according to Laozi.

15

The entry code at the corporation's office had been changed, so I had to ring the bell. Sun Huan came to the door and without a word or a smile, handed me a brown grocery bag containing my personal belongings. I gave her the CEO Chen–only mobile phone that had been issued to me in Shanghai. She received it solemnly, wrote a receipt, and shut the door in my face. Back on the street, I checked my bank balance at an ATM. The full six months in severance pay plus the dollar value of unused vacation time had already been deposited. This considerable sum, added to the banked salary I had not spent while I was in China, made me quite prosperous. I wondered how much of the windfall the Headquarters admin types would find ways to pilfer. Until they figured that out, I could afford to pay cash for a Maserati. I didn't have to look for a job because I already had one, or so I assumed in the absence of information to the contrary. What now? Should I just wait for Burbank to show himself, or should I try again to make contact? Was I under any obligation to report my news? The last time I tried to keep him posted he ignored my letter and stopped answering the telephone. I felt a twinge of resentment. Should I just forget about Burbank, draw out my cash, walk away from my contract, find an American woman to marry, have kids, live an American life as Chen Qi had recommended, and when the end came, be tumbled into the grave with a rattle of dry bones after every last penny and every drop of life had been squeezed out of me by the system and the wife and kids?

Although I had consumed no alcohol since the Chinese beer I drank with my Peking duck the night before, I felt slightly drunk—woozy, reckless, beckoned I knew not where. I decided to go to New York. Now. I had inherited Mother's apartment there, along with the house in Connecticut, some stocks and bonds, and all her belongings including her jewelry, which she had not worn to her cremation after all. The expense of maintaining the apartment and the house was considerable. I couldn't sell them because of the slump, so why should I pay rent? I withdrew a thousand dollars from the ATM, went back to the apartment and packed my belongings, which fit into one large suitcase and one carry-on, and took the Metroliner to Penn Station. While still in the station, I bought yet another cheap unregistered cell phone and dialed Burbank's number. The result was the same as before—a dozen rings, no pickup. Maybe he too had been fired, or been stricken with cancer, or died when a safe fell on him. Everything Burbank said or did was classified, so it made sense that his death would be stamped top secret. On the way uptown in a taxi operated by someone from central Asia who was just learning to drive, I sent him a text message, telling him in wild cards what had happened and where I was. Again, silence. I shrugged and went on with my existence. I had done what I could, and thanks again, pal, for wasting five years of my life. I thought about the future. Maybe I could become a banker. Or better because even more uninteresting than banking, get a Ph.D. and become a professor of Chinese.

It was good to be in Manhattan, where I had spent the winters of my boyhood, the summers having been daydreamed away in Connecticut.

I immersed myself in the city's money-gulping culture—museums, concerts, theater, movies, basketball games. I joined a gym. I visited bars I had liked when I was a kid, but they were full of kids and drunks, so I drank at home—four ounces of the Macallan before dinner, seldom more, never less. I didn't enjoy dining alone at the bar in loud restaurants at one hundred dollars a plate and being treated like a mendicant, so I usually had a mock-gourmet dinner delivered to the apartment. I didn't want company, and when women struck up a conversation in a public place, I was polite but distant. Nothing had happened to my libido. The problem was, I was looking for a Mei in a world where there was only one Mei. I wanted my Shanghai life, stage-managed though it almost certainly had been, to come back. Maybe I just wanted someone to talk to, certainly I wanted a particular face to look into while making love. My Mandarin, I knew, was flying away. Sometimes in midtown I overheard phrases on the street that I didn't really understand. In dreams I saw a Chinese woman in Central Park who usually turned out to be a Mei who didn't know me from Adam. If it was the real Mei she probably would have told me I should learn another Chinese language. "It's ridiculous to speak only one Han language," she would say in her dream-woman voice, which croaked a little, like Jean Arthur's English. "You should perfect your Shanghainese and learn Yue."

One night in spring, after seeing a play on Forty-fifth Street, I decided to walk home. The weather was warm, the air was still. As I emerged from the theater, I noticed a young Chinese couple. Half hidden in the crowd, they walked along behind me for a few steps, the woman talking on a cell phone. At Sixth Avenue I turned left. The couple kept on going east. There were few pedestrians on the avenue. The yellow moon, almost full but flattened on one edge, hung overhead between two tall buildings. I gazed at it, my head bent far back. This posture was slightly dizzying. For once I was content, free of exasperation. I had enjoyed the play, I was glad to see the moon in such a beautiful phase. Because of the pollution and the glare of electric light, it was a rare night when you could see any of the lights in the sky over Shanghai or any other city in China or for that matter, anywhere else in the world unless you were in the Sahara Desert.

A man's voice said, "Be careful. You're walking into traffic."

I woke up, and I unbent my neck. He was right. I was inches from the curb. I said, "Thanks." But I was on my guard. He was smaller than me, but he might have a gun or a knife or maybe Mace, which was as often a robber's weapon as a victim's defense. There was enough light to see that he was Chinese, like the young couple that might have been following me outside the theater.

He moved into the light of a store window. He wanted me to see his face. He waited for me to recognize him. I did so immediately. He was dressed as he had been the last time I saw him, in that Washington restaurant, but now he wore a leather jacket over his black T-shirt and a baseball cap. What was he doing here? I didn't know whether I wanted him to know I remembered him.

He refused to play the game. "I thought it was you," he said. "The Peking duck. The young lady in distress."

"And Laozi," I said. "I remember. How are you?"

"I'm well, thank you. What are we doing in New York?"

"I was wondering the same thing," I said. "You first."

"A long story," he said. "Shall we walk together?"

If nothing else, this was an opportunity to speak Mandarin. I thought I knew what he was, why he was here, whom the Chinese woman had been talking to on her cell phone. I said, "Why not?"

Neither of us mentioned Laozi again. Nor did we exchange names. For two or three blocks we didn't exchange a word. As before, my companion asked no personal questions, volunteered no personal information. A person who offers no information is the reverse image of one who offers too much—follow the logic? After ten minutes or so, I broke the silence. How did he like New York? It was the greatest city in Christendom, he said. I didn't think I had ever before heard that particular word spoken aloud. He began to talk. Small talk. My new friend was a basketball fan. He watched the Knicks on television and liked a pickup game. So did I, I said. Then I said, "We haven't answered your question."

"What question was that?" he asked.

"'Why are we in New York?'"

"I live here," he said.

"So do I."

"Really? I took you for a man of Washington. A civil servant, perhaps."

We marched on. He was exercising, not strolling. I asked if he knew a lot of civil servants.

He said, "Far too many. I work at the United Nations."

"As U.N. staff?"

"No, in China's delegation," he said.

"Do you find the work interesting?"

"Not especially," he said. "The U.N. is an artificial thing. It makes a lot of its great purpose, but in fact it has no purpose except to be the choo-choo toy of Washington."

"Then what's the point?"

"Someone must protect the small fish from too much handling," he said.

At last we reached my building. Though he may have regarded the address as valuable information, he barely glanced at it, as if he already knew where it was.

He said, "Do you play basketball?"

"I used to. But I'm older now and not as nimble as I used to be."

He handed me his card. "I have access to a gym," he said. "If you feel like playing a little one-on-one, give me a call." He didn't ask for my card. I didn't offer one. I was pretty sure he already knew who I was, that this encounter was not accidental.

I said, "I'm sure you'd beat me."

"Who knows?" he said. "Games are in the lap of the gods. I'm shorter and older and not especially interested in winning. We can bet on the outcome—a dollar a game."

I said, "Maybe we should play *weiqi* instead. Then you'd be sure to win."

"That's an idea," he said. "Also for money?"

I said, "Now you're making me worry. Are you a ringer?"

He knew the outdated slang, he caught the double meaning. I could see it in his eyes. He smiled a disarming smile and, without answering, lifted a hand and walked away, moving even more swiftly than when we had been walking together. I looked at his card. The Chinese characters gave his name as Lin Ming. His title was "economics attaché." Read "Guoanbu." What next?

I didn't call him. Making the first move would be the wrong move. There was little doubt in my mind that there would be, in due course, another chance meeting. I made no change in my habits, so as to make things easier. A couple of days later I realized I was being watched—four mixed-gender, all-Han teams of three people each, just like in Shanghai. Here, they stood out a bit more even though they stayed farther back and there was nothing unusual about seeing three Chinese scattered in any New York crowd. I pretended to be oblivious to their company. Since the goal of tradecraft is a natural appearance, why not just be natural? The adversary will watch you whether you know he's there or not. Let him watch, for who knows who watches the watchman? Just the same, remembering Burbank's lecture on the right to self-defense, I started carrying a can of pepper spray and a short fighting knife, and was careful not to let anyone get too close to me when I went walking after dark.

One afternoon a month or so after bumping into Lin Ming, I stopped at a sandwich shop that served excellent meatball sandwiches, then went to the movies. I saw a Woody Allen film, a very enjoyable one set in Barcelona—amusing story, good acting, beautiful ardent women. I wondered if Mr. Allen realized how much better his movies had become since he stopped casting himself. Lin Ming was far from my mind as I walked, still smiling, out of the theater. I had stopped in the men's room, so the rest of the audience had scuttled away by the time I reached the sidewalk. It was raining—a downpour. Darkness was falling and the cars had their headlights on and their windshield wipers thumping. The rain blurred the scene, you couldn't read the signs on the buses or make out faces. I waited under the marquee for it to let up. After a moment or two my eyes adjusted. A few feet away, also under the marquee, stood Lin Ming, smoking a cigarette and watching the traffic. When he saw me, he dropped the butt, ground it out with the sole of his shoe, and said, "Hello there." No smile of delighted surprise. Meeting by chance in a cloudburst in the middle of a city of eight million was the most natural thing in the world, of course it was.

"Hello yourself," I said.

Lin Ming did not explain himself. In some not so very elusive way he reminded me of Burbank. I imagined telling Burbank this and watching his reaction. The comparison would tell him something about Lin, something about me, something to lock up in a safe.

To Lin Ming I said, "Let me guess. You just happened to be passing by and there I was, coming out of the movies."

Smiling at last, the winner of the game of wits, Lin Ming said, "Actually, yes. I was just getting out of the rain and you appeared as if beamed down like Captain Kirk." How did he know these things? He was carrying a gym bag. He said, "Basketball?" Pointing at my Keds, he said, "You're wearing the right shoes. The gym is right around the corner." I shook my head and smiled regretfully.

The rain was letting up. Lin Ming shifted his gym bag from one shoulder to the other. He looked at his watch. "I'd better go or I'll miss my time," he said. "It was nice to run into you. Big city, small world. Long odds."

"Odds can be odd," I said.

He walked away.

Feigning impulse, I called after him, "Wait up. I could use some exercise."

An hour later, panting and drenched in sweat, I owed Lin Ming three dollars even though I was five inches taller and years younger than he was. Under the basket he was quick, deceptive, a deadeye shooter. He played in the same way that he walked—fast, silent, no expression whatsoever on his face, no movement of the eyes or body to tip off his next move. Besides, I had let him win.

I went home to shower, and as hot water washed away sweat and unknotted muscles, I wondered where and when I would run into my new friend next. And how long it would take him to pop the question.

16

Every week or so I cleaned out the mailbox. The usual yield was a large accumulation of junk mail addressed to my mother, sometimes a bill her executor had forgotten to pay, and almost always, several appeals from dodgy strangers who wanted her to give them money. Mother subscribed to the *New Yorker* and *National Geographic* and most of the other genteel slicks that people of her generation and kind displayed for a while, then threw away after looking at the pictures. She also received a couple of beefcake magazines as well as some soft-porn publications. Rifling Mother's mailbox I learned secrets she never meant me to know, and this evidence of her humanness caused me to love her a little more. It also brought back those long-ago female howls from the master bedroom.

A few days after I ran into Lin Ming under the marquee, I found a small envelope addressed to me in a nymphet hand—the kind in which the letter *i* is dotted with a little circle. This puzzled me, since no one knew I was here except the doormen, Lin Ming, and maybe Burbank in his omniscience. I waited until I was alone in the apartment to open the envelope. Inside was an invitation from Dr. Brook Holloway and

Mr. Henry Smithers to the christening of their infant son, Stanley Austin Holloway-Smithers, at the Church of Saint Luke in the Fields on Hudson Street at ten o'clock in the morning of the coming Friday. Business attire, no gifts, please. Friday was two days away. As I had never known anyone called Holloway or Smithers, I surmised that this was a summons from Burbank. That meant that the place named was a cover name for another place, the day and time likewise. The problem was, I didn't know what the wild cards meant, and therefore I couldn't possibly get to the right place at the right time. There was no RSVP phone number. The return address was a post office box with an Upper West Side zip code. Of course I had the number for the phone that Burbank never answered, but even if someone picked up, I could hardly ask to be told over an open line, in plain English, what "the Church of Saint Luke in the Fields" stood for, what the actual time of the meeting was, and what was the significance, if any, of those tin-ear aliases. I looked in the envelope again and found a smaller card inviting me to a reception following the baptism at an address on Washington Square. Was it possible that at some point in my life I *had* known a Holloway or a Smithers, or both, and that the invitation was puzzling because it was genuine? After playing a few hands of solitaire on my new laptop, I decided to go to Saint Luke in the Fields at the time indicated and see what happened.

Wearing one of my Shanghai suits and a shirt and tie and buffed-up leather shoes, I showed up at the church at the precise time indicated. The doors were locked. I lingered for a few minutes, another breach of protocol, since the unmet agent is supposed to consider himself under observation by the adversary and to slink away without delay. No one approached me. I took a cab to an imaginary address on Eighth Street, loitered until the hour of the reception, and tried to find the address on Washington Square. It did not exist. The amount of time wasted every day by spies of all nations on comedies of errors of this kind would provide hours enough for a terrorist cell composed of two illiterate brothers and a cousin living in a cave to build a nuclear device. By now it was well past eleven. I decided to take a walk around Greenwich Village. Maybe someone would follow me, tap me on the shoulder, and explain this fiasco. It would be easy to keep me in sight. It was Friday, so I was almost the only guy on the street wearing a suit, and as usual, I was taking no noticeable countermeasures.

On Fifth Avenue, a young man was handing out leaflets, but only to men. With each leaflet he shouted, "Here you go, dude, get laid! Only twenty bucks." I gave him a wide berth. This offended him. He yelled "Hey!" and ran after me, then walked backward in front of me, red-faced and shouting, spit flying. Was I too effing good to read a leaflet about the crimes of the secret elite? Was I some kind of effing right-winger? Did I effing love it when some effing American assassin murdered innocent Muslims with an effing Hellfire missile? I stopped in my tracks. He walked toward me, crazy-faced. When he was close, he murmured, "This one is special for you." He handed me a leaflet. I took it. Up close he was a nice, clean kid with freckles who smelled of shampoo and whose loving parents had paid for about ten thousand dollars worth of work on his teeth. He said, "Read this, it will show you the way to the Lord."

As I walked away, I read the leaflet. It was a plain piece of paper on which was printed, in block letters, "LOBBY OF ALGONQUIN. NOW." I was back in touch.

I folded it up and placed it in the inside pocket of my jacket, which closed with a button. On the way uptown, I reflected for the thousandth time on the absurdity of the life I was leading. I asked myself why I stayed with it, how all this nonsense could possibly lead to a result that would change the fate of the world by so much as a milligram, why I had wanted to get involved in the first place. Of course I knew the answers to all these questions. As much as I was tempted to put an end to this farce, to quit, to forget it and try despising some other walk in life, the truth was that I had become a secret agent because I could not bear for another minute the pointlessness of life in the real world. To go back to it would be no escape. It would be a surrender to the destiny I fled when I went on the lam. If the craft meant nothing, at least it was done in something like absolute privacy, as if everything was happening in another time, another universe, another state of consciousness. Its joys were palpable. For years I had been left alone to enjoy the pleasures of learning to speak and read an ancient and beautiful language and the company of a brilliant woman who loved sex. If that wasn't a blessed state of being, what was? What difference did it make if the work I did meant nothing, accomplished nothing, burned up money on an epic scale? What human endeavor was any different?

As the cab pulled up to the curb on Forty-fourth Street, I knew I was kidding myself, but at least I knew that escape was a dream and knowing that for certain was a terrific joke on me, on everybody, and for the moment I was a happy man. Of course, I hadn't yet gone inside.

17

It was lunchtime, so every seat but one was taken in the shadowy lobby of the Algonquin. My stepfather, a *New Yorker* enthusiast who loved this place, used to tip the waiter who worked the room fifty dollars per visit to make sure there would always be a table for him and the people he brought in to commune with the ghosts of the Round Table. I looked around for Burbank. No sign of him. He was the quintessential gray man you might not see in a crowd the first time you looked, so I looked again. This time I recognized the person who was waiting for me. He lifted a hand and smiled. He was dressed like a diplomat in a dark pin-striped suit and the rest of the rig, including cuff links. No wonder I had missed him at first glance. Not only was he not the man I had been looking for, but this Lin Ming didn't much resemble the Lin Ming in jeans or sweats I had known before this moment.

He must have laid a satisfactory tip on the waiter, because the man was at our table before either my host or I had had time to speak a word. I ordered mineral water. Lin Ming was drinking tea. He wore round rimless glasses.

I said, "How come you shoot baskets so well if you're nearsighted?"

"Contact lenses. It's kind of you to come on such short notice."

"The invitation was imaginative," I said.

"I'm glad you thought so."

People were finishing their drinks and drifting toward the dining room across the lobby. The din of their conversation made it difficult to hear Lin Ming. He waited until the people at the next table vacated. Then he said, "I apologize for the charade." He pronounced *charade* as a French word, an odd little flourish.

I said, "No problem. I wonder, though, why you went to so much trouble when all you had to do was waylay me the next time I went to a theater."

"Do you have a theory about that?"

"I have an idea, but I'd like to hear your story."

"Very simple," Lin Ming said with perfect composure. "You have avoided tradecraft so assiduously for the whole time I and certain friends have been interested in you"—that word again—"that you have made these people want to know you better. One would have to know tradecraft and know it well in order to fake its absence. Or so my friends assumed."

"'Tradecraft?'" I said, as if the word were new to me. This was an amateurish move.

Lin Ming thought so, too. He was deaf to the interruption. "Today," he said, "tested our assumption."

"And did I pass or fail?"

"Well, here you are. Why don't we have some lunch?"

We were seated at a good table. Clearly they knew Lin Ming at the Algonquin. He ordered a salad composed of many raw vegetables. On the twenty-year-old recommendation of my stepfather, I had a club sandwich—my first, as far as I could remember, since he took me to lunch here when I was sixteen. Strangers were inches away from us on all sides. Lin Ming talked no business. He had been to a Knicks game since the last time we met. It was enjoyable even though the Knicks lost. Basketball was better when you could hear the players cursing at each other, when you could see the sweat fly off their bodies and smell it. Did he particularly enjoy the smell of sweat? At basketball games, yes. The smell of each race was different. Also the sweat of men and women. Had I noticed?

Lin Ming paid the bill in cash, with a knowing but not showy tip. He played by the rules, as an operative is supposed to do as part of the camouflage. We went back to the lounge. It was deserted now. The waiter brought us coffee and disappeared. "Everyone has gone back to work," Lin Ming said. "So we have the place to ourselves."

He sipped his coffee. Lin Ming noticed that I wasn't drinking mine. He asked if I would prefer something else.

"No, thanks."

"Then I will come to the point," he said in Mandarin. "You speak our language with remarkable fluency. You know our country."

"Only Shanghai."

"No one knows the whole of China. Anyway, that's not a requirement of the job."

"What job? I was just fired from a job in China."

"That's not really the case. Better to look at your situation as a transfer."

"I don't follow."

"I want to offer you a position. The salary would be somewhat higher than your former position paid—and perhaps, depending on results, much higher, and totally tax free. It would require a change in your lifestyle."

I thought, *Here it comes*.

I said, "Like what?"

"You wouldn't be living in China. At least, not right away. Perhaps in the future, if the job requires it."

Lin Ming was going slow. Why, if he was so sure of me? Or sure enough, at least, to organize this morning's charade. Of course it hadn't cost much—little more than whatever his people had paid the crazy kid to hand me the message. Probably they had shown him a photo of me and given him his leaflets and a fifty-dollar bill. Or more likely, a twenty. Or maybe he was an unpaid true believer.

"I don't mean to be pushy," I said, "but what exactly is this job, and who exactly would I be working for?"

Lin Ming said, "Let me tell you that as a whole, rather than in fragments."

"Fine. But you're making me nervous. I think the moment has come to lay the cards on the table."

"Or the stones on the board. We must have that game of *weiqi*. Soon."

We seemed to be having it now. If his purpose had been to take me by surprise, he had succeeded. I could hardly have felt more surrounded, even though this scenario was playing out as though Burbank had written the script. Lin Ming seemed to read my thoughts—with something like a twinkle in his eye. He drank a little more coffee. I didn't think he liked the stuff any better than I did.

Lin Ming said, "Let's be frank. I think you know what the job is. You know what I am and what I am doing, and therefore you know who you would be working for."

He was telling me that this was the moment to break off this conversation if I wasn't interested in what was coming next. It was the moment to save him from embarrassing himself.

I said, "Go on."

"Very well," Lin Ming said. "Here is the proposal. We believe that you are sympathetic to China and interested in China's future in the world as it is intertwined with the future of the United States. You have unusual skills and useful contacts."

I started to interrupt. Lin Ming cut me off. "Please. We wish to work with you. We believe you already have a job, a confidential job, and that is the job you have been doing for the past few years, including all your time in Shanghai. We want you to go back to that job, to go inside and work closely with Mr. Burbank. We will make sure that Mr. Burbank has good reason to be pleased with your work. We will help you. We will provide you with information that will be of great interest to Mr. Burbank and his organization. It will be reliable, truthful, valuable information. In return we would hope that you would offer us your services as a consultant, including the provision of certain information that is likewise interesting and trustworthy. We would handle your situation with great care. Very likely you will be promoted and honored by your agency—and honored and rewarded, with the utmost discretion, by us also. By me. We would work together. For the good of both our countries."

I said, "'Us' being who—Guoanbu?"

At the sound of this word, Lin Ming winced. He said, "The moment has not yet come to discuss details."

I said, "You must be crazy."

"You think so?" Lin Ming said. "No one else has ever suggested that."

"Listen to me. I bled for this country. I'm an American to the bone, descended from generations of Americans. Under no circumstances, none, would I ever consider betraying the United States of America. Or worse, betraying my ancestors."

That outburst, as I intended, was theatrical. But Lin Ming had been acting, too. He still was. Now he exhaled, as if expelling his surprise at my rudeness. As the book of tradecraft prescribed (the manual is the same in every language and in every epoch), he waited for me to calm down. He was a professional, keeping his head, playing the game, doing his thing.

"I understand," he said. "Mei will be very disappointed."

I said, "She will? What's that supposed to mean?"

"The plan was that she would come back to you."

"Why?"

"Because she wants to be with you. Because she would be helpful." He smiled. "Because she would give you the opportunity to speak Mandarin with an intelligent person."

Ah, the bribe of bribes. The thing I wanted most in the world! The clumsiness, the nerve, the contempt, the "Roll over, Rover!" The bastard! But oh, what an opportunity. Using the Method like a Brando, I summoned things that had made me mad in the past—Wojciechowski the Hessian, the brainless coach who recruited him, my father's selfish death—until my face reddened with anger. In a furious silence, I walked out of the Algonquin. Minutes later, as I was turning onto Fifth Avenue, Lin caught up. Walking along beside me, looking up at my profile, he said, "You haven't said no."

"Then I'll say it now. No."

"I can't hear you over the traffic," Lin Ming said. "Wait. Think. Take your time. Let's meet for a game of *weiqi* when you've had more time to consider this new opportunity, and talk some more."

He stopped walking. We were in front of Brooks Brothers. As I strode away, I looked into the store window and saw Lin Ming's reflection. He was lighting a cigarette.

What insouciance. Or, more probably, a signal to his sidewalk people.

18

Counterintuitive though it may seem in a time of terrorism, most employees of Headquarters who still have landline home telephones are listed in the directories for Washington and its suburbs. True, you have to know their names or their wives' or husbands' or bedfellows' names before you can look them up or call them up or blow up their houses or cars, but once you've identified them, the next move is yours. Therefore, walking in on Burbank wasn't an impossible mission. I looked up Burbank, Luther R., in the anywho.com white pages. There he was on Forest Lane in McLean, Virginia, complete with driving directions. I knew there was no point in calling him at the number listed, so I changed into jeans and a sweater, stuffed a book and a sandwich and a bottle of water and a change of underwear into my backpack, then took the bus to Broadway and the subway to Forty-second Street, walked to the Port Authority bus terminal, and took a bus to Washington, last passenger aboard.

It was about midnight when I arrived on foot at Burbank's house. Dark sky, sleeping neighborhood. The downstairs lights were on. I assumed that a state-of-the-art alarm system and surveillance cameras would be in operation, so I just walked up to the front door and rang the bell. No one answered. But I heard someone inside the house, a young woman from the light-footed sound she made, running rapidly up or down stairs. Through the glass above the door, I saw a moving shadow. I heard a dial tone, a low female voice. In an astonishingly short time, two McLean police cruisers pulled up at the house, strobes flashing. Four large cops got out of the vehicles and approached me. All carried nightsticks, each had the other hand on a holstered handgun. Whoever was in the house switched on the outside lights. These included several powerful floodlights that bleached the cops' skin.

The lead policeman, a burly sergeant, assumed the stance of authority and said, "Lemme see some ID." I gave him my passport, in which nearly every page bore incriminating stamps and notations in Mandarin and other unreadable languages. He asked for another government-issued picture ID. I handed over my District of Columbia driver's license. Was the address on the license my current address? "No, officer." Then what was my current address and why hadn't I reported it and gotten a new license? Because I didn't have a new address in D.C. Did that mean I was homeless? I explained that I was staying in New York for the time being. Then what was I doing on foot in McLean, Virginia, at this time of night? Where did I work? I admitted I was jobless. At that, the questions ceased. The sergeant cuffed me. Another cop frisked me while a third read me my rights. I was placed under arrest on suspicion of trespassing in the night. Nobody asked me if I knew the people who lived in this house, and I couldn't have answered the question even if it had been put to me, because I wasn't sure I did. For all I knew, the residents were some other Burbanks—the real ones, and the Burbank I knew was really a Brackenridge or a Bumstead. Or maybe this was a Potemkin house and Luther and family, assuming he had one, had never lived here at all. Also, I was sure that anyone who came to the door, especially Burbank himself, would say that they had never seen me before in their lives. Local cops weren't cleared to know that I knew Burbank or that he knew me. Strictly speaking, they weren't cleared to know me in true name. But now they did.

Other cops booked me at the police station, strip-searched me, confiscated my belongings, including about five hundred dollars in fifties, a drug dealer denomination, and put me in a cell. I asked if I could keep my book. A desk officer examined it carefully for hidden razor blades or poisonous pellets or explosive pages, and to my surprise, handed it over. The cops told me I was entitled to one phone call. I said not right now. I had no one to call except Lin Ming.

An hour or so later, a jailer told me I had a visitor. He opened my cell and led me down the hall to a small windowless room. A well-nourished sleepy-eyed gray-haired man in yesterday's rumpled suit sat at a table. He said, "The bail was three hundred dollars. I posted it. Do you have that much with you?"

"I did when I arrived. Who are you?"

"Your lawyer." He stood up. He was in no mood to be friendly. I asked him what time it was. "It's three-thirty," he said. "A.M. Let's go."

I followed the jailer while my lawyer settled the bill. At the desk, my belongings were returned to me. Everything was there. I signed a receipt.

In the lawyer's car, a well-broken-in, entry-level BMW, I said, "Now what?"

"Now you owe me three hundred dollars."

I counted out the money and gave it to him. He stuffed it into the breast pocket of his jacket and started the car. I said, "What about your fee?" He didn't answer the question.

He said, "The bail money will be returned to you by the police. Eventually. The owner of the house where you committed trespass has decided not to press charges, so you're a free man, no hearing or trial, except that you now have a rap sheet, a public record under what I presume is your own name, that puts you on his doorstep at a specific time and date, with four police officers as witnesses. I advise you to observe the speed limit in Virginia from now on."

I said, "Do you want me to get out of the car now or are we going somewhere?"

"I'll tell you when to get out of the car."

He drove me to a house in a sleeping suburb. Another digital lock. He punched in the numbers and let me in. He followed me through the door and turned off the alarm system. Did all safe houses have the same entry code so that agents wouldn't forget them in the same way they used to lose keys? The lawyer said, "Someone will come to see you." He was still disgruntled. As if I had asked a question, he said, "No, I don't know when. Until they get here, stay put. Do not answer the phone. Do not *use* the phone. Do not memorize the address. Do not open the door if the doorbell rings. Do not order pizza. You can use a bed, take a shower, jerk off, eat the food if you find any. Do not go outside."

Where would I go? I had no idea where I was. All suburban housing developments look alike, and besides, every Yankee who ever crossed the Potomac except Ulysses S. Grant got lost as soon as he reached the Virginia side. I couldn't have found my way to the nearest 7-Eleven.

The lawyer left. I locked the door, turned down the heat, drank a glass of nonfat milk, and microwaved some packaged macaroni and cheese I found in a cupboard. *Busy day,* I said to myself and to the listening devices. I found a puffy recliner chair in the basement television room, sat down, covered up with the Burberry, pulled the handle, and went to sleep.

Burbank arrived after dark the next day. I smelled him coming before he even opened the front door because he was carrying a bag of sandwiches—tofu for him, meatball for me, same as before. How could he remember the meatballs? It had been months. Did he take notes? I was too hungry to ask questions. Apart from the mac and cheese, I had found nothing to eat in the kitchen except a couple of Snickers bars, frozen solid. Burbank brought two bottles of microbrew beer, and this time I drank mine. For fifteen minutes, no noise was heard except the sound of chewing. Burbank had no more small talk than he'd ever had, which was to say, none. He was his original muffled self—no *hello* or *good to see you* or other fake camaraderie, no handshake, not the smallest smile. He was a man who lived without the niceties. *Admirable,* I thought. I wondered if he was the same way at home—silent cocktails with his wife if he had one, mute dinners, wordless copulation. If he was upset by what had happened on his doorstep the night before, he didn't say so. My visit had been a serious breach of security. Maybe his silence indicated displeasure. Maybe he thought the tongue-lashing could wait until I finished my sandwich. It was even possible that he thought I must have had a good reason for doing what I did. That was no excuse for having done it.

When we finished eating and Burbank had stuffed the sandwich wrappers back in the bag and gone though his routine of wiping our fingerprints off everything we had touched, he took from his pocket a small remote, like the ones used for keyless car ignitions, and clicked it. I thought he must be turning the listening devices off or on, because he now began to talk.

"About last night, my apologies," he said. "I wasn't home when you called. The au pair was frightened. She was alone. She's from Colombia, so she tends to be a bit nervous after dark."

I said I hoped the girl was all right now. Burbank said, "So what brings you to town? I assume you have something that won't wait."

Apparently he hadn't gotten my text message or had been too busy to read it. I told him what I had written, in detail. As before, he listened intently and seemed to take it for granted that I was leaving nothing out, since he put no questions to me. He took a photograph from his pocket and showed it to me. It was a very good likeness of Lin Ming, taken outdoors on a New York street. Lin Ming was wearing sweats and a Mets cap. Burbank said, "Is this the man?"

If he hadn't received my texts, how did he guess? I said, "Yes."

"What contact have you had with him?"

I told him about the "chance" encounter in the Washington restaurant, about bumping into him on Sixth Avenue. "Also, we ran into each other last week. . . ."

"Jehovah at work. Where?"

"In the rain, outside a movie theater, and then we played one-on-one basketball at a gym."

"Who won?"

"He did."

"A little guy like that beat you?"

I nodded. "And day before yesterday he tried to recruit me."

"Details?"

I provided them for the second time.

Burbank said, "I wonder why he gave you so much detail. Usually the Chinese are stingy with information."

"You know who he really is?"

"*What* he really is, more or less," Burbank said. "It really doesn't matter whether the name he was born with was Chang or Wang or Wu or Xu or what benighted village he comes from. He hasn't been his original self for a long time. We've caught glimpses of him. He's been posted to Tokyo, Paris, London, always under diplomatic cover. He's cordial, social. It's easy to take a liking to him, as you found. He's baptized an impressive number of sinners."

"Was his method the same as with me?" I asked.

"No. His M.O. is to be quiet, slow, discreet. The question is, why was he not the same as usual with you?"

"Don't ask me."

"I'm not asking you."

"Then let me ask you something. What now?"

"Suspicion," said Burbank. "Prudence. Deception."

The three muses of the craft. Burbank was watching me as if he expected me to say something and I was taking too long to say it.

At last he said, "Tell me, what was in your mind when Lin Ming was making his pitch?"

"Self-congratulation because I thought I had read him right. Although I had always assumed that Mei was on duty, I was surprised—startled— when he revealed that he or his friends controlled her."

"You believed that?"

"I believed he wanted me to believe it."

"A natural reaction, but watch yourself. What else?"

"Having revealed so much, he was coy about being Guoanbu."

"Maybe he isn't Guoanbu. Maybe he's military intelligence, like Alger Hiss's Russian case officer. Or something else we're not aware of."

"Like what?"

Burbank waived the question away. He said, "I feel that there's something more. Something you hesitate to put into words. Am I right about that?"

"Okay," I said. "Yes. What he was offering was so close to what you told me you hoped for from this operation that I wondered if it was a case of great minds, his and yours, running in the same channel."

Burbank blinked, like an actor on cue. He said, "Why ever would you think a thing like that?"

"Sometimes I have unworthy thoughts."

"Thanks for the compliment," Burbank said, getting to his feet. "Interesting mind you have. Keep using it. Go back to New York. Play this fish a little longer. Keep your knickers on. Then we'll see."

And that was all I got out of him. He gave me a new phone number to call, a different accommodation address to write to, and a mobile phone to use when I called so the caller ID would be recognized. All this reminded me of CEO Chen. Why did I keep making these comparisons?

19

Two weeks later I was walking in Riverside Park when I saw Lin Ming on the path ahead, bouncing toward me, arms swinging as though in training for a power-walking marathon. He wore a sweatband with a Knicks logo. I sauntered on. I expected him to thrust out a hand, smile broadly, pause to chat. Instead, eyes front, concentrating on technique, he strode right by me. Snubbed! Would I ever recover? I resisted the temptation to turn around and watch him jounce away into the distance but kept on walking, avoiding designer dogs, trying not to stumble over the shrieking brats in designer rompers who swarmed the path while their nannies gossiped in Spanish and half a dozen other languages.

A week or so after that encounter, I found another invitation-size envelope in the mailbox. It contained a card with a Chinatown address typed upon it in red, along with the following message: "Sorry to be in such a hurry the other day. Nothing personal. Hope Saturday is a good day to play *weiqi*. 6 o'clock? Afterward we can have dinner. *Very* good Sichuan chef." The card was signed, also in red, the color of happiness, in an unreadable scrawl.

The meeting place turned out to be upstairs over a restaurant called Sichuan Delight. A sleek young man with a patch of hair under his lower lip was posted at the door. He said, "Please follow me, sir. When he opened the unlocked door, bright ceiling lights switched on, revealing a steep flight of stairs. I smelled China. The young man told me to knock on door Number 8—one knock only. Because it sounds in Mandarin like the word that means wealth, eight is a very lucky number. I knocked. Lin Ming opened the door. Like me, he wore sneakers, jeans, and a T-shirt, his displaying 機, the character for "opportunity." He smoked an unfiltered cigarette—not his first. The room was blue with smoke. Behind me, the hallway lights clicked off. Lin Ming said, "Come in from the dark. The landlord doesn't like to waste electricity."

The stage set was complete. The *weiqi* board was already set up. So was the teapot. A large poster of Three Gorges dam hung on the wall—meant perhaps to remind me, unsubtly, of the beautiful Yangtze. We sat down immediately, and after drinking tea, began to play. As I had expected, it was the village idiot versus Bobby Fisher. We played three games in less time than it usually takes to play one. Lin Ming tried hard not to humiliate me, but I was so bad he could not find a way to let me win. There was plenty of chatter, almost entirely Lin Ming's. He had given up hope for the Knicks, but the baseball season had begun. Maybe the Mets would surprise themselves and make it to the playoffs.

Minutes after we finished our final game of *weiqi*, a waiter arrived from the Sichuan Delight with a staggering load of dishes. Lin Ming had not overstated the chef's skill. After supper—seconds afterward, Lin Ming must have had some sort of hidden bell under the table or carpet—a busboy came and took away the debris. Lin Ming took out his pack of Camels and offered me one. I shook my head. He drank very little of his maotai, but Chinese host that he was, kept my glass topped up. The genteel American has not yet been born who will not go to almost any lengths to avoid being disrespectful of a foreigner's culture, no matter how silly it seems, no matter how transparent the foreigner's contempt for that American's monkey-see monkey-do behavior might be. Foreigners will spit out our food and drink in disgust, challenge the intelligence of every idea we express, look amazed when we act according to our own etiquette instead of making the hilarious mistake of mimicking what we mistake for their own good manners. In this we are alone among the great powers of history. Ancient China laid its disdain on lesser peoples with a trowel, and modern China does the same. Timur the Lame did not make nice to conquered peoples by acting like a Han or a Turk. When the British or the French in their palmy days Gatling-gunned a few hundred Chinese or other racial inferiors, they didn't apologize. They just told themselves that the slant-eyed beggars obviously placed no value on human life, and had a drink.

I was playing the supine American with this Chinese intelligence officer who was trying to suborn me to treason because that was what I thought he expected. For the moment Lin Ming had stopped making conversation. Glowing Camel between his lips, he looked at the ceiling. He tapped the ash from his cigarette at the last possible moment and put it back between his lips. Squinting through the smoke he said, "Have you been in touch with Mr. Burbank since last we met?"

I told him the truth.

"By telephone?"

"No, I took a trip to Washington."

"Ah. And was he glad to see you?"

"Surprised, I think."

Lin Ming ground out his cigarette in the overflowing ashtray. He said, "May I assume that you told Mr. Burbank about my offer of employment to you?"

"Of course I did," I said.

"In what detail?"

"I told him everything. How else could I keep his trust?"

"You wish to keep his trust?"

"Isn't doing so the whole point?" I asked.

"Excellent," Lin Ming said. "Very, very good. You know how to think ahead. That's very rare. I'm proud of you."

He lifted his maotai glass and wet his lips. Supinely I did the same, striving to stay in character, hoping that I was winning *his* trust, but not betting the farm on it.

Lin Ming's mobile phone rang. He looked at the caller ID and left the room to answer it. A long time passed. He did not return. I took the hint and left. As I descended the stairs, the blinding overhead lights went out. In a Fu Manchu movie, the sinister young cashier would have stepped out of a hidden compartment and driven a dagger into my spinal cord. In this humdrum real world, however, I found the fellow waiting for me in the street below, smilingly holding open the door of the taxi he had fetched for me.

20

I had recorded my conversation with Lin Ming with a dirty-tricks cell phone. When I got home after my evening in Chinatown, I extracted the chip from the phone, placed it in a small plastic pillbox I found in Mother's medicine cabinet, put the pillbox in a padded envelope, addressed it in fictitious name to Burbank's post office box, and dropped the envelope down the mail chute. One of the oddities about the explosion in espionage technology is that the computer has rendered snail mail the least vulnerable of all methods, apart from the cleft stick, for the transmission of secret communications. What geek would ever guess that a letter flying around in plain sight might be less easy to hack than an imaginary byte?

The next morning I took a train to Westport and drove to the house in Mother's decrepit Mercedes, which I had left in the station's parking lot. She had called it her new car because it was new to her. She had driven junks exclusively. When a car stopped running she would call up her used car dealer and ask him to bring her a replacement priced at no more than a thousand dollars including removal of the worn-out vehicle. Both my father and my stepfather had been crazy about fast, costly European cars, and I guess her fondness for derelict vehicles was one of the ways in which she expressed her delight over the expiration of her promises to love, honor, and obey.

Like her mother before her, from whom she learned about men and soils and seeds and fertilizers, Mother had been a keen gardener. Now, with the arrival of spring, her flowerbeds were coming back to life. I visualized them as I drove. I had kept Mother's cook, the recovering crack addict, on as gardener and caretaker, and when I arrived at the house she was kneeling in the backyard, transplanting seedlings. She wasn't a bad-looking woman. It was a sunny day—hot, for the hills of New England—and she wore a sensible gray sports bra and denim shorts. She was barefoot. Her fine hair was escaping strand by strand from the rubber band on her ponytail. The knobs along her spine were prominent, but she had a good body, nice legs, pretty breasts. When she recognized the Mercedes she stood up—her bare knees were muddied—and pulled on a T-shirt. This further tousled her hair. She didn't bother to tuck it in. I waved in a nice-guy way and parked in the driveway. She didn't move a muscle. I walked across the garden, which was a carpet of jonquils and other early flowers whose names I didn't know. She tracked me with a sentinel's eyes as if expecting me to trample something. If she recognized me she gave no sign. She definitely wasn't the smiley type. For a moment I thought she really might not know who I was—I had hired her at the cemetery, and she had seen me only a couple of times before that and then briefly—so I took off my baseball cap and said something like, "Planting flowers, I see." One expects such inanities to be understood as gestures of good intentions. No chance of that from this poker-faced militant. I told her I was sorry to arrive unannounced. In the first sign that she had identified me, she said, "It's your house. You can arrive whenever you feel like it."

Her message was clear. I could send her a check every two weeks if I wanted, but that didn't require her to be agreeable. Had I any orders? I told her to go ahead with what she was doing. She nodded, fell to her knees, and went on with the spring planting.

After using the bathroom—I carried no luggage because I had the clothes and razor and toothbrush I needed stowed away in the house—I sat in the sun and read a book in Mandarin about Shanghai between the world wars. It was refreshing because it barely mentioned the hapless foreigners who were the featured characters of most other histories of that time and place. After a while the garden nymph finished what she was doing, stacked her empty flowerpots, and disappeared into the greenhouse. Water pipes howled. Mother had equipped the outbuilding with a shower and required all grimy people to use it to prevent dirt from being tracked into the house.

Soon the young woman emerged with wet hair pasted to her head. She was now dressed in jeans, sandals, and a clean shirt unbuttoned to her cleavage. She walked over and stood beside my chair. She gave off the odor of Ivory soap. I hadn't smelled it since I made out with Mary Ellen Crowley when I was in the eighth grade. I didn't speak or look up. After a long silence that was the equivalent of a staring contest, she said, "You read Chinese?" I closed the book, marking my place with a finger, looked into her cold eyes, and said, "Are you calling it a day?"

"That's your decision," she said. "If you want dinner I can cook it."

"Good idea. What's on the menu?"

"Tell me what you want and I'll go get it and cook it."

"Anything?"

"Anything Stop & Shop has." I knew it had a lobster tank. I said, "Lobster. The rest is up to you. I'll get the wine from the cellar."

"Fine."

She held out her hand, palm up. I gave her an inquiring look.

She said, "Money."

I gave her two fifties. When she saw my bankroll, the look of proletarian disgust I had noted earlier came back into her eyes. Her upper lip twitched in contempt. The reaction was understandable. Nobody loves the rich, and how could she know that I was okay because Communists had made me rich?

She said, "Do you know how long you'll be staying?"

I told her I wasn't sure, but I'd like it if she made supper every night. She nodded, put the money in her pocket, and remained where she was. She seemed to be thinking something over. I thought she would now turn to go, but she hung where she was. She said, "May I ask a question?"

"Sure."

"Are you here because of my message?"

I said, "No. I didn't know you'd left a message."

She said, "Then I'd better repeat it. Somebody broke into the house."

I flinched, as if I had just seen my name in print on the crime page of the *Shanghai Daily*. I said, "Are you sure?"

She said, "Otherwise there'd be no reason to mention it, would there?"

After a moment I said, "Let me rephrase. How did you become aware of the break-in?"

"A pane of glass in the kitchen door had been broken and replaced."

"Replaced?"

"That's what I just said."

"Tell me more."

Wearily—why hadn't I listened to her message?—she said, "When I let myself in with the key, I noticed broken glass on the kitchen floor—not much, only a few slivers. They glittered in the sunlight. Then I smelled putty and saw that it was fresh and the glass was new, not wavy like the old glass."

"You're a good detective." No answer. I persevered. "Why would they bother to replace the broken windowpane, but leave broken glass in plain sight?"

"I have no idea."

"Did you call the police?"

"That never crossed my mind."

"Why not?" I asked.

"Because I've got a criminal record, possession of crack cocaine. I probably would have been booked as a brain-damaged drug addict looking for something to steal and sell."

"So what did you do?"

"I looked around and saw that the burglars had left other signs of their intrusion."

"Like what?"

"They'd violated everything—stripped the beds and remade them, opened all the doors and drawers in all the rooms, looked under the rugs, took the telephones apart, opened the pill bottles," she said. "They tried to put everything back exactly as they found it, but working in the dark, they didn't always succeed. A lot of things were slightly not where they should be. Also, you could smell them."

"How did they smell?"

"Male sweat. Drugstore aftershave. Urine and fecal matter in the bathrooms."

"They didn't flush the toilets?"

"The stink was in the air, and there were smears in one of the toilet bowls. I also smelled plaster dust, very pungent."

"Plaster dust?"

"This is an old house. The walls are plaster, not Sheetrock."

Obviously she had an uncommonly good sense of smell. I kept the thought to myself. By now I had learned to pay this woman no compliments.

"Anything missing?"

"Your mother's letters and papers," she said.

"All of them?"

"Everything she kept in boxes in the attic. Also her photo albums. Maybe other things, like keepsakes I didn't know about."

"Nothing of value, then."

"She valued what was in the boxes. She kept an armchair and a lamp in the attic so she could go up and read them. She kept her stocks and bonds and CDs in a safe in her closet. But as far as I know she got rid of everything like that before she went into the hospital for the last time."

"Got rid of that stuff how?"

"She put it in a safe-deposit box. Maybe some cash, too."

"Who's got the key?"

"I don't know."

"Did she give you anything before she died?"

"An antique topaz brooch set in opals. A thousand dollars in cash. A pat on the cheek."

"She must have liked you."

No response.

This was food for thought. This burglary was a curious crime. It might not have sent her mind racing as it did mine, but even to a smart amateur, if that's what she was, it had to seem peculiar. I *knew* what it meant—a search team, a very clumsy search team, had conducted what they thought was a clandestine sweep of the premises. They had committed a number of basic mistakes—they hadn't put things back in the exact place where they had found them, they had taken things away instead of photographing them as the rules dictated. These characters apparently assumed that a few old boxes from the attic wouldn't be missed, which meant they thought they could bring them back into this empty house with impunity another night. They had forgotten that you can't assume a damn thing, that you have to stick to the

133

rules, that you should never, ever leave behind the slightest trace of your entry.

"One more thing," the chef said.

"Yes?"

"I found a dozen tiny piles of plaster dust."

Now we were getting someplace. I said, "Did you sweep them up?"

"No. I watch TV. I didn't touch anything that might be evidence."

"Show me."

She led me to my bedroom, to the living room, to my stepfather's basement hideaway. Sure enough, tiny heaps of plaster dust—about a quarter-teaspoon each—lay on the parquet next to the baseboard, as if a mouse or an insect had chewed its way through the wall. But no mouse or termite was guilty of making this mess. What I was looking at was the dust left by a small, fast, super-sharp drill—the kind used by technicians who install electronic bugs. I said, "Hmmm. Have you ever seen a mouse in this house? Or a carpenter ant?"

She said, "No."

I looked at my watch. I said, "You must want to get going to the store."

She said, "I should. What time do you want dinner?" Her voice was softer now, even borderline friendly.

I said, "Seven-thirty?"

"Every night?"

"Yes."

She nodded and left without uttering another word. It was quarter after four. It would take her at least an hour to get to the supermarket through rush-hour traffic and do her shopping and get back to the house. That gave me time to do what I had to do next.

Once again I was in no doubt that I was being listened to and watched as I worked, but I had nothing to lose because the team that did this sloppy job almost certainly belonged either to Burbank or Lin Ming and both of them already knew that I was a spy who recognized spyware when I saw it. I dug five itsy-bitsy cameras and seven audio bugs out of the walls. These I ran through the kitchen disposal to send the message that there was a price to be paid for blatant amateurism. Not that I believed that this was truly the work of amateurs. The blunders were a little too obvious. Maybe what I had discovered so far were decoys. The real bugs would be properly concealed. A good technician can drill through a very thick concrete wall, vacuuming up dust like a dentist as he goes, and stop at exactly the point where nothing remains between the drill and the opposite side of the wall except a coat of paint or the wallpaper. Why anyone would go to so much trouble to bug the empty house of a dead widow who had nothing to hide I could not guess. But maybe I was chasing the wrong suspects. Who knew but what the FBI or some other zealous feds had done this work? I called it a day. There would be time enough tomorrow to check it out.

Dinner was fine—just the right amount of grape-seed oil and lemon in the dressing for the lobster salad, excellent sautéed veal, fresh peas, big Peruvian blackberries with the proper crunch and sweetness. From the cellar I had chosen an Alsatian pinot gris—Mother had liked her glass of wine, and what she saved on automobiles she spent on the grape. Also I found out that the chef's name was Magdalena. She made it plain that no diminutives were allowed. She looked less bony in dimmer light and now that the sun was down smelled faintly of a perfume whose aroma another far more agreeable girl had given me cause to remember.

21

Next morning I arose at first light and resumed my inspection. Sure enough, I spotted the backup bugs and cameras, taking care to look like a guy wandering aimlessly around the house sipping his morning coffee. I let them be. Let my watchers think I had fallen into their trap, that I had mistaken their decoys for the real thing. I had no plans to hold operational meetings in this house or mumble secrets in my sleep. There was no reason why these clowns, whoever they were, or for that matter why the whole world should not watch me shave, cut my toenails, chew my granola, read my books, eat my supper, fix a faucet—even, if there was a merciful and compassionate god, watch me nail the fair Magdalena one moonlit evening after she had done the dishes. Imagine her, imagine mismatched us as infrared images, imagine the moans, the gasps, the rest of the pornography. It had been a long time since Shanghai.

I stayed in the house for a week, and at the end of the week decided to stay a little longer. It would be a good thing, I reasoned, to give Burbank plenty of time to mull the choices offered by my tape of Lin

Ming's recruitment pitch, and for Lin Ming to pile a few more stones on the *weiqi* board. The change of scene not to mention the sense that I was not, owing to Magdalena's daily appearances, all by myself, was good for me. Gradually I stopped seeing the frowning gardener she used to be and started noticing the woman she was. There were things about Magdalena—many things—that made me think there was more to her than she thought she was letting me see. As her behavior softened, my curiosity grew. This was not part of the plan. It just happened. Maybe it was my subconscious at work, demanding payback for earlier affronts. One day as I read another book in the garden while she weeded, she asked me where I had learned Chinese. It was a polite gesture. In return I let her have it: "There is no language called 'Chinese.' People living in China speak two hundred ninety-two languages, most of them mutually incomprehensible. Characters signify different words in different languages. There is also one dead language, Jurchen, that only scholars understand. The language I am reading is Mandarin." Absorbing this spurt of bile, Magdalena was transformed. The change was startling. She looked stricken—in danger of tears, even. She darted away. I was not exactly amazed by her reaction. In my experience, people who dish it out seldom can take it. Magdalena came nowhere near me for the remainder of the day. But supper was especially tasty that night: bouillabaisse, no less. She drove all the way to Great Barrington, to Mother's favorite store across the Massachusetts line, to buy the fish. She spoke no word while serving at table. She wore a skirt and a scoop-neck blouse. Her eyes looked bigger. Mascara? Possibly.

As I ate my chocolate mousse I heard the clatter of china being put into the dishwasher, and also a new sound. Magdalena was humming a tune. Amazed, I rose from the table and went into the kitchen. Her back was turned to me. Even though she could see my reflection in the window above the sink, she went on humming in a pretty but muted soprano voice that sounded trained. She was humming an aria from

Madame Butterfly. I couldn't have been more astonished. Magdalena didn't sing the whole of it, but she sang enough to let me know she could have sung louder and longer if she chose. When she was done, I stifled an urge to applaud, knowing that she would take it for what it was, sarcasm.

Instead, I said, "Where did you train?"

No reply. After a long moment of silence, however, she spoke. With her back still turned to me, she said, "You're straight, right?"

Ah. I said, "Right. You, too?"

She said, "In case you're wondering because of my past, I have no STDs. Not now, not ever."

I said, "What does that mean, you don't sleep with Republicans?"

"It means I have no sexually transmitted diseases. Given my background you've got a right to ask."

"Me either."

"I don't like condoms."

"Neither do I."

What a romantic turn this conversation was taking. Clearly the seduction scenario I'd been putting together in my mind had been a waste of time and imagination. All of a sudden Magdalena turned around, skirt swirling. She could dance, too. She had a little color in her face. She smiled a fleeting little smile. She was a different woman altogether. A certain nervousness—how after all could she know what she was getting herself into?—added to the appeal.

After a small silence and a moment of eye contact, I said, "Where?"

"What about right here?" Magdalena said.

"On the floor, on the center island, up against the sink?"

"Not until we're married. Go upstairs. I'll join you."

I did as I was told, wondering if she would actually follow or if she had sent me to wait upstairs while she slipped out the back door. For long minutes, she did not follow. I took a shower to kill time. When I emerged, Magdalena lay on the bed. With her clothes on she may have looked a bit stringy. Naked, on her back, in this light, she made a different impression. I turned off the bedside lamp, thinking again about infrared images. I really wanted the watchers to watch this, but on my terms. She turned the lamp back on. Expertly she took hold of me. In bed as in kitchen or garden, Magdalena was a no-nonsense woman. She knew everything, and as far as I could tell, she liked everything. In her enthusiasm she reminded me a little of Mei, but only a little, and I shooed the comparison from my head because it didn't seem proper to my inner puritan to think of Mei while copulating with another woman. Or, strangely enough, vice versa. There was a difference—Magdalena was satiable, whereas Mei was not. Immediately after the third orgasm, she got up and left without saying good-bye or anything else for that matter. She came back the next night and several consecutive nights after that. The routine was the same. She wasn't impolite about it, but when she had achieved what she wanted to achieve she departed—brusquely, as if she didn't want to miss her favorite sitcom.

As experience teaches us, all good things come to an end. One night after Magdalena had taken her leave, I lay in bed thinking of a touchdown run the Hessian had made in the mud in the last century. It was the last play of the game. The six points he scored clinched the league championship for our school. Everyone else on the bench rushed onto the field to hug the Hessian. I walked away. The coach kicked me off the team for unsportsmanlike conduct.

In this place and time it was midnight, the weather was warm. The windows were wide open. The curtains stirred. I heard a telephone ringing—not the one in the front hall, but a phone outside the house. It had a novelty ring, like the horn of a Jazz Age car: Ah-*OO*-ga! Ah-*OO*-ga! I had left the special cell phone Burbank had given me in Mother's Mercedes, which was parked in the driveway and had never before heard it ring. In bare feet and pants and a T-shirt I walked to the car, started it up, and drove about five miles north—out of range of the gizmos in the walls. I parked, got out of the car, and dialed the number of the missed call. Naturally Burbank didn't answer. After the fifth ring I switched off.

Burbank replied almost instantly with a text message composed entirely of wild cards that translated as: "Report to Washington immediately. Do not repeat do not go back to the house or the apartment. Make contact when you get here."

It is a greater bother than you might think to travel in bare feet. For one thing, your feet get very dirty very quickly. For another you keep stubbing your toes and stepping on sharp or unclean things (it's no fun to pump gas or enter a public restroom). For yet another, going barefoot in public is frowned upon in bourgeois America. It is no easy matter for the unshod to buy shoes. Most stores post signs forbidding the barefoot to enter. Stores don't open until ten in the morning. When I got Burbank's message it was about half past midnight. You cannot get on a train or a bus, let alone an airplane, without shoes. I stopped at the first rest area on the New Jersey Turnpike. The convenience shop didn't even carry flip-flops. I bought a roll of paper towels and a bottle of soap and washed my feet in the restroom. This drew disgusted glances, but by then I didn't care.

The Mercedes's top speed was about fifty miles an hour, so I heard lots of horns on the turnpike. I regarded this as an advantage, because I figured that few drivers, whether under Guoanbu discipline or not, would be so foolhardy as to drive slow enough to tail me in this bat-out-of-hell traffic. To my surprise the car made it all the way to the Metro station in Vienna, Virginia. I parked it in the lot, wiped it for fingerprints, and abandoned it. Whoever towed it away would trace it to my late mother, whose last name was different from mine. I sent an encrypted text message to Burbank. Rigmarole intervened, but at last Burbank himself picked me up in his Hyundai at the third Metro station to which he directed me. How like the movies was the world I had wandered into.

I hadn't stopped to eat. I was very hungry. This time Burbank had brought no sandwiches. I was tired. Driving a clunker for four hundred miles, thinking every minute that the wheels were going to fall off, had been a fatiguing business. Even with all the windows and the roof open, I had inhaled enough carbon monoxide to euthanize a horse.

I said, "I can't stay awake. Let me know when we get there."

Later—how much later I don't know because I had left my father's Rolex on the bedside table in Connecticut—I was awakened by Burbank pinching my lower lip. We were in the countryside, at the same converted barn we had visited before. Crickets chirped. We went inside, me limping slightly more than usual. The god-awful paintings were still there. The caretaker-painter was still absent, so Burbank must have had the same housekeeper. I tried to picture her, but the woman I saw in my mind's eye was Magdalena. I wondered what she would make of my sudden departure—$20,000 watch left on the table, shoes on the floor, socks and underwear strewn on the rag rug made by my grandmother and her sisters, razor and toothbrush in the bathroom.

Burbank brewed tea. He said, "You're quite informally dressed tonight."

"Your fault," I said.

He said, "Meaning what?"

I told him. I told him about the break-in and the bugs. I told him about Magdalena in her many guises mean and mellow. I described the seduction scene. Taken together, this made her sound like a suspicious character—a simple accomplishment, as any character assassin knows. Burbank listened impatiently, obviously controlling his face with an effort.

He cleared his throat and said, "You do seem to have a way with the ladies."

"With a little help from my friends."

"Well, let's hope this Magdalena is still a friend."

"She's not the type."

"Oh?" Burbank said. "What type would you say she is?"

"Hard to tell," I said.

"She's good at what she does? Apart from the sex."

"No end to her skills. Terrific cook, frugal housekeeper, world-class gardener, very smart. I wouldn't be surprised if she can make pottery or fly a helicopter or read Sanskrit. She was very observant, almost like a trained investigator, in picking up clues about the break-in. I told her she was a born detective, and meant it."

"That also fits."

"Fits what?"

"Our files," Burbank said. "But you left something out. Magdalena, as she told you to call her, is a professional assassin."

Oh, was *that* all? I had to suppress a laugh. At the same time I felt a little sick. I was supposed to believe this? I said, "Are you serious?"

He said, "She has seven kills we know about. Just as you say, she cooks like Escoffier, she leaps from scorn to lust, she screws the target regardless of gender, she crawls on her belly like a snake. She does her thing. The target dies. She disappears. We don't even have a picture of her."

"What's her method?' "

"Poison. Untraceable poison. That's why she's never been caught. That and her all-around talent."

"Which talent?"

"What better profession for a poisoner than chef? What better way to build trust than sex?"

Now I was the one who meditated. Burbank wouldn't kid around about something like this—unless he had an operational reason—or, most unlikely, a personal one—in which case he might very well make up whatever fairy story suited the purpose. I made room in my mind for doubt even though I was under oath to believe anything he might say.

This didn't fool Burbank. He said, "You're skeptical. Good. I wouldn't think much of you if you weren't. But you'd better believe what I'm saying to you. Magdalena always gets her man. Others have tried to escape. In the end she always made the kill."

I said, "Who does she work for?"

"If you've got the money, she's got the poison."

"You think she's been paid to do me in?"

"In the context, it's not such a wild surmise."

"The next line in the script is, 'Who put out the contract?'"

"If we knew that," Burbank said, "we'd know who wants you dead, wouldn't we?"

He seemed to savor his words.

22

By the time federal agents got to the house in Connecticut the following morning, Magdalena was long gone. There was nothing Burbank or anyone else at Headquarters could do about this. Bogeyman fantasies notwithstanding, the U.S. intelligence service has no power of arrest or police authority of any kind, and it is prohibited by law from running operations on American soil against American citizens. It has to rely on other feds who carry guns and badges, like the FBI, to apprehend people like Magdalena. I could imagine her springing into action on finding me gone when she arrived at break of day. She would have seen the signs that I had got wind of her—the abandoned heirloom Rolex on the bedside table, the dirty clothes and all the other telltale signs of a sudden departure. She would immediately have done the professional thing and dematerialized. Sooner or later, somewhere else on the planet, she would pull her molecules together again and continue the hunt. If Burbank could be believed, she took her work seriously. She was under contract. Her reputation, her future, her business prospects, even her sex life, depended on fulfilling the contract. I would see her again—or more likely, *not* see her again. One evening I would come home from the office, microwave a leftover, swallow a mouthful of it and suddenly the world would go dark, this time for real. Or maybe I'd feel a pinprick through the seat of my pants while standing at a urinal at the movies, and then in the mirror see the last thing I would ever see—Magdalena's face over her shoulder as she walked out, disguised as an undersized male. As I drew my last breath would she wink and smile that decimal of a Magdalena smile?

These thoughts were in my mind as Burbank, having dealt with the question of my likely assassination, moved on to the next issue, the one that really interested him—namely how to handle Lin Ming by leading him to believe he was handling me. Burbank did not like to wing it—better to be ready in our minds before we acted, to have a plan, to avoid improvisation, to shun impulse. For Burbank, if something did not take years it wasn't real. If it moved too swiftly, it wasn't an operation. As he explained all this yet again, I fought the urge to fall asleep.

Burbank said, "Are you awake?"

I twitched. "Not really," I said. "Can we continue this in the morning?"

"Unfortunately, no. I'm catching a plane early tomorrow. You've got to stay awake."

He went to the refrigerator, drew a glass of ice water, and carried it back to me. I held it in a nerveless hand. He took a pill bottle out of his coat pocket and shook a tablet into my other hand. "Take this," he said.

I said, "What is it?"

"A wake-up pill."

I saw and heard Burbank as if through a gauze bandage. I had never been so sleepy in my life. But why? This had been a day like any other. Had Magdalena poisoned me after all? Slow-working poisons, Burbank had said. Suspicion moved within me. *The hell with it,* I thought. Anything was better than this. I took the pill.

"Drink the whole glass of water," Burbank said. "It'll take a couple of minutes to kick in." He watched me as if counting the passing seconds on a mental stopwatch. Immediately I began to wake up. Burbank brought me a mug of instant espresso, black. I drank it down. All of a sudden, I was wide-awake, as if adrenaline had been injected into my heart.

I said, "Wow. What is that stuff?"

"I don't know exactly," Burbank said. "But it works."

It sure did. I was even hungry again and said so. Burbank got a supermarket pizza out of the freezer and put it in the microwave.

As we ate the pizza we mapped out the Lin Ming operation. Thanks to the pill, my mind was clear, my spirit tranquil. This was the sequence of the plan: very soon I would move back inside Headquarters and work closely with Burbank. I'd be given a title and Burbank's enthusiastic trust. This would put noses out of joint at Headquarters, but it was necessary cover. I would give Lin Ming information—real but not vital information. Over time I would give him more information. And then, when the dirty trick had been done and the key had been turned in Lin Ming's mind, I would give him the false information that would blow Guoanbu to smithereens. It was a brilliant plan. It was a game of surround. It would change the balance of espionage. We would be the aggressors, the pranksters, the ruthless ones. The winners. Both Burbank and I felt wonderful—in his case, presumably, without a chemical stimulant.

"The key element—always remember the key element—is that nobody, *nobody* can know what we are doing until it's over except you and me," Burbank said yet again. "Just the two of us. No one else."

I was not insensible to the risks of this operation. To begin with, it was crazy, but then so were all really good operations. This one had the potential to put an end to me. If Burbank was killed in a plane crash or developed early Alzheimer's or turned out to be a bastard or a traitor, I was lost and gone forever. No one would believe that Burbank, one of the most trusted and steady figures in the apparatus, had ordered me to do the things I was going to do. My own country would be my nemesis. I would be crushed, locked up, delivered to Magdalena or her equivalent. Even while still feeling the exhilarating effects of Burbank's pill, I didn't in my heart want to do this. Burbank, studying my face, saw this.

"You'll be in danger, no question," Burbank said. "But you've been in danger before and come out the other side. The payback will be that for the rest of your life you will live in a state of satisfaction for having done what you will have done for this country that we love."

This meeting was all but over. Formalities remained. Burbank had yet another new contract for me to sign. I signed it. Just like that I was a staff agent again—but no promotion this time. At dawn, Burbank departed. He left a spare car, an environmentally correct electric one, for my use. I could stay in the house until he got back. No one would bother me. Burbank and I and the caretaker and no one else knew this house existed. The caretaker was on vacation in the Seychelles. After Burbank returned I'd move into something more suitable, more secure, and report for duty at Headquarters.

By midafternoon the pill wore off. I was exhausted again. Burbank had shown me my room. When I put my head on the pillow I felt something beneath it. I slid my hand under the pillow and pulled out a fully automatic ten-millimeter pistol with one of those extra-long gun-nut magazines sticking out of the butt. If nobody knew this barn existed why did I need this thing? I fell asleep before I could answer my own question.

THREE

THREE

23

I realized after a day or two as Burbank's house guest that I could live no longer with the caretaker's psychotic paintings. When I was awake they depressed me—angered me. In dreams I came downstairs in the dishwater light of early day and found mammoth portraits of Chen Qi or Steve or the tenor or sometimes the Hessian in his muddy football suit, silent and still, waiting for me. The house itself was so isolated, so surrounded by forest, so empty of life—not even an insect lived in it with me—that I became pathologically watchful. I half expected to wake up some night and see Magdalena at the foot of the bed, syringe in hand, having just injected the venom of the Dahomey viper between my toes. I moved to a cheap motel in Manassas, and on the next nights to other motels in other towns. I went to the movies. I ate junk food, so I nearly always tasted scorched grease at the back of my throat. On the fourth morning, while I was having a superheated breakfast at a McDonald's, Burbank texted me. We would meet at the barn at ten that evening.

I got there a little early. I did not turn on the lights in the room where the paintings were. Though surely he knew about it, Burbank didn't mention my absence from the house.

He handed me the ID card suspended on a chain that would get me through the gates at Headquarters and into the building in the morning. It was a lot like the one I wore around my neck in Shanghai when I worked in the tower for Chen Qi.

"The daily meeting is at seven-thirty," Burbank said. "Be there at seven on Monday. Use the main entrance. Sally will be there to greet you."

He told me the number of my parking space and gave me a parking sticker. He asked if I had any questions. I didn't. He was brusque. He said, "Let's go. Do you have a credit card or a checkbook on you?"

Both, I said. He dropped me off at an all-night car dealership that sold used and new cars at low but nonnegotiable prices. "Nothing fancy," he said, never one to eschew the obvious. "No bright colors." Using my debit card I bought a gray Honda Civic with eighteen thousand miles on the odometer and not a scratch on it and drove it away. There was some difficulty about the registration because I had no local address, so I had to rent the car for a week to give me time to find a place to live. One of the first things I was told when I joined Headquarters was that espionage was a capital crime in every country in the world, so it was vital to be up-to-date in all your papers, for everything to be strictly legal, even in the United States, so as not to give the cops a pretext to mess with you.

The next morning I rolled through the gates as if the guards had known my Civic and my face since childhood. As promised, Sally was waiting for me in the lobby. She led me through the color-coded labyrinth of doors to a blue one that was new to me. At seven o'clock exactly, Burbank joined us. Sally awaited orders but received none. He left her standing there and pushed open the door. A big room. About a dozen people in suits sat at a polished conference table. Heads turned. All but two chairs were occupied—Burbank's, which was a sort of high-backed throne at the center of the table, and an ordinary one just beside it. He gestured me into the ordinary one. Those attending had an air of entitlement about them—gray heads and bald ones, and in the case of the women, mostly dyed ones. Everybody except me wore reading glasses perched on the bulbs of their noses. I recognized none of these people, but why would I? The silent question they seemed to be asking in unison was, What is this unwashed person doing in this holy of holies?

Burbank explained. "For some time I have felt I needed a younger mind closer to me, and I have decided that this young man is the person I have been looking for," he said. He told them my true name. "He will be my right hand," Burbank said. "He will sit in the office next to mine, which has been unoccupied since Suzie Kane left us. He has my confidence. He reports to me, takes his orders from me and no one else, and is to be regarded as a full and equal member of this group. He has done good work in the field and has just completed an exemplary three-year tour under deep cover in denied territory. He will do more good work in Headquarters."

The others listened with blank faces. I detected no enthusiasm for discussing in my hearing the profound, the unutterable secrets known only to this exalted committee. But they spoke freely, and I learned some things I quite possibly might never have known if Luther Burbank had not come into my life. Most of these family jewels seemed trivial to me, as the deepest and darkest secrets often do. I listened, not too intently, and kept my mouth shut. When the meeting broke up, after an interminable hour, nobody shook my hand and bid me welcome. No one smiled. Nobody paid any attention to me at all. I might as well have been an inflatable doll that Burbank had placed in the seat beside him to make the highway patrol think he wasn't alone in his car as he drove in the HOV lane. Burbank gestured for me to follow him into his office, the one with all the safes, where we could talk. He said, "What did you think of the Gang of Thirteen?"

"Is that what it's called?"

"Not by you, if you're wise," Burbank said. He paused, waiting for me to answer his question. When I didn't answer he said, "Well?"

I said, "I sensed no great enthusiasm for your new assistant."

"Nothing surprising about that," Burbank said. "I sprang you on them. They didn't see it coming. They believe they have a right to see things coming. They can't fit you into the picture. They'll freeze you out, isolate you, put you in Coventry."

"Coventry?"

"Old schoolboy word for the silent treatment. Shunning. Be a man and you'll be fine."

"Yes, sir."

"'Luther' when we're alone, but that's the spirit," said Burbank.

I nodded.

"Sometime tomorrow you will be provided with a computer password," Burbank said. "It will give you access to all CI files. Or almost all. Only myself and the people you met this morning have that level of access." He pointed a finger. "Your office is through the door behind my desk. Come through it only when I buzz."

The tiny windowless office was a far cry from the glass stage set I had occupied when working for Chen Qi. It was about the size of a walk-in closet, a cubbyhole into which were crowded a desk and chair, a computer, a see-through burn basket, a safe. Had I been an inch taller or ten pounds heavier I would not have been able to squeeze my body into the remaining space. Burbank buzzed at four o'clock that afternoon. My day had been idle. I had been given no work to do, so I surfed the Web on my cell phone to pass the time. I read the *Times* and the *Wall Street Journal* and the Chinese newspapers and looked up facts at random, establishing among other things that Luther Burbank, the great nineteenth- and twentieth-century American horticulturist who created some eight hundred hybrid plants, had had no children and so could not possibly be a direct ancestor of the Luther Burbank I knew. A century and a world apart, the two Luthers used similar techniques to tweak nature—grafting, crossbreeding, happy accidents. Plums (113 new varieties) and most other kinds of plants and Shasta daisies in the case of the original Luther, spies and traitors for my man.

The end of the day, a very long one, was near. The promised password had not been issued. Evidently it had been a frustrating day for Burbank, too. His voice was hoarse, his eyes red-rimmed. He slumped. He sipped green tea and held it in his throat for an instant before swallowing. I was standing up. He pointed at the chair. I hesitated because it looked just like the one with the sawed-off front legs. He said, "Different chair. Trust me. Sit down."

Burbank said, "There was some resistance to opening the files to a newcomer. Tomorrow you will have full access. This is a turf thing. Nothing of great importance is in the computer. If that were otherwise it would be a great folly, given the ability of geeks in Nigeria and Nepal, let alone our more dangerous adversaries, to hack into any known system and read the mail. But we've covered that ground already."

Burbank looked at me expectantly, as if he knew I was bursting with curiosity. The higher-ups were talking about me. Why wasn't I asking what they were saying? It wasn't difficult to guess. But I did have one unaskable question, namely why was Burbank antagonizing these people and turning them against me if he wanted me to be useful to him? I could just as well have been another Sally, no threat to anyone. Even if you're dealing with a Burbank, a master of evasion, you learn more by letting the other guy fill the silences. I waited for whatever was coming next.

"What I want you to do for the next few days is go through some of this computerized stuff at random and cut and paste whatever interests you into your brain," Burbank said. "A lot of the data is iffy—*all* unprocessed information is iffy and so is a lot that has been processed—but I want you to find something that intrigues the mind, a lure that a fish named Lin Ming would take, maybe something from a friendly intelligence service that can be attributed to that service, and then I want you to find a second and a third such piece of plausible junk. Include at least one item about Taiwan. And discuss this with me next time I buzz."

I said, "May I ask how much time that gives me?"

"I don't know. And stop saying 'may I ask.' The whole point of this arrangement is that yes, you may ask. So just fucking ask."

Burbank was not usually given to such language. He really must have had a bad day. He finished his tea and got to his feet. He said, "That's all."

As Burbank had warned, the files were a hard slog. The content was mostly gossip, unsubstantiated and nine times out of ten hardly worth substantiating. Many, even most files are like that. On opening them you ask yourself, *What's so secret about this?* But every now and then something catches the eye. The natural reaction to such a find is not to cry hallelujah, but to be twice as skeptical as usual. If it's plausible, it probably isn't true. One of Burbank's famously demented predecessors was so controlled by this idea that he could never bring himself to believe that any defector from an enemy service could possibly be genuine. He refused to listen to them, refused to give them shelter. In his youth he had been badly burned by a turncoat, a secret Communist, whom he had trusted absolutely, whom he admired and emulated, even loved, and when the man turned out to be a Soviet agent, he never got over it. Thereafter he slammed the door in the faces of all defectors from the other side. If he was overruled, as sometimes happened, he would do his best to destroy the defector and discredit his sponsors. In the end he thought everyone in Headquarters was a potential turncoat if not an actual traitor and had the delusions to prove it. In the opinion of some, this made him better at his job. His crotchety spirit still stalked these hallways. I felt him at my back as I read.

The next afternoon, Burbank buzzed on the stroke of four. He seemed to be more like himself today. I waited thirty seconds for him to say something. He remained silent, so I spoke.

"It's no picnic to find something in these files that fits the requirement you laid out for me yesterday," I said. "But I have two or three possibilities for you."

I was still on my feet. Burbank said, "Sit down, you're giving me a stiff neck."

While combing the files I had borne in mind that what he wanted was something that would pique Lin Ming's interest. The first two items I mentioned would not necessarily have had that effect. They certainly did not interest Burbank. I slid over them quickly. Then I described a report about a meeting between a man whom Headquarters knew to be an officer of a Taiwan intelligence service and a second person the source said he knew to be an official of the Chinese embassy in Cairo.

To my astonishment, this was news to Burbank. The perplexed look on his face could not be read in any other way. He said, "Names."

We didn't yet know who the person from the Chinese embassy was. I named the Taiwanese. Burbank nodded, as if he knew the fellow.

"How fresh is this?" he asked

"The report, twelve days. The sighting, not specified."

"I'll ask Cairo to take an interest."

I was dismissed.

Cairo took Burbank's request to watch the Taiwanese case officer seriously. Soon he was never alone. Relays of sidewalk men were with him wherever he went. Either he did not notice them or did not care. He was a trawler who caught what he could when he could. He made his rounds as if he hadn't an enemy in the world. He met other foolhardy people from the Chinese embassy. He loaded and unloaded dead drops.

In photographs taken at diplomatic receptions he was a tall handsome Manchu with a tall beautiful Manchu wife. Besides several of China's languages they spoke the polished East Coast American English that was standard for their class. The wife had been overheard speaking fluent French at a dinner party. The situation was somewhat embarrassing for us because the Manchu had liaised with our stations in several different countries. He was by no means an asset of ours, but over the years he had traded scraps of information with us. He had given us good stuff and we had kept him posted on matters of interest to him. He was regarded as a reliable source, a friend.

As reports from the Cairo station dribbled in I made their contents known to Burbank. His interest in the case, strong from the start, grew stronger. But he took a wait-and-see line. This was something we could work with, but we would bide our time. He explained his decision. We didn't want to compromise our old friend the Manchu. Who knew what he might lead us to? We had to be careful not to step on Cairo's toes or the toes of our own Middle East people. At least not right now, not until we knew more, not until the time was right. There was no deadline. We were learning things it was good to know. That was an end in itself. Locking the product in a safe would be a good enough outcome. Maybe it was the impetuosity of inexperience, but I didn't agree.

Friday came at last.

24

Over the weekend I rented a town house a few miles from Headquarters. It was a clone of hundreds of others in the neighborhood, but it had its surprises. At dawn and twilight herds of white-tailed deer, dozens of animals, grazed outside my window as if the fringe of saplings that separated my "community" from the one behind it was a pre-Columbian wilderness. The cul-de-sac on which I lived showed few other signs of life. With one picture window in the front wall and three small ones at the back, the house was dark, but because I went to work at six in the morning and came home late at night, the murky atmosphere didn't matter. The deer were mute, no birds sang when the sun came up, so all in all there were few noises from outdoors except the distant murmur of traffic, no signs of life except the occasional sound of a car motor starting or someone shooting baskets in a driveway. I liked the silence. I didn't miss the uproar of Shanghai or the sirens of Manhattan. Living in this suburb was like living in a science fiction movie in which telepathic aliens have taken over the bodies of human beings. Even the kids made no noise, coming home as silent as manikins in their soccer uniforms, leaving just as wordlessly in the morning with bulging book bags on their backs.

On Monday morning when I got to my computer, I found that a breakthrough of sorts had occurred. The Cairo station had identified the man from the Chinese embassy who was meeting with the Manchu as a Guoanbu officer who used the pseudonym Xu Anguo. *Anguo* means "protect the country." He was a counselor to the embassy, big game. He and the Manchu met more frequently than is usual in clandestine relationships, always at night at an odd time like 4:27 A.M., always in a poor out-of-the-way neighborhood, always very, very briefly. The station tried picking up their conversations with a listening device and caught a few words. They spoke to each other in Hokkien, the language used in Taiwan. I reported this to Burbank.

"So what do they talk about?"

I handed over a transcript of the disjointed exchanges our techs in Cairo had managed to record. Burbank ran his eye over the Chinese characters. "Not much here," he said.

"But it's interesting in its way," I said. "The guy from the embassy has been telling the Manchu that everything has to be word of mouth only. Every paper is guarded. No one is ever alone with an embassy document. The Manchu says he has a camera that can be concealed in a ring. The other guy says he'd be shot if he showed up wearing a new ring."

"We don't want that to happen," Burbank said. "Draft a cable for my signature telling Cairo to tread softly and keep up the good work."

As the weeks passed, the case file fattened. We learned nothing much that was new and had no idea what secrets Xu Anguo was handing over to the Manchu, but the mere fact that we were aware of something that was none of our business justified the trouble and expense.

One morning after the daily meeting I walked down the hall as usual with Burbank, but instead of leaving him at the door of his office and continuing on to my cubbyhole, I followed him, uninvited, into the room of safes. He sensed that I was right behind him. His shoulders hunched slightly, he walked a little faster—but made no comment. When he got to his desk he sat down and went right on ignoring me. I waited, standing. It would have been presumptuous to sit down, and I didn't want to give him an advantage beyond the ones he already had.

Finally he said, "Yes?"

I said, "I have a proposal."

"Make it."

"I think I should go to New York, wait for Lin Ming to stumble over me in the street, and give him a hint about the Cairo stuff—without mentioning Cairo or the target's name or any of the details."

"Why?"

"First, because it's sensational material and he'd soon confirm that, and that would plant the seed of curiosity."

Burbank looked at his watch. "Go faster," he said.

"It would give us the initiative."

"Why?"

"Because we'd only give him a sniff," I said. "He'd have to give something back before he got the rest of it."

"Why would he do that?"

"Because if there's one traitor in one of their embassies there might be others in the same place or in other embassies. Just like you hoped."

Burbank said, "You realize this might blow our whole primary operation before it gets started?"

"That's one possibility," I said. "Another is that it would jump-start it."

"Why do you think that?

"Because sometimes taking a chance is worth it."

"A thrill seeker," Burbank said. "Just what we need."

He said it nicely, giving no sign that he was displeased. He had been given something to think about and he was thinking about it. I let him think.

After a while he said, "You realize that if you take this to its logical conclusion you're pronouncing a death sentence on that fellow in Cairo?"

"Yes."

A flicker of something—pride in a protégé?—came and went in Burbank's eyes. "Also that you're messing with the Manchu, who has been such a help to us in the past."

"That I regret. But what the Manchu is doing is just a diversion."

Burbank relaxed. This was a visible thing, his muscles unknotted, his eyes focused in a new way. He said, "You're coming along. Remember, keep this between the two of us. Keep thinking."

I said, "What about New York?"

Burbank held up a hand in case I was going to say more. He had no more time to spend on me. He said, "Okay, give it a go. But don't go too far."

25

I traveled to New York like an honest man—the shuttle to LaGuardia, a taxi to the apartment, a chat with the doorman. I found nothing of interest in the mailbox. After taking a nap and showering I walked downtown, thought about looking for a woman in a singles bar but decided against it because I didn't know of any singles bars. I had never been inside one. What were the rules? How many drinks did you have to buy for a lady before making your move? I didn't really know Lin Ming's rules, either. Surely he had noticed that I was no longer roaming the streets. Maybe he wasn't roaming the streets, either. I decided to show myself and see what happened.

In the Sichuan Delight the cashier on duty was the same young man who had shown me upstairs the last time I was here. He glanced at me, registered nothing, and said, "Any table, sir." I chose one in a corner and sat with my back to the wall. The food was good, but not in the same class as the feast Lin Ming had ordered the last time I dined from this kitchen. Another familiar face appeared—the waiter was the same wiry man who had carried the laden tray upstairs to Lin's safe room.

If he recognized me he gave no more sign than the cashier had done. However, the latter had vanished. When he came back half an hour later, entering through the kitchen door, I was working on my chili hot pot. He stopped for a moment to ask me how everything was. When I said it was just fine, he complimented me for having ordered the specialty of the house. With a broader smile he said, as if offering me some exotic delicacy reserved for the restaurant's most sophisticated customers, "Fortune cookies very nice tonight."

Normally I am too conscious of my image to crush fortune cookies, let alone eat them, but on this occasion I slipped them into my shirt pocket. On the subway I cracked them open. The first told me I would have true friends, the second that Confucius say a traveling man and his girlfriend are soon parted. A Manhattan phone number was written on the back of that one. I waited until I got home to call because I wanted Lin Ming to know where I was and the GPS on my cell phone would give him that information. A female voice answered. Without preamble, in Mandarin, the speaker said, "Basketball at the same gym as usual, same time, day after tomorrow."

I arrived at the gym five minutes late. I was not followed, but as I approached the door, a man loitering on the opposite side of the street made a phone call. Lin Ming was waiting for me inside. He was not his usual smiling self.

"You're late," he said, as if I were already under discipline.

"Am I? Then we'll have to play fast."

We did. This time I beat him. Badly. I had different purposes than I had had in our first encounter. He was pretty good, but he had few moves and only two shots, a pretty good hook and a wobbly jumper. He was smaller, slower, older, and he had learned the game as a grown-up, which meant he relied too much on his intellect instead of letting his body do the thinking. I got a little physical—not to the point of bullying, but enough to make him look behind him for another me. The scores were lopsided. At the end he was drenched in sweat, breathing hard. He had lost face. He didn't like it. However, we were in America, so Lin Ming shook my hand like a good sport and said, "Nice game." I couldn't really read him—probably few people could—but I had wanted to make him wonder why I did what I did. By the look of him, I had succeeded. Lately I had made an enemy of everyone I met except Burbank, and who could tell what exactly was going on with him?

After we showered, Lin Ming said, "Shall we go for a walk?"

"Why not?"

We found a park—"found" in quotes because clearly Lin Ming knew exactly where we were going—and sat down on an empty bench. In English he said, "You played much better today."

I shrugged. "Bad days and good days."

He said, "So you are back inside Headquarters as we discussed."

As we discussed? When was that? I said, "Well, I'm back inside, anyway."

"Are you still being completely truthful with Mr. Burbank?"

"Invariably."

"So what does he think of our friendship?"

"Maybe you should judge that for yourself, Mr. Lin."

"No names, please," he said in Mandarin. "Names are bad luck."

"Whatever you say."

Lin Ming smiled at last. The smile was tighter now. Possibly this was just the humiliation of losing at basketball. Maybe, though, it was the particle of doubt about where we stood that I was hoping to plant.

He said, "It is now time for me to ask you if you have considered the offer we discussed the last time we met."

"I considered it when you made it." I said. "I gave you my answer."

"You were serious?"

"Of course I was. So were you, I thought."

"Then why are we meeting today?"

"Because I have a counteroffer."

"A counteroffer? You think we can bargain?"

"Do you want to hear what I have to say?"

Lin Ming absorbed this affront. He said, "I am a listener by profession, my friend."

I told him that a man from one of their embassies was meeting regularly and secretly with a man we knew to be a senior officer of the National Security Bureau, the intelligence service of Taiwan. That we had recorded conversations between the two. That we had photographs. Then I stopped talking. He listened with such an absence of reaction that I knew he was shaken. Heavy silence. No eye contact.

Finally Lin Ming said, "And?"

"And we will give you the details if you will give us something in return."

"This is outrageous," Lin Ming said.

"Just business."

A long pause, then Lin Ming said, "What do you want?"

I told him: the complete Guoanbu file on Chen Qi's only son, Jianyu.

Lin Ming was shocked. His face reddened, his mask slipped—not much, but enough. He truly was outraged—a good sign, I thought. Two men I recognized as sidewalk people who used to follow me around were playing cards a few steps away. A gym bag rested on the table. I didn't doubt that it contained a camera, pointed at us, that recorded sound as well as video.

Abruptly, Lin Ming got to his feet and started to walk away. I stood up with my back to the card players, blocking their view with my bulk. I handed Lin Ming a fortune cookie. He resisted what I saw as the temptation to throw it on the ground and step on it.

"In case you want to shoot a few baskets," I said in a whisper, in English. No wink. Then I walked away. If he opened the fortune cookie he'd have my throwaway phone number. In the dusty trees starlings landed, squawked, and took off.

Thereafter, to make things as easy as possible for Lin's sidewalk crew in case they should come back into my life, I adopted a predictable schedule, going out for a morning run at seven, shopping always at the same grocery on the way home, going to the same gym at the same hour every other day, buying the same sandwich at the same shop at the same hour. It was a metronomic existence, and if Lin Ming was truly annoyed because I had put him on the spot, a chancy one. I did remember the tenor and the acrobats, and watched for them. What they had done in Shanghai, they could do in New York, where they had two rivers to choose from.

The possibility of something worse than a dunking happening was remote. Hollywood and Magdalena notwithstanding, assassination is not routine among spooks. There is no point in killing an agent of the opposition because the opposition will merely replace the dead operative with a new agent you don't know, and then there you are, back at the beginning, trying to identify the new man. Totalitarian types, like the Chinese and the Cubans and the Nazis and the Soviets in the good old days, mainly kill their own people—usually the ones they suspect of treason or even more dangerous crimes such as questioning revolutionary scripture. That was why Lin Ming was annoyed with me. I had put him in a position in which his home office might think it a good idea to reassess him. No doubt he had enemies within Guoanbu. So did I, apparently, though it was early in my career for this to be so.

I felt the need of a refuge, somewhere I could go and not be followed —someplace where I was inaccessible if not protected. There were such places. My university had a club in New York. In theory, if you didn't belong, you could not enter unless you came as the guest of a member. Up to now I hadn't been tempted to join, but I decided it might be a good idea to do so. After supplying the necessary credentials and paying the initiation and membership fees, I was admitted.

On the day I received my membership card I dropped in during happy hour and went immediately to the bar. I had been there years before as the guest of a faculty member. The bar itself was a magnificent mahogany thing, as massive as the poop of a whaling ship. Behind it hung a mirror that was installed when there were a lot of penniless immigrants available to polish it. Apparently there still were, because the thick glass sparkled. Alumni of all ages bellied up to the bar and nearly all of the tables were taken. This was a world I did not know. I had gone straight from graduation to the army and straight from training to Helmand province—and then, as you know, to hospitals, to spookdom, to China, to where I was now—one hermit's cave after another. I was no longer used to good fellowship, but I found a space between two brokers or lawyers or bankers and ordered a single malt whisky, spring water on the side. I studied the crowd—good fellows having a good time together. I imagined that they had all kept in touch from college days, as almost certainly they had, because most people soon discover that the chief benefit of going to a good college is that it provides you with a cohort for life—people you can make money with, people who talk your language, people who know the secret handshakes, people who sound alike. People who will usually help you out even if they don't particularly like you.

A good many women were present, mostly in twos, mostly at tables, mostly attractive, all of them pictures of chic. I reimagined them as kids just out of high school. Freshman year had been a sexual circus, and even though my ROTC connection repelled the more political women, who were usually the ones most interested in mindless sex, I found partners. I looked from face to face hoping to recognize someone about my age, someone perhaps I had known, as the Bible puts it. No luck. Lately I had been thinking a lot about women. There had been no one after Magdalena, and no one for quite awhile before her, so I was in the market for companionship. I was not such an optimist as to think that I would find it here. But it seemed possible that I might. It would be nice for a change to sleep with a woman who was not just doing her job.

I smelled perfume. A woman, almost as tall as I was, stood beside me. She was Chinese. She was striking. The bartender hurried to her without being summoned, a glass of white wine in his hand. With a smile that must have made the poor fellow weak at the knees, she signed the chit in an undecipherable scrawl and said, "Thanks, Guillermo."

Clutching her chardonnay, she started to go, then met my eyes in the mirror, then turned and looked at me. Bright obsidian eyes, thick brows, arched nose. She spoke my name followed by a question mark. I didn't remember her, but I nodded.

She said, "The student soldier. The athlete. The Mandarin major. I used to watch you play tennis. Great backhand. Terrific serve. Incredible match against that guy from Dartmouth."

True, I had been on the tennis team. Searching for her name, I said, "Freddy something. Ponytail. Very good player."

A nice, not quite eager smile. "Yeah, that's the one."

I said, "I didn't know anyone came to the matches."

"What power of concentration. The stands were always full." She had amazing diction, each syllable, each letter perfectly audible. She lifted her glass to me. No rings on her fingers. We drank.

She said, "You don't have a clue who I am, do you?"

"I should be ashamed." I meant it. How could I have forgotten this goddess? Before I could ask her name, she gave it.

"Alice Song. We were in some of the same classes, but I was a couple of years and a couple of rows behind you."

Now I remembered. Hair in braids wound round her head, no makeup. Shy. Silent in class. Aced every exam. A little gawky. Slumped to hide her breasts inside her baggy shirt. All that had changed except the brain.

"Now I remember," I said. "Are you meeting someone?"

She hesitated. Who could blame her? I said, "Well, maybe another . . ."

But she said, "Come on. My friend is a one-drink girl. Then she hurries home to the kids."

Following her to a table where a thin blonde awaited, smiling happily until she saw me. She didn't stay long. After she left, Alice Song asked me a question in Mandarin—something about one of our old professors. I answered in the same language. She said, "My God, listen to you!" We went on in Mandarin during dinner in the club dining room. She spoke it like a native, but with a very slight Queens intonation. She ate with appetite, an excellent thing in a woman, and drank sparingly. Wanting my wits about me, so did I. Like an old-fashioned girl who took her dating advice from *Cosmo,* she got me talking about myself. I told her about my time in Shanghai—not all about it, but enough. She asked why I wasn't still in the army. I told her. She was a lawyer, a litigator. She named the firm. Even I had heard of it. She was single. She had a young daughter from a failed marriage. She hadn't visited the club for more than a year. So talk about coincidences.

The conversation was the standard getting-to-know-you stuff—old times, books, movies, stories, did I remember so-and-so. We spoke English now, so the banter had different dimensions. Alice was a brilliant talker even when she was being careful what she said. I was drawn to her. I thought it conceivable that the evening might not end with the signing of the check and that what happened after that might not be the end of things. It was Friday. Her daughter was spending the weekend with her father, she said. On our way to the front door we switched back to Mandarin. "It's amazing how well you speak the language," Alice said. "If you were Chinese my mother would be crazy about you."

Visions of sugarplums danced in my head. And then I woke up and realized I couldn't possibly accompany her outside and let her, a Chinese woman unsuspecting and alone, walk into Lin Ming's surveillance. So I shook hands and said how nice it had been to run into her after all these years, and moving swiftly, went out the door ahead of her and still walking fast, drew my watchers away. It was late, the street was almost empty, I could see them move, hear one of them cough.

26

At one o'clock the next morning, using maximum tradecraft for a change, I took a bus to Washington, then the Metro, then shank's mare to my town house. Nobody was behind me at any point in the journey, but then why should anybody be? Only in New York was I under surveillance. Whoever was watching me already knew what I did when I was in Virginia, or thought somebody in the government must be keeping an eye on me and didn't want to walk into somebody else's surveillance and find themselves being watched as they watched me. After a shower and a shave and a change of clothes, I went to work.

At Headquarters I intercepted Burbank on his way upstairs—he always used the fire stairs, not the elevator, and ran up the steps. I ran along beside him. He barely gave me a glance. At the top, to my surprise, Burbank steered me into my office instead of his own. With two people in it, my cell seemed even smaller. It had no chair for a visitor, so Burbank sat in my chair. I stood before him in front of my own desk. There was barely enough room for my shoes between the desk and the wall.

Burbank said, "Fill me in." I had sent him bare-bones letters about each development, but now I gave him the details. He listened, asking no questions until I finished.

"How do you read this?" Burbank said. "What's your gut feeling?"

"That it's going to take a long time for this grain of sand to become a pearl."

"Maybe not," Burbank said. "They know they've got a problem with one of their people but they don't know which one. That's a motivator."

Hadn't I mentioned that when last we talked? I said, "True, but they might just investigate everybody, everywhere. They've got plenty of manpower."

"You're discouraged?"

"Impatient. Bored. Idle. Everything takes forever. You've said so yourself."

Burbank lifted his eyebrows. Evidently he thought I needed encouragement. "You're questioning your own idea. You're frustrated by a lack of progress after two weeks?"

"I think Lin Ming is going to have trouble selling this in Beijing. Guoanbu is a bureaucracy. Bureaucracy exists to prevent things from happening."

"Is that what you think?" Burbank said. He walked out of the room. Was the conversation over, had I taxed his patience once too often? But a couple of minutes later he came back carrying a bowl of green tea and sat down again in my chair.

"Forget about how long it takes," he said, as if there had been no interruption. "List the possibilities."

"We can wait forever. We can back off and let the Manchu run his asset in peace and hope he'll share the product," I said.

"What else?"

"We can fold the operation."

"Forget that. It's barely begun."

"We could grab the Manchu's friend and talk to him in private. He may know other malcontents."

"They'd put everybody the suspect knows on a watch list the minute he disappeared," Burbank said. "Besides, it would really piss off the Manchu and his service, neither of whom we want to piss off."

Burbank said, "Let me ask you something. Who does your exgirlfriend know?"

"You mean Mei?"

"Who else?"

"In Shanghai, pretty much everybody."

"Inside the corporation, in the tower?"

Why was he always asking for information he already possessed? I said, "I ran into people she had introduced me to in the tower's elevators."

"What kind of people?"

"Wild by night, spoiled brats of the Party hierarchy."

"Wild in what way?"

"Alcohol, marijuana, loud music, punk clothes, outspoken disdain for the Party leadership. Sex, I suppose, but I wasn't an eyewitness to that."

"They trusted each other?"

"They grew up together, for whatever that's worth. At bottom they were just playing games. By day, they were very serious junior functionaries, and they seemed to take the work seriously."

"Strange," Burbank said. "It makes you wonder."

"About what?"

"Everything. For example, this Mei of yours. If she's who she seems to be, the child of someone who counts in the Party, why would Guoanbu use her as they do."

"Maybe she's not Guoanbu."

"You think she *loved* you?"

I didn't answer.

Burbank said, "Did she over time?"

I said, "She was always herself."

"No change at all? Mood, behavior, habits?"

"Toward the end she was less ebullient."

Burbank meditated, but very briefly. He said, "And you never knew who her father was, never asked?"

"No. I've never put that particular question to anybody."

"Is it possible she has something to resent at home? Something serious?"

"Anything is possible."

Burbank finished his tea. He looked at his watch. He stood up and sidled by me on his way out. For an instant we were breathing on each other.

I said, "Why do you ask me these questions?"

"Because resentment has been a factor, usually the key factor, in ninety percent of the defections of foreign assets in the history of this organization," Burbank said. "Somebody doesn't get promoted or doesn't get the respect he thinks he deserves or can't forgive an insult. Or hates his daddy because the old man did him so many kindnesses or has the wrong expectations. He decides to get revenge. Resentment is the open sesame of our business. It's also the demon when it comes to our own people. It hides, it evades, it smiles at you as if nothing is wrong."

Was he talking about Mei? Or was he talking about me, putting me on edge? Certainly I had my resentments. So probably did Mei. Who didn't? I said, "So?"

Burbank said, "So be aware of the possibilities."

27

It was midwinter before the phone call came, early on a Sunday morning. The familiar female voice told me that I was invited to dinner at six o'clock the following evening at Zorba's Café near Dupont Circle, not far from the Chinese restaurant where Lin Ming and I had met for the first time. I accepted. Around three, snow began to fall. I called the Hilton on Connecticut Avenue and booked a room for the night. By the time I parked in the hotel garage and checked in, two or three inches of snow had accumulated, and it was falling even more heavily than before. It didn't take a weather prophet to know this was going to continue. Washington, whose snow removal capabilities are next to nil, would be paralyzed by midnight. It also meant that the U.S. government, including Headquarters, would shut down for at least a day.

I had just enough time to walk to Zorba's. Inside, I saw myself in a wall mirror. I looked like a snowman, my parka whitened by the stuff. Usually at this hour the place was thronged, but tonight even neighborhood people were staying home, so it was all but deserted. Lin Ming, wearing a puffy, down-filled, made-in-China winter coat with a fur collar, waited at one of the half-dozen occupied tables. He waved. He smiled. He leapt to his feet. No gestures could have been more unexpected. He threaded his way among the tables, shook my hand with yet another smile, and said, "It's good to see you again, my friend."

We ordered at the counter, a Greek salad with chicken for Lin, a yero and oily Greek fries for me, two beers. He paid both tabs, holding up a warning hand to prevent me from even thinking about reaching for my wallet. When our number was called over the loudspeaker, Lin Ming fetched the tray, as if all of a sudden he was the lesser person. We ate in a businesslike way, making almost no conversation. About halfway through the meal Lin Ming remarked that the lamb in my yero had a funny smell. Very greasy. Did it taste the way it smelled?

"Pretty much," I said. "You've never eaten lamb?"

"Never," Lin Ming said with feeling.

Just as we finished, the lights went out. A female voice screeched in the darkness. Lin Ming said, "Let's go for a walk."

I didn't like this situation at all. The streetlights, the traffic lights, the shop windows were dark. I hadn't experienced such pitch darkness since Afghanistan. You could half-see snowflakes falling and hear the snow squeak when you stepped on it. By now it was ankle deep. We walked—slogged—for what seemed to be about half an hour. Lin Ming must have been sweating inside his coat. Because the falling snow stuck to its fur collar, he was faintly visible in the darkness. This was not a particularly dangerous neighborhood, but what a laugh it would be if we were mugged—two blind desperadoes handing over their valuables with knives at their throats. Even a master of martial arts—I didn't doubt that Lin Ming was just such a master—would have difficulty taking a blade away from an assailant if he could see neither the knife nor the assailant.

Lin Ming cleared his throat loudly and spat into the snow. A few steps afterward, he did it again—the aftereffect of smelling the lamb, maybe. Or, who knew, a signal to the assassin who awaited us in the blackness that had descended on the city. This was the most aimless clandestine meeting I had ever had. All the usual stuff—the signals, the double-talk, the solemnity, the darting eyes—was missing. We walked on, neither of us speaking a word although we could have chattered in Mandarin to our hearts' content and the odds were ten thousand to one that no lurker would have understood a word. Lin Ming was mute for reasons unguessable. I kept my mouth shut because I wasn't going to be the first to break the silence. My feet were wet. I was edgy for other reasons. I should have used the urinal before leaving the restaurant, but it was just as dark inside Zorba's as it was outside.

By now my eyes had adjusted. I could see Lin Ming quite plainly—not just as a shape in the darkness, but the man himself, his face inside the hood, his gleaming teeth. Apparently he could see me, too, because he put a hand on my arm and said, "Stop. I think we're here."

He turned on a flashlight, a blindingly bright one, and swept the building before us. He read the number on a door and said, "We've passed it."

We turned around. After fifty steps or so, Lin Ming again switched on his flashlight and this time found the number he was looking for. He lighted our way into a doorway. The door was ajar. No elevators were in operation, of course, so we used the fire stairs. Through the darkness Lin Ming moved upward almost as fast as Burbank. On the fifth landing he switched on the flashlight again, located the door, and shone us through it. This on-and-off business with the flashlight destroyed my night vision, so I practically had to hold on to Lin's belt to find my way down the corridor.

At last we came to a door that showed a thread of yellowish light around its edges. Lin Ming pushed it open—it was unlocked—and stood back to let me go first. An inner door stood open, and through it I could see candles burning—many candles. Lin Ming was behind me, almost pressed against me, like one of the acrobats.

I walked through the door, and there in a puddle of buttery candle-light sat Chen Qi with a glass in his hand. I smelled scotch. I was not surprised. Of course it was Chen Qi, the most unlikely man in the world to be here all by himself. Who else would it be? He stood up, he smiled, he extended a hand and shook mine firmly. He spoke my name. I looked around to see if anybody else was lurking in the shadows, if there were other doors, other ways out. The answer to all these questions was no.

I said, "Good evening, CEO Chen. What a pleasure."

"I agree," Chen Qi said. "Sit down, please. We have things to talk about."

As of old, I did as I was told. Chen Qi did not quite snap his fingers at Lin Ming. But without turning his head he said, "Single malt." To me he said, as if he had some reason to be nice to me, "I think you'll like this whisky. Eighteen years old. Very smoky." Lin Ming, obsequious as a waiter, brought my whisky—two ounces, one ice cube.

Chen Qi was in affable mode, as on the night we dined together in Shanghai and he offered me a job. He hoped that I had been well. He brought me greetings from my former colleagues in the tower. My good work, my American humor were missed.

He said, "I hope you're enjoying your new posting."

"It has its moments."

"It must be stimulating, working so closely with your new chief. So famous for being infamous," Chen Qi said. "You have a way of finding your way to the top. I think you will have a very interesting life. I have always thought so."

"Not nearly so interesting as your own life," I said.

"You shouldn't be so sure about that. You should be on the lookout. Opportunities hide, then leap at a man," Chen Qi said. "I'm sure you remember the young woman you knew in Shanghai."

"Zhang Jia?"

"Zhang Jia has married and is pregnant. A boy, according to the sonogram, so she's a fortunate person."

"I'm glad for her," I said. I was.

"I wasn't asking about Zhang Jia," Chen said. "I meant the earlier one, the first woman you had. What did you call her?"

"Mei."

"Yes, Mei. Now I remember."

"She's well and happy, I hope."

"As far as I know she's well," Chen said. "But happy? Probably not."

"I'm sorry to hear that," I said. I took hold of myself and said, calmly I thought, "What's the problem?"

Chen Qi said, "You've finished your whisky. Did you enjoy it?"

"Very much."

"Then you shall have another."

He gave no order, not even a gesture, but his words were enough to bring Lin Ming and a tray at the trot. He poured one finger of the amber fluid into each of our glasses, and deftly handling silver tongs, added an ice cube.

Chen Qi said, "There's something about your friend Mei—several things in fact—that you may not know."

"There is an infinity of things I don't know about Mei," I said. "She never supplied a single fact about herself. Not even her true name."

"Really? And you never asked for facts? Why not?"

"I thought she was entitled to her privacy."

"How sensitive. Especially for an officer of U.S. intelligence."

His voice roughened. His eyes hardened. That much showed, if only for an instant. Had he been a softer man, his face might have been flushed. I put down my whisky glass. The moment was not right for a friendly drink. Chen Qi noted the gesture and put his glass on the table as well.

"Why were you so incurious?" he asked.

"In her case, at the time in question, who she was was irrelevant. I thought I understood what she was."

"And what was that?"

"A woman who lived her own life as she wanted to live it."

"Like an American woman. Do you know what Chairman Mao said about that? 'Never trust an American girl.'"

I said, "He knew American girls?"

Chen Qi brushed away my words with a gesture. It was Mei he wanted to talk about. "Consorting with an American spy is never irrelevant to the people who may now have this Mei of yours in their hands," he said. "They insist on facts. Believe me, she will supply them. Anyone who is her friend would urge her to supply them."

"In this case, what I was, or was suspected of being, *is* beside the point," I said. "I thought it was possible that Mei was an agent whose job was to observe what I did and report. I also thought any woman in China would do the same—would have no choice."

Chen Qi blinked—actually blinked. I had crossed the line. I was guilty of disrespect. His affability evaporated. I was not dismayed by this mood swing, though a saner man might have been.

I said, "So how long has Mei been in the hands of Guoanbu?"

"Guoanbu?" Chen Qi said, as if the term were new to him. "She was placed under protection shortly after you and Lin Ming, here, had your most recent conversation."

"Do you know where she's being held?"

"If I did why would I tell you? What can you do for her?"

The answer was "nothing." To Chen Qi I said, "Let me ask you a question."

A gesture—*go ahead if you must.*

"What's your interest in Mei?"

Chen Qi said, "I have her interests sincerely at heart."

"I don't doubt it. But why? Is she related to you?"

181

No flicker of a reaction from Chen Qi. No sound. Lin Ming, somewhere behind me, moved—twitched. I could feel it.

At this moment the power came back on, fluorescent tubes flickering and buzzing. Chen Qi paid no attention. The bluish electric glare was less flattering to him than the candlelight had been. With no shadows to conceal the reality, he looked just like the heartless bastard he was. I hoped that I didn't look as sick to my stomach, as strangled by anxiety, as I actually was—Mei in prison, confined, silent, learning, session by session, the *Kama Sutra* of pain and fear that was secret interrogation.

I made the feeling worse with my next guess about her identity. "Your mistress?"

"Don't be ridiculous," Chen Qi said.

But Chen Qi, the invulnerable man, looked caught. He looked as if he wished Mei's mother had drowned the girl in a bucket on the day she was born. How else would he feel? If she actually was his relative, however close or distant, and she was under investigation for sleeping with an American spy, he would be under suspicion himself, because how could she commit such crimes without his approval? Chen Qi got to his feet. Lin Ming rushed to help him into his overcoat.

"Our time together is over," Chen Qi said. "You and Lin Ming will have a chat after I go. But before I leave I have a suggestion to make to you."

Chen Qi looked me in the eyes. "You must do what's best for yourself," he said. "But if you are concerned about this girl—Mei? Is that what you call her?"

"Yes."

"The situation may not be hopeless. Obviously she is in difficulty," Chen Qi said. "But if you were to create an opportunity, so to speak, by reconsidering the offer of employment Lin Ming has made to you, then that might give this Mei an opportunity of her own to make amends, to improve her situation."

His eyes were still locked on mine. I said, "How would she do that, and what would it have to do with me?"

"She is said to be willing, even eager, to return to you, to marry you, even," Chen Qi said. "If you were with us and she were with you, she could be a help to you and you to her. It is an opportunity, a rare opportunity, to have what you want by doing a good thing. In my opinion, it is not impossible that a similar thought might occur to the people who are now deciding what should happen to her. She could come to America, become a citizen, live as an American. Make her own life as you say she wants to do. I see no other way this, or anything like it, could happen."

Lin Ming opened the door. Chen Qi walked through it.

28

Burbank went straight to the obvious question.

"What do they gain from this?" he asked.

"Who knows?" I said.

"Come on!" he said. "*Think*, then answer the question."

I had already thought—all night long in my overheated hotel room, all the next day and another night while I waited for thirty inches of wet snow to be scraped off the streets and highways, and all during the inchworm drive along the one plowed lane of the George Washington Parkway. I arrived at Headquarters at 6:00 A.M. on Tuesday. Burbank was already at his desk—showered, shaved, wide-awake, crisp clean shirt. He had slept in the office. His folding cot and rolled-up sleeping bag stood between the rows of safes. He asked about the weather, unable to check it out himself because his office, like mine, was windowless. I told him it was snowing again. Government workers do not drive in the snow. Before the last straggler arrived we'd probably be alone for hours, maybe all day, maybe longer.

I really didn't want to rephrase my answer to Burbank's question. "Who knows?" *was* the answer. Nobody ever knew Chen Qi's purposes for certain. To Burbank's mind, however, the answer I had just given him had merely obscured the real answer, which was, of course, the hidden answer.

I said, "Try this. Chen Qi has enemies he wants to get rid of. Or wants us to think so."

"And he wants us to get rid of them for him."

"Meaning he knows or guesses what we want to do, namely set up a fictitious network inside Guoanbu, and wants to make sure his enemies are on the list of traitors."

"Or wants us to walk into a trap."

"What makes him think we'd be dumb enough to do that?"

"Because he has a low opinion of us," I said. "Because he wants us to think we're counting on a coup. Because he thinks we'd calculate that doing his dirty work will rid the world of certain people who are enemies of the United States and are stealing its secrets. Because we'd think it would make our organization look good to the White House. Because it would help on the Hill at budget time."

Well, yeah. The usual drawn-out Burbankian pause followed. I waited in silence for it to end.

Finally he spoke. "So should we refuse or accept?"

"Refuse."

This was not the answer he had been looking for. "Explain," he said.

I said, "I don't want to be the go-between in this business."

"Really? Why the sudden change of heart?"

"It's dirty," I said.

"We're paid to be dirty so that the virtuous may be immaculate," Burbank said. "What else?"

"I'm personally involved. Emotionally involved."

"You're talking about the woman?"

"Yes, and the fact that I used to work for Chen Qi and the whole world knows that."

"Start with the woman," Burbank said. "You have feelings for her?"

"You might think that. We had sex every day for two and a half years."

"Every day?"

"No. We took five days a month off."

"Why did the two of you split?"

"She disappeared."

"Because she had carried out her mission and was moving on?"

"That's one possibility. She could have been kidnapped or drowned or locked up by Guoanbu just as Chen Qi told me. For whatever reason, she vanished. I went to work in the tower. Another woman was supplied. You knew all this."

"Not about the annual sixty days of abstinence."

Burbank was amused, an interesting thing to see.

I said, "I'm going to ask you a question about Mei."

He waited.

I said, "I've searched the files. I found nothing to suggest that anyone in this building or in any of the stations knows Mei's true name. Do you know it?"

Burbank hesitated. He gestured at his safes. "Somewhere I have a name for her that isn't a funny name," he said. "The person named fits her description, more or less. Whether or not it's her true name is another matter."

"What is the name?"

"I don't remember," Burbank said. "But I'll find it for you."

Maybe he would. That didn't mean that I'd find Mei among the multitude of Chinese women who had the same name. Burbank was right about that. She was gone, lost, probably in a labor camp in Inner Mongolia. They would never let her out.

Burbank showed no sign of wanting to end our chat. I would have been more than glad to do so. But we did have a lot more to talk about, and thanks to Mother Nature, he had no one else to talk to. The prospect of being snowbound and alone with my chief in this airless, sterile building for two days and nights made the heart sink. It was impossible to know what line of action Burbank might decide on, if any. It might even, for once, end with Burbank doing the rational thing, like refusing to fly into Chen Qi's butterfly net.

Burbank was meditating again. I used the time to look back on the events that had led me to this day. My upbringing. Football. Sex. My show-off decision to take an ROTC scholarship rather than accept my stepfather's generosity. That patrol in Afghanistan when my men—bunched up because I had not done my job and kept them spread out as I was supposed to do—had taken the force of the blast and saved my life because I happened to be crouching behind them when the bomb went off. And everything since. I had been scouted, spotted, selected, trained and conditioned and screwed and tattooed by two intelligence services for the suicidal job they were both offering me, as if they had cooked my fate by mutual agreement. And maybe they had. Both Burbank and Chen Qi had drawn certain conclusions about me, probably the same ones. They thought that I cared so little for myself, cared so little for life, for consequences, for shame, for my ancestors, that I would accept this poisonous offer. Did they have me dead to rights? I wasn't sure.

More quickly than usual, Burbank regained his focus. He said, "Are your reservations about carrying out this mission written in stone?"

Anyone with a brain in his head would have said yes in a loud voice. I said, "Why do you ask?"

"Because there's something in this for us. I've always thought so. You've always thought so."

"Have I?"

"Does memory deceive or were you the one who came up with the idea?"

"A fellow can change his mind."

"Can he now?" Burbank said. "Even if what Chen Qi is offering us almost exactly what we wanted?"

"Especially because that's true."

"You have a peculiar mind," Burbank said.

No argument.

Burbank said, "You think what just happened changes things?"

"Profoundly."

"It's a rare operation in which anomaly doesn't show its face. It's the law of the craft."

How Kiplingesque, that choice of words. But then, if Burbank hadn't been a Kipling character at heart he wouldn't now be the man of mystery and power that he was. Nor would I be sitting across a desk from him, not quite in full possession of my senses, while he offered me the chance of a lifetime to become the king of Kafiristan.

There was no place left to go with Burbank except in circles. For the next couple of hours, around and around we went. By then we began to hear voices outside the door as people began to arrive.

Burbank picked out a safe, opened it, went unerringly to the correct folder, and pulled it out. He had known exactly where this particular file was, exactly what it contained, exactly what the combination of this particular safe was. He handed me the file. It was not a very thick file. "The female in question," he said. "Your eyes only. Bring it back the next time I buzz." Burbank's clockwork day had begun. Every fifteen minutes, from now until closing time, he would have something pressing to do, someone to see, some gnarled issue to decide. There was no way of guessing when he might have time to buzz me again.

The file was labeled WILDCHILD. There was no mention of a true name. I began to read, fast, even before I sat down. Most of the file on

WILDCHILD was rank speculation—and so was my conviction that the woman therein described was the Mei I had known and no other. Like Mei, WILDCHILD had gone to high school in Concord, Massachusetts, and later attended Shanghai University. She spoke fluent English. She dressed like an American, acted like an American, had acquired the bad habits of Americans. Her father, true name redacted, called KQ/RUFFIAN in our files, was said to be a figure of consequence in the Party. As a kid of eighteen he had been an activist during the Cultural Revolution and established the reputation for ruthlessness that had carried him upward. WILDCHILD had become sexually active in her later teens, while in America. She had been withdrawn from her American high school and sent back to China when the family with which she lived complained that she and their teenage son had been discovered in bed together in his room, naked, joined, after the household was awakened in the wee hours of the morning by WILDCHILD's "ecstatic outcries."

After this summary introduction, several pages in the file were missing. These were followed by my own e-mail reporting the bicycle accident to Tom Simpson. Attached was an outraged footnote from admin about the cost of the bike I bought for Mei. Admin wanted to deduct the money from my salary. Burbank had ordered it reimbursed as an operational expense. I was surprised that this exchange hadn't been redacted because it confirmed that Mei and WILDCHILD were the same person, and that Burbank had seen an opportunity in our getting to know each other, and that he had encouraged our relationship from the first. And that I had been left in the dark like an unwitting asset. As the relationship ripened, Headquarters's interest in WILDCHILD—that is to say, Burbank's interest in her—intensified. He ordered the officer in charge of CI operations in Shanghai—his man, not Shanghai's—home for consultations. They met in private. No account was given of what was said, but shortly after the man from Shanghai got back to Shanghai, the file began to be enlivened by reports on WILDCHILD's movements.

These were paper documents, mostly written in Mandarin in several different hands, none of them in Mei's dashing calligraphy. They had been sent by pouch for Burbank's eyes only. Burbank's man in Shanghai was an industrious fellow. His sidewalk people were always with WILDCHILD. One or another of them, apparently, had been stationed at all times outside my door to log the times on her comings and goings. They photographed her, listened in on her cell phone, listened in on our sex life through bugs and cameras they planted in my rooms—just as I had suspected, although I had suspected the wrong suspects. Naturally the file did not reveal who these sidewalk people were or where Burbank's man got them or how they got away with what they did under the all-seeing eye of Chinese counterintelligence. Obviously they were Chinese. But were they Chinese Chinese or Chinese-Americans or Taiwanese or one of half a dozen other types favored by our own China people? Whoever they were, they were always there. Just like the ones who shadowed me in New York, just like the acrobats.

There were no reports on WILDCHILD's activities except when she was with me. If, as I had suspected, she had another lover, if she reported to a Guoanbu case officer, if she had any kind of life at all when we were apart, if she slept in her coffin, Burbank had not been interested. He cared only about Romeo and Juliet. How strange that would have seemed in anyone but him.

29

There were two possibilities. Either someone had slipped something into my scotch and I was hallucinating, or I was truly paranoid. Make that three possibilities. The third was that Chen Qi and Burbank knew each other and were working together, had been doing so all along on some perverse operation and needed an unwitting go-between who could be the fall guy in case things went wrong. If so, I was the designated fall guy. That thought tipped the scales toward paranoia. I knew this. I did my best to dismiss suspicion from my mind. Those who have learned what they think they know about the craft from deluded zealots are convinced that it is a world of deception and distrust in which no positive human emotion or sense of decency is involved. In reality the opposite is true. The entire basis of espionage is trust. Spying could not exist without it. If such trust is imperfect or not quite complete, then it is like all other varieties of trust. Ask yourself—do you, does anyone trust absolutely his spouse, his doctor, his lawyer, his best friend, his employee, his mother? Trust is selective. In practice, the agent trusts his case officer to protect him, to keep secrets that are a threat to his life and the lives of his entire family, to make the promised payments in full, in cash, and on time. In return the case officer trusts the agent not to set him up for capture, torture, imprisonment, and perhaps death at every clandestine meeting, and to provide reliable information or perform certain acts when called upon to do so. Within an intelligence service, colleagues may dislike one another and often do, but they trust one another absolutely. It is part of the contract, part of the mystique. It is the indispensable element. Its perversion makes treason possible and all but undetectable among professional spies, but when uncorrupted it is the code that drives the system. Everyone inside an intelligence service has been investigated to a fare-thee-well and is polygraphed on a regular basis. By these means doubt has been caged, even though every professional knows exactly how unlikely are most investigations, and especially the polygraph, to discover the truth, the whole truth—and most unlikely of all, nothing but the truth.

The idea that our side or their side might kill me never crossed my mind. If I became a problem, Burbank and Chen Qi (I had gone so far as to begin thinking of the two of them as a unit before I buried the thought) would just cut me loose. I could do them no harm. Fox News or the *New York Times* would hang up on me if I called and babbled the truth. A psychiatrist would put me on drugs. I'd live in a virtual world—or in the real one in case I had already been living in a virtual one. No one in Headquarters or Chen Qi's corporation or Guoanbu or any other intelligence service in the world would have anything to do with me. Hardly anyone at Headquarters even knew me. Those who did (remember the Gang of Thirteen) did not wish me well. They would be the Greek chorus: "There was always something funny about the guy. We all saw it even if the shrinks and the box missed it." I certainly couldn't count on the brave support of my few remaining friends on the outside. And wait a minute. "No fear of sudden death?" Did I not remember Magdalena? Oh, yes, I remembered her. But if she had been under instructions to kill me, she had already had a hundred opportunities. Had I been the target, I would not now be alive and trying to figure out what she was up to and whom she worked for. She got next to Mother, then next to me because she wanted access to someone I could get next to. But who? And why?

I told myself a lot of things. The fact was, when it came right down to it, I would go on doing the job no matter what, simply because I didn't want to walk out before this movie was over, no matter how bad it was. Not that there weren't worrisome signs I was loath to discuss with myself. For example, resentment was taking up more and more space in my mind. And you know what Burbank had to say about that.

Most of the above were night thoughts fueled by single malt whisky. In daylight I controlled my fantasies and waited for instructions. These were not long in coming. Late on a Friday afternoon, as everyone else headed for the parking lots, Burbank buzzed. It was the first time he had done so since we had our discussion about my meeting with Chen Qi and Lin Ming two weeks before. When I entered his office to return Mei's file, I found him bent over a small refrigerator. He extracted two frosty bottles of beer. He gave me one. "Cheers," he said. We clinked bottles and drank.

After a medium-long pause Burbank said, "You still have a phone number for your friend the basketball player?"

"If it still works, yes."

"Call him up on your way home and set up a meeting for this weekend. In New York."

I said, "What about Chen Qi?"

"He's in Cairo."

Chen Qi was in Cairo? Burbank read my thought, not that there was anything difficult about that.

"It's probably just a coincidence," Burbank said. "Business. But if it isn't, he'll walk into our surveillance and we'll know something new."

I asked what I was supposed to tell Lin Ming.

Burbank said, "What do you think you should tell him?"

"'No, thanks.'"

"Why should we do that?"

"Because what they offer is of no use to us."

Burbank lifted his beer bottle in another toast. "Right," he said. "Isn't it interesting how seeing the obvious makes things so much simpler?"

I said, "So now what?"

"So now you go to New York, meet Lin Ming, change the climate of your relationship with him."

"How? In what way?"

"You say Chen Qi treated Lin Ming like a servant on the night of the blizzard, humiliating him. You saw that Lin Ming resented it."

"And?"

"Remember what I told you. Resentment makes things happen."

Burbank's lip lifted ever so slightly. He pointed a forefinger at me and clucked his tongue. I took this as positive reinforcement, as a reward for good thinking, as a sign of camaraderie. Or condescension.

I said, "You really think it's possible to turn Lin Ming?"

"Didn't you just suggest that it was?" Burbank said. "Maybe not this weekend but if you play him right, you can get the process started. As I hope you're beginning to realize, these things take time. You know how to do it. Would you say that you and Lin Ming have the embryo of a relationship?"

"Maybe."

"Are you sure? Will it grow, will its heart begin to beat, will it create its own brain and liver and arms and legs? Will it in time create others like itself?"

His face was a mask of earnestness. What was he up to? I laughed. He said, "What's so funny?"

"Nothing," I said. "I just didn't know you had a metaphorical side."

"Everyone has a metaphorical side. The question is, can you rattle his bones with a single question? Are you two friendly enough for that?"

He was grinning—a sight I had never seen before—and watching my reaction.

I said, "Maybe."

"That's the right answer," Burbank said. And then, as if granting me permission to do something I absolutely longed to do, he said, "Okay, go. Go to it. Don't fly. Take the next train. It will give you time to think."

30

By the time the Metroliner pulled into Penn Station I knew everybody in my car by sight. Walking out of the gate, I scanned the crowd: a buck-toothed girl hopping up and down in excitement, a Hasid who greeted another Hasid who had been sitting in the fifth-row window seat, a very short man with gym-rat biceps and a boxer's flattened face. And at the back of the crowd, Lin Ming. Our eyes met. He turned around and walked fast across the waiting room. I followed him up the escalators and into the street, then uptown on Seventh Avenue to the Forties. He kept track of my reflection in store windows. I saw no one worth wor-rying about behind us or across the avenue or ahead of us, and no sign of the sidewalk crew. I wondered if we were headed for the Algonquin, but before we got there Lin Ming for some unfathomable reason walked into an all-night sporting goods store. He headed straight for a rack of warm-up jackets at the back of the store and got behind it. From there he had a good view of the door. The display window was a sheet of light. A stalker could look in, but Lin Ming could not look out. This made him nervous, very nervous. This person was not the relaxed Lin Ming I knew. How pleased Burbank would have been at this sudden change in behavior. I stationed myself on the other side of the clothes rack, facing Lin, my back to the door, as if screening him from a defender while he took his shot at the basket. I took a cheap Mets jacket off the rack, held it against my chest, and raised my eyebrows in inquiry. How do I look? Lin Ming paid no attention. He said, "Take the uptown local to Seventy-second Street and walk down to the river." Then he left. I looked at two more jackets and tried on a Giants cap, then did as I had been instructed.

Forty minutes later, when I sighted Lin Ming, he was still on edge. You could sense a churning within him. A light breeze came off the Hudson. I could smell the river, glimpse New Jersey's polluted sky, faintly hear its clamor over the monotonous hum of the West Side of Manhattan and the counterpoint of its many sirens. After a couple of blocks, Lin Ming turned into the park and found an empty bench. I sat down beside him. He didn't flee.

In a voice I could barely hear he said, "Why are you here?"

"Because we have something to talk about," I said.

"This is not good."

"How do you know? We haven't talked yet."

"It's impromptu."

Inasmuch as Lin Ming himself was nothing if not a devotee of the impromptu, this should have made the contact more interesting to him, but what did I know? No matter how good my Mandarin might be, I wasn't Han and could not think like a Han no matter how hard I tried. We simply had different ways of thinking about thinking.

I said, "If you don't want to do this, I can leave."

"Too late," Lin Ming said. "Say what you came to say."

I did as he asked. Beside me in the half-dark, Lin Ming flinched. In the wash of the streetlamp he looked pale. He grew even more ashen as he listened to my words. Afterward he fell into a stillness. I waited for him to speak, to make a gesture, to leap to his feet and stalk away in anger, to pull out a stiletto and attempt to bury it in my heart or brain. Instead he remained as he was—speechless, inert. He leaned forward and rested his forearms on his thighs. His hands dangled between his knees. This pose of despair was as much out of character as the rest of his behavior. Was he acting, playing a scene? Making a joke of the whole thing? And if all this was genuine, how could Lin Ming of all people have believed that I had come to give him an answer different from the last one I had given him?

He muttered something. I said, "What? I didn't hear you." I spoke a little louder, a little more peremptorily than was absolutely necessary. This was method, one infinitesimal move in the reconfiguration of our relationship. He had to know this. It was a humiliation, however tiny. I felt a flicker of regret. I liked this man. I didn't like what I was doing to him. He had had enough humiliation lately.

Lin Ming gave me a sidelong look. After a minute he leaped to his feet and walked, fast, toward the next streetlight. I caught up to him. Another empty bench came in sight. I took his arm, thinking that he would shake off my hand, but he let himself be steered to the bench. He sat down and turned his head to stare at me.

"Speak," he said.

I told him what we wanted. Names, résumés, assessments of six high-quality targets within China, within the elite—perhaps within Guoanbu, though neither one of us would know about that. These people were so exalted that nobody less trustworthy than the ghost of Zhou Enlai would be cleared to possess such knowledge. Lin Ming did not flinch. What I had asked was too outrageous to register while my words still hung in the air.

Lin Ming laughed. In English he said, "You've got balls, I'll give you that. Just as a matter of curiosity, what do you propose to give us in return?"

"The same valuable goods already on offer."

"You're crazy. You know who these people are—who their fathers are. They are untouchable."

True. I didn't even nod but waited for Lin Ming to go on.

He said, "What you're offering us is chicken feed. One man in one embassy in return for the Party jewels? Be serious."

"How do you know the man we are offering to you is the only one like him?" I asked. "How do you know it's just one embassy? How do you know it's not a network? How do you know what we know and you don't know?"

"How do we know you know what you say you know?"

"You don't. You won't, either, unless you start playing ball."

He smiled—you might have called it a twisted smile, but even so it made Lin Ming look more like himself. "I have already played basketball with you," he said.

Without thinking I said, "Meaning what?"

"Meaning I know you are better than you pretend, that you can fake it when you feel like it," Lin Ming said.

I had thought he might just walk away. He made no such move. He seemed to be waiting for something else. But I wasn't going to request anything more and spoil things. I reached into my jacket pocket and showed him the brand-new cheapo cell phone I had bought for him.

I told him the number of my own brand-new phone. He committed it to memory, I could see him doing this. I said, "Give me a call when you've had time to think this over more carefully and realize just how much to your advantage it could be."

Lin Ming knew exactly what was happening. If he took the phone he would take the first step toward life as a turncoat, because there was no conceivable way he could give me what I was asking for with the permission of his masters. He made no move to take the phone. I continued to offer it. He looked at the ground, he looked over my shoulder at the empty park. On the count of twenty he took the phone from my hand and hurried off into the darkness.

31

It was only eight o'clock. I was hungry. I wanted to be with my own kind. I decided to drop in at the club. It was Friday again and I was dressed down like everyone else in this city and every other city in North America. Human beings cannot even go without a necktie unless they do it in unison. All mammals are the same—happiest when they all look alike, think alike, travel on well-trampled ground. Consider the wildebeests of the Serengeti, walking in their thousands around in the exact same semicircle season after season, all headed in the same direction, all eating the same grass, all watching placidly as reckless young nonconformists reject the blood wisdom of the herd and dash outside it to be killed and eaten by carnivores. I myself felt the pull of the herd. I hoped that Lin Ming would not feel it too strongly. Meanwhile, who knew, maybe I'd run into someone at the club who'd keep me company. On my first visit I had run into Alice Song, hadn't I?

This time the street outside the club was deserted. Inside, the cocktail hour was over, so there were many fewer people in the bar than last time. Not a single woman was among them. There was no babble, no laughter. I recognized a face or two—half-drunk white-haired men with raddled cheeks and whiskey noses. Guillermo the barman was on duty. Clearly he had not memorized my face on our single meeting. I ordered a Belgian wheat beer and drank it and because I had come here in hope, waited for Alice to show up. She did not appear. If she did appear I was sure she would cut me cold. But that might not last. I could break the ice by telling her the truth and making her laugh: I was being followed on the night in question by sinister foreign agents who were always with me and my disappearance was my way of saving her from such evil company. Meanwhile I was still hungry. I asked Guillermo if the dining room was still open. He looked at his watch, nodded, and said, "Better hurry. It closes in ten minutes."

The greeter was not happy to see me. No one was happy to see me today, almost certainly not even the phantasm I called Alice. Half a dozen tables were still occupied. White tablecloths, nice old silver cutlery engraved with the university crest. I ordered fettuccine Putanesca and a glass of a wine that the card on the table identified as Montepulciano d'Abruzzo. The pasta wasn't bad. I bolted it because I had had no other food that day and signed the chit. No one bothered me, but I had company of a kind in the pensioners across the room. We shared memories—the look and scent of the campus on the first warm day of spring and the delusion that the weather had always been like that, the drone of a lecturer, the sweet misery of hangovers. After only two visits I was beginning to like being a club member. It provided a sort of chaperoned aloneness that was new to me.

I heard female voices and went out into the foyer. A group of women, chattering and laughing, was descending the main staircase. There were fewer of them than the decibel level had led me to expect. One of them especially had a bell-like voice—Alice Song, of course. She was in the middle of the pack and some of the women at the front turned around and looked upward at her, as if they wanted to absorb the whole glamorous experience of her—voice, face, mind, the aura of her brilliant career, smashing clothes even if it was dress-down Friday. Certainly that's what I wanted. She was tall. She was striking, with a beautiful face that was not quite a woman's face, as if it were a female duplicate of the face of a handsome father. She spotted me immediately but went on with her story.

At the bottom of the stairs most of the women headed for the exit. Three of them including Alice disappeared into the lavatory. The other two emerged after a long interval and left. Five minutes after that Alice appeared. She walked up to me as if she knew I had been loitering. She looked neither happy nor unhappy—bemused, I thought, by the sight of me. She said, "So, someone paid the ransom?"

"I escaped my kidnappers," I said. "Who are your friends?"

"The house committee. Did you have dinner here?"

"The pasta."

"How was it?" she asked.

"It was okay. The service was a little grumpy, but I came late. There are no male members of the house committee?"

"There used to be," Alice said. "That's why the food was so bad. Men just show up at the mess hall. Women bitch."

"Let me guess," I said. "You're the chairperson."

No response but a level stare—what else would she be? All this was a way of avoiding a discussion of the mystery of the disappearing schmuck. She didn't want to suggest that she gave a damn about my running away by asking for an explanation. I couldn't apologize, couldn't explain. Alice wasn't exactly overjoyed to see me, but at least she was talking to me.

I said, "Can we have a drink together?"

"Not here," Alice said. "The bar closes at ten."

The club's grandfather clock whirred and struck the three-quarter hour. We went to a place down the street. Alice was a cautious drinker but voluble nonetheless. We spoke Mandarin—she started it. We talked about China. She had never been there, though she had lived in a replica of it while growing up in her parents' house in a Chinese neighborhood. Facts were her thing, though she knew as only a lawyer can know there is no such thing as immutable truth. She had been in court all week defending a company that had poisoned an entire river in Massachusetts with chemicals from its paper mills that turned the water green or magenta or yellow, killing everything that lived in it and making people who lived on its banks sick. In her heart she hoped her clients would be impoverished by the jury's verdict, but she was trying hard to keep that from happening because such an outcome would cost her firm money. The practice of law, she said, was morally exhausting. She said she would never say that in English. Neither would I regarding my own profession, or in Mandarin either. Alice asked what I did for a living. I told her I worked for the government.

"In which part of it, doing what?" she asked.

I said, "I'm not a civil servant. I consult under a contract." All of which, technically speaking, was the truth.

"Consult about what?" Alice asked.

"The mysterious East."

"Poor darling."

She let it go at that. I guess she thought she already knew all she needed to know about me from the classroom, the tennis court, the hallowed halls of yesteryear even though we had barely known each other in college. As a sexual possibility she became more intriguing by the moment. My girlfriends had always been on the small side. I had never known a woman who looked anything like Alice, who was so tall, who had so much voice, such a brain, who got so much more likeable as the evening wore on. She reminded me of no one.

We exchanged cell phone numbers. I put her in a taxi at 2:00 A.M. She had a dinner party the next night. We made plans to spend Sunday together, maybe drive up to Connecticut or somewhere and have lunch, then go for a walk in the fresh air. She had to be home by five, when her ex-husband would bring their child back. She had only the one kid. She liked it that way. Her daughter, whose outside name was Caitlin (in Mandarin, at home, Liling) was a nice person for a six-year-old, but Alice felt like a slacker because the child did not have a sibling. She said she might be better off living in China, where she would have no choice in the matter.

32

Next morning I listened to Mandopop while I ate breakfast and read the newspapers. The music activated a mental slide show—Mei in daylight, Mei in the dark. To pass the time I played solitaire on the laptop. By setting the level of difficulty at "beginner" I managed to win 8 percent of my games. The computer refuses to be cheated, and that takes away a lot of the fun of the game, but even so solitaire opens the mind. That was the problem—more Mei, more Chen Qi, more Yangtze. After an hour or so I surfed the Web and found one of those ads that invites you to track high school classmates. I clicked on it and typed in the name of Mei's high school. She had told me she played volleyball, so I tried "girls volleyball team." No luck. I tried different class years, and on the third try, there in the team photograph was sweet seventeen-year-old Mei in gym shorts, kneeling first row center. She was identified as Susan Peng. I typed this name into the search box and found her graduation picture—apparently the book had gone to print before she was thrown out of America on a morals charge. The caption said: "She is full of vim and vigor and is always on the go." Her nickname was "SuSu." She was a member of the National Honor Society and had participated in volley-ball, skating, debating team, Shakespeare Society, math club, waltz club, class play, school newspaper, and more. She was president of the math club. She was a princess of the homecoming queen's court. She was elected class brain and class madcap. I couldn't believe my luck. Never had a Headquarters file told me so much about her. Had she stuck to rules and lied to me about where she went to high school, I would never have tracked her down. The information was useless, of course, because the name she used as a student could not be a true name. Had Burbank recruited her when she was in high school and sent her back to China to lie in wait for the sucker who would give him entrée into the shadow land that was Guoanbu headquarters? This was an old question. There were no new answers.

With half a day and an evening to kill and a lot to think about, I lunched at the meatball sandwich place and went to a popcorn movie at the theater around the corner. Emerging from the theater at dusk I half expected to see Lin Ming in the crowd with his gym bag, but he wasn't there and neither was anyone else I had ever seen before. A light rain fell. Headlights bounced off the shiny pavement. I walked back to my building. The rain intensified. Although it's easier to follow some-one in the rain because the target's mind is on not getting wet, there were no signs of surveillance, just lots of people hurrying through the downpour.

The doorman stood under the awning with his big black umbrella. As he opened the door for me he said, "You got a delivery." He unlocked a drawer in his desk and withdrew a padded envelope and the ledger in which he recorded deliveries. "Came in at three fifty-seven," he said as I signed the book. "By messenger," he added.

"What did the messenger look like?"

"Guy on a bicycle. Skinny."

"American?"

"How can anybody tell anymore?" he asked. He thought, then shook his head. "Just a guy," he said.

Inside the apartment, I examined the envelope—my name and address typed on a plain label, no return address. I slit the sealed end with a kitchen knife and shook the contents onto the kitchen counter. A thumb drive fell out. There was nothing else in the package. I inserted the drive in my laptop. A photograph of Da Ge, Mei's favorite princeling, popped up. His real name was Chen Jianyu and he was, as I already knew, the son of Chen Qi. There followed a narrative of many pages, with references to other semiprincelings, including Mei as an unnamed subject. In some of the pictures she was with Chen Jianyu, in others with me. In the ones with Chen Jianyu she was radiantly happy. I had always supposed and now I was certain that there was something between the two of them.

I read for hours. It was a workout. Mandarin bureaucratese is no less convoluted than the same kind of gibberish in any other language, and I sometimes had to use the dictionary, so it was slow going. Toward dawn I made some tea and ate some cereal. As I chewed the Raisin Bran I tried to think. When at last I was done reading, I felt a great unease. Was this file a document or a forgery? Why the indecent haste to put it into my hands, mere hours after I had horrified Lin Ming by asking for this material?

Someone was trying to tell us that we had set the hook in Lin Ming's lip. Maybe we had—anything was possible. *The wise man does not believe in triumph,* I thought, inventing a Laozi proverb. I was tired, eyesore, completely sober. My stomach was sour. My eyes hurt. I turned everything off—Mei first, then the rest. I flopped on the unmade bed without bothering to undress. What a busy day I had had, what dark dreams I had to look forward to if I could talk myself into falling asleep.

When I woke at midmorning my mind was on Lin Ming, as though continuing a thought that had begun while I was asleep. Still abed, I called the number of the cell phone I had given him in Riverside Park. He did not pick up.

"Hey buddy," I said in English to his voice mail. "I've got an extra ticket to the game right here in my hand. Good seats. Gimme a ring before twelve if you're interested."

This message had hidden meanings, wild cards on which I had briefed Lin Ming when I gave him the phone. "Extra ticket" meant I wanted to meet, "right here in my hand" meant urgent. "Good seats" meant the Museum of Natural History at the entrance to the Planetarium. "Gimme a ring" meant cough twice if the coast is clear. "Twelve" meant three o'clock because its two digits added up to three. "If you're interested" meant *really* urgent. Could Tom and Huck, swearing a blood oath in McDougal's cave, have been more devious?

It was ten-forty now. After showering and shaving for the first time in two days, I poached two eggs in the microwave, remembering to prick the yolks with a needle. I made some toast and heated milk for instant hot chocolate. I tried to read the *Times* but failed because yesterday's ideograms still fluttered in my head like moths.

At two-thirty I headed for the Planetarium, the thumb drive containing Chen Jianyu's file in the watch pocket of my jeans. According to my maternal grandfather, who in 1943 parachuted into Lombardy for the OSS, the Gestapo never looked for the watch pocket when frisking a captured American agent because Old World pants did not have watch pockets. That's where the men of the OSS hid their suicide pills, said Gramps.

The museum was mobbed, just as it had been on Sundays when I was a kid. Shrill adolescent voices bounced off the walls. Inside this clamor, quiet and still, stood Lin Ming. The hood of his Knicks sweatshirt was up, making him hard to recognize or even to tell that he was Chinese. He saw me and coughed twice, his all-clear signal. I saw but did not hear the cough.

And then, with a twist of the bowels, I remembered Alice Song and our date for lunch. I looked at my own watch—not a signal to Lin Ming that the coast was clear, though maybe he took it for that, but a spasm of embarrassment and guilt and panic. I was an hour and forty minutes late: strike three. I walked into the crowd, trying to escape from my own stupidity. Lin Ming followed. *Asshole!* I called myself. *Idiot!* Because of the noise it was impossible to call Alice, and anyway how could I make amends and why would she pick up after she saw my name on caller ID? I paused in front of a glassed-in display of American birds. The skylarking crowd surged beyond us, reflected in the big backlit pane. All the kids seemed to be wearing baseball caps and costly sneakers. Lin Ming obviously thought this was no place for a clandestine meeting. Actually, it would have been perfect had we continued on into the darkened Star Theater. When the stars and planets and galaxies were out and everyone else's eyes were fixed upon the ceiling, it was an ideal place to pass documents and money. Plus, the microphone that could filter our voices in this bedlam had not, as far as I knew, yet been invented.

In a loud voice I asked Lin Ming a question. He could not hear me. I asked it again, even louder. He still could not hear me. I pulled the thumb drive out of my watch pocket and showed it to him.

"Put that away," Lin Ming said, genuinely shocked by this breach of security. "Are you crazy?"

"Please answer the question." I was still bellowing.

Lin Ming said, "Let's get out of here."

"Not yet. *Did* you send me this?"

"I'm going. You can follow me if you wish."

He walked away. I followed. Lin Ming threaded his way through the screeching, rowdy, chaotic mob, never slowing down but never bumping into anyone either. Outside, he led me into Central Park, then slowed his steps until I caught up and was walking beside him.

He said, "So what was it you wanted to know?"

"The provenance of the material I received yesterday."

"Ultimate or immediate? How was it delivered?"

"By bicycle messenger."

"At what time yesterday?"

"Three fifty-seven."

"In the afternoon?"

Lin, who had been so depressed only two days before, was now making fun of me. This is not the way humble assets are supposed to behave, but Lin Ming was no garden-variety asset. He was used to being the case officer. In his mind he had been born to be the case officer and that was what he still was and always would be. He was certain that he was a lot smarter than I was. Such hubris was supposed to give me the advantage, but I wasn't so sure about that. Chances are he was right. He started to say something.

I interrupted. "It's a simple question," I said. "What's the answer?"

"I was about to tell you," Lin Ming said. "The package came from me. The guy on the bicycle is a man I sometimes use for errands. He's a recovering addict, he's not Chinese, he's unwitting, he has no curiosity, he rides fast. He charges twenty dollars a delivery, anywhere in Manhattan."

Just like the psycho who, a while ago, was handing out flyers at the right time and place in Greenwich Village.

I said, "Name?"

"The guy on the bicycle. Have you read the material?"

"Yes."

"The whole thing?"

"Yes."

"You know that many ideograms?"

"I have a dictionary," I said. "I also have a question."

"Ask it."

"I only asked for the information day before yesterday. It arrived yesterday."

"True. What's that got to do with anything?"

"A lot," I said. "How did you produce it so fast?"

"It already existed."

"So all you had to do was copy it?"

Lin Ming shrugged. What business of mine were these trivial details?

I said, "I've been told that in your service no one is allowed to be alone with a classified document, that only one copy of any document exists in any one place, that they are never taken outside of the safe room where they are stored, and that making photocopies is regarded as prima facie evidence of treason. So how did you happen to have an extra copy on hand?"

"My, my," said Lin Ming. "If those really are the rules, you're a lucky man to have that thumb drive in your watch pocket."

He was smiling—smirking. The subdued Lin Ming I had bullied in Riverside Park had turned himself into a different Lin Ming. Now he was turning into a third version, this one a comedian.

I said, "You expect us to believe that this file was created in a matter of hours?"

"No," Lin Ming said. "As I've already said, the file already existed."

"Why?"

"Because it was obvious that you would ask for it sooner or later. You Americans are a very strange people. You're always in a hurry and then when something happens fast you get suspicious. Do you imagine you're the only quick people in the world?"

"So how many more of these files already exist?"

"To find that out, you must give me something," Lin Ming said. "Like you, I must give my superiors reasons to trust me."

"I'll be in touch," I said.

"Make it soon."

"I'll call when the time comes."

"No more Planetarium, if you don't mind," Lin Ming said.

He strode away to the east. I went in the opposite direction, seething. Around Seventy-fifth Street my everyday cell phone rang. It was Alice Song. Apologies welled up in me. I spoke her name. Before I could say more she cut me off and said, "How much ransom are they demanding this time?" Her voice was cheery but extra loud, as if she were waking up a dozing juror. I could have heard her perfectly well in the Planetarium. She said, "Listen. There's a nice snooty little California cuisine restaurant." She named it. "Look it up on your iPhone," she said. "If you're not seated at the table by seven o'clock, it's all over between us."

I said, "Will I need a jacket?"

"They probably wouldn't let you in if you showed up in one," Alice said.

33

Dinner at the snooty restaurant consisted of microportions of organic stuff arranged on oversize square plates by some Zen abstractionist in the kitchen and haughty service by a meager young man who clearly thought I didn't deserve and couldn't possibly appreciate the extraordinary creations he placed before me. The courses, four of them, were mere specks of color on the bone-white crockery. The food had no odor, little taste. Decidedly, The Quail, as the restaurant was called after its specialty (two tiny birds, disjointed and garnished with what looked and tasted like steamed leaves of the gingko tree), was in the front line in the battle against morbid obesity.

However, the company was good. Alice, watching me as I ate the two forkfuls that comprised tonight's special, grinned and said, "Do you eat like this every night?"

"Usually it takes a little longer to finish."

"What's your favorite food, just so I'll know next time?"

"There's going to be a next time?"

"Why wouldn't there be?" Alice asked.

"Well, I stood you up twice. Usually that's grounds for an unhappy ending."

"Being kidnapped is always a defense," she said. "So what's your favorite food?"

I told her. She looked amused. She looked as if she had been prepared to be amused.

Because the wait between courses was long in order to provide time for meditation, the meal lasted a couple of hours. Afterward we sipped herbal tea, of which The Quail offered a great variety. The check came. Alice grabbed it. I was not surprised, because I had been given the menu that did not show the prices. She paid it in cash—three hundred dollars and change.

"Next time, me," I said.

"Great!" Alice said. "I love Subway."

It was raining again. Just as we walked out the door a taxi pulled up. "Our lucky night," Alice said. A couple got out of the cab and dashed toward The Quail. Alice got in. I leaned over and gave her a little wave good-bye through the cab's open door. She said, "What's that for?"

"Thanks for dinner. I enjoyed the company a lot."

"So you've had enough enjoyment for one night?"

She was not smiling. A car splashed by in the other direction, its headlights lighting up her face. Her almost-black eyes were filling up with scorn, as in an animated film. What was the matter with this guy? It was nine o'clock. I had planned to take the next train to Washington so as to brief Burbank bright and early the next morning. Instead, I got into the backseat with Alice.

"Sorry about that," I said. "I thought I was still on probation."

"You are," Alice said. "But there's such a thing as time off for good behavior."

She gave the driver an address on Park Avenue. I didn't get a look at her apartment, which felt large and smelled of books, because she did not turn on the lights, but holding my hand, led me to the bedroom. In the next few hours I learned a lot about being in bed with a six-foot woman. Like Mei, though less acrobatic, Alice was an originator. She didn't talk or make any sounds at all while things were happening, but in between she liked to chat. She did not murmur and cuddle as did nearly every other female I had ever slept with, but propped herself up on one elbow and conversed in her customary half shout. For the first hour or so this was disconcerting, but as the night wore on I grew used to it. It was a treat, in its way, to hear every word she spoke instead of the usual muffled commentary into the pillow. Although Alice had had no small talk when fully clothed, she now expressed her opinion about just about everything except Kierkegaard. Things like, "In college I had a professor—Wendell Pitt, do you remember him?"

"No. I was warned."

"You were lucky to have such thoughtful friends," Alice said. "Wendell Pitt said that *Finnegan's Wake* had to be read as if it were music. What do you suppose he meant by that?"

"He didn't tell the class?"

"No, he just read aloud from the thing. Every day. It was torture. The music sounded like a truckload of pots and pans falling off a truck. Listen." She quoted Joyce from memory, her gem-cut diction almost proving Professor Pitt right by turning Joyce's Dadaesque gibberish into a vaudeville routine. "I hope I haven't bored you," she said.

"Don't worry," I said. "Have you read the book since you took the course?"

"Are you kidding?"

"I've never heard of anyone memorizing that stuff. How did you do it?"

"I have positive reinforcement to thank. Regurgitate and you get an A. Come here."

There was a fast train to Washington at 6:00 A.M. At four-thirty I slipped out of bed. Alice lay on her side in a wash of feeble streetlight, a living Velázquez—curved hip and spine, glorious legs, luminous skin, fan of silken hair on the pillow, as if it had been combed instead of just falling naturally into place. I wanted a shower but did not want to wake her up. Then I realized it would be a bad idea to leave without saying good-bye, so I took the shower. When I returned, Alice was wide-awake. She had turned over. Naked and supine, one knee raised, she had become a different woman. Her face was softer, her eyes, filled with sleep, had changed from umber to chocolate, her movements were languid. She had made love with languor, the opposite of Mei's ride-'im-cowboy style. This was the first thought I'd had of Mei since Alice took off her clothes.

Once again Alice said, "Come here."

I thought I was going to miss my train, but all she wanted to do was to sniff me. She said, "You smelled better before you took the shower."

"Sorry about that," I said.

"You've got nothing to be sorry about." She turned on the bedside lamp. "I didn't realize you were so furry," she said, stroking my chest hair.

I started to tell her she had been a surprise to me, too, but thought better of it. I told her I was going to take the train to Washington. Early appointments.

Her demeanor changed. Suddenly she was all-business. She said, "You'll never get a cab at this hour. Get dressed and I'll be right with you."

Still naked, she walked out into the apartment. Seconds later she called to me. I found her in the hall. She was wearing a trench coat and Keds. In the elevator she gathered her hair into a ponytail and bound it with an elastic ring she pulled out of the pocket of the raincoat. In the basement garage we got into an Audi convertible—spoils of the divorce, she said. She drove fast to Penn Station, and as if under an enchantment found a parking space a block away from the entrance. She went inside with me. We had half an hour to spare. At the gate Alice said, "Wait here." She vanished and in minutes came back with a fast-food bag. I could smell the meatball sandwich inside.

"Breakfast," she said. "You must be famished."

We were standing quite close together. I could smell the bed on her skin. It was ten till six. The announcer called my train.

Alice said, "I don't think we know each other well enough yet to kiss good-bye."

This made me smile. She smiled back, as if we had a secret. I felt the greatest goodwill for this woman. Words, I thought again, would spoil the mood. Alice had no such inhibitions.

She said, "Let me ask you this. If I invite you to a dinner party next Saturday, the twenty-third day of the month, will you show up?"

"That would certainly be my intention."

"Not good enough. You have to say 'no' now or show up then. Eight o'clock. My place. I'm not going to remind you."

"What's the address?"

She handed me her business card, street address and apartment number already written on the back in a dashing hand. Then she walked away, wiggling her fingers over her shoulder. As she went I glimpsed her legs winking through the vent in her Burberry, bare under the raincoat like the rest of her body.

34

The train was only twenty minutes late, so it was not yet eleven o'clock when I got to Headquarters. Burbank buzzed before I could sit down. Later I stood in front of him. He didn't tell me to sit down but, without looking up, continued to work on a paper he was annotating in red ink. No wonder he ignored me. I was unshaved and, thanks to Lin Ming and Alice Song, bleary-eyed after two more or less sleepless nights. The jeans I had worn in New York were wrinkled and stained, my shirt was smelly. Everybody in CI was supposed to dress like a banker. I had missed the Gang of Thirteen meeting. I had not called in to say I was running late. However, when at last Burbank dropped his document into his out basket and looked up at me, his expression was neutral.

He said, "Speak."

I described my meeting with Lin Ming. Burbank listened with his eyes closed. When I got to the thumb drive and its contents, the deep-set pale blue eyes snapped open.

"This is Chen Qi's son you're talking about?"

"Supposedly."

"You know him." No question mark.

"We met several times in Shanghai," I said. "He was, I suppose he still is, a friend of Mei's."

"How close a friend?"

It cost me something to answer this question. "Quite close," I said, "if you believe the pictures in the file."

"Do you believe them?

"They tend to confirm old suppositions."

A look, half amused, half contemptuous, crossed Burbank's face. If I was a cuckold, that fit right in with my being late and unshaven. He held out his hand. I dug the thumb drive out of my watch pocket and handed it over. Burbank rolled back his chair and fiddled with something on the back of his desk. I was still standing up, so I could see him punching an access code into a keypad on a bottom drawer—evidently even his desk was a safe. He took a laptop out of the drawer, switched it on to battery power—no wires for Burbank—inserted the thumb drive, and scrolled through the file until he got to the photographs of Chen Jianyu. He looked at the rest of the pictures, lingering over some, then switched off. He made no attempt to read the text.

"Have you read this?" he asked.

"Yes."

"All of it?"

I nodded.

"Did you understand all of it?"

"The surface, yes."

"Have you analyzed it?"

"If you mean have I gone through it with a fine-tooth comb and an all-seeing eye and cross-checked it with other sources, the answer is no," I said. "It took me all night just to read through the thing."

"Who originated the file?"

"No identifying marks. It's sterile."

"So what does it say about this young man?" Burbank asked.

"He was rebellious, defied his father. As a child he wet the bed. He started fires. He killed a cat. . . ."

"How?"

"Beheaded it with a cleaver."

"At what age?"

"Seven. He was rebellious, disrespectful to his father—who is never named in the file even by a pseudonym, by the way. He had a quick mind—did well in school, transcripts of marks and teachers' reports appended. As a teenager, lots of drugs and girls and rock music. He was arrested at seventeen for possession of LSD but the cops let him go after a scare and a lecture. He was a good boy for a while after that, or at least didn't get caught. Kept up his marks, kept his nose clean. After graduating from Shanghai University with an engineering degree, he went to Purdue for an MBA."

"Skip that stuff," Burbank said.

"Are you sure you want me to do that?"

Beneath his unruffled surface Burbank was annoyed. He made an impatient gesture: spit it out.

"Whoever in Guoanbu assembled this file thinks it's possible that he was recruited by us while he was in Indiana."

"Do they believe that actually happened?"

"It's the theme of the file. Everything—his childhood, his look-at-me behavior, his rebellious nature, his disrespect for his father, the wild life he led at Purdue, is treated as part of a pattern."

"What kind of wild life?" Burbank asked.

"The usual grad school kind—alcohol, cocaine, weed, girls, girls, girls, loud music. He paid for two abortions in a single semester. The girls are named."

"All of them?"

"The file does not say otherwise."

"How would anyone know them all?"

"I wonder," I said. "But Chen Jianyu wasn't the only Chinese at Purdue."

"Tell me more."

"Chen Jianyu made friends with a professor the Chinese regard as a spotter for U.S. intelligence."

"Name?"

"Milo D. Fletcher, East Asian studies."

"Background?"

"Not specified, except that he has fluent Mandarin and has published what the file calls 'reactionary capitalist-imperialist anti-PRC propaganda.'"

"Why do the Chinese think he was a spotter?"

"Because two other students reported that Fletcher had introduced them to a stranger who took them out for dinner and made a pitch."

"Did they say yes?"

"The file doesn't say. Nor does it name them. But if Beijing knew about the attempted recruitment, it follows that the students might have said yes on instructions from Beijing."

"Or no for reasons of their own."

"Not if they wanted to serve the motherland by penetrating this Headquarters, or were ordered to do so."

"Thanks for the tutorial," Burbank said. "So why did Chen Jianyu let himself be cultivated?"

"According to the file, because that's the way Chen Jianyu is," I said. "Anything that might outrage or embarrass his father is the thing he wants to do."

"Why?"

"Resentment?"

Burbank broke wind, a string of little detonations, a shocking sound coming from him, and leapt to his feet. "Stay put," he said and hustled from the room. He was gone for a while, and when he came back he unlocked another desk drawer, shook a couple of pills from a drugstore bottle, and swallowed them.

"So how did the professor go about cultivating this fellow?"

"The usual—invitations to parties, introductions to girls and eminent professors, a sympathetic ear, a willingness to treat the target as an intellectual equal. Fletcher cultivates an erudite manner, which the file says made a great impression on Chen Jianyu. The one thing he reveres, apparently, is learning. To him, Fletcher was a figure out of Henry James—a gentleman and scholar, a living contradiction of everything he had ever been told about Americans."

"Speculation."

"No," I said. "Two of the informers at Purdue reported Chen Jianyu had said this in so many words, and not just once but several times."

"So what do you make of this?" Burbank asked. "Don't cover your ass, just answer the question."

I said, "I don't know what to make of it."

Burbank sat forward, as if to interrupt. I held up a palm. He looked displeased. I was telling him when he could speak? Who did I think I was? I raised my voice slightly.

"There are two ways to go," I said. "If you believe the file is genuine. . . ."

"Do you believe that?" Burbank said.

"It smells genuine, but if it's a forgery that's the way it would smell," I said. "The little I know of Chen Jianyu confirms the file. Unless he was playing a role when we met."

"Unless, unless, unless, the almighty *unless*," Burbank said. "Did you study Latin in school?"

"I showed up for class. I remember very little."

"How about the word for *unless*?

"Sorry."

"*Nisi*," Burbank said. "That should be the motto of our craft. *Nisi, nisi, nisi.*"

He pulled the thumb drive out of his laptop and handed it back to me. "Take good care of this," he said. "You know the drill. Mention it to no one. Share it with no one. Do not leave it in your safe. Carry it with you. Make no copy. Go through it again, this time with that fine-tooth comb. Keep an eye out for lice. Research it. Think upon it. Come to a conclusion. Do you have anything else?"

The answer was yes, but I had had enough of this, so I didn't say so. I had already told Burbank in passing about the unbelievable speed with which Lin Ming had delivered this file. I had told him about Lin's mood swing. There was no need to tell him again, but I thought the least he could do was show some curiosity, ask a question or two. This did not happen.

We were done. Burbank took a paper out of his in-basket and said, "Work at home for the rest of the day. You look like you've been sleeping under a bridge in a cardboard box."

FOUR

35

Somehow I did not forget to call Alice Song before I fell asleep that afternoon. When she heard my voice she said, "It's you? How come you didn't say 'surprise!' instead of 'hello?'" I was too tired to think of a comeback. Alice went on with the kidding. I held the receiver well away from my ear. Two tin cans connected by a string would probably have done as well as our smart phones in transmitting her speech from New York to Virginia. I told her with only a touch of insincerity that I was looking forward to her dinner party.

"Good," Alice said, "because you're the guest of honor."

I laughed.

"Don't laugh. A guy who works in my law firm is dying to meet you."

"Why? Is somebody suing me?"

"He worked in Shanghai, too, at about the same time you did. He's heard a lot about you."

"That sounds ominous."

"Maybe it is," Alice said. "Ole says he's got something to tell you."

"Ole?" I said.

"That's his name, Ole Olsen."

"What does he want to tell me?"

"He didn't say," Alice said. "I think it's a secret."

"Why do you think that?"

"His manner suggests it. Got to run. See you at dinner."

I said, "Wait."

"Can't." Tomorrow, in court, she had an expert witness to dismantle and she needed her sleep. The next sound I heard was the dial tone.

I had other things to think about than somebody named Ole Olsen. He was out of mind almost as soon as Alice hung up on me. For the rest of the week I was glued to the computer, checking out every possible reference in Chen Jianyu's file. Nearly every detail of the material he gave me was confirmed, including the decapitated cat. How Lin Ming had obtained such intimate, detailed information on his early life I could not imagine. The files did not assign a pseudonym to the source or sources. That could mean that we had an investment in this juvenile delinquent, that he was someone we valued and wanted to protect even from ourselves. It could mean nothing or anything. Reading the rows and rows of tiny Mandarin characters under the jumpy light of the fluorescent ceiling fixtures irritated my eyes. I was lying behind my desk on the floor, putting drops into them, when Burbank opened the door between our offices, looked in, and said to himself, "Where the hell is he?" Before I could decide whether to sit up and answer the question, he retreated and slammed the door. I got to my feet and knocked. Burbank replied by buzzing me. Feeling like Pavlov's dog, as Burbank probably intended, I opened the door and walked through it.

"Where did you come from?" Burbank said.

I pointed over my shoulder with a thumb.

"You weren't there ten seconds ago."

I said, "Well, here I am now."

Burbank pointed at the visitor's chair. "Tell me something new," he said.

I sat down and said, "On the whole, it checks out."

"What parts don't check out?"

"Practically none," I said. "In fact we already have almost all of the information Lin Ming gave us in our own files."

Burbank blinked. This was like watching a statue scratch its nose. The expression on his face, which is to say the lack of expression on his face, did not change. But his eyes did, ever so slightly. Or maybe I imagined this.

Burbank said, "We do? What, for example?"

I told him, in brief.

"So what don't we have?"

"The identity of the source or sources of this information. No indication that it was ever sent over to the analysts or shared internally in any way."

"What does that suggest to you?"

I said, "What it suggests, Luther, is that something funny is going on."

"Define 'something funny,'" Burbank said.

"I just did."

Burbank took a deep breath. He shifted to sarcastic mode. "You're the designated thinker on this one," he said. "You've read the files. You run the asset who gave you this document. You've found something suspicious. For the fun of it, let's say that you've come to some sort of conclusion, or to the starting point for a conclusion—let's call it a hunch. I haven't read the files. I can't read Mandarin well enough to decipher them. Therefore I must rely on you to brief me. I *am* relying on you. I'm cleared to know everything. So tell me about your hunch. Please."

I said, "I think the answer is obvious. This file is phony. It doesn't suggest the man I know. Lin Ming is trying to sell us junk from our own files and at the same time trying to write a death sentence for Chen

Jianyu. Either somebody inside our Headquarters furnished Lin Ming with this information, which may very well be fabricated, or the Chinese have hacked into our files."

"What do you mean, 'fabricated?'"

"Fed by a Guoanbu agent to a credulous case officer, or just hacked into our files by some computer virtuoso in Beijing."

"Are you serious?"

"You asked me to describe my hunch," I said. "That's what I've done."

Burbank faded away into his secret garden of thought. The meditation lasted quite a long while. Was this habit real or did he just hide out when he didn't know where to go next in the conversation? Had I told him something he already knew but did not want to hear? I told my inner paranoiac, who never listened, to back off.

Burbank's eyes came back into focus. He moved—lifted a hand, swiveled his head. He said, "What did you think of Chen Jianyu when you knew him in Shanghai?"

"I didn't know him all that well."

"Granted. But you knew him. It's possible you and he were sleeping with the same woman. What did you think of him?"

"I thought he was a run-of-the-mill B-list princeling," I said. "A little less ridiculous than some of the others. Smarter than most. He seemed actually to think, to have convictions."

Burbank said, "Nothing more?"

"About Chen Jianyu? What more is there?"

"You do know that bed wetting, playing with fire, and torturing animals in childhood are almost invariably the warning sign of a potential serial killer?"

"I think I read that somewhere," I said. "But as I understand it, not everyone who does those things grows up to be a serial killer."

Burbank looked at his watch. So did I. By now it must be dark outside. We had been talking for longer than I realized. Quitting time had come and gone. I listened to the building. Headquarters was hushed, emptied out, closed for the weekend.

Burbank said, "Why don't you come to my place for dinner around seven? The caretaker is there. She's a good cook—better than good. I'll give her a call, ask her to leave dinner in the oven, then disappear. Can you find the way?"

It was dark by the time I reached the hidden drive that ran through the woods to the converted barn. It was little more than a footpath. Tonight it was choked with rutted snow that was axle deep. About a hundred yards in, my headlights bounced off a black Range Rover coming from the opposite direction, headlights flashing, horn blasting. I put my car in reverse and stuck my head out the window. When I reached the paved road, I caught through tinted windows a blurry glimpse of the other driver, possibly a female, maybe the mysterious caretaker. The Range Rover, scattering gravel, roared onto the slippery macadam, tires spinning, vehicle fishtailing as it made a ninety-degree turn and sped away. The driver did not switch on the lights until the vehicle was far enough down the road that the license tags could not be read. Who was this idiot?

Burbank had told me to just walk in when I got to the house, so that's what I did. I found him standing in front of the dining room fireplace, in which a roaring fire burned, and drinking red wine from a large Burgundy glass. He had changed into a cardigan and slippers. He poured me a glass of the wine from a bottle on the table, which was set for two with nice china and silverware. Mother would have approved. An appetizer, unrecognizable from where I stood, had been placed at either end of the table. Candles burned.

"Sit ye down," said Burbank. "You're a bit early. Hence the heavy traffic in the driveway." He shook his head, laughed as if something amusing—endearing—had occurred.

The dinner was excellent. It ended with key lime pie with billows of whipped cream on top. Burbank cut the pie in fourths. He watched my face intently as I took my first bite. He asked me how I liked it. I said it was terrific. He grinned. "Best in the world. The caretaker may not be the new Rembrandt or much of a driver, but in the kitchen she's matchless. Matchless." He gave himself another piece of pie.

Throughout the meal Burbank did all the talking but said not a word about business. He was so animated I wondered if he had taken a pill. He talked about himself. When as a young officer he had been posted to Paris, he and a fellow spy and a couple of *filles de joie,* always one natural blonde and one brunette, went on an annual gastronomic tour of France. Each August in a different region of France, they hit all the Michelin three-star restaurants, having made reservations two years in advance. Like the regions, the girls changed every year, and after the first week he and his buddy swapped partners. They ate *croques monsieur* and drank beer for lunch at cafés and gorged on haute cuisine at night. The men had a budget—so much for the *chatte,* so much for the girls' suitable new clothes, so much for dinners. To pay for all this, each man deposited a certain monthly amount into a joint account in the embassy's credit union. "Like your grandmother's Christmas club, but hush-hush," Burbank said. They stayed at modest hotels so they could afford better wines. Burbank fairly glowed as he rattled on, menu by menu, *poule* by *poule.* This Proustian tour of old happy moments was touching in its way. Burbank was a good storyteller, which was not surprising considering his eye for detail. He actually made me laugh, the last thing I had expected ever to happen while in his company.

Finally, when it was quite late, we moved into the living room and got down to business. Burbank seemed reluctant to do so. I expected a long inquisitorial session, but he was not eager to start. He stretched, yawned, sipped the last of the wine.

"So tell me," he said. "Where does this thing go next?"

He expected me to do the talking yet again? My spirits sank. At this point I would have been glad to be given instructions. I had hoped for instructions. I was tired of doing all the thinking, making all the meetings, taking all the responsibility, setting myself up for all the blame if things fell apart.

I said, "You tell me."

Burbank said, "Sorry, I can't do that. This is your baby. It's up to you to get the stroller across the street."

My instinct, almost irresistible, was to rise to my feet, thank Burbank and the absent caretaker for a lovely dinner and an enjoyable evening, quit my job, and walk out. Just go. Find another way of earning a living, start over again in some honest low-stress occupation like foreclosing mortgages on poor widows while writing poetry by night in an idyllic small town. Marry a sweet local girl without too many smarts, get laid every third night. Have kids. Shoot baskets with them in the backyard, sing in the choir, drink beer and eat pizza while watching football on TV with the idyllic village's other bachelors of arts. Every spy's daydream. But instead of acting on my impulse, I answered Burbank's question.

"Apart from more of the same," I said, "I haven't got a clue what's next."

"You asked that fellow in New York for six case histories," Burbank said. "He delivered the first one the next business day. You should be encouraged. Motivated."

Really?

"Are you not curious about the fact that Lin Ming acted so fast?" I said. "That he gave us information that was already in our files? Don't you want to know who gave it to *him*?"

"That's the entire purpose of this meeting. But do you think that what we already know will lead us to the culprit?"

"No. It will lead us around the mulberry bush."

"So get more information. Get the other five files from your guy. Plod. Dig. Make comparisons."

"And if I fail?"

"So far you've succeeded beyond any reasonable expectation," Burbank said. "Beyond my expectations, which I admit were and are anything but reasonable."

I said, "Suppose information is not enough?"

"Then do what you have to do."

"Meaning what?"

"Just do it."

"Are you telling me to use my own judgment?"

"Up to now that's worked out pretty well."

"Up to what limits do I use my own judgment?"

"Short of treason, premeditated homicide, or grand theft of government funds, there are no limits."

"I can go where I want, see whoever I want to see, do as I see fit?"

"You're as free as a bird," Burbank said. "You know the mission. Accomplish it."

He smiled like a fond father sending his boy off to school after stuffing him with good advice. He all but patted me on the head.

36

On Saturday evening I was the first to arrive at Alice's place. She opened the door and said, "You! Early! What next?" A firm dry handshake, a whiff of the same perfume I had smelled on the night we met in the bar of the club. The light in the hall was low. In her black dress against this dark background she looked like one of those half-smiling rich women in a Sargent portrait—dark, tall, aloof, hair dressed, face painted, beautifully gowned, and richly bejeweled, the favorite wife of the King of Qin. She gave me a drink and disappeared. I heard her talking to someone, another woman, in the kitchen.

I wasn't the only punctual one. Soon the other guests began to arrive, two by two. All the rest except one blonde wife were Chinese. Everyone was better dressed than me. My best Shanghai suit and a good shirt were shoddy in comparison to the Armani suits and designer dresses on display, not to mention the jewelry. Since abandoning my father's Rolex I wore a Timex.

No one went quite so far as to look me over and make a face. This was a well-mannered crowd. The conversation was in Mandarin. Everyone except the blonde seemed to assume that I knew the language. She took pity on me and spoke to me in English. Her name was Fiona Wang. She and her husband, a neurosurgeon at Mount Sinai, were just back from a medical conference in Hong Kong. Caitlin was an endocrinologist. The couple had met in medical school—Harvard, actually. She had chosen her specialty because it gave her time to be a mother, and her beeper rarely went off during the night. Wesley, on the other hand, was forever leaping out of bed to repair some motorcyclist's damaged brain. The Wangs had a girl and a boy aged five and seven. Did I have children?

Before I could answer her question the last couple arrived. Alice brought them directly to me and introduced them in Mandarin—Ole and Martha Olsen. The husband's unwavering eyes were blue. This created an odd Siamese cat effect in what was otherwise a standard Han face. Clearly his Norse father had passed along very particular genes. Ole Olsen seemed uptight, condescending. He looked me over and didn't like what he saw.

In Mandarin Olsen said, "Are you the person of the same name who used to work for Chen Qi?"

How did he know that? I hadn't mentioned it to Alice. "I was one of many who worked for CEO Chen, yes," I said. "Do you know him?"

"Does anyone?" Ole asked. "I spent some time in the tower just after you left, but in the bowels of the ship, not upstairs like you."

"Doing what?"

"Legal matters."

I barely registered his words. My mind was absent, pondering how he knew about me and what he knew and why he wanted to tell me what he knew. Now that I had met Olsen I was uneasy. My time with Chen Qi was no secret, but it was infected by other secrets.

Olsen said, "What did you do for CEO Chen?"

"I often wondered," I said. "Do you work with Alice, Mr. Olsen?"

"Ole, please," he said. "Alice and I are at the same law firm. She's a litigator, I'm a backroom type. I handle the boring stuff. I heard quite a lot about you in Shanghai. When I arrived your name was on everybody's lips."

"Why was that?"

"Topic One at the watercooler was that you had been sleeping with Chen's niece or maybe his daughter and he'd rescued her from disgrace or worse by hiring you and fixing you up with a different woman to channel your animal instincts."

"No kidding."

"Some were surprised he hadn't drowned you in the Yangtze," Olsen said. "Apparently that was more his style."

As he spoke these words, he watched my face closely. I tried to look amused. I said, "Obviously the conversation was more interesting downstairs than upstairs."

"It could get pretty interesting."

I said, "What was this daughter's or niece's name?"

"You tell me."

There was no lightness in Olsen's tone. He wasn't bantering. On the contrary, judging by the look of moral distaste on his face, he looked as if he was annoyed with me for religious reasons.

I started to turn away. Olsen took hold of my arm. "The story was that when the maiden came to her senses and was out of danger he sent you to the States and then fired you," he said. "The substitute comfort woman, Zhang Jia—is that name correct?—was given a bonus, a promotion, and a suitable husband. Also a transfer. The rumor was that she was a professional, hired for this one particular job."

He was enjoying this. I thought it was unlawyerlike. Maybe Martha, Olsen's wife thought so, too. She touched his hand, a little warning, but he paid her no attention.

Out of the corner of my eye I saw someone in an apron, a female, peek out the kitchen door. She wore a white Nehru-type chef's cap, her hair concealed beneath it. Her hand, which held a napkin—she was touching her nose with her thumb—concealed the lower portion of her face. I had seen that gesture before. Catching the signal, Alice announced that dinner was served.

To me Olsen said, "Anything you want to say to all that?"

Alice had been listening. She answered for me. "I think the answer to that question is no," she said. "But I have a question for you, Ole."

"Ask it."

"Are you drunk or is this your idea of small talk?"

"Small talk," Olsen said. "The white man's name for avoiding the truth. So the answer to that question is also no. This isn't small talk."

Apparently he had more to say. He pointed a forefinger at me and started to speak, but Martha took his hand, smiled brightly, bent Ole's finger back into place, and said, "Dinnertime, dear." She led him into the dining room.

Alice took my arm and walked me to the table, as if we were dining in a country house on *Masterpiece Theater*. She sat at one end of the table, a gleaming expanse of inlay and veneer, and I sat at the other end, as far away from either Olsen as she could put me. The woman on my right immediately began talking about a new Broadway play. Apart from the conversation there was nothing Chinese about the dinner, but it was very good indeed. A waiter in a tuxedo served, assisted by a short plump woman who also wore a tuxedo. He was Chinese. Although he wasn't the same man, he reminded me of the waiter who had balanced that enormous tray on the night that Lin Ming and I dined together in the safe room upstairs from the Sichuan Delight. Everybody in the world, except maybe Ole Olsen, looked a little like someone else. The figure in the apron, the one who had materialized in the kitchen door, found her way back into my mind. I knew her, but how? With the help of my imagination, this mental image became a little more detailed than the one I had actually seen. Now I put my finger on a clue. She had touched her nose with her thumb. In that small way she resembled Magdalena, who when Mother was alive used the same gesture to signal when dinner was ready. Maybe it was something all chefs did. Chewing sliced duck breast as these thoughts passed through my mind, I wondered if I would die before morning with the lingering taste of this food on my tongue. The woman next to me—I hadn't caught her name—was telling me more about the Broadway play. It was called *The Death of Gershwin*. Gershwin was an unhappy woman, not the composer, and death was what she called her marriage to a banker because it had taken the music out of her life.

As the evening wore on the conversation got livelier, more gossipy. Alice made sure I talked to everyone except Ole Olsen. This was the first time since I left Shanghai I had been in a roomful of people who were all speaking Mandarin. I felt contentment, as if I had escaped back into some idyllic parallel existence, as if talk was making sense for a change.

Around ten-thirty, as everyone said their good-byes in the front hall, Olsen smoldered. Martha Olsen held tightly to his arm. I thought he might have something more to say to me—after all, he had never told me whatever it was he wanted to tell me, so I walked over and said good night to Martha.

When I held out a hand to Olsen himself, he ignored it and said, "I'd like a word alone with you before I go."

He walked back into the empty living room, and placing himself where he could see the door and the people milling about and kissing one another in the hall, he put a hand on my shoulder. He seemed to be a little drunk. His eyes blinked, his speech was slurred, he was having trouble with his balance.

He said, "Sorry the conversation went wrong a little while ago, but this is awkward for me. There's something I feel I need to tell you."

"Why? You don't even know me."

"I know Alice. I think I know what you really are and that bothers me. . . ." He lost his balance. I grabbed him. Over his shoulder I saw Martha hurrying toward us. ". . . but I have to break a professional confidence to tell you the facts. That's hard for me to do."

"Then maybe you shouldn't tell me. Maybe you should take it to the FBI."

"You think I haven't thought of that? You think they'd listen?" He wobbled, took hold of my forearm to steady himself. He said, "You think I'm drunk. I'm not. I don't know what the fuck is wrong with me, but listen to me, I'm trying to give you a chance to—what? I can't think of the fucking word."

I said, "I hear what you're saying to me, Ole, but maybe you should sleep on this. We could get together another time for a drink or something."

"No, Listen to me. The Yangtze was nothing compared to what's coming. These people are going to destroy you. You've got to get away."

Olsen's wife took him by elbow. "Time to go, Ole," she said in loud English.

"Not yet," Olsen said. "There's more."

"That's enough, Ole," Martha said.

Olsen really looked sick—addled, as if he didn't know where he was or who this woman was. Martha dragged him out of the room, Ole loose as a rag doll, Martha saying not a word to me. I followed them into the hall. All the others had left, though voices could be heard in the corridor outside the apartment door. Martha, keeping her grip on Ole, placing herself between him and me, thanked Alice for a lovely evening. Alice patted her on the cheek, then air-kissed both Olsens good night and walked them the five steps to the door.

Alice and I went straight to bed. We were too well mannered to talk about Ole Olsen. I told myself he was drunk, that he had been playing a sick prank. But he knew something, and even if what he knew was a useless crumb of gossip, I'd run him down tomorrow and get it out of him while he was still hungover and vulnerable.

At four in the morning Alice's phone rang. She felt for her reading glasses (I could hear her doing this in the dark), found them, picked up the phone, read the caller ID, grunted, and answered it.

"Martha," she said. "*What?*"

She switched on the lamp, and wearing nothing but her reading glasses, leaped out of bed. She fired the questions into the phone, then said, "I'm on my way to you."

I knew what she was going to tell me before she uttered the words.

"Ole Olsen died an hour ago," she said. "He collapsed on the way home in the car. The Wangs were with them. They worked on him on the way to the hospital, but he's gone. An aneurysm, they think, but they're not sure."

As she spoke she pulled clothes out of a closet—underwear, jeans, a sweater, shoes, her Burberry. She was dressed and on her way out before I could get out of bed. "Be sure the door is locked when you leave," she said, and left. A moment later she was back. "What was Ole trying to tell you?" she said.

"I don't know," I said. "He didn't finish."

All I could think about was that female chef, standing in the kitchen door, touching her nose with her thumb.

37

Standing in the mouth of an alley off the Bowery, Lin Ming coughed twice, then once again. Half a dozen derelicts lay on the pavement behind him, sleeping or drunk or both—or maybe the tenor and his acrobats or their equivalent. I asked Lin Ming why he had given the all-clear signal despite the presence of all these unknown people strewn on the pavement. "They're just bums," Lin Ming said. "Relax. Capitalism's victims are everywhere." We walked away and found an empty doorway. Lin Ming stepped into it, hiding himself, as the asset is supposed to do. I stood outside and kept a sharp lookout, as the case officer is trained to do.

Lin Ming immediately switched roles. "I assume you have something for me," he said. He spoke in tones of authority, as if I were working for him.

"What would that be?" I said.

"The name you promised. My friends are anxious to talk to the person in question."

"Our arrangement was based on the expectation of a swap of things of equal value," I said. "You gave us nothing that was remotely equal in value."

For a long moment Lin Ming was silent. His face was masked by the darkness, not that I had ever been able to read it anyway.

He said, "I am puzzled. Confused."

"I don't see why you should be. What you gave us was boilerplate. We might as well have Googled it." I was not at liberty to tell Lin Ming that we knew that his information had been cribbed from our own files. *Never tell the asset what he should not know even if he already knows it.*

Lin Ming said, "There seems to be a misunderstanding. You are acting like the case officer and treating me like an agent. You did this the last time, but I thought it was my imagination. I wasn't feeling well that day."

"So?"

"So why do you have this delusion?"

"In what way is it a delusion?"

"We made an agreement," Lin Ming said. "In this city, on a certain day in a certain park."

Which was recorded by a chess-playing cameraman and soundman. I assumed that Lin Ming was recording this conversation, too. Therefore he was choosing his words carefully. So was I, because I, too, was making a record for the file. In fact there was no particular reason to be careful. There was a good chance that the chip on which our conversation was being recorded would get lost in Guoanbu's archives. Even the Chinese did not have enough manpower to sort out, in time to do anyone any good, the tens of thousands of aimless conversations in a Babel of languages—any nuggets well buried—between their horde of case officers and their multitude of informants. As for my own recordings, only Burbank knew about them, and even he did not know about all of them. They didn't exist as far as the rest of Headquarters was concerned. I kept them in a safe place in case I ever needed them.

Breaking the silence, Lin Ming said, "You do remember that day in the park, and other days and nights as well, do you not?"

"Vividly," I said. "But I remember nothing about agreeing to become the property of whoever or whatever you work for."

"Then you should reremember. Think carefully. Go carefully."

"What I remember, Lin Ming, is that we agreed on an exchange of information."

"That was later," Lin Ming said. "On the day in question, and on other days, we talked of you as someone who would work for world peace and friendship between our two countries from inside Headquarters, who would receive certain benefits in return for certain information. You even spoke enthusiastically of the importance of winning the confidence of your targets inside your Headquarters. How could all that slip your mind?"

"It seems you have misinterpreted my words, whatever you think they were."

"And so you renounce our agreement?"

"There is no agreement to renounce. The deal was, you'd give me something that is equal in worth to what I was, and still am, prepared to give you."

"Why? So you can win and keep the confidence of the reactionary gangsters you work for?"

We weren't going to be polite? Fine. I said, "You sound like a Maoist, my friend. That's out of style. You should be careful."

"And you should be careful who you betray."

His voice quivered with anger. The usual question arose: was this real or was he just playing a part? More likely the latter, not impossibly the former. After all, his backside was on the line. He remained deep in the doorway, wrapped in shadow. I still could not see his face or for that matter his body. I would not have been able to detect a sudden move. I was surprised by a little involuntary shiver. I was exposed. If Lin Ming was truly angry, if he was convinced that I was of no further use to him, if he was the murderous type, he could easily spray cyanide into my face or shoot me dead with a silenced pistol or even stab me in the heart. Or cough and bring another team of acrobats on the run. I told myself to cool it. Lin Ming wasn't the murderous type, at least not on foreign soil.

"Betray," I said. "That's a strong word."

"In this case, not too strong," said Lin. "Believe me when I say that. You're playing with fire."

I had never before heard anyone speak that cliché aloud, and certainly not in the language we were speaking. I laughed. While I was still chuckling, Lin Ming said something I did not catch. Between one breath and the next, his voice had regained most of its normal agreeable timbre. What had just gone on between us was out of character for this typecast smoothie. He *was* playing a role. He was always playing a role, of course. That was his job: shake the foreign devil up.

"All I ask," Lin Ming said, "is that you acknowledge reality."

I said, "Same here. I'll tell you what. Forget the nonsense about my being your creature or ever becoming your creature. I don't give a rat's ass"—this, too, was a nice translation problem—"how you describe your relationship to me."

"I have just described it, exactly as it is," Lin Ming said.

"If you think that," I said, "you need therapy. If you keep your end of the bargain, we'll keep ours. If not, we'll use the information we have, the information you want and must have, in our own way."

Lin Ming stepped out into what little light there was on this backstreet of a great city that was too broke to turn on all of its streetlamps.

He said, "Is that your last word?"

"Yes."

Lin Ming smiled. He had remarkably straight teeth for a Chinese who had been a poor kid during the Cultural Revolution. He put a hand on my sleeve.

"If that's the way you want it, fine," he said. "But a word of advice. Have your horoscope updated."

He turned away and walked into the murk in his usual half-stagger, half-quickstep style, as if carrying a load on a pole with the help of the ghost of an ancestor at the other end of it. Despite what had just passed between us, it was difficult not to like him, difficult to take him seriously as a tough customer who would not hesitate to do whatever was necessary to get the job done, even though I knew that was exactly what he was. He made his exit, heading downtown. When he was a block or so away he stopped, turned his back to the light wind that was tumbling papers west to east, and lit a cigarette. I could see his face quite plainly in the flare of his lighter. He was looking at me, too—eyes lifted, hands steady. The flame went out. He faded into the darkness.

Less than a minute afterward I heard men walking in step with me. There were maybe half a dozen of them, marching in quick time, as if stepping off to fast music. When they were right behind me, almost touching me, they stopped moving forward and marched in place for a couple of moments, soles slapping, leather boot heels punching the concrete. Then they split into four groups, two men close behind me, one at each elbow, two close in front, just as the tenor and his acrobats had done in Shanghai. They wore matching black sweats, black caps, black shoes. The two in the lead carried baseball bats at shoulder arms. All were Han. They marched on for a full block with me wedged in among them, then they halted in front of a store window and marched in place again. Two of them broke formation, and batting righty and lefty and on command from the leader, swung at the display window.

The plate glass rang, quivered and turned into huge shards that hung for an instant as if held in place by some giant thumb and finger, then fell like blades. The gang broke formation and scattered, shouting. Had all this meant anything? Were they a Chinatown gang, rented by Min Ling for an hour, or just a bunch of wild and crazy guys out on a lark? They had done me no harm, so what did it matter? Nevertheless—someone could be watching—it seemed important to act as if nothing had happened. I walked on as coolly as I could, though with nothing like the nonchalance with which Harold Lloyd might have played the scene before the introduction of sound.

38

So far it hadn't been a very pleasant weekend, apart from the abbreviated night with Alice. If what Olsen said to me about the connection between Mei and Chen Qi was true, if she was Chen's niece or his daughter, then we were not dealing with Guoanbu at all. We were in ancient China. Whatever was about to happen to me was personal revenge. Chen Qi's plan was to destroy me in the most humiliating way possible. I knew this. To murder me after torturing me was not enough. He wanted me alive and in his power, so that he could remove my bones from my flesh one at a time. That was the message Ole Olsen had delivered.

In the swaying, trash-strewn, all-but-empty club car of the train to Washington I remembered my way back to the beginning—not just the weekend but the complete phantasmagoria right back to the day Mei crashed her bike into mine—and tried to convince myself I was imagining things. When the train pulled into Union Station and squealed to a shuddering stop, I woke from my reverie as if from a long sleep. Had I in fact been asleep all the while without knowing it? As my brain began to function normally again I feared that by waking up when I did, I had just missed discovering something important. When I picked up my car from the parking garage it was 5:30 A.M., the city was still dark and so hushed that I could hear the Civic's tires humming on the pavement. Would Alice be awake in Manhattan? Probably. I knew she rose early to get her child ready for school, do her exercises, eat her organic granola, rehearse the questions she was going to ask in court that day. My car had a hands-free telephone that worked through the sound system. I pushed the button and spoke Alice's number in the voice of an anchorman, or as close as I could come to it. The device understood me for once and placed the call. Alice picked up on the last ring before the answering machine kicked in.

"What?" she said.

"It's me."

"I know. Why is it you?"

I really didn't know. There was nothing more to be said about Ole Olsen. I had my own theory about his death, but Alice was the last person with whom I wanted to share it—or next to last, counting Burbank. I said, "What are you doing?"

"Shivering," Alice said. "I'm all wet from the shower."

"I'm calling on an impulse," I said. "In my imagination you are now drying off."

Alice said, "Phone sex before dawn? Have you been a pervert all along, or did you just think this was a good moment to let me in on your secret?"

I said, "I am now going to change the subject."

"Good. You've got thirty seconds to grow up before I hang up."

I said, "I have a question about the woman in your kitchen the other night."

"You do?" Alice said. "What, is the chef an old flame?"

249

"I just glimpsed her but she looked familiar. Have you used her before?"

"No. She was part of the caterer's package. Very efficient, not a talker. She did what she came to do and left."

"What did she look like?"

"Skinny but shapely. Thirtysomething. Big ears with her hair tucked under her hat. Maybe five six, not a lot more than a hundred pounds. Light blue eyes. Very capable. Intelligent face, not a beauty but not plain. With makeup, the right hairdresser and the right clothes she'd be quite sexy."

"Voice?"

"Slightly hoarse. Why are you asking all these questions?"

I said, "Name?"

"Name, name, name," Alice said. "Started with a consonant, three or four syllables long. I can't remember more than that. Anyway it was probably an alias. Those people do that, you know, in case a customer doesn't like them and warns all her friends not to hire her."

"Who was the caterer?"

"Stella's Moveable Feast. There's a Web page. Did you sleep with this woman in the past or what?"

"Good luck in court today," I said.

"Same to you if your day ever comes."

Suddenly I knew what came next. I pulled over to the curb and booked a flight to China.

39

It was almost as hot and sticky in Shanghai as in Washington, which is to say that Kinshasa could not compete. The immigration and customs inspectors at the airport paid no particular attention to me. My papers were in order—one more entry and exit remained on my visa. They didn't even ask if I was still a student before stamping my passport. Demonstrative suspicion had long since gone out of style here. If Guoanbu was interested in you it preferred that you remain as relaxed as possible. Long before you landed it would just arrange for you to be put into a bugged hotel room with watchers in the lobby buzzing around you like gnats. I stayed in a cheap hotel in a bad neighborhood because I was paying for this trip out of my own pocket and because the staff here might be a bit less used to keeping tabs on people who interested the security services. I was not difficult to follow, being white and four or five inches taller than almost everyone else, and as usual not really caring whether or not I was followed.

After a long afternoon nap and a lukewarm shower I got dressed and went into the street. My objective was to find Chen Jianyu. Finding him was possible, I thought, despite the vigilant father and the teeming crowds that screened him from me. However, I was by no means confident I would succeed. I had only two weeks to do what I had to do in a culture that had a very long history of confounding its enemies by wasting their time. However, the situation was not hopeless. *"If you wait by the river long enough, the bodies of your enemies will float by,"* says Laozi. I had no idea where Chen Jianyu lived and no way of finding out. I would never get through the door if I did find out. But I knew he worked in the tower, where punctuality was an ironclad law. Therefore he would have to get to work on time in the morning and leave at quitting time in the afternoon. I also knew his hangouts and the hours he was likely to be there. I knew the hours he was likely to be at one or another of them—his cohort of princelings might live in what it thought was anarchy, but for all its make-believe their gang ran on a tight schedule. If I visited all the hangouts for fourteen nights I had a reasonable chance of finding him. Interception was my whole plan, catching him on the fly. After that, everything depended on his turning out to be what I hoped he was, and what his social life suggested he was—a secret American. The world was full of them.

It was about three miles to the tower. No taxis cruised in this part of town. If I walked the whole distance I would be very sweaty by the time I got there. I needed change for a bus so I bought a fried egg embedded in a pancake from a vendor, who held up four fingers for bus No. 4 when I asked him which one went east. I should have known better than to take a bus. I did know better. Passengers, with more getting aboard at every stop, were packed in like, well, sardines. The temperature was well above body temperature. I had an advantage because my head stuck up above the crowd and I had a little more air to breathe than anyone else. Within seconds, however, I was drenched in sweat, my own and that of many strangers. I kept my right hand on my wallet and my left fist balled so that slipping off my WalMart wristwatch would be more difficult. The

Chinese eat a lot of cabbage. Gas escaped from the intestines of many passengers and mingled with untold amounts of recycled bad breath. By the time I got off, a block from the tower, no bloodhound could have detected my original scent beneath the rank odors my clothes and skin had absorbed from the many bodies that had been crushed against mine for the last half hour.

The building, magnificent and vulgar, stood not far from the harbor. A weak breeze from the sea wafted over the crowd, and I cooled off somewhat while I waited for Chen Jianyu to make an appearance. It was rush hour and I was a rock in a flowing stream of humanity, so it was difficult to stand still. Every third person, it seemed, tried to push me out of the way, but I had a weight advantage on most of them, so I was able to hold my ground. After about twenty minutes I spotted Chen Jianyu inside a midnight blue 7 Series BMW sedan that emerged from the tower's underground garage. The crowd ignored it. Chen Jianyu did not bother to blow the horn or flash the lights. Instead, he inched into the throng. Mostly people got out of his way when nudged by the car's bumper, but most refused to yield the right-of-way. The car pulsed with rock music playing at very high volume. I pushed my own way to the passenger-side front window. Inside the BMW, Chen Jianyu was smoking a cigarette and seemingly talking to himself as he chatted on the hands-free telephone. I rapped on the window. He paid no attention. Probably he could not hear me over the music, but even if he could, he probably knew no one who traveled on foot, so he just wasn't curious. I tried the door handle. He saw who I was and unlocked the door. I got in. A woman's voice came over the speakers. I overheard just a syllable or two before Chen Jianyu disconnected.

He looked me up and down, betraying no surprise. He turned down the music and said in English, "Nice aftershave."

"Can I hitch a ride?"

"Where to?"

"Where are you headed?"

"Quite a long way as soon as I run over all these people."

Now he blew the horn, he flashed the headlights. Pedestrians shouted, banged on the hood and the roof. Chen Jianyu paid no attention. He sounded, he looked, he dressed—in designer suit and necktie—as if showing up for a photo op.

I said, "Can I ride along?"

"Suit yourself," he said. "I can't promise you a ride back. Where are you staying?"

"You wouldn't know the hotel."

"Ah, traveling incognito." He turned up the sound system—the Foo Fighters' greatest hits. "Let's observe silence while I'm driving," he said, putting a finger on his lips.

It took us two hours on a six-lane superhighway that looked like a mock-up of the Interstate—same signage, same tollbooths, same everything—to drive to Suzhou, a city about sixty miles from Shanghai. Not a word passed between us the entire way. We parked by a large lake. By now the sun, hanging behind the city's perpetual scrim of pollution, was a red blister in the west.

Once we were out of the car, Chen Jianyu spoke, this time in Mandarin. "Have you been here before?" he said.

"No. This is Suzhou?"

"'Heaven on earth,' they call it because of its gardens," Chen Jianyu said. "Birthplace of the Wu culture. The Yangtze flows through the city. But you know all that."

"There are a lot of things I don't know," I said.

"A common complaint," he said, switching back to English. "What specifically do you want to know that you don't now know?"

I told him, straight out. All of a sudden he was no longer a lounge lizard. He listened to my questions with what seemed to be keen interest, as if he were learning something interesting—which of course he was.

When I had finished—I didn't have all that many questions and they were all short and to the point—he said, switching back to English, "The answer to all your questions except one is, 'Be patient.'"

"What about the one you can answer?"

"Okay," he said. "Yes, I was approached by some spook who thought he spoke Shanghainese when I was at Purdue. One of my professors set up the meeting. I told the spook to get lost. I'm not crazy, even if hanging out with you would suggest otherwise."

"What about the others that professor approached?"

"How would I know? But they're not crazy, either."

He looked at the sun, which was sinking rapidly, lighting a path across the lake. It would be dark in a matter of minutes. Chen Jianyu said, "Let's go for a walk."

We strolled along the lake—Taihu Lake, the signs said—and into a park. Thousands of others were taking the evening air, half of them watching the sunset with oohs and ahs and the other half taking pictures of it with their cell phones. One slim woman stood apart with her back to the spectacle and watched us approach. The light was behind her, so it took a moment before I made out her face.

Mei.

40

The sunset had everyone else's attention, so had that been my impulse I could have swept the love of my life into my arms and kissed her hungrily. It was not my impulse. This had nothing to do with confused emotions. I knew exactly what I felt—astonishment and relief that Mei was alive and free, rage but no surprise that Chen Qi had lied to me about her fate, certainty that Mei had never loved me, resentment that I had never been more to her than a target and possibly, if she hadn't been faking it, a sexual toy. The facts that I had not loved her until I lost her, that I would have deserted her and never looked back if so ordered by Headquarters, that I had used her with a cold heart as a cheap teacher and a convenient lay, that I was worse than she was, didn't count. I stood where I was, five steps away from her, rooted to the ground, unsmiling, seething, staring. It was, in short, a very human moment. What right did she have to ambush me like this? What right, what motive did Chen Jianyu, who had her to himself now, have to taunt me in this way? Mei, up to her old tricks, locked eyes with me. I looked away, searching for Chen Jianyu. He was nowhere to be seen.

With a jerk of her head, Mei beckoned me closer. I took four steps in her direction but remained out of reach. She did not stir. "You've got a problem," she said, "or are you just surprised to see me?"

I had not heard her speak English since I forbade her to do so on the day we met. She still had the Boston accent. In Mandarin I said, "You're looking like yourself."

This was the truth. She hadn't aged a day or gained or lost an ounce, her hair was done in the same way as before and was just as lustrous, she had the same belle of Shanghai face and manner. True, some of the mischief had gone out of her eyes, or so it seemed to me in the failing light. She wore trousers, loose white ones, so I had to reimagine her legs. What my brain produced was the image of Mei sprawled in Zhongshan Road, her miniskirt awry, her sweet bottom in its good-girl underwear, her honey-colored thighs and calves. My mind and body responded now as they had responded then.

"Speak English," she said. "If we talk in Mandarin we'll attract even more attention."

The sun dropped below the horizon. Show over, everyone turned around. About half the crowd spotted me at once. You could read their questions in their faces. They were all the same. What was this foreigner, this *laowai,* doing here all alone and not in a tamed group of other foreigners as a *laowai* was supposed to be? Why was that pretty Chinese girl talking to him? What was the matter with her? The light was fleeing. They squinted in unison. It got darker, then it got dark. Weak lamps switched on along the paths.

"Walk with me," Mei said. "I have things for you to hear."

Walking away from the already curious, we awakened curiosity in almost everyone else we encountered. Someone would certainly go for a policeman. Within minutes, Mei would have questions to answer in addition to the ones I meant to ask her.

I said, "Let's start with this. How come Chen Jianyu brought me to you?"

"Out of the goodness of his heart," Mei said. "He phoned me from the car as soon as he saw you knocking on the window."

"Why?"

"Maybe he thought that the hope of finding me was why you were in Shanghai. He asked if I wanted to see you. I said yes."

"So he wanted to help. That seems like a strange motive in his case."

"Why?"

"Isn't he the lover you left me for?"

She laughed explosively, arms hanging helplessly, as if the joke had stolen their strength. She stopped walking. So did I. People behind us bumped into us and into one another.

She said, "My lover? Is that what you think?"

"You two were lovey-dovey enough."

"He's my brother, you nitwit."

The crowd was flowing around us now, rubbernecking, asking one another what ghost-people language this ill-matched couple was speaking, why they were together.

I said, "Chen Qi is your father?"

"Jianyu's, too. Different mothers."

"So you're half siblings?"

"We never made the distinction," Mei said. "There were just the two of us, we thought, but who can be sure? Chen Jianyu is two years older than I am. His mother was the official wife. My mother was somebody my father kidnapped. We all lived together in the same house, wives as best friends, sisters in misery, like in the Xia dynasty."

"What do you mean, 'kidnapped?'"

"Kidnapped. He saw, he lusted, he confiscated. It was the Cultural Revolution. To make things easier, her father and mother were sent to a commune in Yunnan for reeducation. My father was the Red Guard leader who made the arrest, the one who put a dunce cap on my grandfather's head. In his mind he saved my mother from sharing her father's humiliation. She was fifteen."

"Wasn't that against the rules?"

"'Rules?' The whole idea of the Cultural Revolution was that there were no rules."

"Just days ago someone told me you were Chen Qi's niece," I said. "Chen Qi himself said you two were related—distantly, he implied."

"He said that to you?" Mei said. "For him that's the same thing as a full confession."

"Why would he tell me, of all people?"

"He has his reasons. He always does. But he never speaks the whole truth. Ask my mother. He told her that her parents would be well treated on the commune and she would be reunited with them when their reeducation was complete. They both died of hunger and exhaustion. She never saw them again, never had a letter."

"You sound like you hate your father," I said.

"That's why this is your lucky night," Mei said, "so listen to me."

I did as she asked. Her English was far better than I had imagined. She sounded like she had been born and brought up in Concord, Massachusetts. After a moment I stopped being impressed by her fluency, started listening, and realized she was telling me things I desperately wanted to know. As if reading from a checklist, she informed me of matters I realized might save my life—and might very well cost her hers, no matter who her father was, or more likely, because he was who and what he was.

I didn't like listening to these revelations in the presence of ten thousand eavesdroppers.

"Old Chinese proverb," Mei said when I complained. "There's safety in numbers. We're lost in the crowd instead of being in plain sight."

But how did we know that one or more of the myriad who were using their cell phone cameras were not taking our pictures in support of their local police? How did we know that the little old lady sitting on a bench, wrinkled and hunched and so short that her feet didn't touch the ground, wasn't a Guoanbu informer? I spoke these thoughts aloud.

"You should remember to take your medication," Mei said. "Listen, in the right circumstances, everybody in China is an informer, a spy, a danger to everyone else. In the U.S.A., too, except in that country they usually sell their story to the *National Enquirer* instead of going to the secret police. It's the same everywhere—the Eskimos, the Khoikhoi of the Kalahari Desert. Remember the Russians, the East Germans. Everyone informed on everyone else—husbands, wives, lovers, best friends, Party comrades. Especially Party comrades or fellow Christians. Or lovers. It's in our DNA. Get over it."

Her upturned face was deadly serious, an expression new to me. God, but she was a beauty. She must look like her mother. She certainly didn't resemble Chen Qi. Mei resumed talking—more softly, so it was difficult to hear her voice above the babble. I mimed turning up the volume. She shook her head. I slouched, so as to put my ear closer to her mouth. Still, I had to listen so hard that I could think of nothing else. No doubt that was the idea.

"About a month before I went away I missed a period," Mei said. "This didn't seem possible because I had always taken two kinds of precautions. Like an idiot I hoped for the best instead of doing something right away. Then I missed another period."

I started to speak. Mei stopped me. "Don't ask," she said. "You were the only suspect. That was the problem. I saw a doctor, someone I didn't know and who didn't know me, and had the thing done. But I had to show identification."

Chen Qi found out about the abortion in a matter of days.

"He already knew about you," Mei said. "Why he didn't kidnap me but just let us happen, I don't know. He knew what and who you were. He knew that the baby was an abomination, half me, half *laowai*. The worst of it was, now others knew, too—people high in the Party, people who could do him harm, who were already doing him harm by making a joke of his name. These people were being overheard by the lowest people in their offices. Whisperers everywhere. He knew this. He had lost face—lost it as if a chimpanzee had attacked him and chewed it off."

Apt choice of words.

For a weekend, Mei was left in peace. Then Chen Qi's assistant called. Mei's father wished her to join him for dinner that night. A car would come for her at six-thirty. Dinner would be at seven-thirty, the regulation Shanghai time. The car arrived precisely on time. Chen Qi was in the backseat.

"He was in a rage," Mei said. "He trembled like someone who was totally out of control. His face was bright red, he shouted, spit flew out of his mouth. His eyes were distended, the whites were reddened, as if his anger had ruptured the blood vessels. He was like a crazy talking animal in a cartoon. He told the driver to get out of the car and turn his back to it. As soon as the front door slammed, my father grabbed me—this was the first time he had touched me since I was small—and slapped me, first one cheek then the other very hard, as if he was trying to knock the baby out of me. Probably he would have succeeded if the child had still been inside my body. He's a strong man. My head snapped this way and that. I thought my neck was going to break. I thought he was going to kill me, then drive to the Yangtze Bridge with my corpse beside him on the leather seat and personally throw it into the river."

However, Chen Qi did Mei no more violence. He did what he did next in total silence. He rapped on the car window. The driver got back in, put the car in gear, and without being given an order, drove to Suzhou. When Chen Qi and Mei arrived at the house where she now lived, her mother was there to greet her. She bowed to Chen Qi like a woman whose feet were bound. Three other women and two men, Mei's "chaperones," stood in a row behind her mother. Without a word, Chen

Qi departed. Mei had not seen him since, nor did she expect ever to see him again.

"Suzhou is a place where nothing happens," Mei said. "I know no one in the whole city except my mother and the watchers who live with us. Two of them are always awake. My father has marooned me. My mother, too. We might as well be in Tibet. Mother is happy. I'm back, I'm a big child now, a Barbie with a heartbeat. We live in a nice house, we have good food and several television sets, but no books and no work to do. We play mahjong. We sew. We talk about my childhood. I can never leave. Unless you rape me in front of all these witnesses I will never again have a sex life that involves another person. I am out of sight, out of memory."

"You can come with me," I said.

Mei snorted. "Where to? I have no passport, I have no visa. People watch me."

"We can marry. The consulate can do it. Then you'd have an American passport."

"Ha," said Mei. "I wouldn't be an American for very long."

"Why not?"

"Because I'd be a widow instead of just losing a friend. Face the facts. You've made an enemy who can do what he likes with you, in China or anywhere else in the world. You will never lose him, you will never overcome him, you can't prevent him from doing whatever he plans to do to you. Whatever that turns out to be, death would be a better fate."

"Better than what, specifically?" I said.

"My brother will explain," Mei said. "He's waiting where he left you. Can you find the right gate?"

"I think so," I said. "You won't reconsider?"

Mei didn't answer the question. "I'm out of time," she said. "I have to get on my bike."

Without another word or gesture, she walked away.

I shouted, "Wait."

She stopped but did not turn around. The crowd flowed around her in the watery light like a school of fish eddying around coral.

I said, "Before you go I'd like to know your name. The real one."

She looked over her shoulder.

"Mei," she said.

One breath later she was absorbed by the crowd.

41

The park was emptying. It was almost eleven o'clock when Chen Jianyu's BMW arrived. It stopped some distance away, beyond the edge of the crowd, and I wriggled my way to it. Apparently the rule of silence inside the car was still in force, because Chen Jianyu said nothing to me when I got in and buckled my seat belt. I couldn't have heard him anyway over the deafening music. In the light from the instrument panel I studied his profile. He did resemble Mei—hairline, eyebrows, chin, and when, feeling my gaze, he turned his head and looked at me, his eyes might have been Mei's, large for a Han, smart, bright, lit by mockery.

We headed out of town. After an hour or so, Chen Jianyu exited the highway and threaded his way among the inevitable rows and rows of high-rise apartment buildings. He turned into a gas station. He parked, got out of the car, and walked briskly toward the men's room. As we emptied our bladders into adjoining urinals, Chen Jianyu broke his silence. "Do you have anything at your hotel that you can't afford to leave there?" he asked.

We were still speaking English. "No, not really," I said.

"Then I think you should go directly to the airport," Jianyu said. "There's a flight to Los Angeles in three hours."

I said, "My ticket is nonrefundable."

"So is your life. Go."

My *life*? As if Jianyu had just uttered a perfectly ordinary remark, I said, "I'd never get aboard on such short notice."

"They have one business class seat available, but you have to call them before midnight and pay for it."

I didn't ask how he knew this. People like him knew such things in his country. I looked at my watch—eleven forty-two. I said, "Business class? How much?"

"Five thousand U.S. and change."

"You've got to be kidding."

Chen Jianyu said, "You've got a credit card, haven't you? Call the airline and pay for the ticket now and get on the plane. Get out of China. Tonight."

He was serious. Yet I knew that what happened to me was a matter of indifference to him. He was urging me to leave, scaring me into leaving, in order to protect Mei—or so I was supposed to believe. And did believe. Still at the urinal, I called the airline, paid for the seat, memorized the confirmation number.

I said, "Chen Jianyu, let me ask you this. You've never liked me. Why the sudden concern for my welfare?"

To my surprise, Jianyu answered the question. "Mei asked me to save your skin," Chen Jianyu said. "What other reason could I have?"

"What about your father?"

"What about him?" Chen Jianyu said.

"You think he's going to whack me, send me to a labor camp, what?"

"Not yet," Chen Jianyu said. "But he could be afraid someone else might get to you before he does and deprive him of the pleasure."

"This someone else being who?"

"Use your imagination. And like you said, you're not the most popular *laowai* who ever came to Shanghai."

"So why are you telling me all this?"

"I just told you why. For my sister."

"You're telling me you're saving me because she has feelings for me?"

"She didn't say that, but I think she at least feels responsible for you."

"Why?"

"Wake up. She slept with you for two years and more. She hates her father and he hates you. He's a vengeful person. You humiliated him— or rather, Mei humiliated him with your help, which is a lot worse. So he wants to humiliate you right back. Tear the wings off the fly."

"How, exactly?"

"I have no idea. CEO Chen doesn't share his plans with me. But this much I do know—whatever he decides to do won't be proportional to your offense. Daddy doesn't do proportional." Jianyu looked at his watch. "If we're going, we should go now."

We rode the rest of the way without speaking. The car pulled up in front of the Hongqiao railway station. We got out. Jianyu said, on the sidewalk, "You know how to take the subway to the airport?"

"Yes. All this is very good of you. You have my thanks even if it's all for Mei."

"Some of it, not much, is personal," Jianyu said. "I owe you something for introducing you to my father when he invited you to dinner. I knew he was out to get you. It was a dirty trick."

"No problem," I said.

"'No problem?'" Jianyu looked at me in mild bewilderment. Was I really that stupid?

"Okay," I said. "If you still feel you owe me something, tell me more."

"What exactly? Why should I tell you anything?"

"I can't think of a single reason," I said.

Chen Jianyu hesitated, bit his lower lip. We moved farther away from the car, sidling out of range of the bugs he thought his father had planted in it. I wasn't the only paranoiac in the world.

Finally he said, "What do you know about the Dreyfus affair?"

"The bare details," I said. "What everyone knows."

"You should study his case, take it to heart. Look for parallels."

I must have looked skeptical, though I was merely puzzled.

Chen Jianyu said, "I'm serious. Listen to me." He beckoned me closer and whispered a name in my ear. He stepped away, and still whispering, said, "That man is my father's friend. They're old friends, close friends, like-minded friends who have worked together for years. This American has sinned. He thinks the FBI is on his scent. He fears exposure, ruin. He is what Esterhazy, the real spy, the actual traitor, was to Dreyfus, the fall guy. You're Dreyfus. The *laowai*."

Of course I was. I saw the connections as if a strip of film had just developed in my brain. I wasn't crazy after all.

I said, "Thank you."

"Good luck," Chen Jianyu said. "You're going to need it."

42

When I got back to my town house I checked my balance in the bank I had used when I worked for Chen Qi. In the day and a half I was in China, $250,000 had been deposited to my account. The source of the money was listed as something called Hanyu Consultants Group, otherwise known as Chen Qi. Counting the Chinese money that was already in my account, I now had more than half a million dollars on deposit and I could not account for a penny of it. That meant I could easily afford the five-thousand-dollar business-class ticket I just used. It also meant that I was a dead duck. American banks are required by law to report any single deposit larger than ten thousand dollars to the United States Treasury. Therefore bells were ringing at the IRS, and because Headquarters had a unit embedded in that agency, bells would soon be ringing at Headquarters. And most thought provoking of all, very loud bells would peal at the FBI, which also posted a squad of special agents to the Department of the Treasury.

There is a kind of bullet, jacketed with soft copper, that expands to the size of an eggplant when fired into the entrails. Receiving this windfall was something like being shot with such a bullet. I panicked. The power of this threat overwhelmed thought, reason, breath—everything. My enemy might be a Shanghai tycoon, but thanks to him I was now in the grip of my own country's system, from which few have ever escaped once caught. I knew my life was over even though my heart might keep on beating for the next fifty years. I went into the bathroom, just making it to the toilet bowl, and fell to my knees.

By the time I rinsed my toothbrush I was on the point of falling asleep. You may think this was a strange reaction to the prospect of life in solitary confinement or worse, but with Chen Jianyu as my astrologer I had had my horoscope updated as Lin Ming had recommended and flown twenty hours without sleep. My bones ached, my head throbbed, my throat was sore. My hands trembled. These were blessings in their way because they distracted me from the feeling that an enormous white-hot bullet was pressing against my heart. I took three aspirin and fell into bed. I went to sleep immediately. If I dreamed, as I must have, I didn't remember the details when I woke up ten hours later, wondering what was the matter with me.

I needed someone to talk to. There were no obvious candidates. I didn't have the habit of confession. I had never shared the secrets of my soul with anyone, had never since the onset of puberty asked for advice or another opinion. Would I be able to do so now, when that might well mean throwing away my last and only chance ever to go outdoors again? And if I did suddenly develop the knack for spilling my guts, to whom would I spill them? Everyone I knew by name in the United States or in China was tainted. I was on speaking terms with no one who was clean, no one who could be trusted absolutely to listen to my suspicions—my profound convictions—and keep them secret. Priests had been eliminated. A psychiatrist? No doubt a shrink would find it interesting that I believed I had no friend in the world, but he or she would regard every word I uttered as a code word for the clinical, the real, the hidden truth. I had no one to turn to.

Or did I? I picked up the phone and dialed Alice Song's cell phone. If anyone on the planet might be sane enough to realize that I wasn't as crazy as I seemed, it was Alice. Chances were that she was clean. That glimpse of Magdalena (by now I was sure it was Magdalena) in her kitchen notwithstanding, there was no reason to suspect her of playing a double game. No one could use Alice, of that I was certain. Our first meeting in the club bar was clearly pure coincidence. What else could it be? She could not possibly have known that I was there. I had never been there before. She had taken me as I was, she had put up with what she took to be my atrocious manners. She had gone to bed with me. When I remembered her—anything about her brain, body, that voice—I entered into a state of delight. She may have regarded me as a curiosity—who wouldn't?—but she had taken me as I was. She had never tried to reprogram me. Besides that she was a brilliant lawyer, a formidable courtroom operative, and everything you told her, if you were paying for her services, was stamped top secret the instant it fell from your lips. Just like me, she was under oath to keep her mouth shut no matter what. How much that would be worth in the long run was another question.

Alice's voice mail picked up. "Please don't leave a message," her voice said. "Call me back."

An hour later I tried Alice's number again and was told once more not to leave a message. Finally I realized there was no point in calling her again. Sooner or later she would see my number when she checked for missed calls and get back to me. Or not.

With time to squander, I went for a drive, no destination in mind. I needed a new line of thought. I didn't need to think any more about Albert Dreyfus. I understood the parallel. I knew the reason for my problem, and thanks to Chen Jianyu, I even knew who my Esterhazy was and who his case officer was, and in rough outline, I knew the fate Chen Qi had in mind for me. But how to act on these apprehensions? My situation was like Fermat's Conjecture—a theorem universally regarded by mathematicians as provable even though its solution eluded them for 358 years. Even if my own conjecture was solved in half that time, assuming that anyone but me was interested in its solution, I would still have ample time to serve the life sentence that was staring me in the face. Who would believe my proof even if I published it? Going to the FBI might make me feel better, it might hatch a conspiracy theory that political loonies could ponder for decades if not centuries, but it would not save me. Or cause justice to be done.

In real time I was alone on a long dark road, no headlights in the mirror. Suddenly I knew where I was going and why. Alice could wait.

Around one in the morning I parked on the shoulder of the road half a mile away from Luther Burbank's barn and sneaked closer to it through swampy woods. As I went, I assumed I was being picked up by motion detectors, even by cameras, but I put my hopes in the possibility that Burbank was meditating and therefore temporarily blind and deaf. After ten minutes or so I came to the last line of trees and the house came into sight. Burbank's Hyundai and the black Range Rover that had chased me out of the driveway on my last visit were parked side by side on the gravel. Inside the house, the lights were on, though dimmed. Through the windows I could see fragments of the awful paintings. Also two human figures moving in a rhythmic way. I heard, just barely, the sound of music and realized that these people were dancing. I couldn't make out their faces, so I moved closer. The man was unmistakably Burbank. He wore tuxedo trousers with a scarlet cummerbund and a white silk shirt. The woman, who was as slim as Burbank, was a brunette. She wore a knee-length skirt of shiny material that ballooned and swung prettily when they turned. Her dark shoulder-length hair, cut straight across, swung in synchrony with the skirt. Her face was hidden in the hollow of Burbank's neck. They were excellent dancers, almost professional—erect as a couple of honor guards, brisk in their movements, attuned to each other. I wondered if Burbank and this woman entered weekend ballroom competitions under assumed names or dreamed of making it on *Dancing with the Stars*. Obviously they had studied and practiced together. Had Burbank been a little younger—it wasn't possible to guess the woman's age because I still couldn't see her face—they could have been an adagio act on a cruise ship. The music changed. They tangoed—thrusting machismo and sultry femininity, legs entwining. The light by which Burbank and his partner were dancing was only slightly brighter than candlelight. Even though the two of them were farther apart now, I still could not make out the lady's face.

It was a typical Virginia summer night, temperature and humidity both in the nineties. Fireflies blinked. Mosquitoes bit. I crushed them when I could reach them instead of slapping them because I feared to make a noise. My mind wandered and when it came back into focus, the lights were off in the house. I heard the front door open. Burbank emerged. He still wore his white shirt, so I could make him out in the darkness. A second, smaller white blur moved beside him. I heard a sound I couldn't quite identify, but then, as Burbank's movement triggered the floodlights, I realized that what I had heard was the inquisitive whine of a dog that smells something it does not recognize. The smaller white blur—not so very small on closer examination—was a pit bull. Where had it come from? No dog had ever before been part of this picture. The pit bull barked—a long string of baritone woofs. It growled deep in its throat, then barked again, louder.

Burbank could see me as plainly as I saw him. He said, "You. Stand up with your hands above your head or I'll turn the dog loose."

At this moment Burbank's dance partner came outside, also still wearing her dancing costume. She carried the gun-nut machine pistol Burbank had put under my pillow on my first visit to this house.

She handed the weapon to Burbank, who handed her the dog's leash in return and pointed the weapon at me. I stood up and put my hands above my head.

"Approach," Burbank said. "Slowly."

I was, say, a hundred feet away. Though I have good eyesight I couldn't quite make out Burbank's face. The floodlights had switched on and were so dazzlingly bright that they hindered vision. After I had taken maybe twenty steps, Burbank and the woman came into focus. At the same moment so did I, apparently, because the woman told the pit bull to lie down, and it obeyed her instantly. I looked at the woman. For a fraction of a second I saw her as if she were captured in a freeze frame. Then she turned her back, whirling as if executing a tango step, and rushed into the house, taking the pit bull with her.

Quick as she was, different as she looked in her dancing clothes and her new hair color, I made her. I knew who she was. There was no mistake. By this time I was beyond surprise, but wasn't it odd, wasn't it intriguing, wasn't it extraordinary, the way I kept on catching glimpses of Magdalena in the strangest places?

43

Burbank led me through the dark house to a tiny study. An antiqued print of *Old Ironsides* under full sail, ensign blowing the wrong way, hung on one wall. A print of the Godolphin Arabian, a foundation sire of the Thoroughbred breed, was displayed on the opposite wall.

"Sit ye down," Burbank said. "I'll be right back." A moment later I heard the pit bull's toenails clicking on the bare floor, then heard the front door open and close and the Range Rover's throaty engine start up and the car drive away. Soon after that Burbank reappeared, now wearing pajamas and carrying two bottles of artisanal beer. He handed one bottle to me and took a long pull from the other.

"Thirsty work, doing the tango," he said. "I thought you were on R and R."

"I am, but I need to talk to you," I said.

"Is that why you're here at this ungodly hour? It's after two."

I said, "This won't take long."

"Then spill it," he said. "Some of us have to get up in the morning."

"I was out of town for a while," I said, "and when I got back yesterday I checked my bank balance." I paused.

"And?" Burbank said.

"And I discovered that something called the Hanyu Consultants Group had deposited two hundred and fifty thousand dollars in my checking account."

Now I had his attention, but he was still Mr. Cool. He sipped his beer, wiped his lips with the back of his hand, and said, "In return for what?"

"Your guess is as good as mine."

"What's the Hanyu Consultants Group?"

It would have been untruthful for me to say that I had no idea, so again I shrugged. I said, "Never heard of them."

"Never consulted for them?"

"No."

"Then why are they dropping a quarter of a million dollars into your checking account?"

"I don't have a clue. I thought you might be able to help me figure it out."

"Why me?"

Burbank was looking at me as if I might be carrying a concealed weapon.

I said, "Because you're my superior officer, my only friend at Headquarters, and I don't know who else to report this to. Because I think the deposit may be an attempt to ruin me."

"'Ruin' you?'" He whistled softly. "How? Why? Who?"

Head cocked, he was smiling in a worried sort of way. Had I lost it altogether?

I went on. "I think the FBI or the IRS or both will investigate as soon as they get word of this. So will CI as a matter of reflex. I think the results of such an investigation could be unfortunate for me and embarrassing for Headquarters and for you as the man I work for."

"Why unfortunate for you if you're innocent of wrongdoing? Have you considered just reporting this to the FBI?"

He actually said this—bluffed on the first card dealt. Now his smile was soothing, his tone of voice infinitely reasonable, as though he might be humoring a wife who was working herself up to accuse him of adultery.

I said, "No. I'm reporting it to you."

"Why not go straight to the Bureau, if you think there's something fishy about it?"

"Because Headquarters wouldn't like that. Because whatever illusions may exist about American justice, nobody is ever considered innocent by the Bureau after being taken into custody. Because very few people arrested by the FBI have ever been proved innocent. Because nobody accused of the kind of crime this payment suggests I committed has ever had a friend in the world."

"Whoa," Burbank said. "Hold on, there. Have you considered the possibility that the deposit is a mistake? Banks make them all the time. What bank are we talking about?"

I told him. He asked how much I had in my account. I told him that. If he thought that half a million dollars was an unusual amount for a GS-13 making $89,023.00 a year before payroll taxes and deductions to have in a checking account, he did not say so. I was certain that he already knew everything I had just told him. Even so, a sign of surprise, however tiny, would have been a seemly gesture. Burbank made no such sign.

He said, "I see your problem. I think you may be giving it a little more weight than it can bear."

"I'm paranoid? Wow, that's a load off my mind."

Burbank was displeased by the sarcasm and he amended his performance to let this show. His reaction—a frown, a sad shake of the head—resembled spontaneity, a quality I had not previously observed in him. I felt I was making progress. He was human after all. It was possible to get to him. I thought I had the key to opening him up, I thought I was in luck. I thought that my latest glimpse of Magdalena was the key. So far tonight nearly everything that had happened was unexpected. I had come here with the intention of penetrating Burbank's shell if I had to waterboard him to do it, but with no plan in mind. I was winging it. I had no idea what I was doing or what might happen next. This was no great change from the life I had been living for months—years, even— and maybe, I thought, the whole dog's breakfast of this operation, the whole inside-out life into which I had stumbled, was a training exercise for the new Afghanistan in which I was now waking up, wondering where I was.

All during this train of thought, Burbank stared over my shoulder, as if there were someone behind me (Magdalena, syringe in hand?) who was going to tell him in sign language what to do about this psychopath who had somehow gotten into the house. He looked a little wan. He looked, yes, unsure of his next move or mine.

I said, "I've been thinking about the obvious."

Burbank swiveled his gaze and looked into my eyes. He was looking wary but trying to conceal it.

"So far you haven't sounded that way," he said. "But tell me more."

I said, "I know it has occurred to you that the ideal way to penetrate an intelligence service is through its counterintelligence division."

"And why would that be?"

I said, "CI is above suspicion by definition because suspicion is its turf. It has the need to know everything about everyone, but no one else has the need or the right to know anything about it."

"That's true in a twisted sort of way," Burbank said. "As you know, we've had some experience with being penetrated. We learned from the experience. It can never happen again."

"You believe that?"

"I *know* that."

"How do you know it?"

"Because the last fellow was a clown doing a clown's work and we now know how to take clowns seriously."

"Then one of the clowns is still inside the little trick car in the center ring, because I think it *has* happened again."

"Meaning what?"

"Meaning that I have reason to believe that Guoanbu has an agent within Headquarters, within CI."

"Do you now?" Burbank said.

He smiled a dead-eyed smile. He looked at the clock on his desk. He yawned. He turned the clock around so I could see it. Too many gestures, too much disinterest.

I said, "Will you listen?"

"All right," he said. "Tell me more. Five minutes, my friend."

He pronounced *five* as *fahv,* in an LBJ drawl.

Scientists have established the existence of a parasite called *Toxoplasma gondii* that is transmitted from the feces of cats to human beings, rats, and other mammals. *T. gondii* invades the brain and rewires it, rerouting the connections among neurons. It impels rats to run toward the cat that is hunting them instead of fleeing as instinct would command. In humans, the parasite causes its host to behave in wildly reckless ways, leading to such self-destructive actions as reckless adultery, deliberately crashing cars, or shoplifting. It is suspected of triggering schizophrenia. I had never gone anywhere near a cat turd if I could avoid it, but in Burbank's study I had a *T. gondii* moment. Something leaped in my brain from one neuron to another, and in the nanosecond this took I was transformed into a nutcase who didn't know the meaning of the word *consequences.* Had I been standing on a balcony thirty floors above the ground I probably would have leaped onto its parapet and gone for a walk.

I said, "This will take a little more than five minutes."

Burbank glared at me—*how dared I contradict him?*—and pushed back his chair with a squeal. He started to get to his feet.

I said, "Sit down."

Burbank, who probably hadn't been given a direct order in twenty years, looked startled. I was bigger than he was and years younger and my forearm was larger than his calf, and possibly I had a look on my face that gave him pause. In any case he sat down. Maybe he had a panic button under the desk that would bring a goon squad into his study in a matter of minutes, or some kind of concealed weapon that would fire an instantaneous knockout dart designed for tigers and suicide bombers into my body. I didn't care. I just wanted this whole masquerade to end—now and not a minute later. Enough was enough. Burbank sat down.

"Let's go back to the beginning," I said. I was a little surprised at how steady my voice was, how reasonable my tone. Burbank, apprehensive but cold-eyed, playing the man of stone, waited for me to go on.

"The original assignment," I said, "was to identify half a dozen Guoanbu agents who were giving us trouble and then find a way to denounce them to Beijing as American spies, yes?"

No response from Burbank. Maybe he wasn't listening—probably he wasn't listening. He didn't really have to listen because every word I spoke was almost surely being recorded. I was fine with that. I wanted this encounter to be on record. I was recording it myself with the spyware cell phone in the pocket of my shorts.

"However," I said, "what we wound up with was six B-list princelings who have never done America harm and probably never will. You seemed to be satisfied with that result. Why?"

Again no response. I lifted Burbank's desk a couple of feet off the floor and dropped it. The keepsakes on its surface flew off in all directions.

Outwardly at least, Burbank remained calm. Unperturbed. As if nothing unusual had happened to his desk he said, "Because you struck out."

"So why didn't you fire me?"

"Compassion. Patience. I thought that was not quite the best you were capable of doing and that we might as well see where it led us."

"But you thought I had failed."

"Everyone falters from time to time," Burbank said. "In this business, a lot of things don't work out. As I've told you over and over, it can take years to put an operation together. Your spoiled brats might not be dangerous now, but who knows what they might grow up to be? As often as not an operation never really comes together. It almost never turns out exactly the way we thought or hoped. But I supposed you'd learn from this experience and do better next time. After all, the operation was still alive. There might be a breakthrough, a game changer if you kept at it, believing you had a chance of coming through. I thought you should be given time and space to make something happen. I believed you could do that. That's why I gave you a free hand and the chance to be creative. Even now I think you can amount to something in this business. I really do."

So Burbank had had nothing but avuncular intentions toward me all along, and still had them even after I had revealed the real me to him in the last ten minutes. To give him his due, benevolent uncle had always been the part he played best. He was just staying in character.

I didn't ponder the alternatives. After an interval of heavy silence I said, "Are you familiar with the Dreyfus affair?"

Burbank's eyes widened, an unfeigned reaction at last. In a flat voice he said, "The what?"

I said, "The Dreyfus affair."

"I read Zola when I was a kid."

I said, "What's your recollection of the details of the case?"

"What does that have to do with the price of anything?"

"Indulge me."

He shrugged. If I insisted on being humored, he'd humor me. He summarized the Dreyfus case. Naturally he aced the details—the false (Burbank used the word *mistaken*) accusation that Alfred Dreyfus, a Jew from Alsace, therefore the perfect patsy, had passed military secrets to the German embassy in Paris. He knew all about Dreyfus's court-martial on a charge of treason, about his five years in solitary confinement on Devil's Island, about the attempts of the French army command to quash new evidence that showed him to be innocent, about the final vindication. He knew about Esterhazy.

"So now that you know I know all that, what do you think you know?" Burbank said.

I said, "I know that I'm Dreyfus. That you're Esterhazy."

I'd like to report that Burbank reeled in guilt and surprise. But his face betrayed nothing, his voice did not change, no muscle moved.

He said, "You're serious?"

"Absolutely. That's what this masquerade is all about. You're a spy for China. If the allegation is ever made, you've got a fall guy. He gets to wear the handcuffs, he goes to jail or the guillotine, you go right on doing what you do."

Burbank's smile broadened with every sentence I uttered. He said, "Ingenious. I was right about you. You really do have the knack."

"Thank you."

"However, you poor bastard, you're demented. Anyone can see that."

He got to his feet. "As of this moment you're on indefinite administrative leave," he said. "You are relieved of all duties. Your clearance is suspended. Your access to Headquarters is terminated, your ID is canceled. However, your salary will continue and your medical insurance will still be good. The Headquarters shrinks will be in touch with you first thing in the morning with the names of outside psychiatrists who are cleared to handle cases like yours. Unless you've got an imaginary Chinese submarine waiting for you offshore, it would be futile to attempt to leave the country. Now I'm going to bed. Get out of my house. Go home."

I said, "I'll leave, but I won't go away."

"I wouldn't be too sure about that," Burbank said.

He walked me out. Not a pinpoint of light fell through the windows. He opened the door for me and stood back to give me room, as if I were a guest departing after a good dinner and an interesting conversation. For a moment I thought he was going to shake hands with me, but that did not happen.

44

Alice Song listened intently while I told her all this. I had booked a private dining room at the club, so we were alone and Alice's elocution was not the factor it might have been in a crowded dining room. Like Burbank the night before, she was absolutely still. Nothing moved—not her eyelids, not her hands, not the muscles in her face. Her body did not shift in her chair. After a while the waiter arrived, looked at our untouched plates, and asked if everything was all right.

"Everything's lovely," Alice said. "Could you clear the table, please?"

As soon as the waiter was out of the room, Alice said, "Is that all of it?"

"So far."

"And the crux of the matter is that this mysterious character called Chen Qi wants to destroy you because you knocked up his daughter, and that this same Chen Qi is a Chinese spymaster who is spying on U.S. intelligence through the eyes of the man who is the chief of U.S. counterintelligence?"

"Yes."

Alice, still frozen in place, said, "Then I guess it's time to ask why are you telling me all this."

"Because I think I'm going to need legal advice."

"I think so too, unless this is some kind of joke."

Well, that was exactly what it was in its own way, but I didn't think I could explain that to a stranger to the craft, so I just said, "My hope is that you will agree to represent me. If you believe me."

"If I represent you it won't matter whether or not I believe you," Alice said. "And on the basis of what I've learned about spooks in the last hour, I have no reason not to believe you. Everything you've told me is so crazy that it doesn't even matter if it's the truth. But there are problems. For one, the case doesn't exactly fall within my area of expertise."

"I don't care about that."

"What do you care about?"

"Your smarts. Your courtroom manner. Your knowledge of me."

"But I just found out I don't know anything about you."

"No, you just found out that there was something about me you didn't know. Big difference."

"There's another issue," Alice said.

"Is there some kind of ethical question because we've slept together?"

"No. But I'm emotionally involved," Alice said.

I was thrilled by her words. Even though I knew I would probably never sleep with her again, I said, "You are? That's wonderful."

"Isn't it, though? In your interests I should recuse myself. I can find you an excellent lawyer."

"Thank you, no. No Ole Olsens. It's you or no one."

"If it's no one, you'll end up as dog food. A competent lawyer can at least raise enough doubt to keep you alive."

"That's the optimum outcome?"

"You be the judge," Alice said. "Do you have any proof that this creature you call Burbank is the traitor you say he is? Documents, tape recordings, witnesses, anything at all?"

"No witnesses. Tape recordings of everything except Chen Jianyu whispering Luther Burbank's name in my ear."

"So that includes what?"

"Every meeting with Burbank, every meeting with Lin Ming, with Chen Qi, with Mei and Chen Jianyu three days ago, everyone involved in the operation."

"Where is this material?"

"In the mail, addressed to you."

"Tape recordings are iffy things."

"Maybe to judges, but they're catnip to the FBI."

"Meaning what?"

"If the Bureau investigates me, they'll have to investigate Burbank," I said. "Even if I go down, he goes down with me. He can't be allowed to go on selling the country out to Guoanbu."

"That's the plan, stopping him?"

"More like a forlorn hope," I said. "But it might work."

"And if it does, everything will be right with the world?"

"Maybe not quite everything. But I'll settle for what we can get, as long as we get Burbank."

"The simplest thing for these enemies of yours to do is to kill you," Alice said. "People get murdered for no apparent reason all the time."

"Headquarters doesn't do that kind of thing."

"Tell that to al Qaeda," Alice said. "What about Burbank or Chen Qi or Guoanbu?"

"My sudden death is not enough for Chen Qi. He wants me to die by inches. "

Alice drew a deep breath, then another, as if oxygen was an antidote to exasperation. "Even if the plan works, the government will pursue the charges against you," she said. "You will have caused them too much trouble for them to do otherwise. Given the evidence you've laid out tonight, you'd need twelve twisted minds on the jury to get acquitted. In fact the jurors will be normal people to whom the activities you take for granted will sound like a day in Satan's workshop. In the end the jurors will think one of two things—either you're the vile traitor the prosecution will say you are and you're trying to save yourself by destroying your innocent boss, or you're insane. In any case, you'll be locked up. Forever."

I already knew that. I told Alice I just wanted to get the facts, deformed as they might be, on the record. In the short run, Headquarters might protect Burbank and sacrifice me to cover its own fanny. But the possibility that I was right about him would not go away. It would flit from mind to mind, inside Headquarters and inside the news media, and sooner or later, the hornets' nest would wake up. Burbank would be kicked out of Headquarters. Even if he didn't go to jail, even if Chen Qi didn't have him assassinated to make sure of his silence, he would do no more harm to his country. That was an outcome I could accept.

"You really mean that?" Alice asked.

"Yes. If I don't have a chance of beating the charges, and I know I don't, then I'll settle for getting the bastard in the end."

Alice thought it over, her eyes boring into mine. Then she said, "Okay, I'll take the case, but much as I might wish to do so, the firm probably won't let me do it pro bono. Given the complexity, the essential hopelessness of your situation, you're looking at maybe a couple of million dollars. Can you cover that, leaving aside the Chinese money, which the government will seize?"

"I can come close," I said. I had the house in Connecticut, the apartment in the city, and the stocks and bonds and jewelry Mother had left me.

"Okay," Alice said. "You may even have something left over in case of a miracle. Give me a list of your assets and I'll draw up the papers posting them as collateral. Are you all right with that?"

I said, "Go ahead. I'm assuming everything I've told you tonight or will tell you in the future will be protected by lawyer-client confidentiality."

"Correct. That's why it's costing you so much money. Now let's talk some more."

She opened her purse and rummaged around in it. "Want an energy bar?" she asked, tossing one onto the table for me. I unwrapped it and ate it. Somehow Alice ate hers without spilling a single crumb.

The rest of the conversation was Q & A. She was an even tougher customer than I had thought. It was very reassuring to imagine Burbank, who had been immune to questions for such a long time, trying to stand up under cross-examination by this remorseless inquisitor. For me it was liberating to tell the truth, the whole truth, and nothing but the truth for the first time in years, to hide nothing, to remember lies and crack them open to get at the facts within, and to do this because it profited me and advanced the operation. It was a strange process, baring the soul. I had been told about defected spies weeping with relief, wetting their pants, clinging in gratitude to their interrogators as if to a priest after spilling everything they knew, so great was their relief to cleanse their consciences.

At eleven o'clock the club closed. No gong sounded, Alice just knew what time it was. As we walked down the stairs together, the last two people in the place except for the watchman, Alice said, "We're hungry, no?"

"Yes. Want to go to Subway?"

"Let's go to my place and order a pizza," Alice said.

A last sleepover. My heart sang.

At the bottom of the steps that led from the sidewalk to the door of the club, two persons in black baseball caps and matching warm-up jackets waited. One of them flashed ID and said, "FBI." He then spoke my name as a question. I said yes, that was me. The other agent, a female, also flourishing a badge, repeated my name and said, "You are under arrest on suspicion of espionage under the provisions of 18 U. S. Code, section 793." She then read me my Miranda rights. The other one shackled me, wrists and ankles.

Alice said, "I am this man's attorney. Where are you taking him?"

They told her.

"I'll follow," she said. To me she said, "You know what to do. Say nothing to these people, repeat nothing, apart from stating your name, which you have already done. There is no need to be polite or congenial. Do you understand?"

Before I could do so much as nod in agreement, I felt a hand on my head as Special Agents XX and XY put me into the backseat of a large black Ford that smelled of Lysol. The plan had worked, but far more quickly than I had imagined. Being taken into custody by America's equivalent of the secret police was like slipping into unconsciousness after being wounded in combat. Would I ever wake up again? To my utmost surprise I suddenly felt bottomless fear, worse than anything I had known in Afghanistan or in the dreams I had brought home with me from that godforsaken place.

45

Eventually I got over being terrified. Thanks to Alice Song's skills and a criminal justice system that was more interested in big fish than in small fry like me, I did better than Dreyfus. About a year after my arrest, only dimly aware of how Alice had managed to lead the government to the fundamental, undeniable truth that Luther Burbank was the real traitor and I was merely the babe in the woods, I pleaded guilty to a single felony charge. I was sentenced to three years' imprisonment. As ritual dictated, I expressed my heartfelt remorse for my crime though I wasn't sure what exactly I was being charged with. With credit for the time I had already spent in jail, I served two weeks less than two years in a minimum-security federal prison camp in Tennessee. The experience was something like ROTC summer camp except that the guards were less drunk with power than the instructor NCOs had been and I didn't get nearly as much exercise. Otherwise, all was familiar—barracks that smelled faintly of dirty socks and armpits, good guys and bad guys, dumb jokes, tight routine, unseasoned food, time oozing by. My Timex had been confiscated. I never looked at the clock in the recreation room, just listened for the announcements to tell me when to eat, when to sleep, when to be counted. Gradually I regressed to a Stone Age consciousness in which measurement scarcely existed, knowing only day and night, long and short, rain and shine, cold and warmth, hunger and food, sexual arousal and self-help. After a spell in the kitchen scrubbing pots and pans, I worked on the paint gang, an enjoyable job.

Meanwhile the case moved toward conclusion, inch by inch. Alice called me when there were new developments, but isolated as I was, it was hard to splice the pieces together. I felt that I was watching through the window of my cell as disconnected snatches of an eight-millimeter movie based on the true story of my life flickered on a distant screen. At last came the moment when the climactic scene played, the screen went to black, the music stopped, and a series of captions detailing the after-the-movie life of the characters appeared:

Burbank was indicted on eighty-six counts of espionage, but he was not tried on these charges because he declined to do the patriotic thing and plead guilty and the evidence against him was too sensitive and too damaging to U.S.-China relations to be revealed in open court.

He was also indicted for evasion of income taxes on the millions Chen Qi had banked for him in Singapore, and a trial was scheduled.

Burbank, who was under house arrest while awaiting trial, was found dead, seated at the dinner table in his home in rural Virginia with the crumbs of a piece of key lime pie, his favorite dessert, on the plate before him.

Two months later, a tourist for whom she had once catered a dinner in New York sighted Magdalena in Suzhou, People's Republic of China. She was never seen again by American eyes.

Nor was Mei.

The captions dissolve into a final scene. Alice Song meets me outside the gates of the prison camp on the day I am released after serving my sentence—or if you prefer, after completing my penance for inconveniencing my betters. She is wearing shorts and sneakers and a Chinese red T-shirt with 雙喜, the character for "double happiness," printed on it, her hair cut shorter than before but otherwise looking just the same. I am thinner, calmer—the result, maybe, of 716 days of staring fixedly like a Zen monk at a certain invisible stain on the wall. We drive away, Alice at the wheel. It is late morning on a sunny day in spring—songbirds in flight, crows cawing, blue skies, puffy white clouds, and after we reach the Interstate, flowering trees in the grassy median strip. Somehow all this awakens the memory of Burbank and Magdalena dancing in the dark. And I wonder if Burbank, who knew so many things that nobody really needed to know, ever realized until he took his last bite of key lime pie, who his caretaker, his Ginger Rogers, his matchless chef really was.

"So how was it?" Alice asks.

"Not so bad," I reply.

"Your thoughts?"

"Mostly I thought about the power of coincidence," I say. "The bomb not killing me in Afghanistan. Mei crashing into me on her bike. Her father being the psychopath he was."

"And still is, don't forget," said Alice.

I pretend not to hear her. I go on with my thought: "Chen Qi's connection to Burbank. Burbank's connection to my father. Bumping into Lin Ming on a dark street in Manhattan. Running into you the first time I walked into the club. I could go on. People may scoff, but if you think about it, the unforeseen is what makes the world go around."

Alice takes her eyes off the road and looks me up and down, as if she had known me up to now only in a photograph.

"Say again? What makes the world go around?" she says.

"Coincidence."

"Ah, the white man's word for fate," says Alice.

Contents

Introduction to

Washington DC

Washington DC is a monumental city on a grand scale, filled with lovely Neoclassical buildings arrayed along triumphal boulevards, war memorials honoring centuries of fallen soldiers, some of the finest museums in North America, and scads of high-powered politicians, lobbyists, and bureaucrats charting the course of the country, as well as the world. You would hardly expect anything less from the nation's capital.

But that doesn't mean the city is unapproachable. Indeed, much of what you see is free; getting around is quite easy, aided by an efficient public transit system; and you'll eat and drink well too. A wide range of cuisines is on display, from inexpensive Ethiopian and gourmet Italian, to Nouveau American and good old steaks and burgers, and the odd pocket of lively, bohemian nightlife can be found as well.

The sights that everyone comes to see are primarily lined up along either side of the National Mall, including the Washington Monument, the National Gallery of Art, and many of the museums of the country's greatest cultural collection, the Smithsonian Institution. Just off this central showpiece, the gleaming white symbols of America's three branches of

▼ Columns, Union Station

When to visit

The best times to visit Washington DC are **spring** and **autumn**, when the weather is at its most appealing – with moderate temperatures, partly sunny skies, mild precipitation, and in April, cherry trees in bloom. By contrast, DC's hot and humid **summer** days are made even less hospitable by the throngs of visitors packed cheek-to-jowl at the major attractions, while **winter**, though less crowded, is equally unpleasant, with ice-cold temperatures and plenty of snow and rain.

◄ Jefferson Memorial

government – the White House, US Capitol, and Supreme Court – dominate the landscape; for some, the spectacle of so much power in such a small space can prove quite daunting. Fortunately, though, a living, breathing city exists beyond the institutional core.

You'll have to leave that core anyway to find the best places to eat, drink, and sleep, but dipping into the eclectic array of neighborhoods provides other rewards. There's Dupont Circle, with its galleries, gay clubs and stately embassies; Georgetown and its nineteenth-century row houses and red-brick mansions; the Upper Northwest, home to the National Zoo and towering Washington National Cathedral; and the historic Old Town of Alexandria, Virginia. Even Downtown, which separates the federal center from the northerly

▼ Museum of the American Indian

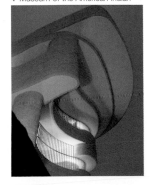

neighborhoods, is not the barren zone it once was, boasting some stylish restaurants and niche museums in what's now called the Penn Quarter. Across the city, DC's Latin American and African-American communities offer their own rich culture in contrast to the sanitized federal version, adding to the vibrant mix outside the compact tourist center.

▲ Rowers under Key Bridge, Potomac River

Washington DC
AT A GLANCE

▲ The National Mall

Federal Triangle

Where much of the day-to-day activity of the federal government takes place, in giant, Neoclassical structures that also house attractions like the National Archives and the Old Post Office – now a Romanesque Revival shopping arcade.

The National Mall

An elegant, two-mile-long strip of greenery that's home to famous war and presidential memorials, Smithsonian museums, and a Reflecting Pool that serves as America's axis of political protest.

Capitol Hill

The country's political nerve center, crowned by the dome of the US Capitol and thick with congressional offices, heroic statues, and key institutions like the Supreme Court and Library of Congress.

▲ Fountain, Dupont Circle

▲ Rotunda, US Capitol

Dupont Circle

Perhaps the most renowned of DC's many traffic-circle parks, in the middle of a hip, energetic enclave full of fashionable boutiques, frenetic clubs, and Victorian-era mansions.

Colorful Victorians, Georgetown

Adams-Morgan

Still off the beaten path for many tourists, a gentrifying neighborhood with a bohemian vibe, ethnic restaurants, and off-kilter shops offering everything from underground books to palm readings.

Georgetown

The oldest extant part of Washington, where you can tour DC's oldest house, gaze at early-American mansions, and take in some of the city's best dining and shopping.

Eternal Flame, Arlington Cemetery

18th Street, Adams-Morgan

Arlington

Just west across the Potomac, this Virginia city is best known for its famous military cemetery, which features endless rows of white crosses and the poignant grave of JFK.

Old Town Alexandria

A well-preserved slice of early Americana along the Virginia waterfront, Old Town features cobblestone streets lined with renovated manor houses, old-fashioned taverns, and other historic treasures and curiosities.

Ideas

The big six

Washington's major attractions are familiar from postcards and the TV news, but when you actually get to DC, what's most striking is not their size, architecture, or symbolism, but just how cozy they all are – tidily arranged around the National Mall in a lineup of the greatest hits of American democracy. It's a circuit that's sure to be at the top of every visitor's list.

▼ The White House

The president's Neoclassical mansion is a compelling sight and can be visited on a tour or viewed from nearby Lafayette Square.

P.87 ▸ THE WHITE HOUSE AND FOGGY BOTTOM

▼ US Capitol

The home to Congress is an unquestioned architectural treasure, crowned by a huge cast-iron dome that's kept by law as the highest building in town.

P.68 ▸ CAPITOL HILL

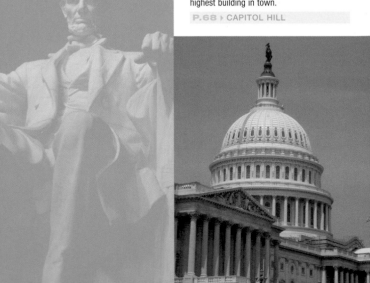

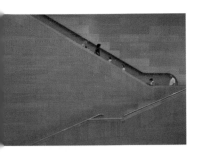

▼ Lincoln Memorial

At the best-loved and most dramatic of the city's presidential memorials, the white-marble statue of a solemn-looking Lincoln is surrounded by engraved renderings of his most famous speeches.

P.56 ▸ THE NATIONAL MALL

▲ National Gallery

Enormous in scope, the museum possesses one of America's premier collections of Western art, housed in two completely different buildings, with a quirky modern sculpture garden set in between.

P.60 ▸ THE NATIONAL MALL

▲ Vietnam Veterans Memorial

This dramatic, black-granite chevron carved into the earth and flanked by a sculpture of three young servicemen is arguably the most affecting war memorial to be found anywhere.

P.57 ▸ THE NATIONAL MALL

▼ National Air and Space Museum

The most popular sight in Washington, this museum is an essential stop for anyone interested in historic airplanes and spacecraft – from the Wright Flyer to Apollo 11.

P.63 ▸ THE NATIONAL MALL

Historical and cultural museums

It goes without saying that the historical and cultural museums in Washington DC are among America's most prominent and best-loved institutions. Whether you're interested in spy gizmos right out of a James Bond movie, artifacts from native cultures, or old-fashioned trains and buggies, there's likely a museum that has them on display.

▼ National Building Museum

The former Pension Building is now a prominent architectural museum that's most famous for its colossal atrium – easily one of DC's greatest spaces.

P.107 ▶ OLD DOWNTOWN AND FEDERAL TRIANGLE

▼ US Holocaust Memorial Museum

Disturbingly unforgettable, this site provides a harrowing look at Nazi Germany's crimes against humanity, unveiled through vivid, unflinching multimedia displays.

P.79 ▶ SOUTH OF THE MALL

▲ National Museum of American History

Featuring Dorothy's ruby slippers, the actual Star-Spangled Banner, and other curiosities from nearly four centuries of national history, this museum is an entertaining celebration of Americana.

P.58 ▶ THE NATIONAL MALL

▼ City Museum of Washington DC

Set in the grand former city library, this institution showcases Washington's growth from a swampy backwater to a marble-and-granite showpiece.

P.108 ▶ OLD DOWNTOWN AND FEDERAL TRIANGLE

▲ Navy Museum

This favorite of nautical buffs resides in the Washington Navy Yard, where you can view historical displays and artifacts, such as a decommissioned destroyer floating out back.

P.83 ▶ SOUTH OF THE MALL

▼ International Spy Museum

This treasure trove of antiques and curiosities used for surveillance, subterfuge, and sedition pays loving tribute to the golden days of spying.

P.110 ▶ OLD DOWNTOWN AND FEDERAL TRIANGLE

Memorials and monuments

There seems to be a war memorial or presidential monument no matter where you turn in Washington. From the exalted to the obscure, countless historic figures are honored in statues, friezes, and emblems throughout the city, and new sculptural icons are dedicated every year. Although there are too many memorials and monuments to see in a brief visit, these – along with the Lincoln and the Vietnam Veterans memorials, detailed in "The big six" – constitute must-see viewing.

▼ FDR Memorial

The twentieth-century's greatest US president is honored with a series of outdoor rustic-stone galleries, adorned with stark Depression-era statues and war-related friezes.

P.54 ▸ THE NATIONAL MALL

▼ Grant Memorial

Stone lions guard the archly dramatic equestrian statue of the Civil War general and later president, poised atop a towering block of marble.

P.71 ▸ CAPITOL HILL

▲ Jefferson Memorial

A lovely, round, Neoclassical temple on the shore of the Tidal Basin, set in a grove of cherry trees, commemorates the third American president.

P.53 ▸ THE NATIONAL MALL

▶ Arlington National Cemetery

A myriad of white crosses (and some Stars of David) sit in perfect rows to mark the graves of nearly a quarter-million US soldiers at the nation's most famous military cemetery.

P.158 ▸ ARLINGTON

▼ National World War II Memorial

The newest entry on the Mall, the long-awaited cenotaph for the soldiers of World War II is a powerful reflection on duty and sacrifice.

P.54 ▸ THE NATIONAL MALL

HERE IN THE PRESENCE OF WASHINGTON AND LINCOLN, ONE THE EIGHTEENTH CENTURY FATHER AND THE OTHER THE NINETEENTH CENTURY PRESERVER OF OUR NATION, WE HONOR THOSE TWENTIETH CENTURY AMERICANS WHO TOOK UP THE STRUGGLE DURING THE SECOND WORLD WAR AND MADE THE SACRIFICES TO PERPETUATE

Parks and gardens

As a complement to the grand boulevards and towering monuments, Washington has been laid out with an excellent array of parks, gardens, and public squares. The range of activities found in these spaces is also impressive, whether you're decamping on the magnificent National Mall, examining meticulous displays of horticulture, or hopping from one civic plaza to the next, each overseen by a commanding statue of a famous politician or Revolutionary or Civil War hero.

▲ Rock Creek Park

Set along a forest and gorge, the park offers rugged trails for hiking, winding paths for cycling and rollerblading, and nineteenth-century oddments like a functional gristmill.

P.145 ▶ UPPER NORTHWEST

▲ The National Mall

Washington's centerpiece, this two-mile-long concourse of water and greenery is the site of many of DC's great museums and memorials, as well as the massive protest marches that descend upon the city.

P.3 ▶ THE NATIONAL MALL

▼ National Arboretum

Marvelous displays of azaleas and bonsai, as well as an incongruous group of sandstone columns that once supported the US Capitol, make this out-of-the-way gem worth seeking out.

P.135 ▶ ADAMS-MORGAN, SHAW, AND OUTER NORTHEAST

▲ US Botanic Garden

See thousands of plants in different climate-controlled settings, highlighted by the dense greenery of the Jungle Room.

P.72 ▶ CAPITOL HILL

▼ Lafayette Square

The finest of DC's many public squares is the site of dashing statues, like that of Andrew Jackson, and a pleasant spot to stretch out on the grass and gaze at the White House.

P.91 ▶ THE WHITE HOUSE AND FOGGY BOTTOM

▲ C&O Canal

The 184-mile-long historic canal, once a key commercial artery, echoes its past with quaint bridges, preserved old buildings, and mule-drawn boat rides.

P.150 ▶ GEORGETOWN

Power dining

There's little doubt that DC is one of the nation's prime spots for power dining. In select restaurants, backroom promises are made over a slice of filet mignon, lobbyists make their cases to pals on Capitol Hill, and mere plebs can gaze at obscure politicians as if they were Hollywood stars. The "in" spots of the moment tend to vary by party and administration, but these places are always good for a thrill – and a high-priced bill.

▼ The Palm

The Washington branch of the New York steakhouse serves up prime cuts of beef and delicious lobster and draws politicians and celebrities who want to be seen being seen.

P.127 ▸ NEW DOWNTOWN AND DUPONT CIRCLE

▼ Café Promenade

Tucked in the grand *Mayflower* hotel, offering the pinnacle of power-breakfasts and lunches to practically anyone cutting deals at the nearby White House.

P.127 ▶ NEW DOWNTOWN AND DUPONT CIRCLE

▲ Citronelle

This huge new player on the dining circuit presents artful French cooking with a California Cuisine twist, and caters to well-heeled honchos in Georgetown.

P.156 ▶ GEORGETOWN

▼ The Monocle

A well-known spot for Congressional aides and their bosses to plot strategy while dining on tasty steaks and crab cakes amid stylish decor.

P.77 ▶ CAPITOL HILL

▲ Old Ebbitt Grill

A DC fixture for nearly 150 years, with a plush mahogany-and-leather ambience; it's a great place for steak, oysters, and even burgers, and you can't help but run into some politico or other.

P.113 ▶ OLD DOWNTOWN AND FEDERAL TRIANGLE

Art museums and galleries

With the National Gallery in town, many visitors get their fill of High Art and overlook some of the city's other standout venues for painting, sculpture, and photography. Indeed, Washington has art that caters to every taste, not just those with a yen for eighteenth-century presidential portraits, and offers a broad range of works, from Ming Dynasty China to the Peruvian Andes to postwar New York.

▲ Renwick Gallery

With the Smithsonian American Art Museum closed until 2006, this handsome Victorian mansion displays many of its holdings in a colossal Grand Salon, where the towering walls feature paintings stacked four and five high.

P.93 ▸ THE WHITE HOUSE AND FOGGY BOTTOM

▲ National Museum of Asian Art

Spread through two Smithsonian galleries – the Freer and the Sackler – are displays of Japanese, Chinese, and Southeast Asian art, with a few rooms devoted to painter James Whistler.

P.66 ▸ THE NATIONAL MALL

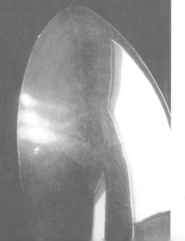

▼ Hirshhorn Museum

This giant concrete drum on the National Mall is a storehouse of modernist treasures, especially good for its Abstract Expressionism and Pop Art.

P.64 ▸ THE NATIONAL MALL

▲ Textile Museum

Kente-cloth from Ghana, colorful ponchos from Chile, mudcloth from Mali, and postmodern tapestries from America are among the fascinating garments and textiles to examine here.

P.125 ▸ NEW DOWNTOWN AND
DUPONT CIRCLE

▼ Corcoran Gallery of Art

The city's oldest art institution is a noteworthy spot for America-style Impressionism, but best for grand canvases by the likes of Thomas Cole and Albert Bierstadt.

P.93 ▸ THE WHITE HOUSE AND
FOGGY BOTTOM

▲ Phillips Collection

One of the city's favorite showpieces for American work by artists such as Milton Avery, Philip Guston, and Mark Rothko.

P.123 ▸ NEW DOWNTOWN AND
DUPONT CIRCLE

Shops and markets

Washington may not rank high on the list of US cities for shopping, and it certainly has no retail corridor rivaling New York's Fifth Avenue or LA's Rodeo Drive. It does, however, sport an appealing range of fun and funky bohemian zones where you can pick up vintage clothing and used vinyl, stylish and trendy spots for the latest fashions, and a number of prime areas for gourmet food and wine.

▼ Eastern Market

Delis, butchers, seafood sellers, and weekend antique stalls mix in and around a historic red-brick building that's been here for 130 years.

P.75 ▶ CAPITOL HILL

▲ Connecticut Avenue NW

A smart and swanky strip for upscale clothing and gourmet eats that is at its most relaxed and appealing around Dupont Circle.

P.117 ▸ NEW DOWNTOWN AND DUPONT CIRCLE

▼ Washington Fish Wharf

Throngs of fishmongers hawk the likes of bass, mackerel, perch, lobster, and, of course, crab at this longstanding waterfront favorite.

P.82 ▸ SOUTH OF THE MALL

▼ M Street and Wisconsin Avenue NW

Shops nest in historic nineteenth-century digs along two busy retail corridors in Georgetown, the former home to a chic selection of national chains, the latter to some of DC's best independent boutiques.

P.149 & P.152 ▸ GEORGETOWN

▲ go mama go!

Eighteenth Street in Adams-Morgan holds most of the area's funky shops, but this entry a few blocks east is the colorful equal of anything on that strip.

P.125 ▸ NEW DOWNTOWN AND DUPONT CIRCLE

African-American DC

DC has had a significant African-American presence since the nineteenth-century, when thousands of newly freed slaves migrated from the South, and – away from the corridors of power – has been a predominantly black city since the 1930s. The first US institution of higher learning to enroll African-Americans can be found here, alongside sights encompassing the legacy of statesman Frederick Douglass, the art and artifacts of Africa, and classic haunts for music and dance.

serade

▼ Frederick Douglass National Historic Site

The preserved Victorian residence where the civil-rights pioneer lived in his 60s and 70s displays key mementos from his life and artifacts like Abe Lincoln's cane.

P.84 ▶ SOUTH OF THE MALL

▼ Howard University

Founded just after the Civil War and boasting numerous famous graduates, this premier black college is also worth a look for its striking 1930s buildings.

P.133 ▶ ADAMS-MORGAN, SHAW, AND OUTER NORTHEAST

▲ Bohemian Caverns

Hear traditional jazz as well as more adventur-
ous, modern stylings at the latest incarnation
of this legendary supper club and jazz hotspot.

P.138 ▸ ADAMS-MORGAN, SHAW,
AND OUTER NORTHEAST

▼ National Museum of African Art

One of the best museums on the National
Mall, featuring sculptures from ancient
Benin, carved icons from the Gold Coast, and
modern art from across the continent.

P.65 ▸ THE NATIONAL MALL

▲ Anacostia Museum

The least known of DC's Smithsonian museums, this storehouse of African-American
history and culture showcases folk-art
quilts, historic photographs, and influential
speeches and documents.

P.85 ▸ SOUTH OF THE MALL

Bars and pubs

A trip to Washington wouldn't be complete without sampling its high-powered bars, funky watering holes, and Irish-style pubs. Along with these old favorites – attracting everyone from three-martini-lunching attorneys to hipsters in black leather – DC's bars also drink in the recent rage for microbreweries, giving you the chance to enjoy handcrafted ales, stouts, and porters, and in some cases even watch the beer being made.

▲ The Brickskeller

This brick-walled basement saloon famously claims to serve "the world's largest selection of beer," some eight hundred brews from around the world.

P.128 ▶ NEW DOWNTOWN AND DUPONT CIRCLE

▼ Capitol City Brewing Company

Shiny copper vats set the tone at this popular microbrewery, which helped establish DC as a place for more than mere corporate-brand chugging.

P.78 ▶ CAPITOL HILL

▼ J. Paul's

This stylish "American Dining Saloon" dishes up a mean crab cake and pours its own homebrewed beers, the highlight of which is its renowned 1889 Amber Ale.

P.156 ▶ GEORGETOWN

▲ Hawk 'n' Dove

Cheap beer and food, along with Redskins football, bring regulars into this longstanding favorite.

P.78 ▶ CAPITOL HILL

▲ Murphy's Grand Irish Pub

A fine Old Town fixture in which to knock back a foaming pint of Guinness and soak up the sounds of brogue-sporting musicians belting out Irish drinking songs.

P.173 ▶ DAY-TRIPS

Washington women

Although the White House still awaits the first female president, extraordinary women have left their mark on Washington since its earliest days: civil rights advocates protesting for social justice, senators and congresswomen representing their constituencies on Capitol Hill, and First Ladies and dowagers who have contributed significantly to DC's cultural life. Fittingly, the capital is home to a number of memorials and museums honoring those women who have served their country either at home or abroad.

▼ Bethune Council House

Once the home and headquarters of one of DC's most prominent African-American women, this restored Victorian is now preserved to honor her legacy.

P.120 ▸ NEW DOWNTOWN AND
           DUPONT CIRCLE

▼ Daughters of the American Revolution Museum

The Daughters of the American Revolution have devoted a century to collecting historic memorabilia, from toys and books to quilts and pottery, and proudly display the cache in their museum and period salon rooms.

P.95 ▸ THE WHITE HOUSE AND
          FOGGY BOTTOM

▲ Sewall-Belmont House

One of the city's oldest private residences, this "living monument" to Equal Rights Amendment author Alice Paul houses a museum dedicated to the women's rights movement and leaders such as Paul and Susan B. Anthony.

P.74 ▸ CAPITOL HILL

▽ National Museum of Women in the Arts

This Smithsonian outpost displays works by famous and lesser-known women painters, photographers, and sculptors from the Renaissance to the present.

P.111 ▸ OLD DOWNTOWN AND FEDERAL TRIANGLE

▲ Vietnam Women's Memorial

A short distance from the larger Vietnam memorial, this simple bronze grouping of three battle-tested nurses, set in a sylvan grove, pays tribute to the 11,000 women who served in that war.

P.58 ▸ THE NATIONAL MALL

Religious DC

Although officially separated by American law, religion and politics make convenient bedfellows in Washington society, and most modern politicians can scarcely get elected without dropping in on an evangelical prayer breakfast or appearing regularly at a famous cathedral. For all this self-conscious mixing of God and country, there are plenty of truly inspiring spots that present an evocative glimpse of the divine.

▲ Washington National Cathedral

The sixth-biggest cathedral in the world took eight decades to construct, its stunning limestone structure complete with flying buttresses, vaults, stained glass, and gargoyles.

P.143 ▶ UPPER NORTHWEST

▼ National Shrine of the Immaculate Conception

Simply put, the biggest Catholic shrine in the US and a towering monument to Christian faith; it really has to be seen to be believed.

P.134 ▸ ADAMS-MORGAN, SHAW, AND OUTER NORTHEAST

▼ St John's Church

This quaint yellow structure with a tasteful dome and Greek Cross layout has been hosting presidents since 1816 and reserves a special pew for them.

P.92 ▸ THE WHITE HOUSE AND FOGGY BOTTOM

▲ Metropolitan AME Church

This massive red-brick, Gothic Revival church saw the funeral of statesman Frederick Douglass in 1895, a decade after it was completed.

P.119 ▸ NEW DOWNTOWN AND DUPONT CIRCLE

▲ St Matthew's Cathedral

JFK's 1963 funeral Mass was held at this grandly inspiring and wonderfully built church, where many prominent Catholic politicians go to take Communion.

P.116 ▸ NEW DOWNTOWN AND DUPONT CIRCLE

DC calendar

As it should be in a national capital, Washington offers so many festivals and events throughout the year that it can be difficult to keep track of them, let alone pick the best and most deserving ones to attend. With its mix of cultures and peoples from around the world, DC hosts many fine ethnic festivals of food, music, and drink, alongside spirited celebrations of events from American history and lore. Those listed here are but a few of the many highlights.

▼ Independence Day

Appropriately enough, DC is the place to be if you're going to be anywhere on the Fourth of July, with a spirited parade along Constitution Avenue NW, free music and concerts, and, of course, a grand display of fireworks.

P.192 ▶ ESSENTIALS

▼ George Washington's Birthday

The district's namesake is celebrated with commemorative events and upbeat concerts at his Mount Vernon home, as well as a spectacular parade and other events just up the road in Alexandria, Virginia.

P.192 ▶ ESSENTIALS

▲ Smithsonian Festival of American Folklife

One of the country's biggest festivals rolls into town in early summer, with American music, crafts, food, and folk heritage events on the Mall.

P.192 ▸ ESSENTIALS

▼ Easter Egg Roll

Toddlers descend upon the White House in droves to toss eggs in this annual race, held on the South Lawn.

P.192 ▸ ESSENTIALS

The music scene

Finding a swinging club or live-music joint in Washington is the exact opposite of finding a good museum – go where the tourists aren't. The best spots to hear hard-driving indie rock, old-school funk, or top blues acts are well away from the Mall, in places like Dupont Circle, Adams-Morgan, and Shaw's U Street corridor; meanwhile, in Foggy Bottom, you can enjoy an uplifting DC music institution, at a gallery no less, if you're in on a weekend.

▼ Gospel Brunch

Passionate odes to Jesus and plenty of good food make this signature event at the Corcoran Gallery's *Café des Artistes* worth waking up for on Sundays.

P.98 ▶ THE WHITE HOUSE AND FOGGY BOTTOM

▼ The Black Cat

Catch the latest tunes from alternative bands at this gritty Logan Circle institution, owned by Dave Grohl of Nirvana and Foo Fighters fame.

P.129 ▸ NEW DOWNTOWN AND DUPONT CIRCLE

▲ IOTA Club and Café

Head across the Potomac to this warehouse-style club for indie-rock, blues, and folk acts as well as bistro-style food and a drink at the great bar.

P.163 ▸ ARLINGTON

▼ Habana Village

This neighborhood favorite draws throngs of Latin music-lovers to dance to frenetic salsa, tango, and merengue beats – and if you don't know the steps, you can always take lessons.

P.138 ▸ ADAMS-MORGAN, SHAW, AND OUTER NORTHEAST

▲ Blues Alley

This thirty-year stalwart on the blues scene draws some of the bigger names in the field – but reserve ahead, as the pricey tickets can sell out quickly.

P.157 ▸ GEORGETOWN

The dark side of DC

Needless to say, Washington DC isn't all about celebrating democracy and showcasing fancy museums and monuments. The city also has a disturbing dark side linked to political scandal, historic injustice, and shocking violence. Aside from sites like the US Capitol being partly built with the aid of slave labor, other attractions have their own checkered pasts, legacies that may not be advertised in their pamphlets but nonetheless color their history.

▲ Ford's Theatre

The theater where Abraham Lincoln was gunned down by Confederate assassin John Wilkes Booth remains the most notorious of any American theater.

P.110 ▶ OLD DOWNTOWN AND FEDERAL TRIANGLE

▼ Old Executive Office Building

Along with being a garish monstrosity, this Washington landmark was the job site for all manner of White House schemers, from Watergate-era crooks to Iran-Contra document-shredders.

P.92 ▶ THE WHITE HOUSE AND FOGGY BOTTOM

▲ Carlyle House

Although a Colonial jewel, the onetime residence of a plantation-owner and slave-trader who lived in splendor while his servants toiled in dirt is also an icon of early American injustice.

P.166 ▶ DAY-TRIPS

▼ The Watergate

The residential and commercial complex whose name lives in infamy as a synonym for political dirty tricks first saw the illegal entry of Richard Nixon's "plumbers" and later housed Clinton intern and mistress Monica Lewinsky.

P.96 ▶ THE WHITE HOUSE AND FOGGY BOTTOM

Chic hotels

Every day Washington hosts legions of visitors from around the nation and world, all of whom need to decamp somewhere for the night. Of DC's most chic and stylish hotels, there are a handful that really stand out for their verve, design, and amenities – places where you can guzzle a martini in a posh cocktail bar or peer out at the White House from the balcony of your room.

▼ Hay-Adams

This early twentieth-century charmer features one of the city's best views – directly across from the White House on Lafayette Square.

P.180 ▶ ACCOMMODATION

▼ Willard

Monumentally grand hotel that has been a Washington landmark for 150 years.

P.182 ▶ ACCOMMODATION

▲ Hotel Monaco

A Greek Revival masterpiece dating to the 1840s, Washington's first-ever marble building, created by renowned architect Robert Mills, is now home to a stylish, modern hotel.

P.182 ▶ ACCOMMODATION

▲ St Regis

A luxury hotel with an impressive pedigree – Calvin Coolidge dedicated it in the 1920s, and it's been beguiling visitors with its Renaissance-styled splendor ever since.

P.181 ▶ ACCOMMODATION

▼ Mayflower

If there's such a thing as a power-hotel, this is it – one of the nation's most famous draws for foreign leaders and political bigwigs, with an opulent lobby and elegant suites.

P.181 ▶ ACCOMMODATION

▼ Hotel Rouge

Visiting hipsters descend on this Dupont Circle hotel for its dramatically moody lounge and red-infused rooms decorated with quirky art and photography.

P.181 ▶ ACCOMMODATION

Government in action

The heavy wheels of bureaucracy grind their way across much of the city, from the waterfront to Foggy Bottom. Although the vast corridors of office buildings bordering the National Mall usually offer little attraction for visitors, several government sites can actually be quite enjoyable to witness firsthand – though the real decisions, of course, are made well away from prying eyes.

▲ Library of Congress

The world's most voluminous library draws researchers as well as visitors eager to see the opulent interior spaces and artifacts on display, from ancient 78 rpm records to famous, hand-scrawled speeches.

P.73 ▶ CAPITOL HILL

▼ Supreme Court

The nation's ultimate arbiter of legal disputes, civil and criminal, is housed in a monumental 1930s Neoclassical building that's regularly open to the public.

P.72 ▶ CAPITOL HILL

▲ Bureau of Engraving and Printing

The avaricious thrill of being so tantalizingly close to so much money draws the crowds to this tourist favorite, where more than $300 million in US currency is minted every day.

P.81 ▶ SOUTH OF THE MALL

▲ National Archives

One of the visual glories of Washington, this site holds the Holy Trinity of the US government: the Declaration of Independence, Constitution, and Bill of Rights.

P.103 ▶ OLD DOWNTOWN AND FEDERAL TRIANGLE

▼ Embassy Row

Many of the world's countries have established their official US presence in grand, century-old mansions, like that of Indonesia, sprinkled throughout Dupont Circle and Kalorama.

P.122 ▶ NEW DOWNTOWN AND DUPONT CIRCLE

Casual eateries

Although Washington is perhaps best-known for its fancy, high-powered restaurants, the city also dishes up a solid set of inexpensive cafés, diners, and casual eateries where you can grab a morning snack before hitting the museum scene, chow down on local favorites from chili half smokes to crispy chicken, and sample good ethnic cuisine without breaking the bank.

▼ Firehook Bakery

Breads, cakes, cookies, and excellent coffee are all on offer at DC's favorite coffeeshop.

P.146 ▶ UPPER NORTHWEST

▼ Clyde's

This saloon-restaurant features checked tablecloths, Art Deco lampshades, and a burnished wood interior to accompany its American bistro fare – a prime lunch and brunch spot.

P.156 ▶ GEORGETOWN

▲ Ben's Chili Bowl

U Street's classic haunt still doles out the city's best chili half smokes – DC's inspired take on the humble hot dog – cheese fries, and shakes.

P.136 ▸ ADAMS-MORGAN, SHAW, AND OUTER NORTHEAST

▼ Queen Bee

You'll have to head to Virginia for the area's best Vietnamese, but this restaurant's renowned spring rolls, grilled shrimp and pork, and steaming bowls of noodle soup are well worth the trip.

P.163 ▸ ARLINGTON

Sports and outdoor activities

It may seem most passionate about its politics, but Washington can be a pretty rabid sports town, too, and not just for big-league spectator sports. Indeed, the city is just as devoted to outdoor pursuits, and, as one of America's greenest cities, DC has a fine selection of parks where you can get your heart pumping.

▼ Cruise the Potomac

This winding watercourse hosts a broad range of waterborne activities, including windsurfing south of Alexandria, white-water kayaking north of town around Great Falls, and canoeing and rowing – with rentals available in Georgetown.

P.151 ▸ GEORGETOWN

▼ Biking the C&O Canal

The old tow-path for mule-drawn canal boats provides a prime stretch for pedaling along the fetching, 184-mile historic waterway.

P.150 ▸ GEORGETOWN

▲ Jogging along the Mall

The Mall's imperial buildings and monuments provide an inspiring backdrop for a daily workout – and the gravel path around the city's mammoth front lawn is kind on the knees.

P.3 ▸ THE NATIONAL MALL

▼ A game at the MCI Center

If hockey or hoops is your thing, head to DC's downtown sports complex and catch the Capitals, Wizards, or Mystics in action.

P.108 ▸ OLD DOWNTOWN AND FEDERAL TRIANGLE

▼ Hiking on Roosevelt Island

Take an enchanting trip on foot along the trails of this island nature-park, which sits halfway between Washington and Arlington in the Potomac but feels much further away.

P.161 ▸ ARLINGTON

▲ Rollerblading on Beach Drive

This forested six-mile strip through Rock Creek Park serves as a training and cruising ground for in-line skaters of all kinds, and rewards a visit for its gently hilly contours.

P.145 ▸ UPPER NORTHWEST

Hidden DC

Although the Washington area's major sights are often readily accessible on mass transit, a handful of fascinating spots take a bit more effort to reach. If you've got the time and inclination, these four spots – from a little-known museum set in the hills northwest of Georgetown to a renowned Virginia concert space devoted to American music in all its native forms – handsomely reward the effort required to seek them out.

▲ Kenilworth Aquatic Gardens

Perhaps the most obscure national park in the district, this unfairly overlooked twelve-acre marvel of aquaculture features graceful water lilies and beautiful lotuses.

P.135 ▸ ADAMS-MORGAN, SHAW, AND OUTER NORTHEAST

▼ Takoma Park

Architecture buffs should head to the DC–Maryland border for its well-preserved Victorian homes, from Colonial Revival mansions to Craftsman bungalows to Queen Anne cottages.

P.134 ▶ ADAMS-MORGAN, SHAW, AND OUTER NORTHEAST

▲ Kreeger Museum

Set in a stylish building designed by modernist Philip Johnson, this storehouse of art from the late nineteenth to mid-twentieth century holds key works by the likes of Picasso, Beckmann, and Kandinsky.

P.153 ▶ GEORGETOWN

▼ Barns at Wolf Trap

Near West Falls Church, VA, this concert venue, consisting of several evocative stages in two restored eighteenth-century barns, is one of the area's premier showcases for folk, blues, and country music.

P.174 ▶ DAY-TRIPS

Places

The National Mall

Laid out along two miles between the US Capitol and the Potomac River is nothing less than the cultural and political axis of the country, the National Mall. Long serving as a choice venue for protest movements of every stripe, it's also the prime target for nearly every visitor to DC. The showpiece expanse is dotted with big-ticket attractions, including nine Smithsonian museums, the National Gallery of Art, and several of the city's most famous monuments and memorials, among them stirring tributes to Lincoln, Jefferson, Washington, and the fallen soldiers of the Vietnam War. Flanked by memorials on the western half of the Mall is the iconic Reflecting Pool, a gleaming body of water that was supposedly inspired by the pools and canals at Versailles and the landscaping at the Taj Mahal.

Washington Monument

15th St NW at Constitution Ave ☎1-800/967-2283, ⊛www.nps.gov/wamo. Daily 9am–5pm. This unadorned marble obelisk, built in memory of the first US president, is simple, elegant, majestic, and huge: immediately recognizable from all over the city, it provides the Mall and the capital with an unmistakable icon. Like seemingly everything else in town, though, the monument is getting revamped for security, which in this case means the grounds have been blocked off for re-landscaping. You can still visit by queuing up for free tickets at a kiosk (daily 8am–4.30pm) on 15th Street; these can run out early in the day, so plan accordingly or call the above number to reserve in advance ($2 charge).

The monument is the tallest all-masonry structure on the planet, 55ft wide at the base, tapering to 34ft at the top, and capped by a small aluminum pyramid. The elevator up takes seventy seconds and deposits you at the 500-foot level, from

▼WASHINGTON MONUMENT

Free admission

Unless otherwise noted, every memorial, monument, and museum in this chapter has no charge for admission.

where the views are tremendous, glimpsed through narrow windows on all four sides.

It took quite some effort for the monument even to be built, despite the ardor that Washington, as America's Revolutionary War general and first president, rightfully inspired. When the cornerstone was finally laid on July 4, 1848, it was on a bare knoll 360ft east and 120ft south of the true intersection – which explains why the monument looks off-center on the map. By 1853, when funds ran out, the monument was just 152ft high and stayed that way for almost 25 years. Even today, you may notice a slight discoloration between the off-white shades of marble that separate the lower third and the upper two-thirds – testament to the break in construction work and change in marble types that were used over the years.

The Tidal Basin

West Potomac Park, between Maryland and Independence aves. The Tidal Basin occupies much of the space between the Lincoln and Jefferson memorials. This large inlet, formerly part of the Potomac River, was created in 1882 to prevent flooding and is best known for its famous cherry trees – a gift from Japan – which were planted around the edge in 1912. The National Cherry Blossom Festival is held each spring in early April to celebrate the trees' blooming with concerts, parades, and displays of Japanese lanterns. To take it all in from the water, you can rent a pedal boat from the Tidal Basin Boat House, 1501 Maine Ave SW (March–Sept Mon–Fri 10am–6pm & Sat–Sun 10am–7pm; two-seaters $8/hr, four-seaters $16/hr; ☎202/484-0206) – a real treat

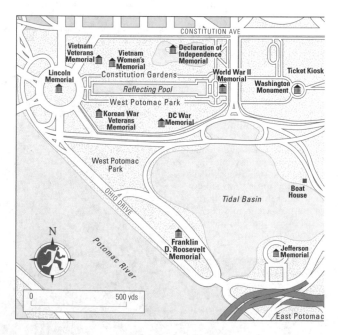

for children and a great way to experience waterside views of several famous monuments and memorials. Also worth your time is a stroll around the perimeter of the basin, where the striking landscape of trees and flowers is at its most picturesque in the springtime, with the Neoclassical buildings in the distance as a nicely evocative touch.

Jefferson Memorial

Southeast bank of the Tidal Basin near 15th St SW and Ohio Drive ☎202/426-6841, ⊛www.nps.gov/thje. Daily 8am–midnight. Given that Thomas Jefferson was a man of countless accomplishments – third president of the United States, prime author of the Declaration of Independence, inveterate architect and inventor, and agent of the Louisiana Purchase and Lewis & Clark Expedition

– it took a very long time for his monument to arrive. When the Jefferson Memorial was finally completed in 1943, some 150 years after his presidency, it was greeted with protestors complaining of the loss of cherry trees, Tidal Basin views, and other seemingly important issues. Such complaints have long been forgotten, and this circular, colonnaded edifice stands as one of Washington DC's most visually memorable buildings, its shallow dome housing a nineteen-foot-high bronze statue of Jefferson and lined with several of his signature quotations. The memorial's style was influenced by the Neoclassical styles Jefferson had helped popularize in the United States after his stint as ambassador to France in the 1780s, and also closely echoes the character of Jefferson's self-designed

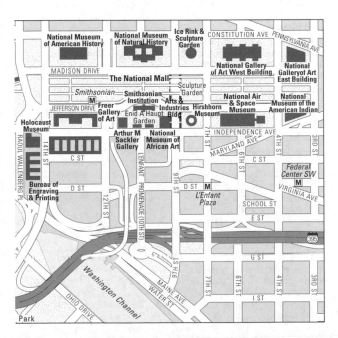

country estate at Monticello, in Charlottesville, Virginia.

As most visitors discover when they enter through the building's grand marble columns, this is one of the most harmonious structures in the city – a white marble temple, reminiscent of the Pantheon, with steps down to the water's edge and framed by the cherry trees of the Tidal Basin. The standing bronze statue of Jefferson (by Rudulph Evans) gazes determinedly outward, while the inscription around the frieze sets the high moral tone, trumpeting "I have sworn upon the altar of God eternal hostility against every form of tyranny over the mind of man." Inside, on the walls, four more texts flank the statue, most notably the seminal words from the 1776 Declaration of Independence – the original copy of which can be viewed under glass at the National Archives (see p.103).

FDR Memorial

Southwest bank of the Tidal Basin
☎202/426-6841, ⊛www.nps.gov/fdrm.
Daily 24hr, staffed 8am–midnight.
DC's most recently constructed presidential memorial honors Franklin Delano Roosevelt, "FDR," the 32nd chief executive in American history and widely considered to be the third-best US president behind Lincoln and Washington. As architect of the New Deal and wartime leader, Roosevelt's underlying political spirit is captured in a series of carved quotations that define the twelve years of his presidency, perhaps most famously "The only thing we have to fear is fear itself." Dedicated in 1997, the memorial spreads across a seven-acre site on the banks of the Tidal Basin and is made up of a series of granite outdoor galleries punctuated by waterfalls,

statuary, sculpted reliefs, groves of trees, shaded alcoves, and plazas. It's among the most successful of DC's memorials, with an almost Athenian quality to its open spaces, resting-places and benches, and texts. On a bright spring or fall day, with the glistening basin waters and emerging views of the Washington Monument and Jefferson Memorial, it's also one of the finest places in the city for a contemplative stroll.

The four galleries of rustic stone represent each of FDR's terms of office, though he only served a few months of his final term before he died. Although the memorial's layout was designed by noted architect Lawrence Halprin, its most compelling artworks were created by George Segal; these are the focus of the second gallery, where sculpted figures show the Great Depression of the 1930s in all its bleakness – a farm couple stand in a Dust Bowl doorway, broken men wait in a city breadline, and an elderly man listens to one of Roosevelt's famous radio fireside chats. In the third room a tangle of broken granite blocks represents the war years, alongside a seated statue of FDR and his beloved dog Fala. The memorial ends in the fourth gallery with a timeline of dates and events inscribed in the steps and a recognition of Roosevelt's redoubtable wife Eleanor, a staunch civil rights advocate and ambassador to the United Nations.

National World War II Memorial

17th St SW at Independence Ave
☎202/426-6841, ⊛www.nps.gov
/nwwm. Daily 24hr, staffed 8am–midnight. The National World War II Memorial opened on Memorial Day 2004 to much acclaim – and

great relief. Although some were concerned that the memorial might disrupt the scenic views down the Mall or become an overblown statement of victory, neither fear was realized, and it stands as a thoroughly moving statement of duty and sacrifice, its power and presence as a war monument second only to the Vietnam Veterans Memorial (see p.57).

The site roughly occupies the former footprint of the Mall's Rainbow Pool on the western edge of the Washington Monument, with the Lincoln Memorial reflected in the distance further west. On each side of a central fountain, the memorial features two arcs consisting of 56 stone pillars – representing US states and territories at the time of the war – which are decorated with bronze wreaths. In the middle of each arc, directly across from each other, stand two short towers titled "Atlantic" and "Pacific" to represent the two theaters of war, and within each are four interlinked bronze eagles. The dramatic birds are a statement of victory and are hardly the arrogant symbols that critics feared, but are tempered by the sizable towers and

a pair of sculpted wreaths, which despite their bulk seem to float above you in mid-air.

Beyond the carefully considered architecture and the chiseled quotations on the walls by the likes of FDR and Dwight Eisenhower, the memorial really succeeds as a public space in full view of the Mall's most important sites. With its stone benches and terraces, the site is appropriately evocative and contemplative, especially considering the concave wall of four thousand golden stars nearby. Each symbol represents one hundred US military deaths in the war, making for a total of 400,000 fallen soldiers – surpassed only by the colossal carnage of the Civil War.

DC War Memorial

Perhaps the Mall's most overlooked monument is the DC War Memorial, hidden in a grove of trees just north of Independence Avenue, a bit west of the World War II Memorial. This one is much more of a humble edifice, basically a small, circular Neoclassical temple built to commemorate local soldiers who fought in "The Great War." Usually free from tourists or any visitors

▼DC WAR MEMORIAL

▲LINCOLN MEMORIAL

whatsoever, it offers a quiet and relaxing respite from the hubbub of the Mall, a place to take a break before you wade once more into the throngs of visitors.

Korean War Veterans Memorial

West Potomac Park, southeast of the Lincoln Memorial ☎202/619-7222, ⓦwww.nps.gov/kwvm. Daily 24hr, staffed 8am–midnight. Dedicated in July 1995, this memorial has as a centrepiece a Field of Remembrance featuring nineteen life-size, heavily armed combat troops sculpted from stainless steel. They advance across a triangular plot with alternating rows of stone and plant life, meant to resemble both a rice paddy and a mine field, and head ultimately toward the Stars and Stripes positioned at the vertex. Beyond this assemblage is a reflective black granite wall, inscribed "Freedom is not free" and etched with a mural depicting military support crew and medical staff.

Although not as well known or as popular as the Vietnam War Memorial, the memorial commemorates a war that was no less bloody for US soldiers. Between 1950 and 1953, almost 55,000 Americans were killed in Korea (with another 8000 missing in action and more than 103,000 wounded), but unlike those who fought in Vietnam, the soldiers sent into battle by President Truman on behalf of the South Korean government went in the name of the United Nations. Thus the memorial also lists the fifteen other countries who volunteered forces, with Britain, France, Greece, and Turkey in particular suffering significant casualties.

Lincoln Memorial

West Potomac Park at 23rd St NW ☎202/426-6841, ⓦwww.nps.gov/linc. Daily 24hr, staffed 8am–midnight. The Lincoln Memorial needs no introduction. As one of the country's most recognizable symbols, it is both a representation of its political ideology (Athenian, Neoclassical architecture) and social activism (speeches, protests, etc.). Hardly a year goes without some memorable march or event taking place here. The site's most famous speech occurred on August 28, 1963, when Dr Martin Luther King Jr chose the memorial to the Great Emancipator as the spot from which to make his "I have a dream" speech to 200,000 people gathered here and along the Mall. Aided by backdrops of the Potomac and Arlington to the west and the Reflecting Pool to the east, it's also one of the best places in town to take a stirring photograph without really trying.

Climbing the steps to the memorial is one of DC's more profound moments, its 36 columns symbolizing the number of states that made up the Union at the time of Lincoln's death, with bas-relief plaques on the attic parapet commemorating the 48 states of the Union that existed when the memorial was completed in 1922. As you enter the building you'll notice murals on the north and south walls, representing Fraternity, Unity of North and South, Charity (north wall), and Emancipation and Immortality (south wall), directly under which are carved inscriptions of Lincoln's two most celebrated speeches. On the north wall is the Gettysburg Address of November 19, 1863, while on the south is the measured eloquence of Lincoln's Second Inaugural Address of March 4, 1865, in which he strove "to bind up the nation's wounds" caused by the Civil War. The momentous centerpiece is, of course, the seated statue of Lincoln himself, created by Daniel Chester French, which faces out through the colonnade. French certainly succeeded in his intention to "convey the mental and physical strength of the great war President": full of resolve, a steely Lincoln clasps the armrests of a thronelike chair with determined hands, his unbuttoned coat falling to either side; the American flag is draped over the back of the chair. It's a phenomenal work, one which took French thirteen years to complete, fashioning the 19ft-tall statue from 28 blocks of white Georgia marble.

Vietnam Veterans Memorial

Henry Bacon Drive and Constitution Ave at 21st St NW ☎202/634-1568, ⓦwww.nps.gov/vive. Daily 24hr, staffed 8am–midnight. The Vietnam Veterans Memorial is one of the most poignant monuments to be found anywhere. Consisting of a polished black-granite chevron cut into the earth, the memorial is inscribed with the names of the 58,191 American casualties of the Vietnam war in chronological order (1959–75). Each name has appended either a diamond (a confirmed death) or cross (missing in action and still unaccounted for – about 1100

▼VIETNAM VETERANS MEMORIAL

names). The words are etched into an east and west wall that each run for 250ft, slicing deeper into the ground, until meeting at a vertex 10ft high. It's a sobering experience to walk past the ranks of names and the untold experiences they represent, not least for the friends and relatives who come here to take rubbings of the names and leave memorial tokens at the foot of the walls. Directories list the names and their locations for anyone trying to find a particular person, and a ranger is on hand until midnight to answer questions.

A national competition was held in 1980 to determine the memorial's design, and Maya Lin, then just a 21-year-old Yale student, won. (The original design is sometimes displayed in the Library of Congress' Jefferson Building.)

When it was built, the memorial's nonpolitical stance came to be seen as a political act itself by some ex-soldiers. Concerned that these somber, dignified walls made no overt reference to military (as opposed to personal) sacrifice, successful lobbying led to the commissioning of a separate martial statue to be added to the site, just to the south. Later lobbying led to the establishment of the **Vietnam Women's Memorial** in 1993, which stands in a grove at the east end of the main site. Few realize that 11,000 American women served in Vietnam (eight were killed), while almost a quarter of a million provided support services during the conflict. The bronze sculpture shows one nurse on her knees, exhausted; one tending a wounded soldier; and a third raising her eyes to the sky.

Constitution Gardens

On the north side of the Reflecting Pool, Constitution Gardens is a pleasant, fifty-acre area of trees and dells surrounding a kidney-shaped lake. A plaque on the island in the center commemorates the 56 signatories of the Declaration of Independence, and every September 17, Constitution Day, the signing of the document is celebrated with, among other things, an outdoor naturalization service for foreign-born DC residents.

National Museum of American History

14th St NW and Constitution Ave ☎202/357-2700, ⊛www .americanhistory.si.edu. Daily 10am–5.30pm. The ever-popular National Museum of American History is not so much a scholarly center as it is an entertaining hodgepodge of castoffs and antiques from nearly four hundred years of American and pre-American history – eighteenth-century farming equipment to computer chips, jukeboxes to washing machines, harmonicas to train engines. Each floor

▼US FLAG, MUSEUM OF AMERICAN HISTORY

▲NATIONAL MUSEUM OF NATURAL HISTORY

has something unique and fascinating, whether it's George Washington's wooden teeth, Jackie Kennedy's designer dresses, or the ruby slippers Judy Garland wore in *The Wizard of Oz*; these items are set among more didactic displays tracing the country's development from colonial times. As a sanctuary for vanishing Americana, the museum is a real storehouse for the glories of the past, and may in its various exhibits show you anything from a rebuilt eighteenth-century house to the original Star-Spangled Banner itself – now looking a bit worse for wear and slowly being preserved by workers laboring on an overhead lift.

Beyond this, two central exhibits draw your attention, the first of which is the "The American Presidency," devoted to presidential life in and beyond the White House. Its fulcrum is the walk-through Ceremonial Court, designed to resemble the Cross Hall of the White House as it appeared after its 1902 renovation, with displays of glass, porcelain, tinware, and silver from the White House collections. Especially interesting is the cabinet displaying personal items of the presidents: Washington's telescope, Grant's leather cigar case, Nixon's gold pen, Wilson's golf clubs, Jefferson's eyeglasses, and Theodore Roosevelt's toiletry set. The other main area worth a look is the recently opened "America on the Move" exhibit, loaded with modes of transportation from various parts of the country, including an urban elevated train, a massive 260-ton locomotive engine, and automobiles from Model Ts to modern hot rods.

National Museum of Natural History

10th St NW and Constitution Ave ☎ 202/357-2700, ⊛ www.mnh.si.edu. Daily 10am–5.30pm. Although not advertised as one of its strong points, the National Museum of Natural History is unquestionably one of the best places for children visiting the nation's capital, and any visit to the museum will doubtless be accompanied by the yelps of school kids on field trips or with their parents. If you can handle such an atmosphere, the institution is well worth a look, providing an eye-opening array of displays on subjects from biology and paleontology to mining and geology. You'll need to go early to avoid the worst of the crowds, especially in summer and during school holidays.

This is one of the oldest of DC's museums, founded in 1911, with its early collection partly based on the specimens that the Smithsonian commissioned from the game-hunting Theodore Roosevelt on his African safaris of 1909–10. The museum's imposing three-story entrance rotunda is built around a colossal African elephant, and hundreds of other animals, tracing evolution from fossilized four-billion-year-old plankton to dinosaurs' eggs and beyond, are displayed in the exhibits. The highlight for many is the section devoted to dinosaurs, their hulking skeletons reassembled in imaginative poses and accompanied by informative text, written with a light touch. The massive diplodocus, the most imposing specimen, was discovered in Utah in 1923, at what is now Dinosaur National Monument. Stay in this section long enough to tour the related displays – on the Ice Age, Ancient Seas, Fossil Mammals, and Fossil Plants – which cover mollusks, lizards, giant turtles, and early fish in exhaustive, engaging detail. Also meriting a visit is a new section nearby that covers the many facets of the world of mammals, showing the furry, milk-producing creatures in all their terrestrial environments, and giving viewers a chance to consider their own relationship

to the warm-blooded beasts.

Finally, no visit would be complete without taking a gander at the Hope Diamond. Found in the stunning National Gem Collection, this legendary 45-carat stone is reputed to be cursed, its various owners (including Marie Antoinette) condemned to early deaths, financial ruin, or other calamities.

National Gallery of Art – West
Constitution Ave between 4th and 7th sts NW ☎202/737-4215, 🖰www .nga.gov. Mon–Sat 10am–5pm, Sun 11am–6pm. The estimable National Gallery is not part of the Smithsonian Institution, despite being located on a prime spot on the Mall and sitting cheek-to-jowl with other Smithsonian museums. Rather, it is the legacy of noted financier Andrew Mellon, who began to buy the works of European Old Masters in his late 20s and later bequeathed to the gallery a score of masterpieces bought in 1931 from the government of the USSR, which plundered the works in the Hermitage to prop up its faltering economy. Now known as the West Building, the original symmetrical, Neoclassical gallery is overwhelming at first sight: on the main floor, two wings stretch for 400ft on either side of a central rotunda, whose massive dome is supported by 24 black Ionic columns. The entire floor contains almost one hundred display rooms, full of masterpieces ranging from thirteenth-century Italian to nineteenth-century European and American art. Down on the ground floor are changing exhibitions from the gallery's virtuoso collection of prints, drawings, sculpture, and decorative art. Since the museum is slowly undergoing a staggered

renovation, with various sections off-limits for months or years at a time, it's unclear exactly what you'll be able to see when you come. The centerpieces of the Renaissance collection include work by Leonardo da Vinci – whose *Ginevra de' Benci* is the only work by the artist in the United States – and Sandro Botticelli, whose devout rendering of the *Adoration of the Magi* dates from the early 1480s. Spanish standouts include pieces by El Greco and Velasquez, while German painters are also well represented by the likes of Albrecht Dürer, whose *Madonna and Child* grafts realistic Renaissance figures onto a northern European landscape, and Matthias Grünewald, with an especially agonized view of the Crucifixion. Fans of seventeenth-century Dutch art will be rewarded with views of exceptional portraits by Rembrandt and Hals and the always-popular genre scenes of Jan Vermeer – whose unprolific career only left 35 extant paintings, three of which the gallery owns. Later French artists also make memorable appearances, from revolutionary-turned-

Napoleonic propagandist David to Impressionists such as Monet, Renoir, and the rest of the lot. Noted American artists include Washington portraitist Gilbert Stuart and heroic landscape painters Thomas Cole and Albert Bierstadt. Especially entrancing is the work of Britain's J.M.W. Turner, which includes a gentle, hazy *Approach to Venice* and *Keelmen Heaving in Coals by Moonlight*, a harbor scene set in the industrial north of England.

National Gallery of Art – East

Constitution Ave between 3rd and 4th sts NW ☎202/737-4215, ⊛www .nga.gov. Mon–Sat 10am–5pm, Sun 11am–6pm. Although it doesn't quite hold the same number of treasures as does its neighbor to the west, the East Wing of the National Gallery of Art is still quite compelling in its own right, and not only for its striking modern architecture designed by I.M. Pei. Built in the 1970s to help accommodate the gallery's ever-expanding collection, this wing's exhibition spaces are often taken up with special shows, so the museum's own holdings may not be on

▼NATIONAL GALLERY OF ART, EAST BUILDING

display when you visit. If any of the artists or works below form part of your reason for visiting, be sure to call first.

Highlights start with the work of Henri Matisse – with restrained early works giving way to the exuberant *Pianist* and *Checker Players* – and Pablo Picasso, who is represented by several diverse pieces, including the Blue Period item *The Tragedy* (1903) and *Family of Saltimbanques* (1905), depicting itinerant circus performers. Post-1945 art is shown downstairs in the concourse-level galleries. Besides Warhol works like *32 Soup Cans*, *Let Us Now Praise Famous Men*, and *Green Marilyn*, there's art by Roy Lichtenstein, Clyfford Still, and Willem de Kooning, as well as artists using huge color swatches: large canvases by Mark Rothko, thirteen massively striped *Stations of the Cross* by Barnett Newman, and the primary colors of Ellsworth Kelly. The museum also features signature work by Robert Rauschenberg, Jasper Johns, and Claes Oldenburg, whose *Red (Hot) Drainpipe* is a huge, soft-red sculpture that looks as much like a drooping phallus as anything under the sink.

The work of Oldenburg and other sculptors is also on display between the National Gallery and the Natural History Museum in an outdoor **Sculpture Garden** (same hours as museum), that doubles as a winter ice rink. Here, a handful of appealing works are situated in a garden setting and crowned by a few key items: an original Art Nouveau arch from the Paris Metro of the early twentieth-century, and, again, one of Oldenburg's oversized pieces – in this case an old-fashioned typewriter eraser wheel blown up to elephantine size.

National Museum of the American Indian

Jefferson Drive between 3rd and 4th sts SW ☎202/357-2700, ⊛www.nmai .si.edu. Daily 10am–5.30pm. Opened to the public in September 2004, the National Museum of the American Indian is the newest of the Mall's many museums and is instantly recognizable by its curvaceous modern form with undulating walls the color of yellow earth – designed to represent the natural American landscape. Planned in the mid-1990s, the museum was nine years in development and occupies the last major site along the Mall. It's designed to recognize and honor the many tribes of native peoples who occupied the continent before the six-

▾NATIONAL MUSEUM OF THE AMERICAN INDIAN

▲WRIGHT FLYER, NATIONAL AIR AND SPACE MUSEUM

teenth- and seventeenth-century arrival of white settlers, including such groups and nations as the Iroquois, Sioux, Navajo, Cherokee, and countless others. The collections reach back thousands of years and incorporate nearly a million objects from nations spread out from Canada to Mexico; on display are woven garments, musical instruments, totem poles, artworks, kachina dolls, canoes, and ceremonial masks, headdresses, and outfits. The museum also sponsors periodic musical and dance events, along with lectures, films, and other cultural presentations.

National Air and Space Museum

Independence Ave and 6th St SW
℡202/357-2700, ⊛www.nasm.si.edu.
Daily 10am–5.30pm. If there's one museum people have heard about in DC, and just one they want to visit, it's the National Air and Space Museum. Since it opened in 1976, the museum has captured the imagination of almost ten million people every year, making it the most popular attraction in the city. The excitement begins in the entrance gallery, which throws together some of the most celebrated flying machines in history, from Lindbergh's *Spirit of St. Louis* and sound-barrier-breaking fighters to spy planes and satellites like Sputnik and Skylab, plus looming Cold War-era missiles. Although the huge institution has many high-ceilinged galleries stuffed with airplanes and aeronautic devices, it's most famous for two core exhibits. The first revolves around the *Wright Flyer*, the handmade plane in which the Wright Brothers made the first powered flight in December 1903 at Kitty Hawk, North Carolina. It's now on display in its own gallery, surrounded by other mementos of the Wright Brothers' inventive ways, including one of their rare bicycles – a product that they first started out making, understandably having no formal training as airplane designers. The other big-name gallery here is devoted to the Space Race – from the time John Glenn became the first American to orbit the earth with the launch of *Friendship 7* in 1962 (his spacesuit is preserved and on display), to Edward H. White's virgin space-walk in 1965 from

the two-seater *Gemini 4* craft, to the famous July 1969 landing when the minuscule *Apollo 11* command module reached the moon.

Fervent devotees of airplanes and spacecraft can also inquire at the museum about taking a shuttle ($7) to the newly opened Steven F. Udvar-Hazy Center, which has the same hours and free admission as its parent institution, though it's located in suburban Virginia. Here you can find everything – from the Blackbird spy plane to the Space Shuttle – that's too big even to fit into the main building on the Mall.

Hirshhorn Museum and Sculpture Garden

Independence Ave and 7th St SW ☎202/357-2700, ✆www.hirshhorn .si.edu. Daily 10am–5.30pm. The concrete cylinder of the Hirshhorn Museum, balanced on 15ft stilts above a sculpture-

▼HIRSHHORN MUSEUM

laden plaza, has been likened to everything from a monumental donut to a spaceship poised for takeoff. Inside is contained the Smithsonian's collection of late-nineteenth- and twentieth-century art, based on the bequest of Joseph H. Hirshhorn, who collected art on a massive scale: the original 1966 bequest was of 4000 paintings and 2600 sculptures; by the time of his death in 1981, the number had risen to more than 12,000 pieces.

Not surprisingly, American art makes a particularly good showing: there are portraits by John Singer Sargent, Mary Cassatt, and Thomas Eakins, as well as works by Winslow Homer, Albert Bierstadt, and Edward Hopper. There are also later pieces by the usual Abstract Expressionist heavyweights, in particular Willem de Kooning – the Hirshhorn collection of his work is one of the most impressive anywhere.

Meanwhile, the sculpture collection runs through the third floor, which starts with figurative paintings from the Victorian era and winds toward Abstract Expressionism and Pop Art; the collection is particularly strong on Henry Moore. Look out for *Kiln Man*, Robert Arneson's self-portrait as a brick chimney, with little cigar-smoking heads of the artist ready for firing inside. It's also hard to miss Nam June Paik's *Video Flag* (1985–96), composed of seventy 13-inch monitors, with a flurry of images spanning the presidents from Truman to Clinton, all the while managing to resemble a fluttering American flag. Particularly enticing is the work of Joseph Cornell, who is honored with an entire room devoted to his art boxes – little found objects and curiosities arrayed behind glass, the most enchanting of them being the *Medici Princess*. Less familiar artists also get their due, among them Lucas Samaras, whose forbidding *Book no. 6* is made of straight pins, and Giacomo Balla, whose vigorously jagged painted-metal pieces look just about ready to tear your hand off if you get too close.

Much of the Hirshhorn's monumental sculpture is contained in the Sculpture Garden, a sunken concrete arbor across Jefferson Drive on the Mall side of the museum. Works include Rodin's *Monument to the Burghers of Calais* and pieces by the likes of Matisse, Moore, Joan Miró, and David Smith. Of the lesser-known works, several stand out, like Gaston Lachaise's proud, bronze *Standing Woman (Heroic Woman)* from 1932. The garden's stagnant pond is fronted by Alexander Calder's *Six Dots over a Mountain* (1956); for a more impressive Calder, make for the museum entrance on Independence Avenue, where his *Two Disks* (1965) sit on five spidery legs tall enough for you to walk under.

National Museum of African Art

950 Independence Ave SW ☎202/357-2700, ◉www.africa.si.edu. Daily 10am-5.30pm. The nation's foremost collection of the traditional arts of sub-Saharan Africa, the National Museum of African Art occupies one of the Mall's most appeal-

ing buildings, its circular motifs and domes recalling a traditional African dwelling. The museum houses some six thousand sculptures and artifacts from a wide variety of cultures, displayed in permanent galleries and bolstered by special exhibitions. One particular highlight is the art of the Nubian trading city of Kerma, which flourished between 2500 and 1500 BC. On display are perfectly round ceramic bowls and delicate ivory animal figures from the ceremonial beds used to carry the dead to the cemetery for burial. Even better is the adjacent gallery's display of royal art from the Kingdom of Benin, home of Edo-speaking people in what is now Nigeria. It's a small collection of highly accomplished works relating to the rule of the Oba, or king, some dating back as far as the fifteenth century. The best pieces here are the copper alloy heads (made using the lost-wax casting technique), some of which depict an Oba, although one is of a defeated enemy. There's also a picture of the current Oba on the gallery wall, in resplendent orange, whose ceremonial headdress and neck-ruff echo those depicted on the copper heads – evidence that the same royal style has prevailed for more than five hundred years.

Other galleries cover peoples from Cameroon to Ghana, whose Asante people are depicted in sculpture with a seated male and female with disk-shaped heads, a form considered to be the aesthetic ideal. One of the most engaging works – a headrest from the Luba people of the Congo – is supported by two caryatid figures with their arms entwined. Finally, the "Art of the Personal Object" displays chairs, stools, and headrests, mostly carved from wood using an adze, as well as

▲ SMITHSONIAN CASTLE

assorted ivory snuff containers (two from Angola with stoppers shaped like human heads), beer straws (from Uganda), carved drinking horns, combs, pipes, spoons, baskets, and cups.

The Smithsonian Castle

1000 Jefferson Drive SW ☎ 202/357-2700, ⊛ www.si.edu. Daily 10am–5.30pm. Easily the most striking edifice on the Mall, the Smithsonian Institution Building is a marvel of ruddy brown sandstone, nave windows, and slender steeples – little surprise, then, that it's widely known as the Smithsonian Castle. Basically, it's the place where you can pick up all the information you need for touring the city's Smithsonian museums and check out models and diagrams of the original plans for Washington DC. More appealing for many visitors, though, are the lovely **Enid A. Haupt Gardens** outside, where you'll also find several topiary bison and well-tended plots of decorative flowers. It's a fitting holdover from the Victorian era, as is the adjoining **Art and Industries Building**, with its playful polychromatic brick-and-tile patterns. However, despite its historic value as one of the Smithsonian's founding structures, the building is undergoing renovation and won't to be open to the public any time soon.

National Museum of Asian Art

Jefferson Drive SW between 10th and 12th sts ☎ 202/357-2700, ⊛ www .asia.si.edu. Daily 10am–5.30pm. The last major institution along the Mall is the National Museum of Asian Art, which encompasses two buildings – the **Freer** and **Sackler galleries**. Formerly two distinct entities, these neighboring galleries have since been merged into one harmonious unit, which is most evident below ground, where the buildings are linked by a passageway. Sackler Gallery highlights include "The Arts of China," with its 3000-year-old Chinese bronzes, temple guard figures of the Tang Dynasty, and Qing Dynasty "scholar's rocks" – natural pieces of stone resembling mountains, meant to encourage lofty thoughts. The art of Silk Road-era cultures encompasses Syrian bowls, Persian plates, and Central Asian swords, while the South and Southeast Asian collection includes a third-century carved head of the Buddha; bronze, brass, and granite representations of Brahma, Vishnu, and Shiva; and a thirteenth-century stone carving of the elephant-headed Ganesha. The Freer Gallery is also quite appealing for anyone with an interest in non-Western art and design, especially its collection of Japanese art, which includes painted folding screens called *byobu*, which depict the seasons or themes from Japanese literature and range from two to ten panels long. Other choice items include a nineteenth-century porcelain dish shaped like Mount Fuji, a twelfth-century wooden Buddha, and gold-leaf Korean ceramics from the tenth to the fourteenth centuries. Other rooms are devoted to Chinese art, ranging from ancient jade burial goods to ornate bronzes, and a stunning series of objects adorned with calligraphy, from hand scrolls to jars, bowls, and even ceramic pillows. The South Asian art collection offers delicate temple sculpture, colorful devotional texts, and gold jewelry inset with rubies and diamonds. Finally, the Freer is also known for its cache of work by American artist James M. Whistler. Along with representative oils (the best are dark, moody, nocturnal waterscapes), the centerpiece is the Peacock Room, a monumental showpiece with blue-painted leather walls and murals representing fighting peacocks – claimed by the artist to represent the relationship of the painter and his patron.

PLACES The National Mall

▼ PEACOCK ROOM, FREER GALLERY OF ART

Capitol Hill

Capitol Hill is, famously, the focus of American lawmaking and a political showpiece without compare – the towering silhouette of the Capitol dome dominates the DC landscape. As a neighborhood, "the Hill" has a more unexpected side. While everyone knows of governmental powerhouses like the US Supreme Court and Library of Congress, less familiar are the casual restaurants and bars lining Pennsylvania Avenue SE, the curious wares of the Eastern Market, and the area's lovely pieces of historic architecture. On the north side of the Hill, Union Station still draws visitors by rail, while the nearby National Postal Museum is one of the Smithsonian's quiet triumphs. To the south, the US Botanic Garden offers a lush, colorful retreat once you've maxed out on museums.

US Capitol

East end of the Mall, between Constitution and Independence aves ☎202/225-6827 tours, ☎202/224-3121 general info, ❀www.aoc.gov. Daily tours 9am–4.30pm. As the focus of American democracy and the seat of the legislature, the white-ribbed dome of the Capitol sits between two similarly imposing edifices for the House of Representatives and the Senate. Though an inviting sight, at first glance it can seem quite daunting: the West Front is guarded and gated in the wake of 9/11, and visitors are not allowed

entrance without a building pass, while the East Front is being completely reconstructed to make way for a new underground visitors center, scheduled to open in 2006.

You'll soon arrive at the **Rotunda**, not only at the center of the US Capitol but point zero of the entire city. Some 180ft high and 96ft across, its dome is decorated by Constantino Brumidi's mighty fresco depicting the *Apotheosis of Washington*, which shows George Washington surrounded by symbols representing American democracy, arts, science, industry,

Visiting the US Capitol

You can access the building by dropping by (as early in the morning as possible) the Capitol Guide Service kiosk, near the southwest side of the complex (close to the James Garfield statue, 1st St SW at Maryland Ave), to obtain free tickets. From there, you'll wait at the South Visitor Receiving Facility, on the south side of the US House, until a tour commences.

For a chance to see the House and Senate chambers, American citizens can try applying to their representative's or senator's office in advance for a pass valid for the entire (two-year) session of Congress. For more information call ☎202/225-6827 or visit ❀www.house.gov or ❀www.senate.gov.

and the thirteen original states. Running around the Rotunda wall is a frieze celebrating American history, which starts with Columbus's arrival in the New World and finishes with Civil War scenes. Below the frieze hang eight large oil paintings, four depicting events associated with the colonization of the country – Columbus again, and the embarkation of the Pilgrims – though the most notable are the four of the Revolutionary War period by John Trumbull. Busts and statues of prominent American leaders fill in the gaps in the rest of the Rotunda: Washington, Jefferson, Lincoln, and Jackson are all here, along with a modern bust of Dr Martin Luther King Jr and a gold-and-glass facsimile of the Magna Carta. In such august surroundings, 29 prominent members of Congress, military leaders, and eminent citizens (including ten presidents from Lincoln to Reagan) have been laid in state before burial.

From the Rotunda, you move south into one of the earliest extensions of the building, which once housed the

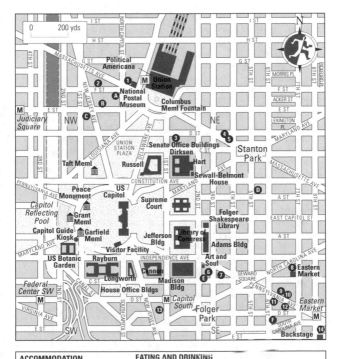

ACCOMMODATION			EATING AND DRINKING				
Bull Moose B&B	D		Bread and Chocolate	10	Las Placitas	14
Capitol Hill Suites	E		Bullfeathers	13	Market Lunch	8
Hereford House	F		Café Berlin	5	The Monocle	3
Hotel George	B		Capitol City Brewing Co.	1	Mr. Henry's	11
Hyatt Regency Capitol Hill	C		Capitol Lounge	6	Murky Coffee	9
Phoenix Park	A		Hawk 'n Dove	7	Remington's	12
			Kelly's Irish Times	2	Two Quail	4

▲GRANT MEMORIAL, WEST FRONT OF US CAPITOL

chamber of the House of Representatives. When the House moved into its new wing in 1857, the chamber saw a variety of temporary uses until Congress decided to invite each state to contribute two statues of its most famous citizens for display in a **National Statuary Hall**. Around forty are still on show here, with the recent focus being the Suffrage Monument, depicting women's-rights pioneers Susan B. Anthony, Lucretia Mott, and Elizabeth Cady Stanton poking their heads out of a large, uncut block of granite – one of only six statues of women in the entire building.

North of the Rotunda, the **Old Senate Chamber** was built in 1810 and reconstructed in 1819 after the British had burned down the Capitol in the War of 1812. The Senate met in this splendid semicircular gallery, with its embossed rose ceiling, until 1859, when it moved into its current quarters. The chamber then housed the Supreme Court until 1935, when it, too, was given a new building. After that the Old Senate Chamber lay largely unused until restored to its mid-nineteenth-century glory

in time for the Bicentennial. The members' desks today are reproductions, but the gilt eagle topping the vice president's chair is original, as is the portrait of George Washington by Rembrandt Peale. Contemporary engravings helped restorers reproduce other features of the original Senate chamber, like the rich red carpet emblazoned with gold stars.

Before 1810, the Senate met on the floor below the Old Senate Chamber, in a room that was revamped in 1819 to house the Supreme Court; the Court remained until 1860, before moving to the chamber just vacated by the Senate. The **Old Supreme Court Chamber** served as a law library until 1950, after which it too was restored to its mid-nineteenth-century appearance. Its dark, comfortable recesses resemble a gentleman's club – which, in many ways, it was. Some of the furnishings are original, including the desks, tables, and chairs, and the busts of the first five chief justices. On the same level as the Old Supreme Court Chamber, underneath the Rotunda, lies the **Crypt**. Lined with Doric columns, it was designed to house a tomb containing George Washington's body, a plan that was never realized. The Crypt instead serves as an exhibition center (provided it's open for tours), displaying the history of the Capitol's construction.

The visitors' galleries of the **House and Senate chambers** are not currently part of the official Capitol tour, and even if you do manage to gain entrance (see box p.68) the chambers may well be empty, or deep in torpor. Still, both are suitably grand: the House is more imposing, with its decorative frieze and oil paintings; from here the president addresses joint sessions of Congress, including the annual State of the Union speech. The Senate chamber is more widely recognized these days, as it was the setting for the 1999 impeachment trial of President Clinton.

▼NATIONAL STATUARY HALL, US CAPITOL

Legislative offices

Paradoxically perhaps, you can get a lot closer to senators and representatives in their own offices than you can in the Capitol itself, and access to these buildings is usually quite open, consisting mainly of guards and scanners. These six office buildings are also where most of the

day-to-day political activity takes place in committee rooms – named for politicians and built from 1908 to 1982 – where the hearings have been open to the public since the 1970s. The Senate office buildings (Russell, Dirksen, and Hart) are north of the Capitol, and the House offices (Cannon, Longworth, and Rayburn) are south. Committee hearings (usually held in the morning) are listed in the *Washington Post*'s "Today in Congress" section: unless you turn up early, you may not get in, especially to anything featured on the TV news.

Grant Memorial

Contrary to what you might expect, the West Front of the Capitol is not graced with a statue of Washington, Lincoln, Jefferson, or anyone else considered to have been a great chief executive, but instead one of the country's worst presidents: Ulysses S. Grant. Of course, Grant's presence is due to his successful generalship in the Civil War, not his scandal-plagued presidency. True to form, the "Galena Tanner" rides a noble steed on a marble pedestal and looks to the west at the National Mall, while directly below the Capitol Reflecting Pool provides a nice spot for relaxation and a good mirror image of the Capitol. The Grant Memorial is quite a stirring sight, with the general guarded by lions and looming above sculptures of an artillery unit moving through thick mud into battle (south side) and a charg-

▲ PALM HOUSE, US BOTANIC GARDEN

ing cavalry unit (north side).
Sculptor Henry Merwin Shrady
spent twenty years on the work,
using uniformed soldiers in
training as his models.

US Botanic Garden

245 1st St SW ☏ 202/225-8333,
ⓦ www.usbg.gov. Daily 10am–5pm.
The US Botanic Garden sits
near a corner of – but not
directly on – the National Mall,
and is always a popular site for
touring the country's horticul-
tural highlights. The centerpiece
is a Conservatory crowned
by an eighty-foot-tall Palm
House, the results of a recent
renovation that transformed the
Victorian-style structure, built
in 1933, into a state-of-the-art
greenhouse – where it's now
possible to grow plants from
almost everywhere in the world.
More than four thousand plants
are now resident here and on
display, and include several climate-controlled rooms devoted
to colorful ranks of tropical,
subtropical, and desert plants.
Especially intriguing are the section showcasing orchids, where
two hundred of the garden's
twelve thousand varieties are
visible at any one time, and
the Jungle Room, stuffed with
equatorial trees and other plants
and humid almost to the point
of discomfort.

US Supreme Court

1st St and Maryland
Ave NE ☏ 202/479-
3211, ⓦ www.scus
.gov. Mon–Fri 9am–
4.30pm. The third
– and easily the
most respected –
branch of Ameri-
can government,
the judiciary, has
its apex at the
US Supreme
Court. Not only is the court
the final judge of what is and
isn't constitutional, it's also the
nation's final arbiter for disputes between states, the federal
government and states, federal
and state judges, and individuals
fighting all kinds of government
decisions, from boundary disputes to death-penalty appeals.
Although the court has moved
around to different chambers
over many decades, in the 1930s
it got its own home, a grand
Greek Revival edifice created
by Cass Gilbert, emblazoned
with the weighty motto "Equal
Justice Under Law." Outside,
the building positively glistens
as natural light bounces off the
bright white marble, while the
wide steps down to 1st Street
are flanked by sculptures of the
Contemplation of Justice and
the Guardian of Law.
  Inside, the main corridor
– known as the Great Hall
– features a superb carved
and painted ceiling of floral
plaques, while its white walls
are lined with marble columns,
interspersed with busts of all
the former chief justices. At
the end of the corridor is the
surprisingly compact Court
Chamber, flanked by more
marble columns and decorated
with damask drapes and a
molded plaster ceiling lined in

gold leaf. When in session, the Chief Justice sits in the center of the bench (below the clock), with the most senior justice on the right and the next in precedence on the left; the rest sit in similar alternating fashion. Curiously, the justices' chairs are made in the Court's own carpentry shop.

The Court is in session from October through June. Between the beginning of October and the end of April, oral arguments are heard every Monday, Tuesday, and Wednesday from 10am to noon and 1pm to 3pm for two weeks each month. The sessions, which almost always last one hour per case, are open to the public on a first-come, first-served basis: arrive by 8.30am to be sure of getting one of the 150 seats. Most casual visitors simply join the separate line, happy to settle for a three-minute stroll through the standing gallery. When Court is not in session, guides give informative lectures in the Court Chamber (Mon–Fri 9.30am–3.30pm; hourly on the half-hour).

▼US SUPREME COURT

PLACES Capitol Hill

Library of Congress

1st St SE at Independence Ave
☏202/707-8000, ⊛www.loc.gov.
Mon–Sat 10am–5.30pm. Based on the original collection of Thomas Jefferson, the Library of Congress has since 1870 been the nation's official copyright library – adding to its shelves a copy of every book published and registered in the United States. Since then, it has become the world's largest library, and with time and technological progress books became just a part of its unimaginably large collection. Today, 110 million items (from books, maps, and manuscripts to movies, musical instruments, and photographs) are kept on 600 miles of shelving spread out over three buildings; it's said that on average ten items a minute are added to the library's holdings – where they stay, as the Library of Congress does not circulate its materials beyond the complex. If you're here to do research, you can register at the Jefferson Building (the main, classical structure on 1st Street) by providing a copy of your driver's license or passport; anyone over 18 is allowed admittance to the domed octagonal Reading Room – adorned with hundreds of mosaics, murals, and sculptures – provided they go through the proper security procedures.

Otherwise, you can wander around yourself or take one of the free library tours (Mon–Sat 10.30am, 11.30am, 1.30pm, 2.30pm & 3.30pm; last tour Sat 2.30pm), which are, unfortunately, more popular than you'd expect and involve some rather long lines during the high season. You'll miss the Reading Room and have to be content with the beautifully vaulted Great Hall, rich with marble walls and numerous medallions, inscriptions, murals, and inlaid mosaics. The other highlight is on the second floor in the "American Treasures" gallery, where themed cabinets – "Civil Society," "Mapping," "Invention and Film," "Technology," and so on – display some of the nation's most significant documents. The exhibits are periodically rotated, but you'll encounter such diverse pieces as Walt Whitman's Civil War notebooks, the original manuscript of Martin Luther King Jr's "I Have A Dream" speech, a copy of Francis Scott Key's "Star-Spangled Banner," and a multitude of music scores, historic photographs, early recordings, magazines, and baseball cards.

Sewall-Belmont House

144 Constitution Ave NE ☎202/546-1210, ⊛www.sewallbelmont.org. Tues–Fri 11am–3pm, Sat noon–4pm. $3. North of the Supreme Court, the red-brick edifice known as the Sewall-Belmont House is among the oldest private residences in the city, built in 1800 by Robert Sewall. The British tried to burn it down in the War of 1812, but unlike the Capitol, it wasn't too badly damaged; enough survived, in fact, for the Treaty of Ghent – the document that ended the war – to be negotiated here. In 1929, the house was sold to the National Woman's Party and was home for many years to Alice Paul, the party's founder and author of the 1923 Equal Rights Amendment. The house is still the party headquarters and maintains a museum and gallery dedicated to the country's women's and suffrage movements. A short film fills in some of the background, after which you'll be

escorted around on a short tour that makes much of the period furnishings; the carriage house, one of the oldest parts of the building, contains the country's earliest feminist library. There are portraits, busts, and photographs of all the best-known activists; other mementos of the famous include the desks of both Alice Paul and Susan B. Anthony, while over the staircase hangs the banner used to picket the White House during World War I as the clamor for universal suffrage reached its apex. The building recently secured $1 million to complete an overdue renovation to preserve its internal structure, and may be periodically closed in coming years.

Folger Shakespeare Library

201 E Capitol St ☎202/544-7077, ⊛www.folger.edu. Mon–Sat 10am–4pm, free 90min guided tours Mon–Fri 11am, Sat 11am & 1pm. The renowned Folger Shakespeare Library provides an unexpected burst of Art Deco architecture, with a sparkling white marble facade split by geometric window grilles and reliefs depicting scenes from the Bard's plays. Inside, however, the expansive 1930s mood is immediately transformed by a dark oak-paneled Elizabethan Great Hall, featuring carved lintels, stained glass, Tudor roses, and a fine, sculpted ceiling. Founded in 1932, the Folger holds more than 300,000 books, manuscripts, paintings, and engravings, accessible to scholars, and has evolved over the decades into a celebration of Shakespearean culture. The Great Hall displays changing exhibitions about the playwright and Elizabethan themes; the reproduction Elizabethan Theater hosts lectures

and readings as well as medieval and Renaissance music concerts by the Folger Consort; there's even an Elizabethan garden outside on the east lawn, growing herbs and flowers common in gardens of the sixteenth century. The library itself – another masterfully reproduced sixteenth-century room – is open to the public only during the Folger's annual celebration of Shakespeare's birthday (usually the Saturday nearest April 23).

Pennsylvania Avenue SE

To most visitors the section of Pennsylvania Avenue running southeast from the Capitol will be much less familiar than the stretch running northwest from it, site of the presidential inaugural parade. Still, over the course of six blocks or so, you can find a good collection of some of the District's more appealing ethnic restaurants and noteworthy bars – practically the only decent food and drink

▼ PENNSYLVANIA AVE SE

to be found in the vicinity – amid a gentrifying scene that attracts increasing numbers of yuppies looking for affordable digs; you'll also see Congressional staff out for a break from the Capitol Hill grind. The avenue runs through some historically important architecture, the likes of nineteenth-century townhouses and preserved Georgian buildings. Keep in mind that while there's a convenient Metro stop here ("Eastern Market" station on the Blue and Orange lines), it's worth being wary after dark – this was where Supreme Court justice David Souter was mugged in 2004, not far from his home.

Eastern Market

7th and C sts SE ⓦ www.easternmarket .net. Tues–Fri 10am–6pm, Sat 8am–6pm, Sun 8am–4pm. If you're taking a stroll east of the Capitol, you may wonder what all the hubbub is around what looks like an ancient brick rail station. This forbidding windowless 1873 structure has nothing to do with trains, but has long been the major commercial hub of the Eastern Market. Designed by Adolph Cluss with less flamboyance than his Arts and Industries Building on the Mall, the market is home to a welter of vendors doing roaring business selling seafood, deli meats, sides of beef, and other foodstuffs. On the weekend, the stalls spill onto the sidewalk, when you can buy produce and flowers (Sat 10am–5pm) or antiques and junk (Sun 10am–5pm). On either side of the market along 7th Street, delis, coffeeshops, and antique and clothing stores make this one of the more appealing hangouts on the Hill – though like Pennsylvania Avenue SE, the place is best avoided after dark.

76

PLACES

Capitol Hill

National Postal Museum

Massachusetts Ave NE at N Capitol Ave ☎202/357-2700, ⊛www.si.edu/postal. Daily 10am–5.30pm. One of the more obscure Smithsonian sites, the National Postal Museum is more engaging than you might expect. Done up in white Italian marble, the interior was the home of the City Post Office

▲EASTERN MARKET

Union Station

50 Massachusetts Ave NE. The magnificent Beaux Arts structure of Union Station is a sight to behold. Some 20,000 square feet larger than New York's Grand Central Terminal, the station's monumental proportions are alive with skylights, marble detail, and statuary, culminating in a 96-foot-high coffered ceiling whose model was no less than ancient Rome's Baths of Diocletian. For five decades, Union Station sat at the head of an expanding railroad network, and hundreds of thousands of people arrived in the city by train, catching their first glimpse of the Capitol dome through the station's great arched doors – just as the wide-eyed James Stewart does at the beginning of Frank Capra's *Mr. Smith Goes to Washington*. These days, Union Station is slowly recovering from several decades of automotive-age neglect but does feature a gallery food court, movie theater, stores, restaurants, money-exchange offices, car rental agencies, and ticket counters – along with an underground Metro station and active rail sheds for Amtrak and MARC trains.

until 1986. Nowadays, its lower levels display the history of the US mail system with, naturally, many collections of stamps, as well as more elaborate exhibits showing archaic means of delivery like a rickety Concord coach and three biplanes hanging from the ceiling. You can also follow the first postal routes, such as the seventeenth-century King's Best Highway between New York and Boston, and check out artifacts from the Pony Express and creaky old mail coaches and other relics. Beyond this, photos and text trace the early racial makeup of the postal service, from the opportunities offered to blacks during Reconstruction to the segregation of the early twentieth century. Elsewhere, there are oddball castoffs such as a collection of weird and wonderful rural mailboxes, including one peculiar example made from car mufflers in the shape of a crude tin man.

Shops

Art and Soul

225 Pennsylvania Ave SE ☎202/548-0105. Handmade clothes and contemporary American ceramics, toys, and crafts by more than two hundred regional artists.

Backstage
545 8th St SE ☎202/544-5744.
Whether you're at a loss on
Halloween or looking for an
elaborate disguise, this costume
shop – teeming with wigs, boas,
and catsuits – just may be able
to help. Also features books on
the theater and make-up, masks,
and dance shoes.

Political Americana
50 Massachusetts Ave NE ☎202/547-
1685. Located in Union Station,
a good spot to pick up everything from historic and topical
buttons and bumper stickers to
gifts, books, and videos on every
side of the political divide.

Cafés

Bread and Chocolate
666 Pennsylvania Ave SE ☎202/547-
2875. Popular bakery and coffee-
house with street-view seating
and solid sandwiches, located
along this strip's main people-
watching zone.

The Market Lunch
Eastern Market, 7th St SE ☎202/547-
8444. Eat-and-go market-coun-
ter meals – sandwiches and
fries, salads, crab cakes, and
fish platters – served to a loyal
band of local shoppers and
suit-and-tie staffers. Arrive early

for lunch or you'll be waiting
in line.

Murky Coffee
660 Pennsylvania Ave SE ☎202/546-
5228. Styled after Italian brew-
making, espresso drinks that
pack an authentic punch and are
straight-up black – not murky.
Also sells pastries and coffee by
the pound.

Restaurants

Cafe Berlin
322 Massachusetts Ave NE ☎202/543-
7656. The perfect, not-too-
pricey spot to fill up on your
favorite gut-busting German
food, with all the staples from
pork Jaegerschnitzel and savory
potato pancakes to spiced her-
ring with onions and apples.

Las Placitas
517 8th St SE ☎202/543-3700.
Great-value Mexican standards
and Salvadoran specials pack the
tables nightly at this no-nonsense eatery. Another Capitol
Hill branch at 723 8th St SE
(☎202/546-9340).

The Monocle
107 D St NE ☎202/546-4488.
Although some criticize this
elegant, somewhat pricey
saloon-bar-restaurant as stuffy,

PLACES Capitol Hill

▼UNION STATION

that's likely what draws the congressional patrons, who duck in for savory crab cakes, steaks, and the like in between votes.

Mr Henry's
601 Pennsylvania Ave SE ☎202/546-8412. Saloon and restaurant with outside patio, charcoal grill, and loyal gay crowd. Even the most expensive choices – the steak and shrimp plates – are typically below $10.

Two Quail
320 Massachusetts Ave NE ☎202/543-8030. Spread over a trio of townhouses, this romantic little bistro serves a changing menu of California Cuisine-styled food, including dinner entrees such as Cornish game hen with chipotle sauce. Lunches are a deal at $10–15.

Bars

Bullfeathers
410 1st St SE ☎202/543-5005. Pol-watchers just may catch a sighting at this old-time Hill favorite, a dark and clubby spot with affordable beer. It's named for Teddy Roosevelt's favorite euphemism for bullshit during his White House days.

Capitol City Brewing Company
2 Massachusetts Ave NE ☎202/842-2337. Prime microbrewing turf, which offers average pub food but solid handcrafted beer, highlighted by the rich Amber Waves Ale and German-styled Capitol Kolsch and Prohibition Porter. Another branch in Old Downtown, 1100 New York Ave NW (☎202/628-2222).

Capitol Lounge
229 Pennsylvania Ave SE ☎202/547-2098. More sophisticated than most of the Hill bars – with cigars and martinis in the downstairs bar – but there's still plenty of life up in the brick-walled saloon thanks to happy hours and colorful campaign memorabilia.

Hawk 'n' Dove
329 Pennsylvania Ave SE ☎202/543-3300. Famous old pub, a bit tatty at the edges now, hung with football pennants, bottles, and bric-a-brac. The young, loud crowd comes (depending on the night) for the cheap beer, half-price food, or Redskins football on TV.

Clubs and live music

Kelly's Irish Times
14 F St NW ☎202/543-5433. Colorful folk music sets the stage from Wednesday to Sunday nights at this boisterous Irish pub, which also features weekend club music on the downstairs dance floor.

Remington's
639 Pennsylvania Ave SE ☎202/543-3113, ⊛www.remingtonswdc.com. Signature gay country-and-western club with four bars and two dance floors, where the events include cornpone singing competitions, spirited hoe-downs, and "cowgirl"-themed drag pageants.

South of the Mall

Since the axis of the National Mall and Capitol Hill is the inevitable focus for most visitors, it's not surprising that other areas in the vicinity are often ignored. The area south of the Mall, along the Potomac and Anacostia rivers, is one such place – and it's easy to understand why: the assorted sights are not united by much other than their proximity to the water and to a handy collection of Metro stations. That said, several are well worth a look, including the Holocaust Museum and the Bureau of Engraving and Printing; the Fish Wharf on the Potomac waterfront; the Navy Museum with its cache of nautical artifacts; and the Frederick Douglass National Historic Site and Anacostia Museum in Anacostia. One of Washington's oldest neighborhoods, Anacostia is unfortunately also one of its most notorious – its pair of attractions are best reached by cab during the day from the Anacostia Metro station.

US Holocaust Memorial Museum

14th St between C St and Independence Ave SW ☎ 202/488-0400, ⓦ www.ushmm.org. Daily 10am–5.30pm. One of the city's most disturbing and unforgettable museums is the US Holocaust Memorial Museum, which opened in 1993 and has since been praised for both the penetrating character of its exhibits and its stark architecture, meant to recall a concentration camp in a stripped-down modernist idiom. The museum, of course, is a close-up examination of the persecution and murder of six million Jews by the Nazis and is aimed at those with both a full understanding or only a sketchy knowledge of this dark period in Western history. Note that despite its bleak subject matter, the museum is one of the more popular attractions in DC, and crowding can be a problem. Tickets for fixed entry times are available free (limited to four

per person) from 10am each day at the 14th Street entrance; you can also book in advance through Tickets.com (☎ 1-800/400-9373). If you arrive without a ticket any later than

▼ US HOLOCAUST MEMORIAL MUSEUM

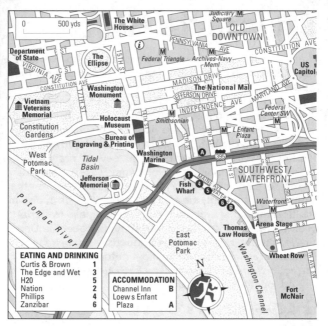

EATING AND DRINKING

Curtis & Brown	1
The Edge and Wet	3
H2O	5
Nation	2
Phillips	4
Zanzibar	6

ACCOMMODATION

Channel Inn	B
Loew s Enfant Plaza	A

mid-morning, you're unlikely to get into the permanent exhibition – the centerpiece of the museum, focusing on the core events of the Holocaust. Beyond this, there are usually temporary displays that are open to all, covering such topics as children's lives under Nazi rule and the grim specter of "doctors" such as Josef Mengele.

Upon entry, each visitor is given an ID card, containing biographical notes of a real Holocaust victim, whose fortunes are followed as the museum unfolds. The permanent exhibition is spread over the second, third, and fourth floors; you start at the top and work your way down, proceeding through the nightmarish history of Europe in the 1930s and on to World War II, when Adolf Hitler and his henchmen carried out their plans for the "Thousand Year

Reich" though the massacre of millions of Jews and other victims, including gypsies, gays, racial minorities, Slavs, and the mentally and physically disabled. This horrifying story unfolds as you continue downward (ending with Hitler's genocidal attempt at a "Final Solution"), and the dark mood is reflected by the museum's design, overseen in part by Holocaust survivors. Half-lit chambers, a floor of ghetto cobblestones, an obscenely cramped barracks building, and an external roofline that resembles the guard towers of a concentration camp all add to the overwhelming feeling of oppression. The themed displays are a mix of personal possessions and photographs alongside historical montages and video presentations, before which visitors stand visibly moved.

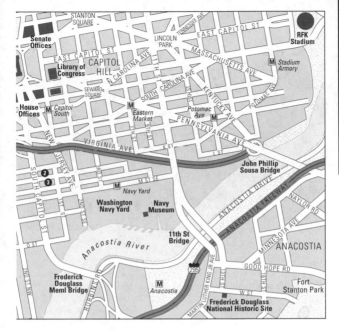

Bureau of Engraving and Printing

14th and C sts SW ☎202/622-2000, ⓦwww.moneyfactory.com. Mon–Fri 10am–2pm. The lone worthwhile entry among the bureaucratic superstructures east of 14th Street and south of Independence Avenue may sound a bit dry, but the Bureau offers up one of DC's most popular tours, featuring a twenty-minute look at what is, effectively, a large printing plant. The difference is that the presses here crank out millions of dollars in currency every day, $120 billion a year (95 percent of which is replacement currency for money already in circulation). As you will no doubt learn in an introductory video, the Bureau is the federal agency for designing and printing all US currency, government securities, and postage stamps. It was established in

1862, when Abraham Lincoln empowered six employees to start up business in the attic of the Treasury Building. By 1877 all US currency was produced by the Bureau, which finally moved into this building in 1914. Nowadays, almost three thousand employees work either here or at a second plant in Fort Worth, Texas. The style of US currency has, of course, changed radically in the last 140 years, and bills these days are being redesigned with all manner of newfangled high-tech methods to deter counterfeiters – color-changing inks, hidden security stamps, watermarks, and micro-printing.

Your perspective on all this money-making comes through claustrophobic viewing galleries looking down upon the printing presses. It's a surprisingly low-tech operation: hand-engraved

▲FISH WHARF

dyes are used to create intaglio steel plates, from which the bills are printed in sheets of 32, checked for defects, and loaded into large barrows. On a separate press, they're then overprinted with serial numbers and seals, sliced up into single bills by ordinary paper cutters, and stacked into "bricks" of four thousand notes before being sent out to the twelve Federal Reserve Districts, which issue the notes to local banks. It's little wonder the presses never stop: the lowliest bill, the humble dollar, lasts an average of no more than eighteen months.

The waterfront

Running due southeast from 14th Street along the Washington channel of the Potomac River, the DC waterfront was originally built around a series of haphazardly developed commercial buildings and piers, which grew up at some remove from the central city in the nineteenth century. These were finally redeveloped during the 1960s. Although the area is hardly a must-see, it is worth-

while for a stroll or a bite. Most people come here to eat seafood at one of the restaurants that line the waters of the Channel, along Maine Avenue or the parallel Water Street SW, west of 7th; all have terraces and patios with views across to East Potomac Park. The district even has its own Metro stop, at 4th and M, which provides for much easier access than if you try to arrive on foot, dodging the maelstrom of automotive traffic around the freeways southeast of the Tidal Basin.

Washington Marina and Fish Wharf

Beyond restaurants, the two main waterfront attractions are located next to each other, near the towering Francis Case Bridge, which crosses the Channel to the pleasant, if isolated, East Potomac Park. North of the bridge, a collection of pricey nautical craft is on view at the Washington Marina, which provides a good backdrop for various summer fairs and events, though is typically off limits to landlubbers. South of the bridge lies the Fish Wharf (daily 7.30am–8pm), the oldest continuously operated fish market in America, conducted from permanently docked boats and trailers. The fishmongers will do their best to sell you their wares, even if you're not buying, and display huge trays of Chesapeake Bay fish, shrimp, clams, oysters, and, especially, Maryland blue crabs, which you can buy live or steamed. There's nowhere to sit and eat, but there's nothing to stop you from heading down the waterside promenade for a picnic.

Thomas Law House and Wheat Row

N and 6th sts SW and 1315–1321 4th St SW, respectively. There are a few pockets of interesting architecture near the waterfront, best seen opposite the Spirit Cruises dock, where the Thomas Law House (built c.1794–96) is one of DC's oldest surviving federal townhouses and has a stately presence that belies its owner's bankruptcy shortly after he built it. If you cut through past here to 4th Street, you can see another strip of federal houses built around the same time, called Wheat Row and maintained within the Harbor Square development at 4th between N and O streets. The structures are elegant gems of early-American design and are also unique for being local survivors of 1960s urban renewal (the rest of the neighborhood is blandly modern) as well as some of the first edifices built on speculation, with the promise of rising property values to come. Unfortunately, no historic buildings along here are open to the public, and the same is true with Fort McNair, a few blocks south, famous as the spot where a penitentiary housed the conspirators in the Lincoln assassi-

nation as they were imprisoned, tried, and executed.

Navy Yard and Navy Museum

805 Kidder Breese St SE ☎ 202/433-4882, ⊛ www.history.navy.mil. Mon–Fri 9am–4pm, Sat & Sun 10am–5pm. The Navy Yard is the US Navy's oldest shore establishment, building ships and producing weaponry continuously from 1799 until 1961. The Yard's activity was interrupted only in 1812 when the commander was ordered to burn the base to prevent the British capturing it. Since the 1960s the base has acted as a naval supply and administrative center and would be of little interest were it not for its splendid Navy Museum. Unless you're an active member of the military, to get access you must reserve in advance at the above telephone number; once you arrive in the Yard, you can find the museum housed in Building 76.

This focused and illuminating collection traces the history of the US Navy from its foundation in 1794, in response to attacks on American ships by Barbary pirates. Dress uniforms, ship figureheads, vicious cat-o'-nine-tail whips, and a walk-through frigate gun-

▼NAVY MUSEUM

deck all illustrate the gradual development of the Navy as a fighting force, while separate galleries deal with every conflict the Navy has taken part in. A painting illustrates the exploits of early naval hero Stephen Decatur (see p.91), who captured three boats during hand-to-hand fighting at Tripoli in 1804. The World War II displays are particularly affecting, featuring anti-aircraft guns in which you can sit, crackly archival film footage, and an account of the sinking by a Japanese destroyer of a PT109 patrol boat – the famous incident in which future president John Kennedy swam ashore towing the boat's badly burned engineer. Also meriting a look is the *USS Barry*, a destroyer docked outside the museum, whose mess room, bridge, and quarters are open to the public.

Frederick Douglass National Historic Site

1411 W St SE ☎202/426-5961, ⓦwww.nps.gov/frdo. Daily May–Sept 9am–5pm, Oct–April 9am–4pm. An undeniable attraction if you're at all interested in American history, and deserving of the effort you'll need to make to get to it (by car, Metro, or taxi), the Frederick Douglass National Historic Site occupies the home of the famed orator and abolitionist leader. He was 60 in 1877 when he moved to this white brick house in Anacostia, and its mixed Gothic Revival–Italianate style, with 21 rooms and 15 acres, was typical of the quality homes built in Uniontown twenty years earlier – though at that time they were restricted to whites. Douglass, newly appointed US marshal in DC, was the first to break the racial ban, paying $6700 for the property and living out the last eighteen years of his life here.

You can reserve a place on one of the free hourly tours of the house by calling ☎1-800/967-2283 ($2 handling fee). The tours begin in the visitor center below the house, where a short docudrama and a few static exhibits fill you in on Douglass's life. You're then led up the steep green hill to the home itself, where Douglass entertained all the leading abolitionists and suffragists of the day, talking in the parlors or eating in the dining room.

▼FREDERICK DOUGLASS NATIONAL HISTORIC SITE

Many brought him mementos, which are now on display – there's President Lincoln's cane, given to Douglass by Mary Todd Lincoln, and a desk and chair from Harriet Beecher Stowe. Most of the fixtures and fittings are original and give a fair idea of middle-class life in late nineteenth-century Washington. Douglass kept chickens and goats outside in the gardens, and the only water source was a rainwater pump, but inside the kitchen the domestic staff had access to all the latest technology, like the Universal clothes wringer. Douglass himself worked either in his study, surrounded by hundreds of books, or in the outdoor "Growlery" – a rudimentary stone cabin he used for solitary contemplation.

Anacostia Museum

1901 Fort Place SE ☏202/287-2061, ⊛www.si.edu/anacostia. Daily 10am–5pm. Though well off the beaten path, the Smithsonian's Anacostia Museum certainly rewards a visit. Still, don't even think about walking here from the Anacostia Metro stop; buses #W2 or #W3 from Howard Road (outside the Metro) stop at the museum, though it's less unnerving to come by taxi. The museum's official mission, as the Center for African American History and Culture, is to devote itself to recording and displaying the life of blacks in America, but particularly the upper South (DC, Maryland, Virginia, and the Carolinas). The museum's permanent collection is mostly historical in nature, holding documents, photographs, books, and objects such as the fur coat opera singer Marian Anderson wore to her famed 1939 concert on the steps of the Lincoln Memorial, after she was denied permission to sing at Constitution Hall by the racially hidebound Daughters of the American Revolution. There's also a small art collection – a sampling of paintings and prints by local artists like Samella Lewis, John Robinson, and Elena Bland; works by folk artist Leslie Payne; and a contemporary quilt collection that touches on both folk and formal art. The museum is perhaps best known, however, for its themed temporary exhibitions (held here and at the Arts and Industries Building on the Mall). Call or check the website to see what's on, or ask for details at the Smithsonian Castle on the Mall (see p.66). Keep in mind that during the installation of new exhibits, the museum may be closed for weeks at a time or longer.

▼ANACOSTIA MUSEUM

Restaurants

Custis & Brown

1200 Maine Ave SW ☎202/484-0168.
A signature Fish Wharf seafood
stand serving giant fried-fish
sandwiches, steamed spiced
shrimp, crab, and lobster, clam
chowder, and oyster platters
to go – all at giveaway prices.
Great for a lunch or picnic
overlooking the Washington
Channel.

H2O

800 Water St SW ☎202/484-6300.
One of the few decent choices
in an area not known for its eateries, a marina restaurant with
swanky, newly remodeled decor,
and attached lounge and stylish
club. The appealing river view is
the main attraction, along with
tasteful, semi-expensive entrees
of crab cakes, steak, and pasta.

Phillips

900 Water St SW ☎202/488-8515.
Another popular seafood spot
on the tour-bus circuit, mainly
worthwhile for those looking to
pack away big, reasonably priced
helpings of fish and crab from
the lunch, dinner, and weekend
brunch buffets. Good location
not far from the Fish Wharf.

Clubs and live music

The Edge and Wet

56 L St SE ☎202/488-1200, ⊕www
.edgewet.com. Frenetic gay-oriented club with multiple bars
and special dance nights – the
Edge is home to Gay Black

Pride, while Wet has foam parties, nude dancing, and other
activities.

Nation

1015 Half St SE ☎202/554-1500,
⊕www.velvetnation.com. A hot,
two-floored club that draws
revelers to a dicey part of town.
During the week you're apt to
hear a broad selection of bands
and artists, while the weekend
brings dance nights, highlighted
by superstar DJs at Velvet Nation
on Saturdays.

Zanzibar on the Waterfront

700 Water St SW ☎202/554-9100.
Waterfront restaurant with a
view draws the international
crowd with live bands and DJs
spinning salsa, R&B, reggae,
and jazz. Also not a bad spot to
watch a sunset.

Performing arts

Arena Stage

1101 6th St SW ☎202/554-9066,
⊕www.arenastage.org. One of the
most popular and well-respected
of DC's major theatrical institutions and a centerpiece of
waterfront redevelopment.
Presents an eclectic selection of
modern, classical, musical, and
avant-garde works on its three
stages.

RFK Stadium

2400 E Capitol St SE ☎202/547-
9077. The former home of the
Washington Redskins is the
place to see DC United soccer games and in 2005 will
become the temporary home of
Washington's new baseball team
(relocated from Montreal).

The White House and Foggy Bottom

The White House is one of Washington's star attractions, and countless throngs proceed past its gates every year, trying to sneak a peek at the commander in chief. Directly aligned with the Jefferson Memorial, and almost so with the Washington Monument, the White House was always intended to be a focal point of the District, even though these days the current occupants do their best to keep people at a distance. The adjacent area known as Foggy Bottom has much to offer by way of culture and history. Along with being a center for international relations (the State Department, World Bank, and IMF are located here), it has some excellent museums and classic architecture, as well as the Kennedy Center and Watergate Complex.

The White House

1600 Pennsylvania Ave NW ☎202/456-7041, ⊛www.whitehouse.gov. Tues–Sat 7.30–11.30am. The core of the self-guided tour of the White House concentrates on the rooms on the ground and state (principal) floors. The Oval Office, family apartments, and private offices on the second and third floors are off-limits; posted guards make sure you don't stray from the designated route. Once inside, your group is allowed to wander one-way through or past a half-dozen furnished rooms – but in many rooms you can't get close enough to appreciate the paintings or the furniture. Most people are outside again well within thirty minutes.

Visitors enter the East Wing from the ground floor and traipse first past the Federal-style Library, paneled in timbers

Visiting the White House

Increasing levels of national security have meant that, with each year that passes since 9/11, regulations for visitors to the White House have only gotten stiffer. Currently, you must reserve tours a month in advance through your Congressional member (representative or senator), and only parties of ten or more are granted access. If you're a foreign citizen, you must seek access through your own embassy in Washington DC; see p.193 for a list. Before your scheduled tour date, call ahead to verify that daily schedules have not changed in the interim since you made the reservation. For more information on this and other touring opportunities in the District (and to check schedules and security requirements) head to the White House Visitor Center, which is housed within the Department of Commerce, located several blocks southeast of the White House at 1450 Pennsylvania Ave NW ☎202/208-1631, ⊛www.nps.gov/whho (daily 7.30am–4pm).

▲THE WHITE HOUSE

rescued from a mid-nineteenth-century refit and housing 2700 books by American authors. Opposite is the Vermeil Room, once a billiard room but now named for its extensive collection of silver gilt; the portraits are of recent First Ladies. From here the tour moves upstairs to the State Floor, where the

EATING AND DRINKING

Aquarelle	10
Art Gallery Bar & Grille	3
Breadline	11
Capitol Grounds	6
Dish	5
Froggy Bottom Pub	4
Kinkhead's	8
Marshall's	2
Melrose	1
Nectar	9
Primi Piatti	7

first stop is the East Room, the largest in the White House, which has been open to the public since the days of Andrew Jackson. Used in the past for weddings and other ceremonies, it's on a grand scale, with long yellow drapes, a brown marble fireplace, and turn-of-the-century glass chandeliers. Between the fireplaces hangs the one major artwork on display: Gilbert Stuart's celebrated 1797 portrait of George Washington, rescued from the flames by Dolley Madison when the British burned the White House. The last rooms on the tour are more intimate in scale. The Green Room, its walls lined in silk, was Jefferson's dining room and JFK's favorite in the entire house. Portraits line the walls, Dolley Madison's French candlesticks are on the mantelpiece, and a fine matching green dinner service occupies the cabinet. The adjacent, oval Blue Room, with its ornate French furniture, witnessed the marriage of Grover Cleveland in 1886, the only time a president has been married in the White House. The Red Room is the smallest of the lot, decorated in early nineteenth-century Empire style and sporting attractive inlaid oak doors. The painted-oak-paneled State Dining Room harks back to the

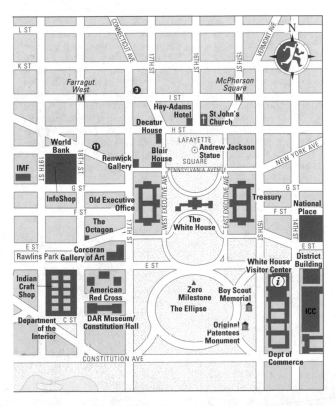

White House architecture

From the outset, the White House was to be the focal point of the executive branch of government, connected to the proposed US Capitol by the broad diagonal sweep of Pennsylvania Avenue. Its design was thrown open to an architectural competition in 1792, and the winner, Irish immigrant and professional builder James Hoban, picked up a $500 prize for his Neoclassical design, which was influenced by the Georgian manor houses of Dublin. It met President Washington's requirement for a mansion that would command respect without being extravagant and monarchical, but the house of gray Virginia sandstone wasn't completed in time to house Washington, whose second term in office ended in 1797. Instead, John Adams was the first presidential occupant, moving into the unfinished structure in 1800. East and west terraces were built during the administration of Thomas Jefferson, who had entered the original design competition under an assumed name; he also installed the first water closets and introduced a French chef to the house. Under James Madison, the interior was redecorated by Capitol architect Benjamin Latrobe, but occupying British forces burned down the mansion in August 1814, forcing Madison and his wife to flee. Hoban was put in charge of its reconstruction after the war and the mansion was again ready for occupation in 1817, but with one significant change: to conceal fire damage to the exterior, the house was painted white.

Throughout the nineteenth century, the White House was decorated, added to, and improved with each new occupant: Andrew Jackson had the first indoor bathroom installed in 1833; Theodore Roosevelt added elevators and an executive West Wing, which incorporated the president's personal Oval Office; the famous Rose Garden was planted outside the Oval Office in 1913; an entire residential third floor was added in 1927, and an East Wing followed in the 1940s. However, all these renovations were completed while the first family of the day was in residence. This meant that changes tended to be finished too quickly, so that by 1948 the entire building was on the verge of collapse. Harry Truman had to move into nearby Blair House for four years while the structure was stabilized; new foundations were laid, all the rooms were dismantled, and a modern steel frame inserted. Since then there have been no significant alterations – unless you count Nixon's bowling alley, Ford's outdoor pool, Carter's solar panels (though these were removed by Reagan), and Clinton's jogging track.

East Room in scale and style and hosts banquets for important guests. The tour loops back through the cross halls, and you exit on the north side of the White House.

The South Lawn

The White House is surrounded by greenery, but its most famous patch is the South Lawn, that expansive grassy stretch that helps provide such iconic views of the White House and which hosts its most famous outside event. The Easter Egg Roll is a longstanding tradition that

▼ANDREW JACKSON STATUE, LAFAYETTE SQUARE

began in 1878 and has continued ever since, though occasionally interrupted by war and foul weather. A White House staffer dressed as the Easter bunny is usually at the scene, along with various department heads reading kids' stories and trying to act goofy. To get your free tickets for this event – which occurs the Monday after Easter – drop by the Ellipse Visitor Center at 15th and E streets at 7.30am on the day of the Roll or on the Saturday before it. Tickets are first-come, first-served, and run out quickly.

The Ellipse

The Ellipse, a large grassy expanse between the White House and the Washington Monument, is a centerpiece of the park plan for the District and offers a few low-key attractions. On the northern edge, the Zero Milestone marks the point from which all distances on US highways are measured. Here, too, is the National Christmas Tree, a Colorado Blue Spruce that's been here since 1978 and is lit by the president every year to mark the start of the holiday season. On the east (15th St) side of the Ellipse, a bronze boy scout marks the site of the Boy Scout Memorial, while nearby, the simple granite Monument to the Original Patentees commemorates the eighteenth-century landowners who ceded land so that the city could be built.

Lafayette Square

Lafayette Square could be considered an unofficial extension of the mansion itself – the place where former inhabitant Andrew Jackson is deified in statue on horseback, and where political protestors can

expect a spot on the nightly news if they put on a boisterous enough demonstration. In the twentieth century, four corner statues of foreign-born Revolutionary generals were added, the most famous the Marquis de Lafayette, the French officer who raised an army on behalf of the American colonists and was made a US general at the age of 19. His statue shows him flanked by French admirals and being handed a sword by a female nude, symbolizing America. At the southwestern corner of Lafayette Square, the **Blair House** was where Robert E. Lee was offered – and refused – the command of the Union Army. It has served as the presidential guest house since the 1940s, and both the Trumans and Clintons used it while White House renovations were in progress.

▼DECATUR HOUSE

Decatur House

1610 H St NW ☎202/842-0920, ⓦwww.decaturhouse.org. Tues–Sat 10am–5pm, Sun noon–4pm. Donation. The oldest house on Lafayette Square is Decatur House. Dating from 1819, this red-brick house was built by Benjamin Latrobe (who had already worked on the White House) for Stephen Decatur, a young American hero who performed with distinction as a navy captain in the War of 1812. The Federal-style first floor, studded with naval memorabilia, is decorated in the elegant fashion of the day. Most of the other period rooms have inlaid floors, furnishings, and decorative arts in the Victorian style – though much of the house is now being restored to its early-American splendor with ongoing renovations. If the museum is open (it's closed several weeks during the year for preservation work), you can take a closer look at it on hourly guided tours (30–45min) that begin fifteen minutes after the hour.

St John's Church

1525 H St NW ☎202/347-8766, ⓦwww.stjohns-dc.org. Mon–Sat 10.30am–2.30pm. Free tours after 11am Sun service. Across H Street from Lafayette Park, the tiny, yellow St John's Church dates from 1816.

▼ST JOHN'S CHURCH

Benjamin Latrobe again did the honors, providing the neighborhood with a handsome domed Episcopal church in the form of a Greek cross, with appealing half-moon windows in the upper gallery of the intimately proportioned interior. Unsurprisingly, St John's is commonly known as the "Church of the Presidents"; all since Madison have visited – sitting in the special pew (no. 54) reserved for them – and when an incumbent dies in office the bells of St John's ring out across the city. Note also the handsome 1836 building just east of the church, a stately edifice with a grand French Second Empire facade, which now serves as a parish building but in the nineteenth century was the site of the British Embassy.

Hay-Adams Hotel

H and 16th sts ☎202/638-6600, ⓦwww.hayadams.com. Across the street from the church, the Renaissance Revival gem of the *Hay-Adams Hotel* (see review, p.180) impresses with its elegant arches and columns, and sits on the former site of the townhouses of statesman John Hay and his friend, historian and author Henry Adams. Their adjacent homes were the site of glittering soirees attended by all the Washington swells, and since 1927 the hotel has been at the heart of Washington politicking and fundraising.

Old Executive Office Building and Treasury Department

On either side of the White House sit two of the most imposing federal buildings in the District, the Old Executive Office Building to the west and the Treasury Department to the east. The Executive is a French Empire riot of hundreds of

GRAND SALON, RENWICK GALLERY

free-standing columns, tall and thin chimneys, a copper mansard roof, pediments, porticos, and various stone flourishes – infamous as the place where Watergate conspirators plotted their deeds and Iran-Contra henchmen shredded documents. By contrast, the Treasury is a colossal work of Neoclassicism, all monumental columns and Greek Revival style. However, for all their pretension and grandeur, respectively, both buildings have been off-limits to the public since 9/11. The Executive offices are only accessible if you can persuade your Congressional representative to get you inside for a look, while the Treasury may be open at some point after it completes its ongoing structural renovations.

Renwick Gallery

Pennsylvania Ave at 17th St NW ☎202/633-2850, ☻americanart.si.edu. Daily 10am–5.30pm. The French style of the Old Executive Office Building was directly influenced by the earlier, smaller, and much more harmonious Renwick Gallery. Built by James Renwick (architect of the Smithsonian Castle) in 1859, the red-brick building served first as the original Corcoran Gallery (see opposite), then was the site of the US Court of Claims, until it was restored in the 1960s by the Smithsonian, which now uses it to display selections of American art.

The building's ornate design reaches its apogee in the deep-red Grand Salon on the upper floor, a soaring parlor preserved in the style of the Gilded Age, featuring windows draped in striped damask, velvet-covered benches, marble-topped cabinets, and wood-and-glass display cases. Even better, with the National Museum of American Art itself closed until 2006, the Grand Salon now features many of its finest works and showcases them in the Belle Epoque style – hung floor-to-ceiling, three to five pictures high. Although your neck may be sore from all the craning, the effect is suitably monumental, and there are almost too many classic works to see in one place. Some of the highlights include portraits by Gilbert Stuart, John S. Copley, and John Singer Sargent; huge landscapes like that of Yellowstone by Thomas Moran; Albert Pinkham Ryder's dark and moody oils; and Frederic Church's entrancing *Aurora Borealis*.

Other galleries are devoted to American crafts – mostly modern jewelry and furniture but also sculpture, ceramics, and applied art – while the first floor hosts temporary exhibits.

Corcoran Gallery of Art

500 17th St NW ☎202/639-1700, ☻www.corcoran.org. Wed–Mon 10am–5pm, Thurs closes at 9pm. $5. A treasure trove of culture, the Corco-

▲ CORCORAN GALLERY

medallion-holding cherubs) make it seem larger than it actually is; the floor-to-ceiling hand-carved wood paneling, gold-leaf decor, and ceiling

ran Gallery's American holdings alone include more than three thousand paintings, colonial to contemporary, plus Neoclassical sculpture and modern photography, prints, and drawings. Over the years, the permanent collection has expanded considerably to include European works, Greek antiquities, and medieval tapestries. A huge new wing in the works – a flowing, sculptural addition designed by Frank Gehry – will go a long way toward accommodating the museum's collection.

For European art, some of the most familiar names hang in the Clark Landing, where you're likely to find mid-level paintings by Degas, Renoir, Monet, and Pissarro. Other works include serviceable French and English paintings of the seventeenth to nineteenth centuries, some outstanding Italian majolica plates depicting mythological scenes, and two large, allegorical wool-and-silk French tapestries. However, the gallery's main European holding is not painting but the room known as the Salon Doré (Gilded Room), which originally formed part of an eighteenth-century Parisian home, the Hôtel de Clermont. Framed mirrors (flanked by

murals are both intricate and sweeping.

The bulk of the American art is usually on the second floor. The gallery possesses a fine collection of grand landscapes, starting with the expansive *Niagara* (1857) by Frederic Edwin Church and Albert Bierstadt's dramatic *The Last of the Buffalo* (1889). In contrast is Thomas Cole's *The Return* (1837), a mythical medieval scene. One room is usually devoted to nineteenth-century portraiture, with formal studies by renowned artists like John Trumbull and Charles Bird King, while the gallery's most notorious piece of sculpture is Hiram Powers' *The Greek Slave* (1846), whose manacled hands and simple nudity so outraged critical sensibilities that women visitors were prevented from viewing the statue while there were men in the room. Moving into late nineteenth-century art, the gallery holds works by John Singer Sargent, Thomas Eakins, and Mary Cassatt, while pre-World War II paintings include those by Childe Hassam, George Bellows, and Edward Hopper, whose yachting picture *Ground Swell* (1939) adds a splash of color along with a hint of menace. Depending on space, contemporary American art gets a glance, too, with examples from big names such as Lichtenstein, Warhol, and de Kooning.

The Octagon

1799 New York Ave NW ☎202/638-3105, ⊛www.theoctagon.org. Tues–Sun 10am–4.30pm. $3. One of the District's oldest homes, dating from 1800, the Octagon does not in fact have eight sides (debate continues as to what the name actually means). It's a classic structure loosely adapted from the Georgian style, with curving interior walls and closet doors, lovely spiral staircase, and several period rooms open for touring. Moreover, there's also an accessible basement, to give you a hint of the kind of drudgery servants and slaves underwent while the house owners lived in splendor above. Now owned by the American Architectural Foundation, the house museum has long been associated with Washington history; having barely survived the flames of the War of 1812, the house later hosted the signing of the Treaty of Ghent that ended the war.

▼THE OCTAGON

DAR Museum

1776 D St NW ☎202/879-3241, ⊛www.dar.org/museum. Mon–Fri 9am–4pm, Sat 9am–5pm. Tours Mon–Fri 10am–2.30pm, Sat 9am–4.30pm. The conservative, patriotic organization Daughters of the American Revolution is unfortunately best known for being the group that, in 1939, denied black singer Marian Anderson the right to sing in its Constitution Hall (nearby on 18th St; see p.99) – a milestone in the civil-rights struggle. Less familiar is the group's curious museum, a hodgepodge of embroidered samplers and quilts, silverware, toys, kitchenware, glass, crockery, and earthenware – much of it dating to the Revolutionary and Federal periods. What they're most proud of, however, are the State Rooms, a collection of 31 period salons, mainly decorated with pre-1850 furnishings, each representing a different state or region. The New England room, for example, contains an original lacquered wooden tea chest retrieved from Boston Harbor after the Tea Party in 1773; the California an adobe house interior; and the New Jersey a set of furnishings fashioned from the wreck of a British frigate sunk off the coast during the Revolutionary War – the overly elaborate chandelier was made from the melted-down anchor.

Department of the Interior Museum

1849 C St NW ☎202/208-4743, ⊛www.doi .gov/museum. Mon–Fri 8.30am–4.30pm. Reserve in advance for tours. The Department of the Interior is one of the many big bureaucratic buildings that crowd the part of town west of the White House known as Foggy Bottom. Unlike most such buildings, which are generally closed to the public and offer little of interest, the DOI offers one signature sight worth a look. Its wood-paneled museum was opened in 1938 and is still very much of that era: rich with fossil and mineral samples, stuffed bison heads, old saddles, and paintings by nineteenth-century surveyors of the West – not to mention five elaborate dioramas featuring the likes of an Oklahoma land office, a coal mine explosion, and a frontier fort. There are also regularly changing special exhibitions of photography, paintings, or sculpture, much of it drawn from the museum's huge stock of 145 million items.

Department of State
C St between 21st and 23rd sts ☏ 202/647-3241, ⊛ www.state.gov. Tours by appointment only Mon–Fri 9.30am, 10.30am, & 2.45pm. No government bureaucracy is more synonymous with Foggy Bottom than the Department of State, and it's hard to see at first glance why anyone would be interested in venturing into this massive hulk; however, the chance to see the Diplomatic Reception Rooms provides one reason. During the 1960s, many of the chambers were redecorated and refurnished to become suitable for the reception of diplomats and visiting heads of state. In came a wealth of eighteenth- and nineteenth-century paintings, decor, and furniture – including the desk on which the Treaty of Paris, which ended the War of Independence, was signed. If you're delighted by the decorative arts, this is an

essential stop; just make sure to reserve your place on a tour at least a month in advance.

Kennedy Center
2700 F St NW ☏ 202/467-4600, ⊛ www.kennedy-center.org. Tours Mon–Fri 10am–5pm, Sat & Sun 10am–1pm, reserve on ☏ 202/416-8340. Simply put, the white-marble colossus of the Kennedy Center for the Performing Arts is the nation's apex of institutional culture. The National Symphony Orchestra, Washington Opera, and American Film Institute have their homes here, and there's an information desk on your way in, so you're free to wander around inside the theaters and concert halls (most are open to visitors 10am–1pm). Free 45-minute tours depart daily from Level A beneath the Opera House and cover most of the sights noted below. The Grand Foyer itself is 630ft long and 60ft high, lit by gargantuan crystal chandeliers with a seven-foot-high bronze bust of JFK. In addition, each of the theaters and concert halls also has its own artwork, from the Matisse tapestries outside the Opera House to the Barbara Hepworth sculpture in the Concert Hall. The Roof Terrace Level holds the Performing Arts Library of scripts and recordings (Tues–Fri 11am–8.30pm, Sat 10am–6pm); while you're up there, step out onto the terrace for scintillating views across the Potomac to Theodore Roosevelt Island, and west to Georgetown and north to the National Cathedral.

The Watergate Complex
2650 Virginia Ave NW. If there's a place that defines modern, political Washington, it's not the White House or the Capitol but the Watergate Complex.

▲ JFK SCULPTURE, KENNEDY CENTER

This unassuming, curving, Italian-designed, mid-1960s residential and commercial complex – named for the flight of steps behind the Lincoln Memorial that leads down to the Potomac – has always been a much sought-after address, both for various foreign ambassadors and for top city brass. The Doles and Caspar Weinberger have maintained apartments here for years, while White House intern Monica Lewinsky lived here before scandal forced her from DC. It's also the site of the *Watergate* hotel (see p.180). But its inescapable association is with events in mid-1972. That June 17, five men were arrested during a break-in at Democratic National Committee headquarters, located at an office within the complex. The links between the burglars and the Committee to Re-Elect the President – and running up to the White House itself – led to the resignation of President Richard Nixon two years later.

Shops

Indian Craft Shop

Department of the Interior, room 1023, 1849 C St NW ☎202/208-4056. One of the city's best gift boutiques in a rather bleak stretch for shopping, where you can purchase rugs, crafts, beadwork, jewelry, and pottery by artisans from different native tribes in the US.

InfoShop

In the World Bank, 1818 H St NW ☎202/458-5454. For serious readers only: an excellent bookstore with a compendious selection of volumes on international relations, the Third World, environment, education, and finance, with many educational videos, too.

Cafés

Art Gallery Bar & Grille

1712 I St NW ☎202/298-6658. Soak up the Art Deco ambience or sit on the outdoor patio as you tuck into breakfast, salads, burgers, sandwiches, omelets, pizza, and grills. Nightly beer specials and jazz also on tap.

Breadline

1751 Pennsylvania Ave NW ☎202/822-8900. Prime bakery making DC's finest loaves and serving flatbreads, samosas, empanadas, and pizza, plus salads and tasty pork sandwiches. Organic ingredients are the rule.

Café des Artistes

In the Corcoran Gallery of Art, 500 17th St NW ☎202/639-1786. Fine museum café with all the usual tasty salads and sandwiches, but highlighted by the signature Gospel Brunch ($24), a famed Sunday-morning event where you brunch to the sound of musical evangelizing.

Capitol Grounds

2100 Pennsylvania Ave NW ☎202/293-2057. Located near George Washington University, a lively spot for gourmet sandwiches and breakfast staples, plus good coffee and a convivial atmosphere. Also at 1455 Pennsylvania Ave NW (☎202/637-9618).

Restaurants

Aquarelle

2650 Virginia Ave NW ☎202/965-2300. Located in the *Watergate* hotel, a reliable choice for Mediterranean cuisine in an upscale setting, with a complex blend

of rice, pasta, and seafood dishes, with some good grilled offerings as well.

Dish

924 25th St NW ☎202/337-7600. Tasty New American versions of classic fare, from fruit cobbler and fried chicken to steaks and pot roast, with fresh and trendy ingredients, but carrying a heftier price tag than you'll find in any old diner.

Kinkead's

2000 Pennsylvania Ave NW ☎202/296-7700. One of DC's favorite, and priciest, restaurants, with a contemporary menu specializing in fish and seafood, from salmon stew to monkfish medallions. Since it's plenty popular and recently renovated, you'll need to book ahead.

Melrose

1201 24th St NW ☎202/955-3899. New-styled American-fusion food – Thai calamari, spicy duck confit, sea bass, etc – at this ultra-chic hotel restaurant that draws crowds of foodies and diners in the know.

▼KINKEAD'S

Nectar
George Washington University Inn, 824 New Hampshire Ave NW ☎202/337-6620. Quality hotel restaurant serving up delicious seafood and New American fare – from sushi and soft-shell crab to foie gras – though a bit on the expensive side at $25 per entree.

Primi Piatti
2013 I St NW ☎202/223-3600. Major-league Italian restaurant with a solid knack for creating savory gourmet pizzas, with ingredients such as goat cheese and prosciutto – and cheaper prices than the expensive meat-and-pasta dishes.

Bars

Froggy Bottom Pub
2142 Pennsylvania Ave NW ☎202/338-3000. Colorful, three-level bar catering to students at nearby George Washington University; worth a visit if you're interested in shooting pool, munching on cheap pub grub, and knocking back a good brew or three.

Marshall's
2524 L St NW ☎202/333-1155. Solid microbrews like Red Hook and beer faves like Guinness, plus a decent menu of steak, pasta, and seafood, make this upscale bar-and-grill a good spot to spend your time; the kitchen serves 'til midnight.

Performing arts

American Film Institute
2700 F St NW ☎202/785-4600, ⓦwww.afi.com. $7. Kennedy Center film heavyweight with regular programs of art, foreign, and classic films, usually built around certain directors, countries, and themes, often with associated lectures and seminars.

DAR Constitution Hall
1776 D St NW ☎202/628-4780, ⓦwww.dar.org/conthall. Widely known as one of the best concert halls in the city, only usurped in the 1960s by the Kennedy Center. Now hosts uneventful mainstream concerts of pop, country, and jazz acts.

Lisner Auditorium
730 21st St NW ☎202/994-1500. Regular classical and choral concerts on George Washington University campus; often quite good, sometimes free.

National Symphony Orchestra
2700 F St NW ☎1-800/444-1324, ⓦwww.kennedy-center.org/nso. Performs in the Kennedy Center, serving up the big names in classical music under the baton of conductor Leonard Slatkin, who's best known for championing American composers.

Old Downtown and Federal Triangle

Until recently, Old Downtown was a pretty bleak place, blighted by crime and deserted at night, with little of interest to anyone other than architecture buffs. In recent years, though, the area has picked up, thanks to a steady flow of urban-renewal dollars, and offers an excellent range of chic restaurants, niche museums, fancy hotels, and other attractions. The same can't be said for the ten-square-block area known as Federal Triangle, where eight colossal government office build-ings hog the duly geometric terrain. It's true the Triangle has its highlights – mainly the Old Post Office and the National Archives – but for most visitors it's little more than a huge buffer between Downtown and the National Mall.

Pennsylvania Avenue NW

Defining the border between Old Downtown and the Federal Triangle, Pennsylvania Avenue NW is one of the District's most famous roads, connect-ing the Capitol with the White House. In the original design, the avenue was supposed to allow for unimpeded views of both structures, but this changed when Andrew Jackson had the Treasury Building plunked down on the western end. Still, the avenue continues to provide a historic backdrop for the trium-phal Inaugural Parade that takes the newly sworn-in president from the Capitol to his residence for the next four years. Thomas Jefferson led the first impromptu parade in 1805; James Madison made the ceremony official; and every president since has trundled up in some form of conveyance or another – except

▼PENNSYLVANIA AVENUE NW

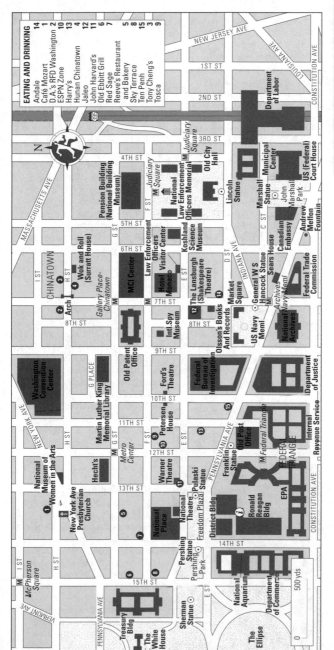

Jimmy Carter who, famously, walked the sixteen long blocks to the White House.

Unless you're really into super-sized office blocks, most of the appealing architecture can be found on or around the north side of the street. Good examples include the preserved 1920s moviehouse of the Warner Theatre, just north at 13th and E streets (see p.115), and the turreted pink stone of the Sears House offices, at 633 Pennsylvania Ave NW. Nearby worthy statues honor Ben Franklin, at 14th Street, and World War I general John Pershing, at 12th Street. By contrast, the giant government buildings on the south side are notable mainly for their size: the Ronald Reagan Office Building, on 14th Street between Constitution and Pennsylvania avenues, is the second-largest federal structure in the US, while the alphabet-soup offices of the EPA, IRS, and FTC, from 12th to 6th streets, do little to make the government seem user-friendly.

▼WILLARD HOTEL

Willard Hotel

1401 Pennsylvania Ave NW ☎ 202/628-9100, ⊛ washington.intercontinental .com. Peering over the north side of Pershing Park at 14th Street stands one of the grandest of Washington hotels, the *Willard*, a District landmark for 150 years. Although hotels have existed on the site since the capital's earliest days, it was after 1850, when Henry Willard gave his name to the place, that the site became a haunt of statesmen, politicians, and top brass – not the least of whom was Abraham Lincoln, who dropped in before his first inauguration. The hotel's opulent lobby attracted countless profit-seekers anxious to press their issues on political leaders; it's even claimed that this provides the origin of the word "lobbyist." In 1901, Henry Hardenbergh – architect of some of New York's finest period hotels – was engaged to update the *Willard* and produced the splendid Beaux Arts building that stands today. It went out of business after the riots of 1968, but a thorough restoration in 1986 recaptured its early style, and the hotel – now the *Willard InterContinental* (see review p.182) – is once again a swank hangout for both the swells and well-heeled political leaders.

National Aquarium

14th St south of Pennsylvania Ave NW ☎ 202/482-2825, ⊛ www .nationalaquarium.com. Daily 9am–5pm. $3.50. Despite its impressive-sounding name and central location, the National Aquarium – the oldest aquarium in America – is one of the city's more disappointing sights. Quite unlike what you might expect, the National Aquarium sits in the bowels of the Department of Commerce, the fish-tank displays seem very dated, and the atmosphere is stagnant and a bit depressing. Save your effort for the National Museum of Natural History, one long block south and east (see p.59).

Old Post Office

1100 Pennsylvania Ave NW ☏202/289-4224, ⊚www.oldpostofficedc .com. Mon–Sat 10am– 7pm, Sun noon–8pm, summer Mon–Sat until 9pm. The survival of this wondrous Romanesque Revival building owes more to the depressed real-estate market of the early

▲OLD POST OFFICE

twentieth century than it does to civic planners' flair for historic preservation. A longtime candidate for demolition, the onetime post office (which only served that function for fifteen years, from 1899 to 1914) has managed to persevere through the decades with its towering granite walls, which make it look suitably cathedral-like, and eye-popping seven-story atrium, now home to ethnic diners and various shops (see "Shops" and "Restaurants" at the end of the chapter). For a really appealing look at this monumental structure, take a free tour of the clock tower (Mon–Fri 9am–5.45pm, Sat & Sun 10am–5.45pm, summer Mon–Fri until 7.45pm; ☏202/606-8691, ⊚www.nps. gov/opot), which is administered by the National Park Service and provides dramatic views of the District from its 270ft observation deck.

Federal Bureau of Investigation

Pennsylvania Ave and 9th St NW. Even if you had somehow never heard of the FBI, the presence of countless DC tourists wearing T-shirts emblazoned with that acronym would still get your attention. Just as eye-grabbing is the Bureau's giant concrete-Brutalist edifice, a clunky modern office that pales by comparison to the Neoclassical Department of Justice across the street. The FBI used to be a favorite spot for visitors with a taste for the X-Files and other such TV programs, but since 9/11 tours have been canceled, and the ongoing renovation of the building has kept it off-limits to nosy interlopers, T-shirts or not.

National Archives

700 Pennsylvania Ave NW ☏202/501-5000, guided tours ☏202/501-5205, ⊚www.archives.gov. Daily 10am–5.30pm, summer until 9pm. The National Archives build-

▲ FBI BUILDING

ing is one of the visual glories of Washington DC, with 72 ornate, 50ft Corinthian columns, plain walls supporting a dome 75ft above ground level, and a sculpted pediment topped by eagles. Even better, the Archives' collection of records governmental, private, and otherwise is of an almost unfathomable quantity: hundreds of millions of pages of paper documents, from war treaties to slave-ship manifests; seven million pictures; 120,000 reels of movie film; almost 200,000 sound recordings; eleven million maps and charts; and a quarter of a million other artifacts. If you're a researcher, you can apply for an official ID to access the collection; otherwise, what everyone comes to see is the Holy Trinity of American historical record – the Declaration of Independence, the Constitution, and the Bill of Rights – which are lined up in the magnificent marble Rotunda within state-of-the-art airtight containers filled with argon gas. The pages are, of course, sizable artifacts from the post-Colonial era, and are written in elegant calligraphy in closely spaced lines – which, given their faded ink, makes them very hard to read nowadays under the low light of the display cases. Other less familiar but significant documents relating to Western US expansion, law, and politics are on view alongside them. Seeing any of these documents can involve a long wait during summer hours, so try to come during non-peak times (winter, mornings, etc). Given that the Archives hold items as diverse as Napoleon's signature on the Louisiana Purchase, the World War II Japanese surrender document, the Strategic Arms Limitation Treaty (SALT I) of 1972, and President Nixon's resignation letter, it's always worth checking the temporary exhibi-

▼ DECLARATION OF INDEPENDENCE, NATIONAL ARCHIVES

SCULPTED FRIEZE, US NAVY MEMORIAL

tions as well in the surrounding chambers. There are also plenty of valuable, intriguing documents and artifacts at the Archives' Maryland depository (to which a shuttle bus can take you), where you can hear selections from the Watergate tapes.

US Navy Memorial/Naval Heritage Center

701 Pennsylvania Ave NW ☎ 202/737-2300, ✪ www.lonesailor.org. Heritage Center open Tues–Sat 9.30am–5pm, also Mon in summer. In a circular plaza covered by an etched representation of the world and circled by low, tiered granite walls lapped by running water, the US Navy Memorial features a statue of a single sailor, kit bag by his side, and inscribed naval quotations from the historic (Themistocles, architect of the Greek naval victory during the Persian Wars) to the tenuous (naval aviator Neil Armstrong's "That's one small step for man…"). In summer, the Navy Band holds a regular series of concerts here. Directly behind the memorial, the Naval Heritage Center can tell you more about the service with its changing exhibits and portraits honoring the various presidents who have served in the US Navy: JFK famously commanded a motor torpedo boat and was

awarded the Navy and Marine Corps Medal for heroism, but Johnson, Nixon, Ford, and Carter all served with distinction, too, while George Bush (the Elder), the Navy's youngest bomber pilot during World War II, received the Distinguished Flying Cross and three Air Medals for his endeavors.

Judiciary Square

East of 5th St, between E and F sts. The idea of having a plaza or section of downtown devoted to law and the judiciary dates from the earliest days of planning for the District, and Judiciary Square continues to be the focus of the city's judiciary and local government. The mayor's offices are at One Judiciary Square, while the unobtrusively Neoclassical Old City Hall on D Street is fronted with the earliest recorded statue of Abraham Lincoln, its plans dating from 1865, just after he was assassinated; appropriately, in 1881 the building saw the murder trial of Charles Guiteau, who shot President James Garfield in the back just four months after his inauguration. Unfortunately, the building itself is fenced off and not open to the public.

Within a few blocks of here stand the US Tax Court, the District of Columbia Court House, the Municipal Center, and the US (Federal) Court House, all uniformly colorless and monolithic. All the courthouse galleries are open to members of the public interested in watching proceedings: the US (Federal) Court House (main entrance on Constitution Avenue) sees the most high-profile action, from the trial of various Watergate and Iran-Contra defendants to that of former DC mayor Marion Barry.

National Law Enforcement Officers Memorial

The impressive National Law Enforcement Officers Memorial occupies the center of Judiciary Square. It was dedicated in 1991, and the walls lining the circular pathways around a reflecting pool are inscribed with the names of nearly 17,000 police officers killed in the line of duty. With symbolic bronze lions overseeing their cubs at the end of the memorial walls, it's a poignant spot in the so-called Murder Capital of the nation. Each May new names are added to the memorial, which has space for 26,000 more – at the present rate (a police officer is killed every other day on average), it will be full by the year 2100. There are directories at the site if you want to trace a particular name, or you can also call in at the nearby visitor center, two blocks west at 605 E St NW (Mon–Fri 9am–5pm, Sat 10am–5pm, Sun noon–5pm; free; ☎202/737-3213, ⓦwww .nleomf.com).

Koshland Science Museum

500 5th St NW ☎202/334-1201, ⓦwww.koshland-science-museum .org. 10am–5pm, closed Tues. $5. One of the newest museums in the District opened its doors in April 2004. Refreshingly, the Koshland Science Museum doesn't soft-pedal or dumb down its displays, but provides an engaging, vigorous presentation of fact, theory, and speculation relating to some of the core science and technology issues of the day. A product of the National Academy of Sciences, the museum has one permanent exhibition covering the latest, and typically controversial, ideas relating to the expansion of the universe, string theory and dark matter, and two temporary exhibits running until 2006. The

▼GREAT HALL, NATIONAL BUILDING MUSEUM

first covers the nature of DNA in various manifestations, from its nucleic-acid construction to its use in tracking down criminals and providing antidotes for pandemic diseases; the second concerns global warming in a fairly complex and multifaceted style, showing the chemical components of greenhouse gases (notably carbon dioxide and methane) and the potential dangers they pose. Both of these exhibits balance their scientific data with hands-on, user-friendly multimedia elements that enable you, for example, to find the right strand of DNA to match one existing in a deadly virus.

National Building Museum

401 F St NW ☎202/272-2448, ⊛www .nbm.org. Mon–Sat 10am–5pm, Sun 11am–5pm. $5. Showcasing what is easily the District's greatest interior, the National Building Museum was constructed in the 1870s as the Pension Building, and unlike what that bland moniker might signify today, the structure was built as a jaw-dropping monument to the soldiers who fought in the Civil War – and were thus owed retirement wages commensurate with their service (hence the original name). Although the grand red-brick face of the building is impressive enough, with its 3ft-high terracotta frieze of battle scenes, the atrium of the Great Hall steals the show, supported by eight columns 8ft in diameter and more than 75ft high, each made of 70,000 bricks, plastered and painted to resemble Siena marble. Above the ground-floor arcade with its central fountain, the three galleried levels are 160ft high and decorated with 244 busts that repeat eight symbolic figures (architect,

construction worker, landscape gardener, etc) representing the building arts. Not surprisingly, the space has been in regular demand, even after the Pension Bureau moved out in 1926: Grover Cleveland held the first of many presidential inaugural balls here in 1885, and every year the *Christmas in Washington* TV special is shot on site. The structure is now preserved as the National Building Museum, which presents changing exhibitions on architecture and building history. The permanent exhibition on the second floor, "Washington: Symbol and City," concentrates on the construction of the city itself with a detailed model showing how many of the District's planned buildings have come to fruition. Free tours (Mon–Wed 12.30pm, Thurs–Sat also 11.30am & 1.30pm; Sun 12.30pm & 1.30pm) give you access to the otherwise restricted third floor – the best spot to view the towering columns' intricate capitals.

Chinatown

Along G and H streets, between 6th and 8th. Washington's Chinatown pales in comparison to those in San Francisco and New York. The vibrant triumphal arch over H Street (at 7th) heralds little more than a dozen restaurants and a few grocery stores. DC's first Chinese immigrants, in the early nineteenth century, didn't live in today's Chinatown (which only became such at the beginning of the 1900s) but in the slums of Swampoodle, north of the Capitol. At that time, H Street and its environs were home to small businesses and modest rooming houses. In one of these, during the 1860s, Mary Surratt presided over the comings and goings of her son John

▲CHINATOWN ARCH

and his colleagues, including a certain John Wilkes Booth – all subsequently implicated in the Lincoln assassination. A plaque marks the site of the house (then 541 H St), now the *Wok and Roll* restaurant at 604 H St NW.

City Museum of Washington DC

801 K St NW ☎ 202/383-1800, ⊛ www .citymuseumdc.org. Tues–Sun 10am– 5pm. $3. Until recently occupying the glorious Heurich House in Dupont Circle, the Historical Society of Washington DC's new digs are just about as historic: the District's former downtown library, this grand Neoclassical jewel with stylish friezes, floor mosaics, and Ionic columns and pilasters was funded by Andrew Carnegie and completed in 1903. It served patrons until the 1970s, when the main branch moved further south. Luckily, the library building has now been reborn as the home of the Historical Society, which displays photos, models, and artifacts from the history of the District, including such relics as an old volunteer fireman's helmet, deeds of slave sales and manumission, and vari-

ous political posters. *Washington Stories*, a daily multimedia show (extra $4), recounts the city's past in the museum's theater, while its Gibson Reading Room (Tues– Sun 10am–5pm; free) recalls the building's former use, giving you access to a trove of photos, documents, books, and memorabilia relating to the development of the nation's capital.

MCI Center

601 F St NW ☎ 202/628-3200, ⊛ www .mcicenter.com. With the opening of the $200-million MCI Center at the end of 1997, professional sports came back to downtown DC: the center now hosts the NBA's Washington Wizards, the WNBA's Washington Mystics, and the NHL's Washington Capitals. To encourage extra visits, the center holds several other attractions, mainly bars and restaurants to grab the suburban and tourist crowds.

Hotel Monaco

7th and F sts NW ☎ 202/628-7177, ⊛ www.monaco-dc.com. Occupying an entire block, the former General Post Office is a Greek Revival masterwork dating back to 1842, made of New York's Westchester marble and modeled on a Renaissance palazzo inspired by the ancient Roman Temple of Jupiter. As the District's first-ever building constructed of marble – created by Robert Mills, esteemed architect of the Treasury and Patent Office buildings – it has a solidity and permanence that has seen several uses since the post office pulled up stakes, including the site of the US Tariff Commission and today's *Hotel Monaco* (see review p.182). With its high-ceilinged offices now remodeled into guest rooms, the luxurious hotel's interiors and public spaces are well worth a look, with wonderfully preserved details and complementary modern touches, including vaulted ceilings, marble columns and checkerboard-marble floors, spiral stairways, and minimalist contemporary decor.

Old Patent Office Building

7th and F sts NW. Catercorner to the *Hotel Monaco* is the second of Robert Mills' great DC buildings, another Greek Revival gem, which dates from 1836 and is among the city's oldest structures. It was designed to hold offices of the Interior Department and the Commissioners of Patents, displaying models of all patents taken out in nineteenth-century America. Thus it became one of the city's earliest museums, featuring models of inventions by Thomas Edison, Benjamin Franklin, and Alexander Graham Bell as well as Whitney's cotton gin, Colt's pistol, and Fulton's steam engine. During the Civil War the echoing halls were pressed into emergency service as a hospital with over two thousand beds. One of the clerks in the Patent Office, Clara Barton, abandoned her clerical duties to work in the hospital, going on to found the American Red Cross in 1881. Despite its heritage, the building was scheduled for demolition in the 1950s, until the Smithsonian stepped in. Today, housing the double museum of the **National Portrait Gallery** and the **National Museum of American Art**, the building is undergoing a major renovation and will reopen on Independence Day 2006. Until then, the Smithsonian's American art collection has partially relocated to the Renwick Gallery, where some of its key paintings are displayed in the stunning Grand Salon (see p.93); check

PLACES Old Downtown and Federal Triangle

▼CITY MUSEUM OF WASHINGTON DC

the museum websites at ⓦwww
.npg.si.edu and ⓦamericanart
.si.edu for more information.

International Spy Museum
800 F St NW ☎202/207-0219, ⓦwww
.spymuseum.org. Daily 10am–6pm,
April–Oct closes 8pm. $13. One of
DC's newest, and despite the
steep entrance fee one of its
more popular attractions – call
ahead as tickets can sell out days
in advance – the International
Spy Museum is crammed full
of the type of Cold War-era
gizmos, weapons, and relics that
will make readers of Robert
Ludlum and Tom Clancy beam
with delight. The museum offers
a playful and mildly informative array of items and displays
from thousands of years of
spycraft, beginning with a small
model of the Trojan Horse
and going on briefly to cover
ancient Rome, imperial China,
Elizabethan England, and Civil
War-era America. Of course, it's
the twentieth century – or more
specifically from the beginning of World War II to the
end of the Cold War – that the
museum really focuses on, with
a sizable assortment of multimedia exhibits, walk-through
re-creations, dioramas, and video
presentations.
Providing just
enough infor-
mation to get
you started,
there's a broad
range of top-
ics on view,
from Hol-
lywood stars
fighting the
Nazis (nota-
bly Marlene
Dietrich), to a
cramped ver-
sion of an East
Berlin escape

tunnel, to a darkened "interrogation room" for captured spies,
to a video game based on the
spy-coding Enigma machine.
These are all interesting enough,
but the museum's standouts are
undoubtedly its artifacts from
the height of the Cold War in
the 1950s and 1960s, presented
in glass cases and broken down
by theme – "training," "surveillance," and so on. Some of
the many highlights include
tiny pistols disguised as lipstick
holders, cigarette cases, pipes,
and flashlights; oddments like
invisible-ink writing kits and a
Get Smart!-styled shoe phone;
a colorful and active model of
James Bond's Aston Martin spy
car; bugs and radio transmitters
hidden in ambassadorial gifts
(such as a Great Seal of the US
given by the Russians); ricin-
tipped poison umbrellas used to
kill Warsaw Pact dissidents; and
a rounded capsule containing a
screwdriver, razor, and serrated
knife – ominously marked "rec-
tal tool kit."

Ford's Theatre
511 10th St NW ☎202/347-4833,
ⓦwww.fordstheatre.org. In 1861
Ford's Theatre was opened in a
converted church by theatrical

▼FORD'S THEATRE

entrepreneur John T. Ford. It proved popular until April 14, 1865 – during a performance of *Our American Cousin* – when it became the site of the dramatic assassination of Abraham Lincoln by John Wilkes Booth, actor and Confederate sympathizer. During the play, which Lincoln was watching with his wife from the presidential box, Booth yelled out "Sic semper tyrannis" (Thus ever to tyrants) and shot the president once in the head before escaping. Initially draped in black as a mark of respect, the theater was closed while the conspirators were pursued, caught, and tried; Ford later abandoned attempts to reopen the theater after he received death threats. The site was converted into offices and only in the 1960s was restored to its previous condition.

Today it's furnished in the style of 1865, and while it still serves as a working theater, it's more notable as a museum dedicated to the night that Lincoln died. Provided rehearsals or matinees aren't in progress (usually Thurs, Sat, & Sun), the theater hosts entertaining talks (hourly 9.15am–4.15pm; free) recounting the events of that fateful night. You can then look at the damask-furnished presidential box in which Lincoln sat in his rocking chair; most of the items inside are reproductions. In the basement, the Lincoln Museum (daily 9am–5pm; free; ☏202/426-6924, ⊛www.nps .gov/foth) puts more flesh on the story. The actual weapon – a .44 Derringer – is on display, alongside a bloodstained piece of Lincoln's overcoat and Booth's knife, keys, and diary, in which he wrote "I hoped for no gain. I knew no private wrong. I struck for my country and that alone."

Petersen House
516 10th St NW ☏202/426-6924, ⊛www.nps.gov/foth. Daily 9am–5pm.
After Lincoln was shot, the unconscious president was carried across the street and placed in the back bedroom of a house belonging to local tailor William Petersen. Built of the same red brick as the theater, the Petersen House has also been sympathetically restored, and you can troop through its gloomy parlor rooms to the small bedroom to see a replica of the bed on which Lincoln died – though in a concession to taste, the original bloodstained pillow that used to be laid on the bed has been moved to the theater museum. Lincoln's immediate family and colleagues were present in the house during his last night, but not all could cram into the tiny room at the same time – something ignored by contemporaneous artists who, in a series of deathbed scenes popular at the time, often portrayed up to thirty people crowded around the ailing president's bed.

National Museum of Women in the Arts
1250 New York Ave NW ☏202/783-5000, ⊛www.nmwa.org. Mon–Sat 10am–5pm, Sun noon–5pm. $8.
Housing one of the world's most important collections of art of its kind – more than 2500 works by some 600 artists, dating from the sixteenth century to the present day – the National Museum of Women in the Arts features silverware, ceramics, photographs, decorative arts, and paintings. Even the building itself, a former Masonic lodge, is interesting for its trapezoidal shape, brick-and-limestone facade, and elegant colonnade. The highlights of the museum's collection start with works from the Renaissance, like

▲PLAQUE, PETERSEN HOUSE

those of Sofonisba Anguissola, considered the most important woman artist of her day. From a noble family, she achieved fame as an accomplished portraitist before becoming court painter to Phillip II of Spain; her *Double Portrait of a Lady and Her Daughter* is one such work on display. A century or so later, Dutch and Flemish women like Clara Peeters, Judith Leyster, and Rachel Ruysch were producing still lifes and genre scenes that were the equal of their male colleagues, while in France, women like Elisabeth-Louise Vigé-Lebrun held sway as court painters, depicting the royalty fluttering around Marie Antoinette.

Nineteenth-century highlights include scenes by Mary Cassatt, who was intrigued by the forms and colors of Asian art; *The Bath*, an etching of mother and baby using crisp swatches of pale color, was influenced by an exhibition of Japanese woodblocks she had seen in Paris. Twentieth-century artists and works include the Neoclassical sculpture of Camille Claudel, the nature symbolism of Georgia O'Keeffe, and a cycle of prints depicting the hardships of working-class life by the socialist and feminist Käthe

Kollwitz, part of her powerful *A Weaver's Rebellion* series. More curious is Frida Kahlo's *Itzcuintli Dog with Me*, in which she poses next to a truly tiny, strangely adorable mutt. The last gallery reaches into modern times, with striking photographs of figures from the entertainment and literary worlds by Louise Dahl-Wolfe, some compelling sculpture by Dorothy Dehner and Louise Nevelson, and a series of studies for the *Dinner Party*, by Judy Chicago, a groundbreaking feminist work from the 1970s.

New York Avenue Presbyterian Church

1313 New York Ave NW ☎ 202/393-3700, ⊛ www.nyapc.org. Daily 9am–1pm, guided tours Sun after 8.45am & 11am services. The red-brick New York Avenue Presbyterian Church is a clever 1950s facsimile of the mid-nineteenth-century church in which the Lincoln family worshipped. The pastor at that time, Dr Gurley, was at Lincoln's bedside at the Petersen House when he died, and conducted the funeral service four days later at the White House. Ask in the office on the New York Avenue side and someone should be on hand to show you the president's second-row pew, while downstairs in the "Lincoln Parlor" you can see an early draft of his Emancipation Proclamation and portraits of Lincoln and Dr Gurley.

Shops

Hecht's

1201 G St NW ☎202/628-6661. The best place in Old Downtown to get your fix of name-brand clothing, fragrances, electronics, and other mainstream goods.

Old Post Office Pavilion

1100 Pennsylvania Ave NW ☎202/289-4224. A good bet for cheap Indian, Greek, and Mexican food, where you can also gaze up at the building's massive atrium, around which are arrayed a number of gift and knickknack shops.

Olsson's Books and Records

418 7th St NW ☎202/638-7613. One of the premier spots for buying retail books downtown, with a solid selection of fiction, history, and politics (some of it touching on the District), along with a café and a respectable number of CDs.

Cafés

Café Mozart

1331 H St NW ☎202/347-5732. Worth seeking out if you have a flair for German food, this combination eatery and deli serves the requisite schnitzels, bratwursts, roasted meats, and other favorites, plus sweets, cakes, and desserts.

Reeve's Restaurant and Bakery

1306 G St NW ☎202/628-6350. In business since 1886, this classic diner has an all-you-can-eat breakfast and fruit bar, crispy chicken at lunchtime, and famous fruit pies.

Restaurants

Andale

401 7th St NW ☎202/783-3133. Federal Triangle eatery with fine, fairly authentic Mexican cuisine, including the likes of pepper-roasted seafood and chicken and some good mole sauces.

Harry's

In the *Hotel Harrington*, 436 11th St NW ☎202/624-0053. Old-fashioned meals of tasty comfort food (meat loaf, spaghetti and meatballs), with even cheaper prices at the adjacent self-service *Harrington Café*.

Hunan Chinatown

624 H St NW ☎202/783-5858. Sleek Chinese restaurant heavy on spicy flavors; the tea-smoked duck is one of the highlights. You probably won't need appetizers, as the portions are large, though the wonton in chili sauce is tasty.

Jaleo

480 7th St NW ☎202/628-7949. Renowned upscale tapas bar-restaurant with fine flamenco dancing and seafood and plentiful sangria to wash it down with. Limited reservation policy makes for long waits during peak hours.

Old Ebbitt Grill

675 15th St NW ☎202/347-4801. In business in various locations since 1856, this plush re-creation of a nineteenth-century tavern features a mahogany bar (serving microbrews), gas chandeliers, leather booths, and gilt mirrors. Professional/politico

▲D.A.'S RFD WASHINGTON

clientele feasts on everything from burgers to oysters, breakfasts to late dinners.

Red Sage

605 14th St NW ☎202/638-4444. Nuevo-Southwestern restaurant serving rotisserie-grilled meat, fish, and veggie specials. The funky café-bar is less exclusive, though its menu is more conventional. Reservations essential for the restaurant.

Sky Terrace

In the *Hotel Washington*, 515 15th St NW ☎202/638-5900. A romantic spot to enjoy a sweeping view of the city, along with a simple sandwich. While the food is nothing special, it's a bargain considering the outdoor perch above the White House.

Ten Penh

1001 Pennsylvania Ave NW ☎202/393-4500. Slick, high-profile Asian-fusion restaurant in the Federal Triangle, serving up pricey dishes like roasted duck and pork wonton ravioli. Many dishes are worth the cost, but head north to Chinatown for more authentic entrees.

Tony Cheng's

619 H St NW ☎202/842-8669. Good-value, all-you-can-eat Mongolian barbecue downstairs; upstairs, a pricey Cantonese seafood restaurant with daily dim sum. The upstairs dining room has been visited by every president since Carter.

Tosca

1112 F St NW ☎202/367-1990. Upscale Northern Italian eatery with well-prepared meat and pasta staples from the Old Country, along with tasty desserts and flavorful juice drinks.

Bars

D.A.'s RFD Washington

810 7th St NW ☎202/289-2030. The leading edge in DC micro-breweries, with three hundred bottled beers and forty locally crafted and international brews on tap. Centrally located near the MCI Center, so watch for heavy post-game crowds.

ESPN Zone

555 12th St NW ☎202/783-3776. Sports fanatics will delight in the sports empire's DC branch, with hundreds of TVs – even above the urinals – showing every sporting event under the sun, plus tables outfitted with individual audio feeds and, of course, beer.

John Harvard's

In the Warner Theatre building, 1299 Pennsylvania Ave NW ☎202/783-2739. Upscale basement brewhouse and restaurant, with half a dozen solid beers on tap; also a good place to power down home-styled food favorites like chicken pot pie and meat loaf.

Clubs and live music

Dream

1350 Okie St NE ☎202/347-5255, ⊛www.dcdream.com. A huge, four-level lounge-and-club playing hip-hop and Latin music, with all the usual attitude. One of several mega-clubs that have appeared in recent years, still going after the others have closed. Take a cab, though – this is in one of DC's dicier areas, a fair distance from major sights.

▼WARNER THEATRE

Performing arts

National Theatre

1321 Pennsylvania Ave NW ☎202/628-6161, ⊛www.nationaltheatre.org. One of the country's oldest theaters, it's been on this site (if not in this building) since 1835. Features flashy new premieres, pre- and post-Broadway productions, and musicals.

Shakespeare Theatre

In the Lansburgh building, 450 7th St NW ☎202/547-1122, ⊛www.shakespearedc.org. Four plays a year by Shakespeare and his Elizabethan and Jacobean contemporaries. Each June the company stages free, outdoor performances at the Carter Barron Amphitheatre in Rock Creek Park (see p.148).

Warner Theatre

1299 Pennsylvania Ave NW ☎202/628-1818, ⊛www.warnertheatre.com. Glorious 1920s movie palace that's been remodeled and now stages post-Broadway productions, musicals, and major concerts.

Woolly Mammoth Theatre

7th and D sts ☎202/289-2443, ⊛www.woollymammoth.net. Increasingly popular theater troupe that's recently moved to splashy new downtown digs. Stages budget- and mid-priced shows of contemporary and experimental plays.

New Downtown and Dupont Circle

Many visitors will bear at least passing acquaintance with New Downtown, if only because that's where many of the better hotels are – and have been since the late-Victorian era, when businessmen and hoteliers first saw the advantage in being just a few blocks from the White House. More than anything, New Downtown is DC's corporate district, though some thoroughfares, like 16th Street and Connecticut Avenue, have some appeal in their architecture or the odd museum. Farther northwest, Dupont Circle has come into its own only in recent decades – it's the place to go for hip restaurants, gay-friendly clubs, charming old buildings, and modern-art galleries. East of Dupont, up-and-coming Logan Circle boasts an alternative theater scene and some quirky shops.

St Matthew's Cathedral

1725 Rhode Island Ave NW ☎202/347-3215, ✆www.stmatthewscathedral.org. Mon–Fri & Sun 6.30am–6.30pm, Sat 7.30am–6.30pm. While not quite on the same gigantic level as the National Shrine of the Immaculate Conception, St Matthew's Cathedral is still monumental and is an essential stop for anyone interested in things spiritual or architectural. The centerpiece above the altar is a towering, 35ft mosaic of the church's patron saint, while other features include a grand organ with seventy tin pipes, a white-marble altar and pulpit, and four more mosaics depicting the four evangelists (Matthew, Mark, Luke, and John) with their respective symbols. The cathedral is perhaps best known as the place where JFK's funeral Mass was held in 1963, and there's a memorial in front of the altar. When he was alive, Kennedy made frequent appearances

▼ST MATTHEW'S CATHEDRAL

here, and later (Protestant) presidents have also dropped by on occasion, along with just about any notable Catholic politician in Congress. If you want to peer at the political-bigwig worshippers, church services are open to all; for a better look at the building itself, free tours, which you can reserve in advance, occur Sunday at 2.30pm.

Connecticut Avenue NW

You could conceivably cover most of DC's major sights on just two roads: Pennsylvania Avenue NW, starting at the US Capitol and proceeding through Old Downtown to the White House, and from there on to Connecticut Avenue NW, leading from New Downtown to Dupont Circle and up to Adams-Morgan and Upper Northwest. Connecticut Avenue is arguably the most appealing of all the District's thoroughfares, if only because it links so many interesting neighborhoods – from chic and swank to funky and bohemian – and takes you past all manner of excellent eateries, nightspots, boutiques, booksellers, museums, and galleries. Moreover, it's easy to navigate, and even if you get lost all you have to do is roll downhill (southbound) and eventually you'll find yourself back at Lafayette Square, where the road begins its journey.

Mayflower Hotel

1127 Connecticut Ave NW ☎202/347-3000. Connecticut Avenue has since 1925 been graced by the double bay-fronted *Mayflower Hotel*, whose first official function was President Calvin Coolidge's inaugural ball but which has subsequently been used as a site for countless official and unofficial events; indeed, FDR lived here

for a while after his inauguration, while J. Edgar Hoover lunched here every day when he ran the FBI. Designed by the New York architects responsible for Grand Central Terminal, the hotel's showcase is its remarkable, 500ft-long Promenade. It's rich in rugs, oils, sofas, gilt, and mirrors, as is the hotel's Grand Ballroom, in which a dozen incoming presidents have swirled around the dance floor over the years. Now part of the Renaissance chain, the hotel will cost you a good amount for a stay (see review, p.181), but you can always troop through the marvelous public spaces and peer in at the swells taking lunch in the hotel's uber-chic *Café Promenade* (see p.127).

▼BATHYSPHERE, NATIONAL GEOGRAPHIC SOCIETY

National Geographic Explorers Hall

1145 17th St NW ☎202/857-7588, ⓦwww.nationalgeographic.com/explorer. Mon–Sat 9am–5pm, Sun 10am–5pm. Situated with the group's headquarters near 17th and M, the hall presents excellent rotating exhibitions in the tradition of the magazine's globe-trotting coverage, as well as child-friendly geography displays.

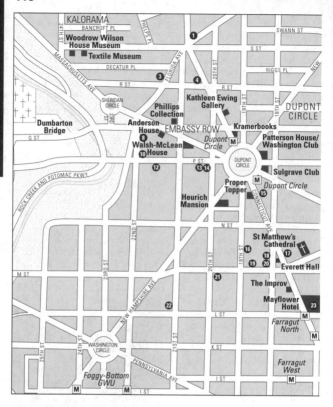

Together these exhibits cover a range of diverse topics, including rainforest protection, indigenous cultures, and the latest trends in science and technology. There are frequent events featuring explorers, photographers, scientists, and filmmakers as well as occasional concerts. Also on hand is the National Geographic store, which vends a wide selection of maps, globes, videos, photography books, and souvenirs.

B'nai B'rith Klutznick National Jewish Museum

2020 K St NW ☎ 202/857-6583,
🌐 bnaibrith.org/museum. Mon–Thurs
10am–3pm, by reservation only. $5.
The exemplary B'nai B'rith

Klutznick National Jewish Museum presents a captivating look at Jewish life through historical, ceremonial, and folk-art objects. The galleries cover almost every aspect of the Jewish experience, and everything from eighteenth-century circumcision instruments and tax permits to painted Italian marriage contracts and linen Torah (liturgical scroll) binders are on display. The oldest items are 2000-year-old incantation bowls, whose Hebrew inscriptions were believed to cast a protective spell over whomever the words were dedicated to. Other pieces show extraordinary workmanship; note the silver spice containers adorned with turrets,

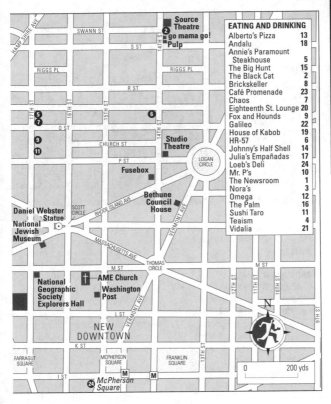

EATING AND DRINKING

Alberto's Pizza	13
Andalu	18
Annie's Paramount Steakhouse	5
The Big Hunt	15
The Black Cat	2
Brickskeller	8
Café Promenade	23
Chaos	7
Eighteenth St. Lounge	20
Fox and Hounds	9
Galileo	22
House of Kabob	19
HR-57	6
Johnny's Half Shell	14
Julia's Empañadas	17
Loeb's Deli	24
Mr. P's	10
The Newsroom	1
Nora's	3
Omega	12
The Palm	16
Sushi Taro	11
Teaism	4
Vidalia	21

PLACES New Downtown and Dupont Circle

and the micrographic writing on miniature Bibles. Enthusiastic docents point out the significance of particular objects; slender metal Torah pointers, for example, are designed to avoid having a human hand touch the sacred scroll itself. The museum also has a hall of fame celebrating Jewish-American contributions to sports and goes into some detail about diaspora groups around the world.

Metropolitan AME Church

1518 M St NW ☎202/331-1426, ⊛www.metropolitanamec.org. Mon–Sat 10am–6pm; services Sun 7.30am & 10am, Wed noon. The large Gothic red-brick Met-

ropolitan African Methodist Episcopal (AME) Church was built and paid for in 1886 by former slaves, becoming home to the largest black congregation in the nineteenth century. It was here that the funeral of Frederick Douglass took place in February 1895. The statesman and orator was brought to lie in state in the place where he had often preached. On the day of the funeral, crowds swamped the street outside, black schools closed for the day, and flags in the city flew at half-mast. A formidable-looking edifice, the church is one of the District's ecclesiastical high points, with its striking,

▲ WASHINGTON POST BUILDING

narrow arches and spires and handsome decorative trim of granite.

Washington Post

1150 15th St NW. Hourly tours Mon 10am–3pm, by advance reservation only at ☎202/334-7969. The District's daily newspaper, the *Washington Post*, has built its reputation squarely on the investigative coup of its reporters Bob Woodward and Carl Bernstein, who brought to light the Watergate scandal that led ultimately to the resignation of President Richard Nixon in 1974, and who continue (in Woodward's case) to score the occasional insider's story. Free tours of the offices are available for groups of ten or more, by request in writing (call ahead for more information). If you take one of the tours, you can get a glimpse of how one of the country's most respected publications is put together – nothing surprising, perhaps, but worthwhile if you have any interest in local journalism behind the scenes.

Bethune Council House

1318 Vermont Ave NW ☎202/673-2402, ⊛www.nps.gov/mamc. Mon–Sat 10am–4.30pm. In the Logan Circle neighborhood – located between the corporate towers of New Downtown and the grittier confines of Shaw – the Bethune Council House is a restored Victorian townhouse that commemorates one of DC's most prominent African-American residents. Mary McLeod Bethune was born on a cotton farm in South Carolina in 1875, one of seventeen children of poor parents, both ex-slaves, and persevered to found Florida's Daytona Educational and Industrial School for Negro Girls (later Bethune-Cookman College). In 1935 she was honored by the NAACP and soon after became FDR's special advisor on minority affairs. Later, as the director of the Division of Negro Affairs in the National Youth Administration, Bethune became the first black woman to head a federal office. This house was bought by Bethune in 1942 to serve both as her home (she lived here for seven years) and as headquarters for the National Council for Negro Women, which she founded in 1935. Now administered by the National Park Service, the house serves as a research center and archive, and if you have any interest in digging into American race relations during this period, Bethune's letters and writings will help bring them to life. You're also welcome to tour the restored rooms, which are decorated with Victorian flair and contain a few mementos of Bethune alongside period photographs.

Dupont Circle

Strictly speaking, Dupont Circle is the great traffic roundabout formed at the intersection of such major boulevards as Massachusetts, Connecticut, and New Hampshire avenues, along with 19th and P streets. Beyond the circle itself, it's an amiable, relaxed neighborhood with a good blend of hipsters, yuppies, and old-timers. This is also one of the District's best places for a walk, loaded with gorgeous townhouses and mansions from the nineteenth and early-twentieth centuries, along with a number of compelling museums, bookshops, galleries, restaurants, bars, and clubs. Along with

Connecticut Avenue NW, the major stretches for nocturnal entertainment are P Street west of the circle and 17th Street east of it, which both tend to be gay-oriented.

There are almost too many notable works of historic architecture to mention here, but one of the highlights is the Neoclassical building at 15 Dupont Circle NW and Massachusetts Ave – though now the **Washington Club**, it was once known as the Patterson House, where the Coolidges, camping out while White House renovations took place, entertained Charles Lindbergh, fresh from his solo transatlantic crossing. The swanky **Sulgrave Club** is another upscale, private entity, at 1801 Massachusetts Ave, with an elegant Beaux Arts design with terra cotta details that seems to tower above the commoners. Although these structures are closed to the public most of the time, some are open during the first weekend in June, when a consortium of ten area museums sponsors the Dupont–Kalo-

▼SULGRAVE CLUB

rama Museums Walk Weekend (🅦www.dkmuseums.com), featuring free concerts, historic-house tours, and craft displays.

Heurich House

1307 New Hampshire Ave NW
☎202/429-1894, 🅦www.heurichhouse
.org. Tours Wed 12.15pm & 1.15pm. $5.
One historic residence around Dupont Circle that is regularly open to the public is the won-drous Heurich House, built in 1894 for German-born brewing magnate Christian Heurich, and a stunning jewel of the Richard-sonian Romanesque popular at the time. With its rough-hewn stone turret and castellations, richly carved wood-and-plas-ter interior, and forbidding yet perfect facade, the mansion – known as "The Brewmaster's Castle" – resembles a miniature medieval fortress plunked down in a leafy suburb. Formerly occupied by the Historical Society of Washington DC, the house is once again in the possession of the only family that ever lived there, the Heurichs and their descendants, and to their credit they still allow weekly tours of the place. These take you through many of the restored rooms, dwelling on the mansion's lav-ish decor and the lifestyle of its occu-pants. On display are the formal parlor, drawing room and dining room, a music room with a mahogany musi-cians' balcony, and the basement *Bier-stube* (beer room),

carved with such Teutonic drinking mottos as "He who has never been drunk is not a good man."

Embassy Row

Massachusetts Ave, NW of Dupont Circle. This attraction makes Washington DC unique among American cities: countless for-eign embassies lined up in rows, and on intersecting streets as well. Displaying outside their front entrances many differ-ent flags – familiar and obscure – the embassies are marked by plaques (some in English) and can be anything from deserted outposts to heavily guarded fortresses, depending on the country. Again, an architecture guide will go some distance toward sorting them all out, given that most of the embassies are in grand mansions from the turn of the last century; one of

▼HEURICH HOUSE

▲ ANDERSON HOUSE

the clear standouts is the Indonesian Embassy, 2020 Massachusetts Ave NW, which occupies the magnificent Art Nouveau **Walsh-McLean House**, built in 1903 for gold baron Thomas Walsh. It's a superb building, with colonnaded loggia and intricate, carved windows, and it saw regular service as one of Washington society's most fashionable venues, with soirees presided over by Walsh's daughter Evalyn, the last private owner of the Hope Diamond (now in the National Museum of Natural History). Visit Ⓦwww.embassyevents.org for a listing of art shows, lectures, food fairs, films, and displays taking place at selected embassies here and elsewhere in town. Alternatively, you can drop in on the Goodwill Embassy Tour (pre-booked $30, $35 on the day; ☎202/636-4225, Ⓦwww.dcgoodwill.org), held on the second Saturday in May, in which some of DC's finest embassy buildings throw open their doors for one day

Anderson House

2118 Massachusetts Ave NW
☎202/785-2040, Ⓦwww
.thesocietyofthecincinnati.addr.com.

Tues–Sat 1–4pm. Another historic treasure, the Anderson House is a veritable palace built in 1905 as the winter residence of Larz Anderson, who served as ambassador to Belgium and Japan. As a Beaux Arts residence it has no equal in the city, its graystone exterior sporting twin arched entrances with heavy wooden doors and colonnaded portico. Inside, original furnishings – cavernous fireplaces, inlaid marble floors, Flemish tapestries, diverse murals, and a grand ballroom – provide a suitably lavish backdrop for ambassadorial receptions. Some of this you'll be able to see for yourself, since the house was bequeathed in Anderson's will to the Society of the Cincinnati, established in 1783 and the oldest patriotic organization in the country, which maintains a small museum of Revolutionary memorabilia.

Phillips Collection

1600 21st St NW ☎202/387-2151, Ⓦwww.phillipscollection.org. Tues–Sat 10am–5pm, Sun noon–7pm, Thurs closes at 8.30pm. $8. Calling itself "America's first museum of modern art," the Phillips Collection occupies part of the brownstone Georgian Revival building that was the family home of founder Duncan Phillips, heir to a steel fortune who bought nearly 2400 works over the years. During the 1920s, he and his artist wife, Marjorie, became patrons of artists such as Georgia O'Keeffe and Marsden Hartley, and later of everyone from Renoir to Rothko. The museum is strong on temporary exhibitions, so any works mentioned from the voluminous permanent collection may or may not be on view when you come. A recent, ongoing renovation may also keep some works from being displayed.

The main entrance is in the Goh Annex, on 21st Street, where permanent-collection pieces include a handful of Abstract Expressionist works, including a set of paintings by Rothko and abstract items by Richard Diebenkorn and Philip Guston. On the second floor, there's a wistful Blue Period Picasso, Matisse's *Studio, Quai St-Michel*, a Cézanne still life, and no fewer than four van

▲MICROPHONE, WOODROW WILSON HOUSE

Goghs, including the powerful *Road Menders*. Top billing generally goes to *The Luncheon of the Boating Party* by Renoir, where straw-boatered dandies linger over a long and bibulous feast. Phillips bought the painting as part of a two-year burst of acquisition that also yielded Cézanne's *Mont Saint-Victoire* and Honoré Daumier's *The Uprising*. There's an interesting spread of works by Degas, too, from early scenes like *Women Combing Their Hair* to a late ballet picture, *Dancers at the Bar*.

Kalorama

The leafy, well-tended streets of the exclusive district of Kalorama stretch out to meet Rock Creek Park, about a half-mile northwest of Dupont Circle. Here the city's diplomats, senators, cabinet secretaries, presidential advisors, and top-notch lobbyists and businesspeople hide behind lace curtains and bulletproof glass in row after row of multimillion-dollar townhouses, embassies, mansions, and hibiscus-clad gardens. As in all rich American ghettos, there is little to see other than a few interesting, if blandly similar, buildings. One exception is the residence of the French ambassador, 2221 Kalorama Rd NW, a Tudor Revival country manor built for a mining magnate and sold to the French in 1936 for the then-expensive sum of almost half a million dollars. Not surprisingly, they've clung to it tightly ever since.

Woodrow Wilson House

2340 S St NW ☎ 202/387-4062, ⊛ www.woodrowwilsonhouse.org. Tues–Sun 10am–4pm. $5. After his term in office ended in 1921, ailing ex-president Woodrow Wilson moved into a fine Georgian Revival house that's now open to the public. It's a comfortable home – light and airy, with high ceilings, wood floors, a wide staircase, and solarium – which, despite his incapacitating stroke in 1919, Wilson aimed to use as a workplace where he could write and practice law. However, he only lived another three years, and after his death was interred in Washington National Cathedral.

There's plenty to see, not least of which is the bedroom, furnished by his second wife, Edith, as it had been in the White House. The canvas-walled library of this most scholarly of presidents once contained eight thousand books (they were donated to the Library of Congress after his death); those that remain are the 69 volumes of Wilson's own writings. Frozen in the 1920s, the fully equipped kitchen is a beauty, with black-lead range and provisions stacked in the walk-in pantry.

Textile Museum

2320 S St NW ☎202/667-0441, ✆www.textilemuseum.org. Mon–Sat 10am–5pm, Sun 1–5pm. $5. Spread over two equally grand converted residences, the Textile Museum presents temporary exhibitions drawn from its 15,000-item collection of textiles, garments, and carpets. The museum had its roots in the collection of George Hewitt Myers, who bought his first Oriental rug as a student and opened the museum with three hundred other rugs and textile pieces in 1925. Based in his family home, the museum soon expanded into the house next door; today both buildings, and the lovely gardens, are open to the public. Rotating displays might take in pre-Columbian

Peruvian textiles, Near and Far Eastern exhibits (some dating back to 3000 BC), as well as rugs and carpets from Spain, South America, and the American Southwest.

Shops

Everett Hall

1230 Connecticut Ave NW ☎202/467-0003. Big-name designer for men's Italian suits and contemporary sportswear, outfitting countless high-rollers, celebrities, and athletes – and you too, if you have the money.

Fusebox

1412 14th St NW ☎202/299-9220. A chic and popular spot to sample the latest in avant-garde artwork in a variety of media, with a strong bent toward the abstract, irreverent, and inexplicable.

go mama go!

1809 14th St NW ☎202/299-0850. Funky home-furnishings store featuring cool and swanky Asian-styled art, wall hangings, and dinnerware, some of it designed by the store's owner.

Kathleen Ewing Gallery

1609 Connecticut Ave NW ☎202/328-0955. Highly regarded gallery featuring vintage nineteenth-century photography and prints, abstract and representational sculptures, and paintings by contemporary artists as well. Worth dropping in to see the latest exhibitions, even if you're not buying.

Kramerbooks

1517 Connecticut Ave NW ☎202/387-1462. In a central location near Dupont Circle itself, one of the District's most noteworthy booksellers, with a wide and

▲KRAMERBOOKS

eclectic selection, plus a decent café-restaurant.

Proper Topper

1350 Connecticut Ave NW ☎202/842-3055. The sleek and sassy spot to create a new look for yourself, with a stylish assortment of purses, bags, makeup, hats, watches, and knickknacks and accessories.

Pulp

1803 14th St NW ☎202/462-7857. Eye-popping, purple-fronted shop in Shaw thick with trinkets and oddball souvenirs, but best for its wide selection of greeting cards – from the mundane to the freakish, or you can create your own.

Cafés

Alberto's Pizza

2010 P St NW ☎202/986-2121. Little more than a basement-level take-out stand, but draws lines for the excellent deals on thin-crust pizza. Open 'til 4am Fri and Sat.

House of Kabob

1829 M St NW ☎202/293-5588. Delicious and cheap Middle Eastern fare prepared according to Islamic rules. The meat and veggie kebabs are the main draw, though the cramped setting offers zero atmosphere.

Julia's Empanadas

1221 Connecticut Ave NW ☎202/861-8828. Savory Mexican turnovers stuffed with international flavors from curry to spicy sausage, and so cheap you'll barely notice the money leaving your wallet.

Loeb's Deli

832 15th St NW ☎202/371-1150. New York-style delicatessen, one of the better places in the District to get a decent pastrami sandwich, and featuring all the usual bagel-and-lox staples.

The Newsroom

1803 Connecticut Ave NW ☎202/332-1489. Coffee, snacks, and pastries are served at this newsstand, which carries one of DC's best selections of hipster magazines, British and French imports, and hard-to-find newspapers. They also have Internet access upstairs.

Teaism

2009 R St NW ☎202/667-3827. Serene Dupont Circle teahouse

serving Japanese bentos, Thai curries, ginger scones, and, of course, lots of good tea. Also at 800 Connecticut Ave NW, New Downtown (☎202/835-2233), and 400 8th St NW, Old Downtown (☎202/638-6010).

Restaurants

Annie's Paramount Steakhouse
1609 17th St NW ☎202/232-0395. A gay-friendly, Dupont Circle institution that's been in business since the 1940s, serving inexpensive steaks, good burgers, and brunch – including a midnight brunch on weekends.

Café Promenade
In the *Mayflower Hotel*, 1127 Connecticut Ave NW ☎202/347-2233. A serenading harpist and pricey but scrumptious Mediterranean menu set the tone in this elegant hotel restaurant, where you can expect to see all types of political heavyweights.

Galileo
1110 21st St NW ☎202/293-7191. Superb Northern Italian cuisine has made this spot into a favorite for discerning foodies. Risotto makes a regular appearance on the changing menu, service is snappy, and the wine list impressive. Book well in advance.

Johnny's Half Shell
2002 P St NW ☎202/296-2021. Retro 1920s decor and a swank marble bar sit well with this bistro's down-to-earth menu, featuring local specialties like crab cakes, fried oysters, and seafood stew – go for the gumbo or, in summer, the soft-shell crabs.

Nora's
2132 Florida Ave NW ☎202/462-5143. Housed in a converted store with walls decorated with folk-art quilts, this is one of DC's best eateries, with prices to match. The all-organic fare includes oddball items like veal-and-cashew curry and Amish duck confit.

The Palm
1225 19th St NW ☎202/293-9091. This "power meatery" is renowned for its New York strip and lobster – and for the power players and celebrities who wine and dine here. Reservations required.

▼GALILEO

▲JOHNNY'S HALF SHELL

Sushi Taro

1507 17th St NW ☏202/462-8999. One of DC's best Japanese restaurants; if raw fish isn't your thing, choose from the selection of tasty curries and noodles.

Vidalia

1990 M St NW ☏202/659-1990. The New American cuisine dished up with a Southern twang has garnered this eatery a reputation as one of the District's best. Be on the lookout for barbecued pork, fried chicken, and the shrimp-and-grits combo.

Bars

The Big Hunt

1345 Connecticut Ave NW ☏202/785-2333. As well known for its eccentric decor – including a tarantula candelabra – as for its beer. More than 25 brews on tap, a good jukebox, and a groovy crowd. Always busy during happy hour.

The Brickskeller

1523 22nd St NW ☏202/293-1885. Renowned brick-lined basement saloon serving "the world's largest selection of beer" – as many as 850 different types, including dozens from US microbreweries.

Fox and Hounds

1537 17th St NW ☏202/232-6307. Smack in the middle of the 17th Street action, this easygoing bar draws a diverse crowd of different races and orientations, who are here mostly to kick back and enjoy the stiff and cheap drinks.

Mr P's

2147 P St NW ☏202/293-1064. Longest-serving gay bar in the neighborhood, though some say it's seen better days. Mirrored walls and dance tunes downstairs, hustling naked go-go dancers upstairs, plus an outdoor patio decorated with kitsch like pink flamingos.

Omega

2122 P St NW, in the rear alley ☏202/223-4917. Gay-oriented, techno-swanky spot with four bars, pool tables, and a dark video room upstairs. Stop in for happy hour or for a kickoff drink on the weekends. Mostly men.

Clubs and live music

Andalu

1214 18th St NW ☎202/785-2922. Stylish, dress-code-oriented place with a mix of moody deep-house and garage dance beats, and the occasional live musicians dabbling in jazz and electronica. Booze is on the expensive side, though.

The Black Cat

1811 14th St NW ☎202/667-7960, ⓦwww.blackcatdc.com. Part-owned by Foo Fighter Dave Grohl, this indie institution provides a showcase for up-and-coming rock, punk, and garage bands and veteran alternative acts alike, plus a sprinkling of world beat and retro-pop.

Chaos

1603 17th St NW ☎202/232-4141. Free-spirited club at the heart of the 17th Street scene, with inexpensive drinks poured from a finely stocked bar. There's a cabaret show featuring drag kings and queens, plus drag bingo, the latter popular with the straight crowd, too.

Eighteenth Street Lounge

1212 18th St NW ☎202/466-3922. Ultrastylish spot housed in Teddy Roosevelt's former mansion. While the attitude can be a bit thick, the beats – mostly acid jazz, dub, and trip-hop – are a big draw, along with superstar DJs. Look for the unmarked door next to the mattress shop. Dress smart and come early to beat the cover and line.

HR-57

1610 14th St NW ☎202/667-3700, ⓦwww.hr57.org. Small but authentic combo educational-institute/live-music-club where jazz in many of its manifestations – classic, hard bop, free, and cool – is performed on Wed, Fri, and Sun nights, often by newcomers on their way up. One of the essential cultural spots in the Logan Circle neighborhood.

Performing arts

Improv

1140 Connecticut Ave NW ☎202/296-7008, ⓦwww.dcimprov.com. DC's main comedy stage, part of a chain of eight such venues nationwide. Draws both up-and-coming performers and the occasional veteran from the TV humor circuit.

Source Theatre

1835 14th St NW ☎202/462-1073, ⓦwww.sourcetheatre.com. New and contemporary works and classic reinterpretations in this favorite just north of Logan Circle. Promotes the Washington Theater Festival, a showcase for new works, every summer.

Studio Theatre

1333 P St NW ☎202/332-3300, ⓦwww.studiotheatre.org. Independent Logan Circle theater with two stages, presenting classic and modern drama and comedy.

Adams-Morgan, Shaw, and Outer Northeast

Few districts more greatly represent the gap between tourist DC and "real" DC than Adams-Morgan and Shaw. Though they offer little in the way of museums or sights, they boast some of the liveliest street culture, best independent shops, and richest blend of races and cultures in town. Even better, for those so inclined, these are the essential places to party in freewheeling dance clubs, rock- and punk-music venues, and cheap bars. The authenticity is accompanied by a bit of an edge; it's best to take a cab at night between major destinations. Outer Northeast DC offers a handful of appealing destinations, such as the National Arboretum, at some remove from its crime-ridden areas.

Columbia Road and 18th Street

Nowhere is gentrification faster changing the original, ethnic character of a Washington neighborhood than along Adams-Morgan's main drags of Columbia Road and 18th Street – the intersection of which marks the center of the area. Although many new designer restaurants, stylish bars, and hip stores have

begun to outnumber the traditional Hispanic businesses, Spanish signs and notices are still in evidence along Columbia, and the neighborhood certainly celebrates its heritage handsomely at the annual Latin American Festival (July) and Adams-Morgan Day (Sept) shindigs.

South of Columbia, 18th Street is DC's melting-pot axis, where yuppies from Kalorama

▼18TH STREET NW, ADAMS-MORGAN

▲U STREET, SHAW

drop in to sample the funky vibe and snap up street wear for a song, venturesome gays and hipsters from Dupont Circle come to imbibe at bars and browse in secondhand bookstores, and African Americans from Shaw visit to support independent boutiques and other minority businesses. Matching the broad mix of visitors is a wide range of restaurants and stores – Latin botanicas, junk emporia, astrologists and palm readers, vintage-clothing dealers, fringe theaters, you name it.

U Street

One of DC's oldest residential neighborhoods, Shaw has its focus along U Street between 10th and 16th streets. The area's early twentieth-century heyday is long gone, when pool halls, churches, cafés, theaters, and social clubs dotted the landscape; a shopping strip developed on 14th Street; and U Street evolved into the "Black Broadway." By the 1960s, the older streets in Shaw were antiquated, and the riots of 1968 finished them off. The assassination of Dr Martin Luther King Jr sparked three days of arson, rioting, and looting that destroyed businesses

and lives along 7th, 14th, and H streets. A dozen people were killed, millions of dollars of property were lost, and the confidence of nearby businesses in Old Downtown jolted so severely that within a decade that area, too, was virtually abandoned.

That said, signs of revival are now evident – revitalized U Street has a Metro station and once again features on the city's nightlife scene, while 14th Street has blossomed as an alternative theater district. The requisite corporate chains (Starbucks and the like) are taking root, and redevelopment is slowly taking place – albeit more slowly than in Adams-Morgan. There's good fun in a night out on U Street or a stroll around the area's historic sights and landmarks, but take a cab to get here and avoid wandering aimlessly or alone in the neighborhood, which can change from sketchy to threatening in a few blocks.

African-American Civil War Memorial and Museum

1200 U St NW ☎ 202/667-2667, ⊛ www.afroamcivilwar.org. Mon–Fri 10am–5pm, Sat 10am–2pm. Right at the 10th Street Metro exit is the African-American Civil

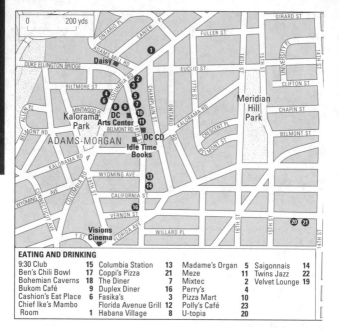

EATING AND DRINKING

9:30 Club	15	Columbia Station	13	Madame's Organ	5	Saigonnais	14
Ben's Chili Bowl	17	Coppi's Pizza	21	Meze	11	Twins Jazz	22
Bohemian Caverns	18	The Diner	7	Mixtec	2	Velvet Lounge	19
Bukom Café	9	Duplex Diner	16	Perry's	4		
Cashion's Eat Place	6	Fasika's	3	Pizza Mart	10		
Chief Ike's Mambo		Florida Avenue Grill	12	Polly's Café	23		
Room	1	Habana Village	8	U-topia	20		

War Memorial, the country's
only monument honoring the
209,000 African-American soldiers who fought for the Union.
The Spirit of Freedom sculpture
stands in the center of a granite-
paved plaza, partially encircled
by a Wall of Honor, along which
you'll find the names of the
black troops (and their seven
thousand white offi-
cers) who served in
the war. Sadly, these
brave troops were
not included in the
celebratory Grand
Review of the Union
Armies along Penn-
sylvania Avenue after
the war's end, an early
sign that the battle
for equality had only
begun.

Three blocks west
of the memorial, in
the five-story Ital-

ianate True Reformer Building,
the museum tells the soldiers'
little-known story as part of
its small permanent exhibition,
"Slavery to Freedom: Civil War
to Civil Rights." Composed
largely of photographs and documents, the collection begins
its rendering of African-American history with the original

▼EXHIBIT AT AFRICAN-AMERICAN CIVIL WAR MUSEUM

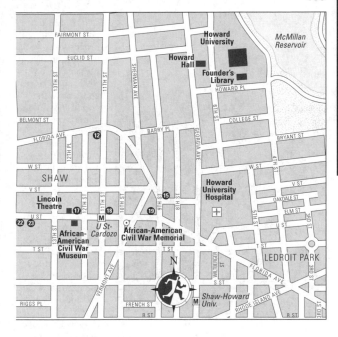

bill of sale for an 11-year-old girl. Other features include a descendants registry and a computer search that employs the Civil War Soldiers and Sailors Names Index to identify troops and the history of their regiments.

Howard University

Main entrance at 2400 6th St NW. Call ☎202/806-2755 in advance for campus tours. Perhaps the most prestigious black university in the country, Howard University was established in 1867 by a church missionary society to provide a school for blacks freed after the Civil War. Its first faculties were in law, music, medicine, and theology, though nowadays hundreds of subjects are taken by some 13,000 students from more than a hundred countries. Famous Howard alumni include Toni Morrison, Thurgood Mar-

shall, and Andrew Young. Sadly, none of the original campus buildings remain except one – Howard Hall, at 607 Howard Place, a handsome French Second Empire structure dating from the 1860s. Apart from this, many of the buildings are from the 1930s, in historic-revival styles. Few are better than the Founder's Library, a monumental edifice modeled after Philadelphia's Independence Hall.

LeDroit Park

Just north of intersection at Florida and Rhode Island avenues. Short of money just a decade after its founding, Howard University sold a plot of land to the south to developers who built an exclusive parkland suburb of sixty detached houses. By 1920 LeDroit Park was established as a fashionable black neighborhood, and though much of it

▲FOUNDER'S LIBRARY, HOWARD UNIVERSITY

US. Its grand Byzantine design, broad dome with multicolored mosaics, and towering Roman arch above the entrance would alone make the Shrine an eye-grabber, but added to this are a sleek bell tower, lovely bas-relief panels, several large buttresses, and a huge circular Celtic *triqnetra*, symbolizing the Trinity – and that's just the exterior. Inside the church is astoundingly big, with some 75 chapels or alcoves for statues, intricate mosaics showing a fight against a seven-headed serpent (among other scenes), a big pipe organ and even larger baldachino with four great marble columns, and looming above it all – its eyes seeming to follow you around the church – a jaw-dropping mosaic of Jesus clad in a striking red robe, with jets of flame shooting out from his golden halo.

has decayed over the decades, the area has been declared a historic district, with the finest surviving group of houses along the 400 block of U Street. Prominent black citizens continue to be associated with the area – the family of DC's first black mayor, Walter Washington, has owned a house here for years, while Jesse Jackson also maintains a property in the area. Neo-Gothic, French Second Empire, and Victorian styles predominate.

National Shrine of the Immaculate Conception

400 Michigan Ave NE ☎202/526-8300, ⊛www.nationalshrine.com. Daily Nov–March 7am–6pm, April–Oct 7am–7pm. Red Line, Brookland Station. Constructed in the 1950s, the National Shrine of the Immaculate Conception is the largest Catholic church in the

Takoma Park

⊛www.historictakoma.org for maps, tours, and information. Red Line, Takoma Station. If you have an interest in architecture, Takoma Park, America's first planned suburb for commuters, is worth seeking out for its original 1880s houses and design. Notable examples of some of the stylish historic homes in the area include the Bliss House, 7116 Maple Ave, an Italianate charmer made of wood but with a painted brick-and-stone facade; the bungalows along Willow Avenue north of Tulip Street, which cover a wide range of Victorian building trends; the Zigzag Art Deco structure at 7000 Carroll Avenue; and the grand Cady Lee Mansion, Chestnut Avenue at Eastern, the best of several textbook examples of the Queen Anne style, rich with gables, wraparound porch, slate roof, and gingerbread detailing.

National Arboretum

3501 New York Ave NE ☎202/245-2726, ⊛www.usna.usda.gov. Daily 8am–4.30pm, summer Sat & Sun closes 5pm. About two miles northeast of the US Capitol, the sprawling National Arboretum is an oasis of green amid an otherwise grim part of the District. The best time to visit is from mid-April to October, when plenty of plants are in bloom and park access is made easier by direct bus service (#X6; Sat & Sun every 40min;

▼SHRINE OF THE IMMACULATE CONCEPTION

$1.10) from Union Station and by tram tours (April–Oct Sat & Sun, 10.30am–4pm; $4). At the entrance at 24th and R streets you'll find the visitor's center, where you can pick up a visitor's guide, which includes a map, seasonal plant information, and descriptions of the gardens. The Arboretum's undeniable highlight is its surreal gathering of "Capitol Columns," which stand in a meadow at the heart of the grounds, supporting open sky. Once part of the US Capitol, these sandstone Corinthian pillars presided over every presidential inauguration from Jackson to Eisenhower. (They were put out to pasture in the 1950s after a renovation of the Capitol building.) Other Arboretum highlights include its collections of azaleas and dogwoods, best seen in bloom on a late spring afternoon, as well as the renowned National Bonsai and Penjing Museum (daily 10am–3.30pm).

Kenilworth Aquatic Gardens

1550 Anacostia Ave NE ☎202/426-6905, ⊛www.nps.gov/kepa. Daily 7am–4pm. Orange Line, Deanwood Station. Well off the beaten path, Kenilworth Aquatic Gardens is on the eastern fringe of the District (accessible by the I-295 freeway), but is definitely worth a look if you're curious about horticulture or natural preserves. Set on seven hundred acres of protected marshlands, the twelve-acre gardens are rich with water lilies and lotuses, and you can take an up-close view of them on an elevated boardwalk that hovers over the waterline. Alternately, there are several good paths for exploring this wet terrain, as you're able to see what was once the pristine state of the Anacostia River – hard

▲KENILWORTH AQUATIC GARDENS

to imagine in other parts of the District. The lilies are in bloom from May to September but are at their height in late July, when the park's Waterlily Festival provides a very good reason to visit.

Shops

Daisy
1814 Adams Mill Rd NW ☎202/797-1777. Stylish women's shop in Adams-Morgan that features hot items from the latest designers and an ass-kicking selection of grrrl shoes.

DC CD
2423 18th St NW ☎202/588-1810. One of the better bets in Adams-Morgan for new and used vinyl and CDs – from the mainstream to the utterly obscure.

Idle Time Books
2410 18th St NW ☎202/232-4774. Adams-Morgan favorite for used and vintage titles, with a bent toward fiction, left-leaning politics, science, and the off-beat. Late hours.

Cafés

Ben's Chili Bowl
1213 U St NW ☎202/667-0909. Venerable U Street hangout, serving chili dogs, burgers, milk shakes, and cheese fries at booths and counter stools.

The Diner
2453 18th St NW t☎202/232-8800. Open 24hr. A high ceiling and weathered tile floor make this Adams-Morgan oasis more stylish café than greasy spoon. That said, you can't go wrong with old favorites like omelets, pancakes, and bacon.

Duplex Diner
2004 18th St NW ☎202/234-7890. Classic comfort foods such as mac and cheese and meat loaf go toe-to-toe with spruced-up favorites such as salmon quesadillas – though everything on the menu is fairly affordable.

Pizza Mart
2445 18th St NW ☎202/234-9700. Adams-Morgan clubgoers mop up an evening's drinks with the hefty slices at this hole-in-the-wall pizzeria.

Restaurants

Bukom Café

2442 18th St NW ☎202/265-4600.
Delicious African fare like goat-meat broth with ground melon seeds and spinach, and chicken yassa, baked with onions and spices – most for about $10 – plus a decent selection of African beers.

Cashion's Eat Place

1819 Columbia Rd NW ☎202/797-1819. Renowned for its clever takes on New Southern cuisine, where old-time dishes like casseroles, tarts, corncakes, grits, sweet potatoes, and fruit and nut pies are transformed into taste-bud-altering delights – for a rather high price.

Coppi's Pizza

1414 U St NW ☎202/319-7773. Chic little pizza joint with a brick oven, doling out all-organic pies with a range of fancy ingredients – goat cheese, pancetta, etc – along with spicy calzones. Prices a bit higher than you might expect for a pizza place.

Fasika's

2477 18th St NW ☎202/797-7673. Most upmarket of the local Ethiopian places, a twenty-year institution with sidewalk seating, live music three nights a week, and spicy stews for $12 or so. Also try the *doro wat* – chicken in pepper sauce – and Ethiopian steak tartare.

Florida Avenue Grill

1100 Florida Ave NW ☎202/265-1586. Southern-style diner serving cheap and hearty meals for almost half a century to locals and stray celebs. Especially known for its eggs, ham, and grits.

Meze

2437 18th St NW ☎202/797-0017. A wide array of delicious Turkish meze (similar to tapas), both hot and cold, is served in a fashionable restaurant-lounge setting. Kebabs, grape leaves, and apricot chicken are among the highlights.

Mixtec

1792 Columbia Rd NW ☎202/332-1011. Drab setting, but serving great-tasting, low-priced Mexican food – tacos and tortillas, plus roasted chicken and mussels steamed with chilis. Near the heart of Adams-Morgan.

Perry's

1811 Columbia Rd NW ☎202/234-6218. In-crowd restaurant serving sushi and Asian-influenced American entrees. Rooftop tables are always at a premium and the drag queen brunch (Sun 11am–3pm) is a blast.

Saigonnais

2307 18th St NW ☎202/232-5300. Gourmet Vietnamese food in a cozy townhouse – try the steamed fish, spicy chicken, or savory rice crepes. One of the better choices in Adams-Morgan.

U-topia

1418 U St NW ☎202/483-7669. Arty, romantic bar-restaurant with regular live blues and jazz, art exhibits, good veggie dishes, and a popular weekend brunch. Entrees are eclectic, ranging from pasta and gumbo to steak and sausage.

Bars

Chief Ike's Mambo Room

1725 Columbia Rd NW ☎202/332-2211. Ramshackle mural-clad

bar with live bands or DJs hosting theme nights. It all makes for an unpretentious, fun spot to dance. The bar upstairs has indie music and a pool table.

Columbia Station

2325 18th St NW ☎202/462-6040. One of the better places in the area to listen to live jazz, along with blues, presented nightly in a supper-club setting.

Habana Village

1834 Columbia Rd NW ☎202/462-6310. Intoxicating Latin dance joint infused with the eclectic spirit of the Adams-Morgan of old. Tango and salsa lessons are available, and a good downstairs lounge/bar serves a fine mojito.

Polly's Café

1342 U St NW ☎202/265-8385. Neat little brick-and-board café-bar with a few outdoor tables, good food, tap beers, and bottled microbrews. Live music on Wednesdays.

Clubs and live music

9:30

815 V St NW ☎202/393-0930, ⊛www.930.com. Famous DC venue for indie rock and pop, local, national, and foreign. There's a separate no-cover bar, too. Book in advance for big names. It's not in a great part of town, but it is two blocks from the U Street-Cardozo Metro; take the Vermont Ave exit.

Bohemian Caverns

2003 11th St NW ☎202/299-0800, ⊛www.bohemiancaverns.com. Legendary DC jazz supper club, reopened after three decades. The jazz happens in a basement grotto, below the stylish ground-level restaurant. Cover runs to $15 or more, with a limited number of reserved tickets for bigger acts.

Madame's Organ

2461 18th St NW ☎202/667-5370, ⊛www.madamsorgan.com. Straightforward Adams-Morgan hangout featuring live blues, raw R&B, and bluegrass; small cover. Upstairs, there's a pool table and a rooftop bar.

Takoma Station Tavern

6914 4th St NW ☎202/829-1999, ⊛www.takomastation.com. Laidback club with jazz several nights a week, featuring mostly local acts, with the occasional big name. On some evenings reggae acts, comedians, or poetry slams take the spotlight.

Twins Jazz

1344 U St NW ☎202/234-0072, ⊛www.twinsjazz.com. Celebrated neighborhood jazz haunt drawing talented musicians Tues through Sun. Also serves decent Ethiopian, American, and Caribbean food.

Velvet Lounge

915 U St NW ☎202/462-3213, ⊛www.velvetloungedc.com. Schmooze-and-booze in a relaxed setting, with an eclectic range of live performance – everything from spoken-word musings to percussion-heavy worldbeat to frenetic alt-rock thrashing – and a weekly open-mike session, too.

Performing arts

The Dance Place

3225 8th St NE ☎202/269-1600, ⊛www.danceplace.org. Contemporary and modern dance productions, both mainstream and experimental. Hosts the Dance Africa festival every June. Accessible from Brookland Metro station.

DC Arts Center

2438 18th St NW ☎202/462-7833, ⓦwww.dcartscenter.org. Performance art, drama, poetry, and dance are held in this small northern Adams-Morgan space. Cheap tickets, too.

Lincoln Theatre

1215 U St NW ☎202/328-6000, ⓦwww.thelincolntheatre.org. Renovated movie/vaudeville house featuring touring stage shows, concerts, and dance, with a focus on multicultural productions.

Summer Opera Theater Company

Michigan Ave and 4th St NE ☎202/526-1669, ⓦwww .summeropera.org. Independent company staging two operas each summer, usually June, July, and/or August. Performs in Hartke Theater at the Catholic University (accessible from Brookland Metro station).

Visions Cinema Bistro Lounge

1927 Florida Ave NW ☎202/667-0090, ⓦwww.visionsdc.com. Excellent spot that's one of the few places in DC showing independent and foreign films; the attached bistro serves good food and potent drinks, which can be taken into the theater. Also features *Bar Noir*, with dance DJs, and Midnight Movies on weekends.

Upper Northwest

The swank neighborhoods of Upper Northwest comprise some of the most exclusive territory in Washington. The upper- and middle-class flight here first began with a series of nineteenth-century presidents who made the cool reaches of Woodley Park their summer home. Few others could afford the time and expense involved in living a four-mile carriage-ride from downtown until the arrival of the streetcar in the 1890s; within three decades both Woodley Park and Cleveland Park had become bywords for fashionable living, replete with apartment buildings designed by the era's top architects. Scattered about the hilly, spread-out area are the National Zoo, Washington National Cathedral, and the wooded expanses of Rock Creek Park, largest and most enjoyable of the city's green spaces.

Woodley Park

The first Upper Northwest neighborhood you'll likely encounter will be Woodley Park, which is marked at the intersection of Calvert and Connecticut Avenue with a pair of wondrous hotels that give a hint of the serious money that lurks in the surrounding hills. The massive, vaguely Colonial Revival *Wardman Park Hotel* (see review, p.182) was built in 1918, and its red-brick tower still dominates the local skyline. From its earliest days it has attracted scores of high-profile politicians and social butterflies who entertained guests in the grand public rooms and rented apartments. Within a decade a second landmark followed, the hybrid Art Deco–style *Shoreham* (see review, p.182), built in 1930 for $4 million. The hotel has held an inaugural ball or gala for every president since FDR, and in 2004 hosted a Republican fundraiser that snagged $35 million. It's also the spot where Truman played poker,

JFK courted Jackie, Nixon announced his first cabinet and, in the hotel's celebrated **Blue Room**, Judy Garland, Marlene Dietrich, Bob Hope, and Frank

▼WARDMAN PARK HOTEL

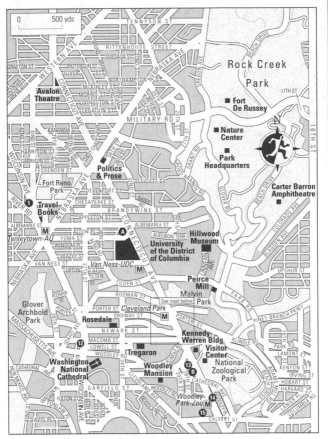

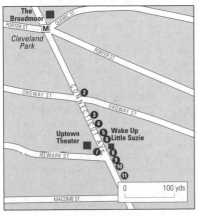

EATING AND DRINKING

Ardeo	11
Aroma	5
Cactus Cantina	12
Firehook Bakery	6
Ireland's Four Provinces	7
Krupin's	1
Lebanese Taverna	14
Nam Viet	4
Nanny O'Brien's	9
New Heights	15
Sala Thai	2
Spices	8
Vace	10
Yanyu	3
Zoo Bar - Oxford Tavern	13

ACCOMMODATION

Days Inn	A
Kalorama Guest House	B

▲ WOODLEY MANSION

Sinatra entertained the elite. For a view of where the nineteenth-century presidents passed their summers, head up Connecticut Avenue to Cathedral Avenue and walk west past 29th Street to the Georgian, white-stucco Woodley Mansion, now the Maret School. It was built in 1800 for Philip Barton Key, whose nephew Francis was later to pen the "Star-Spangled Banner," and occasionally hosted (middling) antebellum presidents such as Martin Van Buren, John Tyler, and James Buchanan.

Cleveland Park

Cleveland Park is a stylish suburb marked by a few eye-grabbing buildings along Connecticut Avenue, including the Kennedy-Warren Apartments (no. 3133), a soaring Art Deco evocation of 1930s wealth; the Art Deco movie house of the Uptown Theater (no. 3426), which has been showing movies since 1936; and the Broadmoor (no. 3601), a residential development from 1928 with a grand scale and angular Art Deco spin on classical motifs. However, it's farther west into the hills

where you can find the really historic treasures that make this neighborhood unique. Worth a look are such old-time estates as the Rosedale, 3501 Newark St NW, featuring the area's oldest structure – a weathered stone building – that dates from 1740, amid later Colonial and early American additions; and the Tregaron, 3100 Macomb Ave NW (tours by appointment only at ☎202/243-1827), a stately Colonial Revival charmer that's now used as the campus of the Washington International School. For more on local architectural highlights, contact the Cleveland Park Historical Society (☎202/363-6358, ☜www.clevelandparkdc.org), which also provides information on occasional tours of area homes.

National Zoo

3001 Connecticut Ave NW ☎202/673-4800, ☜www.natzoo.si.edu. Grounds daily: April–Oct 6am–8pm, Nov–March 6am–6pm; buildings daily: April–Oct 10am–6pm, Nov–March 10am–4.30pm. The one place in Upper Northwest that inevitably attracts out-of-town visitors is, not surprisingly, part of the

Smithsonian. Home to some 3000 creatures, the National Zoo combines the usual menagerie of giraffes, elephants, lions, and tigers with its own botanic gardens, prairie, wetlands, and aquariums. Just inside the gates from the visitor center, two trails loop down through the park to Rock Creek: the Olmsted Walk, passing most of the indoor exhibits, and the steeper Valley Trail, with birds and the major aquatic exhibits.

Strolling along the Olmsted Walk, you'll notice that the big cats in the Cheetah Conservation Station are fairly sleepy looking much of the time, but beyond here is the first celebrity sighting: the pandas Mei Xiang and Tian Tian, who arrived from China in 2000 and are the constant focus of media interest for their mating activity – or lack thereof. From here the path winds down past bison, elephants, and hippos to the Great Ape House. Nearby, you'll also find the Reptile Discovery Center, with all the usual suspects on hand plus some remarkable komodo dragons. The adjacent Invertebrate Exhibit covers everything from ants to coral and octopus, and beyond here the special

moated island with the lions and tigers marks the end of the big animals, though you might want to duck in and out of the thoroughly unpleasant bat cave before heading back up the Valley Trail.

The best thing on the Valley Trail is undoubtedly "Amazonia," the indoor tropical river and forest habitat, where an undulating aquarium gets you close to the fish – piranhas included. Farther along, seals and sea lions splash in an outdoor pool, and then it's a slow walk uphill past beaver dams, the bird house, an artificial wetland with cranes and herons, and assorted eagles, antelope, and tapirs. On Thursday evenings during the summer, the zoo hosts "Sunset Serenades," events which involve musical and cultural entertainment and draw families and couples looking for more relaxing zoo sounds than the usual primal shrieks and grunts.

Washington National Cathedral

Massachusetts and Wisconsin aves NW ☎202/537-6200 or 364-6616, ⊛www .cathedral.org/cathedral. Mon–Fri 8am–6.30pm, Sat 10am–5.30pm, Sun 10am–4.30pm; $3 donation. Washington National Cathedral is the sixth largest cathedral in the world, a monumental building so medieval in spirit it should surely rise from a dusty European town plaza rather than from a District suburb. The siting of the cathedral was

▼CHEETAH, NATIONAL ZOO

▲PEIRCE MILL, ROCK CREEK PARK

tresses, bosses, and vaults – it shows off some striking stained-glass windows, quirky gargoyles, massive columns, and, as an all-American touch, two rows of state flags hanging below the clerestory level. Along the south side of the nave, the first bay commemorates George Washington, while five bays down is the sarcophagus of Woodrow Wilson – the only president to be buried in the District (though JFK's grave can be found nearby in Arlington; see p.158). At the High Altar there's a splendid view back down along the carved vault to the west rose window; an elevator from the south porch at the west end of the nave ascends to the Pilgrim Observation Gallery, which affords stupendous city views. The 57-acre grounds hold offices, schools, a college, sports fields, and a swimming pool, not to mention an Herb Cottage selling dried herbs and teas, a greenhouse, and the Bishop's Garden, a walled rose-and-herb garden laid out in medieval style.

intentional, though: here, on the heights of Mount St Alban, the architects could have free rein to produce their Gothic Revival masterpiece.

George Washington first proposed the establishment of a "national" church in the city, but it was a century before Congress finally granted a charter for it. In 1907, the foundation ceremony was held and construction commenced; the cathedral was completed only in 1990, though parts have been in use since the 1920s. It's a Protestant church and the seat of the local Episcopal diocese, yet it also hosts services for other denominations and is conceived of as a national church – indeed, this is where Ronald Reagan's 2004 memorial service was held. Built from Indiana limestone and modeled in the medieval English Gothic style – its great spaces supported by flying but-

It's easiest to reach the cathedral by bus #30, #32, #34, #35, or #36 from Downtown DC; if you don't mind a twenty-minute walk, you can take the Metro. From the Woodley Park–Zoo station, turn left from Connecticut Avenue into Cathedral Avenue and right into Woodley Road to reach the lower-level information center; the west door is around the corner on Wisconsin Avenue.

Rock Creek Park

ⓦ www.nps.gov/rocr. Bus #S2 and #S4 run straight up 16th Street to east side of park from anywhere north of K Street NW. Most visitors overlook the attractions of the city's major natural preserve, Rock Creek Park, which divides Upper North-west from Adams-Morgan and the north-central part of the District. Established in 1890, its 1800 acres are little more than a narrow gorge in its southern reaches but spread out above the National Zoo to become a mile-wide tract of woodland west of 16th Street. A road shadows the creek for much of its length, called the Rock Creek Parkway until it reaches the zoo, north of which it's known as Beach Drive. A car is the easiest way to get in and around the park.

There are fifteen miles of trails and paths, along both sides of the creek. They include tracks and workout stations, bridleways, and a cycle route that runs from the Lincoln Memorial, north through the park and into Maryland. On weekends Beach Drive between Military and Broad Branch roads is closed to cars, and rollerbladers make the space their own. The park also features ballparks, picnic areas, and the Carter Barron Amphi-theatre (16th St and Colorado Ave NW), which hosts summer concerts. The sights start at the southern end of the park, a mile above the zoo, where the serene, granite **Peirce Mill** (Wed–Sun noon–4pm; ☎202/282-0927) stands in a beautiful riverside hollow on Tilden Street, near Beach Drive. One of eight nine-teenth-century gristmills in the valley, and the last to shut down (in 1897), it has been restored by the National Park Service and today produces cornmeal and wheat flour for sale to visitors. The **Nature Center** on Glover Road, just south of Military Road (daily 9am–5pm; ☎202/426-6828), acts as the park visitor center, with details of weekend guided walks and self-guided trails.

Hillwood Museum and Gardens

4155 Linnean Ave NW ☎1-877/HILL-WOOD, ⓦ www.hillwoodmuseum.org. Tues–Sat 9.30am-5pm; by reservation only. $12. The 1923 neo-Georgian manor once known as Arbremont was in the 1950s acquired by Marjorie Merriwether Post – heir to the cereal-company fortune – and transformed into a showpiece she renamed Hillwood. These days, the red-brick mansion and its lovely grounds – thick with roses and French- and Japanese-styled gardens – are part of the Hillwood Museum, and while the site is handsome enough, what brings people out here is the cache inside. Through her Russian-ambas-sador husband, Post managed to acquire in the 1930s a trea-sure trove of Fabergé eggs and boxes, Byzantine and Ortho-dox icons, eighteenth-century glassworks, and other priceless items, which today form the core of the museum's collec-tion. There's also an array of French and English decorative-arts items – tapestries, gilded commodes, porcelain cameos, parquet-inlaid furniture, and so on – but it's the loot from Sta-lin's USSR that really attracts the attention.

Shops

Politics & Prose

5015 Connecticut Ave NW, Tenleytown ☏202/364-1919. Located in the northern reaches of Upper Northwest, a good independent bookstore/coffee shop with one of the best programs of author appearances and readings in the city.

Travel Books & Language Center

4437 Wisconsin Ave NW, Tenleytown ☏202/237-1322. Superb travel center and bookstore featuring guides, maps, atlases, software, international cookbooks, magazines, newspapers, and a full program of events and lectures.

Wake Up Little Suzie

3409 Connecticut Ave ☏202/244-0700. Trinket emporium with a broad range of interesting items, including home-made jewelry and ceramics, arty novelty items, curious puppets, and other assorted oddments.

Cafés

Firehook Bakery

3411 Connecticut Ave NW ☏202/362-2253. Breads, cakes, cookies, and excellent coffee are all on offer at this DC institution's Cleveland Park outpost; seating in the garden adds a bit of atmosphere.

Krupin's

4620 Wisconsin Ave NW ☏202/686-1989. Jewish deli-diner with attitude – it's a long way from anywhere, but devotees consider the trek worth it for the true tastes of hot corned beef, pastrami, lox and bagel platters, and other favorites.

Vace

3315 Connecticut Ave NW ☏202/363-1999. Grab a slice of the excellent pizza or tasty sub sandwiches, or pack a picnic from the solid selection of sausage, tortellini salad, and olives and head for the zoo.

Restaurants

Ardeo

3311 Connecticut Ave ☏202/244-6750. Ultra-trendy spot with "Modern American" cuisine – meaning lots of oddball hybrids like duck-confit cannelloni and pork loin with chickpeas – though the pricey experiments work most of the time; a good lobster sandwich, too.

▼FIREHOOK BAKERY

Cactus Cantina
3300 Wisconsin Ave NW ☎202/686-7222. A Tex-Mex treat for Cathedral-goers, with a great veranda and fine eats like enchiladas, tacos, and chiles rellenos as well as grilled dishes cooked over mesquite wood and charcoal.

Lebanese Taverna
2641 Connecticut Ave NW ☎202/265-8681. Delicious Middle Eastern joint with soothingly dark, authentic decor inside. Sample something from the assortment of kebabs and grilled meat platters, or go straight for the leg of lamb.

Nam Viet
3419 Connecticut Ave NW ☎202/237-1015. No-frills eatery in the heart of the Cleveland Park dining scene. The soups are good, as are the grilled chicken and fish, the caramel pork, the Vietnamese steak – you really can't go wrong.

New Heights
2317 Calvert St NW ☎202/234-4110. Fashionable, new-wave American restaurant serving an inventive, seasonal menu where you're liable to be served anything from buffalo to rockfish. Book ahead in summer to sit outside, especially for Sunday brunch.

Sala Thai
3507 Connecticut Ave ☎202/237-2777. Good, fairly traditional Thai noodle dishes and soups, though some are jazzed up with unexpected appearances of trendy items like seared salmon,

Spices
3333 Connecticut Ave NW ☎202/686-3833. Stylish, affordable Pan-Asian place serving spicy bowls of laksa, stir-fried basil chicken, and sushi in a spacious, high-ceilinged dining room.

Yanyu
3433 Connecticut Ave NW ☎202/686-6968. Celebrated for its inventive cuisine – rich with things like sea bass, shiitake mushrooms, and crab – and elegant decor, this Cleveland Park enclave ranks high among DC's upscale Asian restaurants, but a meal can be expensive.

Bars

Aroma
3417 Connecticut Ave NW ☎202/244-7995. For all its swank atmosphere, this Cleveland Park cigar-and-martini bar still manages to feel like a neighborhood watering hole.

Ireland's Four Provinces
3412 Connecticut Ave NW ☎202/244-0860. Rollicking Irish music five nights a week brings in a college crowd. There's a good atmosphere, outdoor seats in the summer, and thirteen beers on tap.

Nanny O'Brien's
3319 Connecticut Ave NW ☎202/686-9189. Cleveland Park's other Irish tavern is a smaller, more personable spot but with the same successful mix of heavy drinking and live music. Monday's jam night is good, loud fun.

Zoo Bar – Oxford Tavern
3000 Connecticut Ave NW ☎202/232-4225. Timeless suburban saloon across from the zoo, with Guinness and microbrews and occasional performances by blues, jazz, and rock acts.

Performing arts and film

Avalon Theatre
5612 Connecticut Ave NW
☎202/966-6000, 🌐www
.theavalon.org. Near
the Maryland border,
a marvelously refur-
bished 1930s movie
palace with hand-
somely redecorated
lobby, lovely ceiling
mural, and old-fash-
ioned charm, now
showing independent
films and Hollywood
classics.

▲UPTOWN THEATER

Carter Barron Amphitheatre
4850 Colorado Ave NW ☎202/426-
0486, 🌐www.nps.gov
/rocr/cbarron. Summer amphitheater in Rock Creek Park
that offers a mix of free and
paid events, including Shakespeare plays, concerts, high-
brow dance and classical-music
performances, and more.

Uptown Theater
3426 Connecticut Ave NW ☎202/966-
5400. The District's other extant
1930s moviehouse, with one
marvelously large screen, plenty
of balcony seating, and slate of
contemporary Hollywood movies. Located in central Cleveland
Park.

Georgetown

After more than two hundred years, the historic character of Georgetown still manages to impress. Well-preserved buildings line cobblestone streets, lending the quarter the air of a bygone era while housing all manner of fancy restaurants and diverting shops. It's as close to a boutique town as anywhere within Washington – a place where well-heeled visitors can rub shoulders with the capital's elite in the media, politics, law, and lobbying. It's also the only place firmly on the tourist map that isn't connected by Metro to the rest of the District, so you'll have to take a cab or hoof it over from Dupont Circle or Foggy Bottom.

M Street

The axis of Georgetown for two centuries, M Street is linked to Foggy Bottom by Pennsylvania Avenue and retains much of its Federal-style and later Victorian architecture, though the ground floors of its buildings have since been converted to retail use. Where new buildings have filled in any gaps, they've tended to follow the prevailing red-brick style, none more noticeably than the elegant *Four Seasons Hotel* between 28th and 29th streets (see review, p.180). Farther along, upscale shops and restaurants proliferate around the M Street/Wisconsin Avenue junction, whose landmark is the gold dome of the Riggs National Bank. Just beyond, the late twentieth century imposes upon the late nineteenth in the shape of Georgetown Park, a high-profile shopping mall at 3222 M Street that used to be a site for storing public-transit "omnibuses" drawn by horses. A block west at Potomac Street, the red-brick Market House has been the site of a public market since the 1860s, even if today the butchered carcasses and patent medicines have made way

for a Dean & Deluca deli. On the western end of M, north on 35th Street, watch for the staircase that appeared in the horror classic *The Exorcist*, one of several Washington locations for the movie. Just to the northwest, at 37th and O streets, is the east entrance to **Georgetown University**, America's oldest Catholic university; call about taking a tour of its historic 1789 campus (℡202/687-3600, ⊛www .georgetown.edu).

The Old Stone House

3051 M St NW ℡202/895-6070, ⊛www.nps.gov/olst. Wed–Sun noon–5pm; tours by reservation only. In the center of the M Street action sits the incongruous presence of the Old Stone House, which has a very real claim to fame of being the only surviving pre-Revolutionary house in DC. It was built in 1765 by a Pennsylvania carpenter and retains its rugged, rough-hewn stone construction, the craggy rocks used for the three-feet-thick walls being quarried from blue fieldstone. It has been restored to the state it probably resembled in the late eighteenth century, and short guided tours lead you through

On the map: Dumbarton Oaks Garden & Museum Ⓐ, Georgetown University Hospital, Tudor Place, Georgetown University, Bryn Mawr Lantern Bookshop Ⓞ, Commander Salamander, Appalachian Spring, Old Print Gallery, Georgetown Park, Francis Scott Key Park, Smash!, Market House, Dream Dresser, Chesapeake & Ohio Canal, Potomac River

0   300 yds

the kitchen and carpenter's workshop downstairs, paneled parlors and bedrooms upstairs.

The C&O Canal

C&O Canal Visitor Center, 1057 Thomas Jefferson St NW ☎202/653-5190, ⓦwww.nps.gov/choh. April–Oct daily 10am–4pm. On a summer day there's no finer part of Georgetown than the Chesapeake and Ohio (C&O) Canal, parallel to M Street a few blocks south, which is overlooked by restored redbrick warehouses, spanned by small bridges, and lined with trees. When it was finished in

1850, the C&O Canal stretched as far as Cumberland, Maryland, 184 miles and 74 locks away, allowing the hauling of barges full of goods. The last mule-drawn cargo boat was pulled through in the 1920s. Today, scores of visitors hike, cycle, and ride horses along the restored

▼THE OLD STONE HOUSE

ACCOMMODATION

Four Seasons	D
Georgetown Inn	B
Holiday Inn	A
Latham	C
Monticello	E

EATING AND DRINKING

Amma Vegetarian Kitchen	8
Au Pied de Cochon	2
Bangkok Bistro	6
Bistro Francais	12
Blues Alley	22
Booeymonger	5
Café La Ruche	23
Ching Ching Cha	24
Citronelle	C
Clyde's	17
Dean & Deluca	16
Furin's	14
Garrett's	13
J. Paul's	18
Martin's Tavern	3
Modern	9
Mr. Smith's	20
Nathan's	19
Old Glory	11
Red Ginger	1
The Saloun	10
Sequoia	25
Third Edition	7
The Tombs	4
Vietnam Georgetown	21
Zed's	15

towpaths of this national historic park; canoeing and boating are allowed in certain sections, too. The prettiest central stretch starts at 30th Street, where the adjacent locks once opened for boats laden with coal, iron, timber, and corn.

To sign up for trips on the 90ft, mule-drawn canal boats – accompanied by park rangers in nineteenth-century costume – stop in at the Visitor Center. Tickets cost $8; three or four trips run daily Wednesday through Sunday from mid-June to early September, with reduced service from April to mid-June and mid-September to late October.

Around the canal

One of the most appealing stretches around the canal is the short section between Thomas Jefferson Street and 31st Street, where artisans' houses have been handsomely restored as shops, offices, and private homes. Jefferson Street itself is lined with attractive brick houses, some in the Federal style, featuring rustic stone lintels, arched doorways with fanlights, and narrow dormers. At Wisconsin Avenue and South Street, one structure that retains its original function is the Gothic Revival Grace Church (1866), where canal boatmen would be enticed by promises of salvation from the earth-bound drudgery of hauling heavy goods.

If you're into boating, head a few blocks south of the canal to the Potomac River, where several boat-rental shops offer the means to explore the calmer waters around the Francis Scott Key Bridge and Roosevelt Island.

▲CANAL BOAT, C&O CANAL

do feature a more creative touch and irreverent spirit – anything from upstart DC designers and hometown coffeehouses to modernist galleries and frenetic clubs.

Tudor Place

1644 31st St NW ☎202/965-0400, ⊛www.tudorplace.org. Tours Tues–Fri 10am–2.30pm, Sat 10am–3pm, Sun noon–3pm. $6. Stately Tudor Place was designed by William Thornton, who won the competition to design the US Capitol. The house displays a pleasing mix of styles, rare for the period, in which Thornton embellished the fundamentally Federal-style structure with a Neoclassical domed portico on the south side. The 1816 exterior has remained virtually untouched since and, as the house stayed in the same family for more than 150 years, the interior has been saved from the constant "improvements" made to other period Georgetown houses. The pleasant gardens are also open (Mon–Sat 10am–4pm, Sun noon–4pm; free); walk up the path and bear right where a white box holds detailed maps ($2) of the paths, greens, box hedges, arbors, and fountains.

Good choices include Fletcher's Boat House, 4940 Canal Rd NW (☎202/244-0461, ⊛www.fletchersboathouse.com), which rents rowboats and canoes; and Thompson Boat Center, 2900 Virginia Ave NW (☎202/333-9543, ⊛www.thompsonboatcenter.com), with its kayaks, canoes, and rowing shells.

Wisconsin Avenue

Georgetown is at its vibrant best where M Street meets Wisconsin Avenue, marking the neighborhood's cultural epicenter, rich with enjoyable saloons, clothing shops, fashionable restaurants, and antique bookstores. Whereas M Street's offerings tend to be more mainstream chain stores and tourist-friendly boutiques, Wisconsin caters a bit more to locals and those with a flair for independent shopping. It's not that the shops along Wisconsin (which is at its most alluring from M to Q streets) are necessarily cheap or obscure, but they

Dumbarton Oaks

1703 32nd St ☎202/339-6401, ⊛www.doaks.org. Tues–Sun 2–5pm. Donation. The grand estate of Dumbarton Oaks encompasses a marvelous red-brick Georgian mansion from 1800, surrounded by gardens and woods. Diplomat Robert Woods Bliss acquired the property in 1920 to house his sizable collection of art; in 1940 the house was given to

Harvard University (the current owners); in 1944 its commodious Music Room saw a meeting of delegates whose deliberations led to the founding of the United Nations the following year.

The only part of the mansion open to the public is its terrific museum, featuring the Bliss collection. Pre-Columbian art was one of the statesman's obsessions, visible with countless gold, jade, and polychromatic carvings, sculpture, and pendants of Olmec, Inca, Aztec, and Mayan provenance – among them ceremonial axes, jewelry made from spondylus shells, stone masks of unknown significance, and sharp jade "celts" possibly used for human sacrifice. Outside the house, ten acres of formal gardens (entrance at 3101 R St; March–Oct 2–6pm; $6) provide one of DC's quietest and most relaxing retreats.

Dumbarton House

2715 Q St NW ☎202/337-2288, ⊛www .dumbartonhouse.org. Hourly tours Tues– Sat 10am–2pm. $5. Built between 1799 and 1804, Dumbarton House is one of the oldest houses in Georgetown. Known for a century as "Bellevue," the elegant Georgian mansion housed the

city's first salon. During the War of 1812, as the British overran Washington, Dolley Madison watched the White House burn from Bellevue's windows – the house was a sanctuary for the fleeing First Family. On the tour you'll be escorted through period rooms filled with Federal furniture and decorative porcelain, and past early city prints and middling portraits. If you don't have an hour to spare, content yourself instead with a seat in the restful garden and ponder this remarkable fact: the building of the bridge over nearby Rock Creek in 1915 necessitated the house's removal, brick by brick, from farther down Q Street to its present site.

Kreeger Museum

2401 Foxhall Rd NW ☎202/338-3552, ⊛www.kreegermuseum.org. Tours by reservation only Tues–Fri 10.30am & 1.30pm, Sat without reservation 10am–4pm. $8. One of Washington's most obscure attractions, the Kreeger Museum is little known mainly because of its location in the hills northwest of Georgetown University, though it well rewards a visit (probably by car) for its splendid array of twentieth-century modernist art.

▼BLISS COLLECTION, DUMBARTON OAKS

▲DUMBARTON HOUSE

The museum has open hours on Saturday but shows its collection on 90min tours the rest of the week. However you see it, you'll be in the presence of all manner of major artists – from Monet and Renoir to Picasso and Frank Stella. Also worth a look are the jagged steel monoliths of David Smith, the lean metallic sculptures of Brancusi, James Rosenquist's huge Pop Art diptychs and triptychs, and Edvard Munch's disturbing Scandinavian brand of Expressionism. It's sometimes hard to predict exactly what will be on view, given that the museum stages periodic temporary exhibitions once a year.

Shops

Appalachian Spring
1415 Wisconsin Ave NW ☎202/337-5780. A colorful array of handmade ceramics, jewelry, rugs, glassware, kitchenware, quilts, toys, and other eclectic examples of American craftwork.

Bryn Mawr Lantern Bookshop
3241 P St NW ☎202/333-3222. Although its stock is donated, this rare and vintage dealer has a great general selection of secondhand books.

Commander Salamander
1420 Wisconsin Ave NW ☎202/337-2265. Funky T-shirts and sneakers, sportswear and party gear, gimcrack jewelry, and various eclectic and oddball items. Open late.

Dream Dresser
1042 Wisconsin Ave NW ☎202/625-0373. One of the racier operations along this commercial stretch, an eye-popping emporium for all kinds of naughty lingerie, corsets, and fetish wear.

The Old Print Gallery
1220 31st NW ☎202/965-1818. A favorite local seller of historic landscapes, antique maps, old charts and prints, plus political cartoons, DC scenes, and early-American artisan work.

Smash!
3285 1/2 M St NW ☎202/337-6274. Punks gasping for air amid Georgetown's well-scrubbed shops can take refuge among the racks of leather pants, zebra-stripe Creepers, and studded belts, or select a vinyl classic from the selection of punk records.

Cafés

Booeymonger
3265 Prospect St NW ☎202/333-4810.
Crowded deli-coffee shop at the
corner of Prospect and Potomac
streets, excellent for its inventive sandwiches like the Gatsby
Arrow – roast beef and brie
– and the Patty Hearst – turkey
and bacon with Russian dressing.

Café la Ruche
1039 31st St NW ☎202/965-2684.
Relaxing bistro with patio seating ideal for dining alone or in
twos in warmer weather. Sample
the onion soup, quiches, and
croque monsieur or drop by for
pastries and espresso.

Ching Ching Cha
1063 Wisconsin Ave NW ☎202/333-
8288. Bright and pleasant tea-
room transports teetotalers to
Old Asia with black teas and
herbal infusions, a tidy menu
of savory items like bentos and
dumplings, and an array of
snazzy collectibles for sale.

Dean & DeLuca
3276 M St NW ☎202/342-2500.
Superior self-service café (and
fantastic attached deli-market
with sushi stand) in one of M
Street's most handsome red-
brick buildings. Croissants and
cappuccino, designer salads,
pasta, and sandwiches.

Furin's
2805 M St NW ☎202/965-1000.
Georgetown's best bet for a
home-cooked eggs-and-fries
breakfast, blue plate deli sandwiches, potato or chicken salads,
and tasty desserts and pastries.

Restaurants

Amma Vegetarian Kitchen
3291 M St NW ☎202/625-6625. A
safe haven for vegetarians and
vegans, this South Indian spot
specializes in *dosa* – lentil and
rice-flour wraps – but also has
very good curries and breads,
along with veggie meatballs.

Au Pied de Cochon
1335 Wisconsin Ave NW ☎202/337-
6400. Cheap, 24hr French bis-
tro-bar serving breakfast (until
noon), $10 early-bird dinners
(3–8pm), and a la carte eggs,
fish, coq au vin, steaks, and the
like. An old, weathered Georgetown favorite.

▼DEAN & DELUCA

Bangkok Bistro

3251 Prospect St NW ☎202/337-2424.
Pitches some style into Thai
dining with a sleek dining room
that's often full. The old favorites (*tom yum*, pad Thai, shrimp
cakes, and satay) sit alongside
spicy beef curries and chili
prawns.

Bistro Français

3128 M St NW ☎202/338-3830.
Renowned for its French cooking, from simple steak-frites and
rotisserie chicken to roast pigeon
and lamb sausage, this bistro stays
open late. Early-bird (5–7pm)
and late-night (10.30pm–1am)
set dinners for around $20.

Citronelle

In the *Latham Hotel*, 3000 M St
☎202/625-2150. Huge player on
the DC dining scene, serving up
French-inspired cuisine with a
California flair – and set-price
dinners starting at $125. Dress
swanky and bring plenty of
attitude.

Clyde's

3236 M St NW ☎202/333-9180.
Classic New York-style saloon-
restaurant and a Georgetown
institution, featuring checked
tablecloths, Art Deco lampshades, and burnished wood
interior. Reservations essential
for weekend dinner and Sunday
brunch.

Martin's Tavern

1264 Wisconsin Ave NW ☎202/333-
7370. Old-fashioned, clubby
saloon that's more than seventy
years old, but still serves up
famous steaks and chops, great
burgers, linguine with clam
sauce, and oyster platters – try
the popular brunch.

Old Glory

3139 M St NW ☎202/337-3406.
Rollicking barbecue restaurant
with hickory smoke rising from
the kitchen. Accompany your
huge portions of ribs and chick-
en with one of the half-dozen
sauces on every table and a shot
of great bourbon.

Red Ginger

1564 Wisconsin Ave NW ☎202/965-
7009. Crab cakes, seafood quesadillas, and oxtail stew are just
some of the culinary features at
this hybrid Caribbean-African
restaurant, with numerous "small
plates" (a la tapas) at affordable
prices.

Vietnam Georgetown

2934 M St NW ☎202/337-4536.
Tourist-friendly Vietnamese
restaurant, with decent food and
solid specials that include grilled
lemon chicken, stuffed crepes,
and shrimp curry.

Zed's

1201 28th St NW ☎202/333-4710.
The place for Ethiopian food
in Georgetown, and an intimate one at that. The set lunch
is cheap but so are the dinner
entrees. The *doro wot* (chicken
stew in a red pepper sauce) is
a good, spicy choice, as are the
tenderloin beef cubes.

Bars

Garrett's

3003 M St NW ☎202/333-1033.
Amid its brick-and-wood interior, Garrett's features a giant
rhino head by the door, pumping jukebox that keeps the
young crowd in a party mood,
and nightly drink specials, along
with a few microbrews.

J. Paul's

3218 M St NW ☎202/333-3450. A
"dining saloon" that offers the

standard grill/barbecue menu, with some famous crab cakes, and a great bar with its own-brewed Amber Ale.

Mr Smith's

3104 M St NW ☎202/333-3104. Most welcoming of Georgetown's saloons, with a splendid garden drinking and eating area, cheap beer-and-burger nights, live bands on weekends, and $1.50 rail drinks during weekday Happy Hour.

Nathan's

3150 M Street NW ☎202/338-2000. Longstanding Georgetown institution known for its sizable bar with plenty of potent choices, and all-American steak-and-potatoes fare in its back dining room.

Sequoia

3000 K St NW ☎202/944-4200. Popular restaurant-bar with one of the best locations in the area – at the eastern end of Washington Harbor, with outdoor terrace seating overlooking the river. Arrive early on weekends.

The Tombs

1226 36th St NW, at Prospect St ☎202/337-6668. Busy basement student haunt, adorned with rowing blades. It's good for catching college football on Saturday afternoons in fall or just soaking up the Georgetown vibe. Occasional live bands and club nights.

Clubs and live music

Blues Alley

1073 Wisconsin Ave NW, Georgetown ☎202/337-4141, ⊛www.bluesalley .com. Small, celebrated Georgetown jazz bar, in business for more than thirty years, attracting top names. Shows usually at 8pm and 10pm, plus midnight some weekends; cover can run to $40. Book in advance.

Modern

3287 M St NW ☎202/338-7027. Upscale lounge and club boasting a stylish bar and fittingly mod decor – all shiny metallic surfaces and posh designs – and mix of hip-hop, house, and other beats.

The Saloun

3239 M St NW ☎202/965-4900. Cozy bar with 75 bottled beers and nightly jazz trios or bands, plus occasional R&B and soul acts. Free admission before 8pm, otherwise small cover charge.

Third Edition

1218 Wisconsin Ave NW ☎202/333-3700. Gung-ho college scene spread across several floors, with bars and second-floor dance club with DJs and periodic live music. It's a cattle-market on weekends, when you'll probably have to wait in line and pay a cover.

PLACES

Georgetown

Arlington

The Virginia suburb of Arlington is directly linked to Washington by the fetching Arlington Memorial Bridge, and it features several of DC's iconic sights, such as Arlington National Cemetery, the Pentagon, and Arlington House, the home of Robert E. Lee. Across the river to the east is pleasant and walkable Roosevelt Island. In addition to a few good Vietnamese restaurants, the town boasts some major malls and a handful of worthwhile bars and clubs. Conveniently, much of the nightlife is found on Clarendon and Wilson boulevards around the Court House and Clarendon Metro stations, and the rest of the sights are equally accessible on public transit.

Arlington National Cemetery

Across Arlington Memorial Bridge ☎703/695-3250, ◎www .arlingtoncemetery.org. Daily: April–Sept 8am–7pm; Oct–March 8am–5pm.
A vast sea of identical white headstones that spreads across hillsides, Arlington National Cemetery honors some quarter-million US soldiers and their dependents, as well as the assassinated Kennedy brothers, whose graves here elevate the cemetery to the status of a pilgrimage site. Primarily a military burial ground – the largest in the country – Arlington's 600 landscaped acres also contain the graves of other national heroes with military connections, from boxing legend (and ex-GI) Joe Louis to the crew of the doomed space shuttle *Challenger*.

The Metro takes you right to the main gates on Memorial Drive. Luckily, the visitor center by the entrance issues maps indicating some of the more prominent graves; the cemetery is absolutely enormous, so if you simply want to see the major sites without doing too much walking, board a Tourmobile for a narrated tour (see Essentials).

The site began as a burial ground for Union soldiers, though as a national cemetery it was subsequently deemed politic to honor the dead of both sides in the Civil War. The Confederate Section, with its own memorial, lies to the west of the Tomb of the Unknowns; other sections and memorials commemorate conflicts from the Revolutionary War to the Gulf War, and the fallen from recent wars in Afghanistan and Iraq continue to be interred here.

The focus of much visitor attention is the marble terrace where simple name plaques mark the graves of John F. Kennedy, 35th US president, his wife Jacqueline Kennedy Onassis, and two of their children – a son, Patrick, and an unnamed daughter – who both died shortly after birth. The eternal flame, which burns here, was lit at JFK's funeral by Jackie. When it's crowded, as it often is, the majesty of the view across to the Washington Monument and the poignancy of the inscribed extracts from JFK's inaugural address – "Ask not what your country can do for you..." – are sometimes obscured; come early or late in the day, if possible. In the plot behind Jack's, a plain white cross marks the gravesite of his brother Robert, assassinated in 1968.

The Tomb of the Unknowns, a white marble block dedicated to the unknown dead of two world wars and the Korea and Vietnam conflicts, is guarded 24 hours a day by impeccably uniformed soldiers, who carry out a somber Changing of the Guard (April–Sept every half-hour, otherwise on the hour);

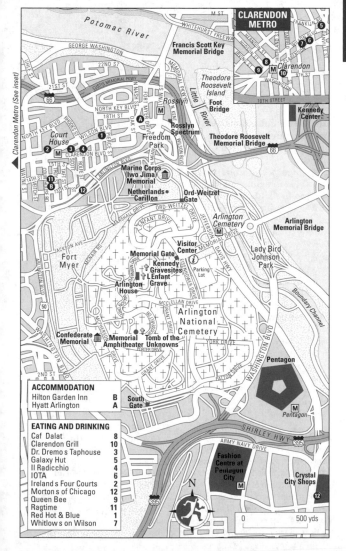

Clarendon Metro (See inset)

ACCOMMODATION

Hilton Garden Inn	B
Hyatt Arlington	A

EATING AND DRINKING

Caf Dalat	8
Clarendon Grill	10
Dr. Dremo s Taphouse	3
Galaxy Hut	5
Il Radicchio	4
IOTA	6
Ireland s Four Courts	2
Morton s of Chicago	12
Queen Bee	9
Ragtime	11
Red Hot & Blue	1
Whitlow s on Wilson	7

▲TOMB OF THE UNKNOWNS

the circular, colonnaded Memorial Amphitheater behind is the site of special remembrance services.

The highest concentration of notable individual graves is found in the myriad plots surrounding the Tomb of the Unknowns: with a map, you'll find the graves of Audie Murphy, most decorated soldier in World War II, and former heavyweight champ Louis (born, and buried here, as Joe Louis Barrow), among others.

The most photographed of the many memorials is the one dedicated to those who died aboard the *Challenger*, located behind the amphitheater. One of the most recent memorials, situated at the main gateway, honors Women in Military Service – the country's first national monument to American servicewomen.

Arlington House

Sherman Drive, in Arlington National Cemetery ☎703/557-0613, ⊛www .nps.gov/arho. Daily 9.30am–4.30pm.
Arlington National Cemetery stands on land that once belonged to General Robert E. Lee, who in 1861 was at home at his Georgian Revival man-

sion – Arlington House – when he heard the news of the secession of Virginia from the Union. Although offered command of the Union Army, Lee resigned his US Army commission and left his Arlington home for the confederate capital of Richmond, where he led Virginia's military forces. The estate was eventually confiscated by the federal government, and the Lees never returned; in 1864 a cemetery for the Union dead of the Civil War was established on the grounds of the house.

Since the 1950s Arlington House has stood as a memorial to the Lee family. A self-guided tour leads you past highlights such as the bedroom where Lee wrote his resignation letter and the family parlor in which he was married. A fair proportion of the furnishings are original. Outside, the views across the river to the Mall are exemplary.

Marine Corps Memorial and Netherlands Carillon

Arlington Blvd, at Meade St ☎703/289-2500, ⊛www.nps.gov/gwmp/usmc .htm. Daily 24hr. Just outside the cemetery to the north is the 78-

foot-high, bronze Marine Corps Memorial, which shouldn't be missed. It's a twenty-minute walk north of the cemetery's main section, through the Ord-Weitzel Gate, though the easiest approach is actually from Rosslyn Metro, from which it's a ten-minute, signposted walk. The affecting memorial commemorates the marine dead of all wars, but it's more popularly known as the Iwo Jima Statue, after the "uncommon valor" shown by US troops in the bloody World War II battle for the small Pacific island. In a famous image – inspired by a photograph by Robert Rosenthal – half a dozen marines raise the Stars and Stripes on Mount Suribachi in February 1945. In summer (June–Aug), the US Marine Corps presents a parade and concert at the memorial every Tuesday at 7pm.

Nearby, to the south, rises the Netherlands Carillon, a 130ft-high steel monument dedicated to the Dutch liberation from the Nazis in 1945. Given by Holland in thanks for US aid, the tower is set in landscaped grounds featuring thousands of tulips, which bloom each spring. The fifty bells of the carillon are rung on Saturdays and holidays from May through September; at those times visitors can climb the tower for superlative city views.

The Pentagon

I-395, at Jefferson Davis Hwy ☎703/695-3325, ⊛www.defenselink .mil. Mon–Fri 9am–3pm; by reservation only. The locus of modern American war-making, the Pentagon is the seat of the US Department of Defense and one of the largest chunks of architecture in the world, with a floor area of 6.5 million square feet and five 900ft-long sides enclosing 17.5 miles of corridors. The building is constructed entirely of concrete rather than the marble that brightens the rest of Washington. Terrorists left their mark on this massive structure on 9/11 when they crashed Flight 77 into its western flank, killing nearly two hundred people and tearing open a hole almost 200ft wide. In the wake of the attack, the military suspended all Pentagon tours, though they've since resumed for veterans and school groups of ten or more people; reserve well in advance.

The Mount Vernon Trail and Roosevelt Island

If you've had enough of official government sites and are inter-

▼ARLINGTON HOUSE

▲ WOMEN IN MILITARY SERVICE MEMORIAL

Potomac, not far from the Rosslyn Metro station.

Shops

Crystal City Shops
Crystal Drive and 23rd St
☎ 703/922-4636. Directly accessible via its own Metro stop, the section of town known as Crystal City hosts this amalgamation of a hundred shops – mostly chain retailers – plus a handful of decent cafés and restaurants.

Fashion Centre at Pentagon City
1100 S Hayes St
☎ 703/415-2400. Another somewhat upscale mall with chain retailers and seven uneventful restaurants; it's also right on the Metro line.

Restaurants

Café Dalat
3143 Wilson Blvd ☎ 703/276-0935. Brisk, Formica-tabled Vietnamese joint with a popular lunch buffet and some tasty specials such as grilled lemon chicken and five-spice pork.

Il Radicchio
1801 Clarendon Blvd ☎ 703/276-2627. The cross-river branch of this pizza-and-pasta chain offers great-value wood-fired pizzas and mix-and-match spaghetti-and-sauce combos.

Morton's of Chicago
1631 Crystal Square Ave ☎ 703/418-1444. Local branch of the chic steakhouse chain, with the

ested in doing a little hiking or biking, the 18.5-mile Mount Vernon Trail runs parallel to the George Washington Memorial Parkway, from Arlington Memorial Bridge south via Alexandria (7 miles) to Mount Vernon in Virginia. The trail sticks close to the Potomac for its entire length and runs past a number of sites of historic or natural interest. For more information, and a free trail guide, contact the National Park Service in Washington (☎ 202/619-7222, ⓦ www.nps.gov). Those looking for a quieter place for a constitutional should head to Roosevelt Island, a nature park with 2.5 miles of trails that meander through marsh, swamp, and forest. Access to the island, which lies at the start of the Mount Vernon Trail, is via a footbridge on the Arlington side of the standard array of delicious cuts of beef and veal, lobster, and a clubby atmosphere good for smoking and boozing.

Queen Bee

3181 Wilson Blvd ☎703/527-3444. The best Vietnamese food around, with renowned crunchy spring rolls, seafood over crispy noodles, grilled pork, and huge bowls of noodle soup. Expect to wait.

Red Hot & Blue

1600 Wilson Blvd, at Pierce ☎703/276-7427. Memphis barbecue joint that spawned a chain, serving the best ribs in the District. A rack, with coleslaw and beans, costs just ten bucks.

Bars

Clarendon Grill

1101 N Highland St ☎703/524-7455. Solid old favorite for boozing, and something of a pickup joint. Music selections (Wed–Sat) include earnest acoustic strummers, alternative rockers, and occasional DJs – but the real focus is convivial drinking.

Dr Dremo's Taphouse

2001 Clarendon Blvd ☎703/528-4660. Microbrews and pool in a converted car showroom, right at the Court House Metro station. The bar's the most fun on Tuesday nights, when the beer is just $1 a glass and "psychotronic" film showings offer nerve-jangling D-grade horror and kitsch classics.

Ireland's Four Courts

2051 Wilson Blvd, at N Courthouse Rd ☎703/525-3600. One of the nicest of the area's Irish bars, drawing a cheery Arlington crowd for the live music (Tues–Sat), dozen

beers on tap, whiskey selection, and filling food.

Clubs and live music

Galaxy Hut

2711 Wilson Blvd ☎703/525-8646. Regular line-up of local DJ talent takes the stage in this tiny neighborhood hangout set in a popular strip for music, with a bevy of beers on tap.

IOTA Club and Café

2832 Wilson Blvd ☎703/522-8340. One of the area's better choices for clubbing, a warehouse-style music joint with nightly performances by local and national indie, folk, and blues bands. A great bar and attached restaurant, too.

Ragtime

1345 N Courthouse Rd ☎703/243-4003. Relaxed bar and grill decorated with antique decor and offering live music several nights a week, often hip-hop, jazz, or blues.

Whitlow's on Wilson

2854 Wilson Blvd ☎703/276-9693. Neighborhood retro lounge on Wilson with good happy hour drinks and food, pool, and wraparound bar, but best for its live rock, jazz, acoustic, blues, and reggae.

Performing arts and film

Arlington Cinema 'n Drafthouse

2903 Columbia Pike ☎703/486-2345. Grab a brew or munch on food while you watch a second-run movie at this combo pub-theater.

Gunston Arts Center

2700 South Lang St ☎703/228-1850. Featuring two theaters, this facility hosts a range of drama, novelties, and cultural events from local and regional troupes.

Rosslyn Spectrum

1611 N Kent St ☎703/525-7550, ⊛www.arlingtonarts.org. Near the last Arlington Metro stop before DC, a good venue for theater, concerts, and cultural events. With classics, multimedia experiments, and off-kilter new plays, you're likely to see almost anything here.

Signature Theatre

3806 S Four Mile Run ☎703/218-6500, ⊛www.signature-theatre .org. Award-winning theatrical group putting on premieres of new works, as well as straightforward revivals and irreverent adaptations of classics and musicals.

Day-trips

Beyond Washington DC and Arlington, the attractions are farther flung but still worthwhile if you have a car or can navigate between Metro and bus lines. In Virginia, in particular, you can go in any direction and find some fascinating slice of history, culture, or entertainment. Excellent day-trips within easy reach include treks to the wonderfully preserved eighteenth-century town of Alexandria – also good for its dining and nightlife – and George Washington's home of Mount Vernon. The latter excursion can be combined with a visit to lesser-known, but still intriguing, Woodlawn Plantation, which is also the site of Frank Lloyd Wright's "Usonian" Pope-Leighey House.

Old Town Alexandria

Yellow or Blue Line, King Street Station. Walk half-mile east or use local DASH bus. The lovely, preserved Old Town of Alexandria, Virginia, alone provides an excellent reason for visitors to venture beyond the confines of DC. Fully seeing all the town has to offer – with its restored shops and taverns, Georgian and Neoclassical houses, and other tourable sites – requires several days just by itself. Along with this, the appealing bed-and-breakfasts, pubs, clubs, and restaurants that populate the place give it a real sense of contemporary vitality, not just ossified museumtown dullness.

Ramsay House

221 King St, Alexandria ☎703/838-4200, ⊛www .funside.com. Daily 9am–5pm. The town's visitor center is located in the Ramsay House and offers pamphlets and information on countless other historic sites and curiosities. The house itself is the oldest in town, built (though not originally on this site) in 1724 for William Ramsay, one of Alexandria's founding merchants and later its first mayor. Ramsay had the house transported upriver from Dumfries, Virginia, and placed facing the

▼OLD TOWN ALEXANDRIA

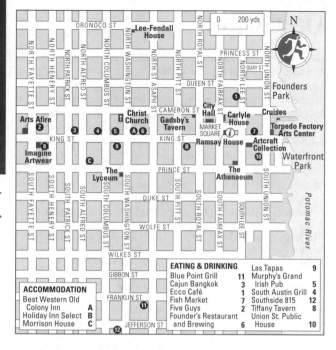

ORONOCO ST

Lee-Fendall House

PRINCESS ST

QUAY ST

QUEEN ST

Founders Park

Cruises

CAMERON ST

Arts Afire 2

Christ Church A 6

Gadsby's Tavern

City Hall

Carlyle House 1

Torpedo Factory Arts Center

KING ST

KING ST

Ramsay House B

Artcraft Collection 10

Waterfront Park

Imagine Artwear 8

The Lyceum

PRINCE ST

The Athenaeum

Potomac River

DUKE ST

WOLFE ST

WILKES ST

GIBBON ST

ACCOMMODATION

Best Western Old Colony Inn   **A**
Holiday Inn Select   **B**
Morrison House   **C**

FRANKLIN ST

JEFFERSON ST

EATING & DRINKING		
Blue Point Grill	11	Murphy's Grand Irish Pub 5
Cajun Bangkok	3	
Ecco Café	7	South Austin Grill 4
Fish Market	1	Southside 815 12
Five Guys	2	Tiffany Tavern 8
Founder's Restaurant and Brewing	6	Union St. Public House 10
Las Tapas	9	

Day-trips   **PLACES**

▼RAMSAY HOUSE

river, where his ships loaded up with tobacco. The water is now three blocks away: the bluff that the town was built on was excavated after the Revolution, and the earth was used to extend the waterfront into the shallow bay.

Carlyle House

121 N Fairfax St, Alexandria ☎703/549-2997, ⊛www.carlylehouse.org. Tues–Sat 10am–4.30pm, Sun noon–4.30pm. $4. In the 1750s, when all the town's other buildings were constructed of wood, prosperous merchant John Carlyle's Georgian, white-sandstone house made an ostentatious statement about its owner's wealth. Accounts of Carlyle's business dealings – he ran three plantations and traded countless slaves – inform the half-hour guided tours of the restored house. Contrast the family's

▲CARLYLE HOUSE

same scenery, along with other historic buildings, bathed in a romantic glow ($20; ☎703/838-4242). Anyone who was anyone in early-American society dropped by for a visit here – from the Marquis de Lafayette to Thomas Jefferson. Some would come to eat, drink, and be merry; others to pontificate at club meetings; still others to perform or watch theatrical productions; and a great many others to dance – in the galleried ballroom, George Washington used to cut a rug at parties thrown for his birthday.

draped beds, expensively painted rooms, and fine furniture with the bare servants' hall, which has actually been over-restored – in the eighteenth century it would have had an earthen floor and no glass in the windows. More than many historic-home tours, this one tries to lay out the authentic historical evidence involving the site. Aside from slavery and domestic matters, the Carlyle House played a role in intercontinental affairs: in August 1755, it was used as General Braddock's headquarters during the planning of the French and Indian War. George Washington was on Braddock's staff, and later he frequently visited the house.

Gadsby's Museum Tavern

134 N Royal St, Alexandria ☎703/838-4242, ⊛www.gadsbystavern.org. April–Sept Tues–Sat 10am–5pm; Sun 1–5pm, Oct–March Tues–Sat 11am–4pm, Sun 1–4pm. $4. Gadsby's Museum Tavern occupies two (supposedly haunted) Georgian buildings, the City Hotel from 1792 and the tavern itself from 1785. Downstairs, Gadsby's Tavern is still a working restaurant (complete with "authentic" colonial food and costumed staff). Short tours by a knowledgeable guide lead you through the old tavern rooms upstairs; candlelight tours in mid-December offer the

Christ Church

118 N Washington St, Alexandria ☎703/549-1450, ⊛www .historicchristchurch.org. Mon–Sat 9am–4pm, Sun 2–4pm. To see the Washington family pew, head to the English-style Christ Church, a working branch of the Episcopal diocese. Identified by a striking red-and-white bell tower, the handsome Georgian edifice was built of brick and finished just before the Revolution, and is set in a beautiful churchyard.

▼GADSBY'S MUSEUM TAVERN

▲ GHOST AND GRAVEYARD TOUR, OLD TOWN

During the Civil War Union soldiers worshipped here, as did FDR and Churchill on one occasion eighty years later; periodically, the sitting president may drop in for a visit, often to coincide with President's Day or Washington's birthday.

Lee-Fendall House

614 Oronoco St, Alexandria ☎ 703/548-1789, ⊕ www.leefendallhouse.org. Tues–Sat 10am–4pm, Sun 1–4pm. $4. A descendant of the Lees of Virginia, Phillip Fendall built his splendid clapboard mansion, the Lee-Fendall House, in 1785. Distinguished Revolutionary War general Henry "Light Horse Harry" Lee composed Washington's funeral oration here (in which, famously, he declared him "first in war, first in peace, and first in the hearts of his countrymen"); although much of the furnishing dates from the Antebellum era (and the house has been remodeled into the Greek Revival style you see today), the place has had other famous residents in later years. The most notable of these was labor leader John L. Lewis, who moved in during 1937 as the head of the United Mine Workers, soon created the Congress of Industrial Organizations as a rival to the American Federation of Labor, and helped merge both groups in the 1940s; he lived here until his death in 1969.

The Lyceum

201 S Washington St, Alexandria ☎ 703/838-4994, ⊕ www.alexandriahistory.org. Mon–Sat 10am–5pm, Sun 1–5pm. The Lyceum houses the town's history museum in a magisterial Greek Revival building dating to 1839. It was designed to be a centerpiece for the town's cultural pretensions, the evocative name harkening back to Greek hubs for learning, discussion, and public oration. Although the place doesn't quite have the same role today, its changing displays, film shows, and associated art gallery can put some flesh on the town's history; varied exhibits range from old photographs and Civil War documents to locally produced furniture and silverware (the latter an Alexandrian specialty in the nineteenth century).

The Athenaeum

201 Prince St, Alexandria ☎ 703/548-0035, ⊕ www.nvfaa.org. Wed–Fri 11am–3pm, Sat 1–3pm, Sun 1–4pm. Like the Lyceum an ancient-styled edifice, the Athenaeum has a similar Greek-influenced look with its mighty columns and high pediment, but like other American buildings with the same style, this was built as a bank. Nowadays, though, it's an art center, where you can check out the latest modern art in a series of galleries, take in performances of music, dance, and theater, or listen in on a lecture devoted to the arts.

Alexandria waterfront

Eighteenth-century Alexandria wouldn't recognize its twenty-first-century waterfront beyond North Union Street, not the least because the riverbank is several blocks farther east, following centuries of landfill. Where there were once wooden warehouses and wharves heaving with barrels of tobacco, there's now a smart marina and boardwalk, framed by the green stretches of Founders Park to the north and Waterfront Park to the south. In front of the Food Pavilion, forty-minute sightseeing cruises depart (May–Aug Tues–Sun, April & Sept–Oct Sat–Sun only; $8); longer trips run to DC or Mount Vernon and back. For information, visit the Potomac Riverboat Company (☎703/548-9000, ⓦwww.potomacriverboatco.com).

Before this area was cleaned up, the US government built a torpedo factory on the river, which operated until the end of World War II. Restyled as the diverting **Torpedo Factory Arts Center** (daily 10am–5pm; free; ☎703/838-4565, ⓦwww.torpedofactory.org), its three floors contain the studios of more than two hundred artists. All the studios are open to the public, displaying sculpture, ceramics, jewelry, glassware, and textiles in regularly changing exhibitions. Take a look, too, inside the center's **Alexandria Archaeology Museum** (Tues–Fri 10am–3pm, Sat 10am–5pm, Sun 1–5pm; ☎703/838-4399, ⓦwww.alexandriaarchaeology.org), where much of the town's restoration work was carried out and where you can see ongoing preservation efforts in a laboratory open to the public.

George Washington Masonic Memorial

101 Callahan Drive, Alexandria ☎703/683-2007, ⓦwww.gwmemorial.org. Daily 9am–5pm. In a town bursting with Washington mementos, nothing is more prominent than the George Washington Masonic Memorial, whose 333ft tower – built on top of a Greek temple – looms over town behind the King Street Metro station. The tower was designed to resemble nothing less than the long-destroyed Lighthouse at (a much further away) Alexandria, one of the seven ancient wonders of the world. The Virginian Freemasons built this memorial in Washington's honor in 1932, deeming him a "deserving brother." Inside, the glorious visual ode continues with a towering, 17ft bronze statue of the general and president, sundry memorabilia, and dioramas depicting events from his life. To see this, and the superb views from the observation platform, you'll have to wait for a forty-minute tour, which leaves from the hall (on the half-hour in the morning, on the hour in the afternoon, last tour 4pm). But even from the steps outside, the views are magnificent, across the Potomac to the Washington Monument and Capitol dome in the distance.

Mount Vernon

3200 George Washington Memorial Pkwy ☎703/780-2000, ⓦwww.mountvernon.org. Daily April–Aug 8am–5pm, March & Sept–Oct 9am–5pm, Nov–Feb 9am–4pm. $11. Set on a shallow bluff overlooking the broad Potomac River, sixteen miles south of Washington DC, Mount Vernon is among the most attractive historic houses in America. The beloved country estate of George Washington, it was his home for forty years, during which he ran it as a thriving and progressive farm, anticipating the decline in Virginia's tobacco cultivation and planting instead grains and food crops with great success. When he died, he was

Visiting Mount Vernon

To reach Mount Vernon via public transit, take the Metro's Yellow Line to Hunting-ton station and then catch Fairfax Connector Bus #101 (hourly; ☎703/339-7200, ⊛www.fairfaxcounty.gov/connector). It's an easy enough route, though it takes over an hour. A cab from the station costs around $20 (call White Top Cab at ☎703/644-4500). Drivers can follow the George Washington Parkway from DC; there's free parking. Alternatively, join a boat cruise in Old Town Alexandria or bike the Mount Vernon Trail, which runs here from Arlington. To beat the crowds, especially in summer, come early or midweek.

buried on the grounds and now lies next to his wife, Martha, in a simple family tomb.

The path up to the mansion passes various outbuildings, including a renovated set of former slave quarters. Ninety slaves lived and worked in the mansion grounds alone, and though there's evidence that Washington was a kinder master than most – for instance, refusing to sell children away from their parents, allowing slaves to raise their own crops, and engaging the services of a doctor for them – they still lived lives of depriva-tion and overwork.

Nearby, a small museum traces Washington's ancestry and displays porcelain from the house, medals, weapons, silver, and a series of striking miniatures, by Charles Willson Peale and his brother James, of Martha and her two children by her first marriage.

Around the corner, fronting the circular courtyard, stands the

mansion itself, with the bowling green stretching before it. It's a handsome, harmonious wooden structure, reasonably modest but sporting stunning views from the East Lawn. The wooden exterior was painted white, beveled, and sand-blasted to resemble stone; inside, the Palladian windows and brightly painted and papered rooms follow the fashion of the day, while the contents are based on an inventory prepared after Washington's death. Four-teen rooms are open to the public: portrait-filled parlors and cramped bedrooms, and the chamber where Washington breathed his last on a four-poster bed still in situ.

After touring the mansion there's plenty more to see on the grounds, including the separate kitchen, stables, smokehouse, overseer's quarters, kitchen garden, and shrubberies. There's also a forest trail nature walk, and you can take a stroll down to the

tomb, where two marble sarcophagi for George and Martha are set behind iron gates. Nearby lies a slave burial ground, while beyond there's a site where demonstra-tions of the crop-growing

▼MOUNT VERNON GROUNDS

▲ PORTRAITS, MOUNT VERNON

and farming techniques used by Washington are occasionally held.

Finally, located three miles west of the estate along Highway 235, **George Washington's gristmill** (April–Oct daily 10am–5pm; $4, or $2 with Mount Vernon admission) provides a glimpse into the tedious labor involved with mashing grain to make it usable for other purposes. Guides in costume go through the rigors of showing how water-power drove the mill and how it produced flour from corn, wheat, and other cereals.

Woodlawn Plantation

9000 Richmond Hwy ☎703/780-4000, ⊛www.woodlawnplantation.org. March–Dec daily 10am–5pm. $7.50. Not far from George Washington's gristmill, near the intersection of highways 1 and 235, lie the expansive grounds of Woodlawn Plantation, which used to be a part of the Mount Vernon estate until, after Washington's 1799 death, two-thousand acres were ceded to his nephew Major Lawrence and Martha Washington's granddaughter Eleanor Custis Lewis. From that sizable parcel grew this impressive red-brick Georgian manor house (finished in 1805), which was built by no less than US Capitol architect William Thornton using Palladian design elements, its decorative trim fashioned from local sandstone. However, the substantial labor involved in the house's making – all the bricks were fired in a kiln at the site – meant that slave labor was used in abundance.

Pope-Leighey House

Woodlawn Plantation, same hours and details, ⊛www.popeleighey1940 .org. Combined Woodlawn ticket $13. Almost incongruously, Woodlawn Plantation is also the site of a house designed by Frank Lloyd Wright, whose broad notions of the democratic spirit enabled him to develop "Usonian" houses meant to be affordable to common people. The Pope-Leighey House is one such experiment, and while the Usonian trend never really caught on, it did allow him to try some rather radical concepts within the strict limitations of budget, size, and labor. The Pope-Leighey was

Events at Mount Vernon

Throughout the year, Mount Vernon hosts a range of festivals and special events. Around the third weekend in February, Washington's birthday is celebrated with a wreath-laying ceremony and fife and drum parades; admission to Mount Vernon is free at this time. Each May, a three-day festival toasts local winemakers in a series of evening events featuring live jazz and visits to the cellar vaults. In December, special Christmas tours re-create the Washingtons' yuletide celebrations, and, on weekend winter evenings (late Nov to mid-Dec), special "Mount Vernon by Candlelight" tours cast a nocturnal glow on this historic site. Book ahead for a candlelight visit or for the wine festival; a special admission price applies.

moved here from another Virginia location when threatened with demolition. Luckily it survived, for this smallish, 1200-square-foot residence says much about Wright's building concepts: the materials are limited to wood, brick, concrete, and glass; the layout is strongly horizontal, with trellises to control direct sunlight; the clerestory windows employ unique cut-out patterns; and the floor plan is open and the ceilings low, except for that of the living room, which rises to thirteen feet and occupies about half the overall space of the house.

Shops

American in Paris

1225 King St, Alexandria ☎703/519-8234. As the name suggests, one of the top spots in town to get your fix of fashionable European designer-wear, as well as unique clothes from local designers.

Artcraft Collection

132 King St, Alexandria ☎703/299-6616. A strange and impressive collection of handcrafted artifacts – furniture painted in bizarre colors, exquisitely detailed atomizers, oddball sculptures, anthropomorphic teapots, and high-heeled doorstops, to name but a few.

Arts Afire

102 N Fayette St, Alexandria ☎703/838-9785. On the west side of Old Town, a major dealer in art glass, with a full complement of work from regional and national designers on display, everything from jewelry and home decor to kaleidoscopes, vases, and trinkets.

Card & Comic Collectorama

2008 Mount Vernon Ave, Alexandria ☎703/548-3466. A few miles north of Old Town, and hardly the type of place you might expect to find in this burg, but worth a trip for its stock of ancient Disney memorabilia, long-forgotten trading cards and rare comics, and all manner of other curious castoffs.

Imagine Artwear

1124 King St, Alexandria ☎703/548-1461. Vivid array of fashions bridging the gap between the aesthetic and the functional – brightly colored and detailed garments that could pass for tapestries, unique handcrafted jewelry and accessories, and more.

Cafés

Ecco Café

220 N Lee St, Alexandria ☎703/684-0321. Fine gourmet pizza and pasta joint with a neighborhood feel, featuring lunch specials, homemade noodles, decent steak and seafood, and a jazz brunch on Sunday.

Five Guys

107 N Fayette St, Alexandria ☎703/549-7991. This Old Town greasy spoon cooks its juicy hamburgers to order, piles on the fixings, and tucks 'em in a heavenly bun. The result? The best burger in the entire region, hands down. One of eight local branches.

Hard Times Café

1404 King St, Alexandria ☎703/837-0050. Four styles of fiery chili; good wings, rings, and fries; tub-thumping country music; and savory microbrews add up to one of Alexandria's better Tex-Mex/American restaurants. Located near the Metro station.

La Piazza

535 E Braddock Rd, Alexandria

⊕703/519-7711. Less than a mile north of Old Town and a solid choice if a hoagie's what you crave, here made with generous portions of meat and cheese, and just enough pepper, spice, and sauces to do the trick.

Restaurants

Blue Point Grill
600 Franklin St, Alexandria ⊕703/739-0404. Fresh, damn good seafood earns this Old Town jewel its reputation as one of Alexandria's best restaurants. In warmer weather pass up sitting in the elegant dining room for a spot on the veranda.

▲ BLUE POINT GRILL

Cajun Bangkok
907 King St, Alexandria ⊕703/836-0038. Incendiary blend of Thai and Cajun fare, with tasty jerk chicken, "crying tiger" (grilled steak with a spicy sauce), and a zesty gumbo.

Fish Market
105 King St, Alexandria ⊕703/836-5676. Brick-walled restaurant with terrace a block from the water, serving oysters and chowder at the bar and fried-fish platters, pastas, and fish entrees, not to mention a mean spicy shrimp meal.

Las Tapas
710 King St, Alexandria ⊕703/836-4000. Best of the local tapas bars, with a wide selection of authentic small plates, plus rich paella, glass after glass of tasty sangria, and regular (free) flamenco sessions.

South Austin Grill
801 King St, Alexandria ⊕703/684-8969. Quality Tex-Mex fare packs lively crowds into this Old Town institution. The Cadillac-sized fajitas, stacked nachos, taste-bud-tingling salsas, and zesty margaritas make the long waits worthwhile.

Southside 815
815 S Washington St, Alexandria ⊕703/836-6222. Deep-fried Southern cooking, heavy with good old-fashioned favorites like biscuits with ham gravy, thick and buttery cornbread, BBQ shrimp, crab fritters, and straight-up crawdads and catfish.

Bars

Founder's Restaurant and Brewing
607 King St, Alexandria ⊕703/684-5397. Recent brewpub arrival serving up a mix of American pale ales and stouts, along with German-style Kolsch and altbier. Also serves decent food and a Sunday brunch for under $10.

Murphy's Grand Irish Pub
713 King St, Alexandria ⊕703/548-1717. Old Town's nightlife revolves around this boisterous pub, pouring the city's best pint

of Guinness. Local solo acts perform upstairs, while a central fireplace and chow like Irish stew add much Emerald Isle atmosphere.

Shenandoah Brewing Co.

652 S Pickett St, Alexandria ☎703/823-9508. A fine combination pub-and-brewing-academy, where you can learn how to make your own beer as well as munch on spicy chili and sample such beverages as Whitewater Wheat, Stony Man Stout, and Old Rag Mountain Ale. Well away from the Old Town action on the south side of town, but worth seeking out.

Union Street Public House

121 S Union St, Alexandria ☎703/548-1785. Hard to miss this red-brick spot with gas lamps – a good steak-and-seafood joint that's just as nice for eating as drinking, with its own handcrafted and hearty microbrews. Very popular on weekends.

Clubs and live music

The Barns at Wolf Trap

1645 Trap Rd, Vienna, VA ☎703/938-2404, ✆www.wolftrap.org. Concerts Oct–May; opera June–Sept. Northwest of Alexandria, via Highway 7, this so-called Kennedy Center of folk music is devoted to American music in all its native forms – blues, bluegrass, jazz, ragtime, Cajun, zydeco, Native American, Tex-Mex, and countless other types and hybrids. Other venues include the modern Filene Center and a theatrical stage; in the summer the barns host local performances of classic operas.

Birchmere

3701 Mount Vernon Ave, Alexandria ☎703/549-7500, ✆www.birchmere.com. A few miles north of Old Town, an excellent, longstanding country, blues, and folk club with an A-list of current and retro acoustic performers, including some up-and-comers. Nightly gigs; ticket prices vary widely depending on the act.

Laporta's

1600 Duke St, Alexandria ☎703/683-6313. Less than a mile west of the main Old Town action, an upscale seafood restaurant with a good range of jazz acts performing nightly.

State Theatre

220 N Washington St, Falls Church, VA ☎703/237-0300, ✆www.thestatetheater.com. Suburban venue and stylish former moviehouse that rewards a drive if you like country, folk, or blues music, often for affordable prices. Sometimes mixes it up with retread rockers and novelty acts as well.

Tiffany Tavern

1116 King St, Alexandria ☎703/836-8844. It's all about bluegrass on the weekends at this Old Town haunt, which also presents open-mike nights the rest of the week, but is best for its folk-flavored local and regional performers.

Zig's Bar & Grill

4531 Duke St, Alexandria ☎703/823-2777, ✆www.zigsbar.com. Although located in a cultural no-mans-land between Old Town and the freeway (a few miles west of the main scene), this is a prime venue for regional bands of all stripes, with good jazz and rock acts, and biweekly Sunday-night "jazz poetry" events.

Accommodation

Hotels

One of the highlights of staying in Washington DC is cozying up in a swank hotel in the historic center and having the entire District at your feet, either literally or through the Metro system. Although the usual chain-hotel suspects are well represented, DC also has its share of marvelous old piles – grand hotels that date back a hundred years or more and still draw the swells and political elite. Of course, unless you're willing to drop $200 or more a night for such features, you may be out of luck. Standard room rates throughout the city start at around $100–120 a night, but there's plenty of scope for negotiation for canny travelers.

There are hotels in all the main downtown areas, though those near the White House, on Capitol Hill, and in Georgetown tend to be business-oriented and pricey. The occasional budget option exists in Foggy Bottom and Old Downtown, while most of the chain hotels and mid-range places are in New Downtown – particularly on the streets around Scott and Thomas circles. Outer neighborhoods tend to have a wider selection of smaller, cheaper hotels and B&B-style guesthouses (see p.183), and it's no hardship at all to be staying in Dupont Circle, Adams-Morgan, or Upper Northwest – you'll probably be eating and drinking in these places anyway. We've also listed a few options in Alexandria, VA, though it's easy to see that city on a day-trip from the capital. Any accommodation not listed on the map in this chapter (p.178) can be found on the relevant chapter map in the Places section.

Adams-Morgan

Courtyard by Marriott 1900 Connecticut Ave NW ☎202/332-9300 or 1-800/321-3211, ®www.courtyard.com/wasnw. The top-floor rooms of this well-located hillside

Accommodation practicalities

Rates in this chapter refer to the approximate cost of a standard double room in peak season – late-spring to mid-summer – and do not include the city's hotel tax of 14.5 percent. Many hotels discount their rates on weekends (some by up to fifty percent), while prices are typically lower from late-autumn to winter. You're more likely to be able to park for free in the outer neighborhoods; garage parking is available at most downtown hotels, but you'll be charged $20–30 a night for the privilege.

Very occasionally, an inn or hotel we list is on the cusp of a slightly iffy neighborhood; where safety is an issue, we've said so, and you're advised to take taxis back to your hotel at night in these areas.

Hotel reservation services

Bed & Breakfast Accommodations ☎413/582-9888, ®www
.bedandbreakfastdc.com
Bed & Breakfast League ☎202/363-7767
Capitol Reservations ☎202/452-1270 or 1-800/847-4832, ®www
.capitolreservations.com
Washington DC Accommodations ☎202/289-2220 or 1-800/554-2220,
®www.washingtondcaccommodations.com

| 0 | 400 yds |

ACCOMMODATION

Adam's Inn	3	Omni Shoreham	4
Carlyle Suites	12	Rouge	16
Channel Inn	36	St. Regis	25
Courtyard by Marriott	9	State Plaza	29
Dupont at the Circle	14	Swann House	11
Grand Hyatt	27	Tabard	17
Harrington	34	Topaz	18
Hay-Adams	26	Washington	30
Helix	19	Washington Hilton	8
HI-Washington DC	23	Washington Intl.	
Hotel Lombardy	24	Student Center	5
Jefferson	20	Watergate	28
JW Marriott	32	Westin Embassy Row	15
Loew's L'Enfant Plaza	35	Willard	31
Marriott Wardman Park	2	William Lewis House	13
Mayflower	21	Windsor Inn	10
Monaco	33	Windsor Park	6
Morrison-Clark	22	Woodley Park	
Normandy Inn	7	Guest House	1

hotel have splendid views. Free Web access, gym, outdoor pool, and good prices for the area, which is a short walk from the heart of both Dupont Circle and Adams-Morgan. $120.

Normandy Inn 2118 Wyoming Ave NW ☎202/483-1350 or 1-800/424-3729, ⊛www.jurys.com. Quiet hotel in upscale neighborhood, with comfortable rooms (each with fridge and coffeemaker) and free high-speed Internet access. Coffee and cookies are served daily, and there's a weekly wine and cheese reception. $120.

Washington Hilton 1919 Connecticut Ave NW ☎202/483-3000 or 1-800/445-8667, ⊛www.hilton.com. Massive, 1100-room, 1960s convention hotel midway between Dupont Circle and Adams-Morgan. Rooms are a bit smallish, but most have good views. Facilities include pool, health club, tennis courts, and bike rental. $240.

Windsor Park 2116 Kalorama Rd NW ☎202/483-7700 or 1-800/247-3064, ⊛www.windsorparkhotel.com. Pleasant, vaguely Victorian rooms outfitted with cable TV, and eight suites, just off Connecticut Avenue. Continental breakfast included. $110.

Alexandria

Best Western Old Colony Inn 1101 N Washington St ☎703/739-2222, ⊛www.bestwestern.com. Affordable choice with the standard amenities (with free breakfast and Web access) that's one of the better chain options for Old Town – which doesn't have as many unique hotel choices as you might expect. $130.

Holiday Inn 480 King St ☎703/549-6080 or 1-800/368-5047, ⊛www.holidayinnwashingtondc.com. Alexandria's best-situated hotel, just off Market Square, makes a great base for exploring. There's an indoor pool, and many rooms have balconies overlooking a quiet internal courtyard. The hotel is pet-friendly, too. $180.

Morrison House 116 S Alfred St ☎703/838-8000 or 1-800/367-0800, ⊛www.morrisonhouse.com Faux Federal-era townhouse (built in 1985) complete with ersatz "authentic" decor like parlor, parquet floors and crystal chandeliers, yet with modern comforts like high-speed Internet connections and designer linens. There's also an acclaimed restaurant. $250.

Arlington

Hilton Garden Inn 1333 N Court House Rd ☎1-800/528-4444, ⊛www.hiltongardeninn.com. Useful chain hotel near a Metro stop, with suites featuring fridges, microwaves, and Internet access, plus business center and gym. Save $30 by coming on a weekend, otherwise $180.

Hyatt Arlington 1333 N Court House Rd ☎1-800/528-4444, ⊛arlington.hyatt.com. Recently renovated corporate property in a prime location near the Rosslyn Metro station, as well as Georgetown and Arlington National Cemetery, with standard chain features plus gym and Internet access. $220.

Capitol Hill

Capitol Hill Suites 200 C St SE ☎202/543-6000 or 1-800/424-9165. Popular converted apartments whose renovated suites are all equipped with kitchenettes or proper kitchens, plus free morning coffee, muffins and juice, Internet access, and daily paper. Busy when Congress is in session – on weekends and in August the price drops $50–70; otherwise $200.

George 15 E St NW ☎202/347-4200 or 1-800/576-8331, ⊛www.hotelgeorge.com. Postmodern design meets 1928 Art Deco architecture, resulting in sleek lines, contemporary room furnishings (dark wood and glass, with copious Washington imagery), great marble bathrooms, in-room CD players, and a trendy bar-bistro. Weekend rates are $40–50 cheaper, otherwise $320.

Hyatt Regency on Capitol Hill 400 New Jersey Ave NW ☎202/737-1234 or 1-800/233-1234, ⊛washingtonregency.hyatt.com. Two blocks from Union Station, an 800-room luxury hotel that features a multistory atrium, pool, and gym – and a few rooms with views of the Capitol. Newly remodeled rooms with sleek black-and-cream furnishings give a modern spritz to formerly staid units. Rates can drop by up to $100 on weekends, otherwise $220.

Phoenix Park 520 N Capitol St NW ☎202/638-6900 or 1-800/824-5419, ⊛www.pparkhotel.com. Elegant rooms in an Irish-owned hotel – loaded with dark wood, paintings, and old-country style –

located across from Union Station. Popular with politicos, who frequent the associated *Dubliner* pub. There's a good restaurant, too, serving hearty breakfasts. $300 for basic room, suites start at $100 more.

Foggy Bottom

Lombardy 2019 Pennsylvania Ave NW ☎202/828-2600 or 1-800/424-5486, ✆www.hotellombardy.com. Red-brick apartment-style hotel, renovated with art and modern furnishings, in good Pennsylvania Avenue location, close to two Metro stations. Spacious rooms, most with kitchenettes and coffeemakers; the café has outdoor seating and is good for breakfast. $180.

State Plaza 2117 E St NW ☎202/861-8200 or 1-800/424-2859, ✆www .stateplaza.com. Commodious, stylish suites with fully equipped kitchens and dining area, plus a rooftop sundeck, health club, and good café. There's often room here when other places are full. $145.

Watergate 2650 Virginia Ave NW ☎202/965-2300 or 1-800/424-2736, ✆www.watergatehotel.com. Iconic Washington hotel synonymous with bad political behavior (see p.96), but otherwise a nice spot with comfortable rooms and suites, some with kitchens, and balconies with river views. New owner has improved the swank factor and jazzed up the rooms, and the complex offers a gym, shops, and services as well as the primo *Aquarelle* restaurant. Expect to save $80 on weekends, otherwise $280.

Georgetown

Four Seasons 2800 Pennsylvania Ave NW ☎202/342-0444 or 1-800/332-3442, ✆www.fourseasons.com. One of DC's most luxurious hotels – a modern red-brick pile at the eastern end of Georgetown – with lavish rooms and suites with views of Rock Creek Park or the C&O Canal. Service is superb, and there's a pool, fitness center, and Garden Terrace bar-lounge. Save $100 on weekends, otherwise $400.

Georgetown Inn 1310 Wisconsin Ave NW ☎202/333-8900 or 1-800/424-2979, ✆www.georgetowninn.com. Stylish, red-brick hotel in the heart of Georgetown offering tastefully appointed rooms (those off the avenue tend to be quieter) with marble bathrooms, plush decor, and high-speed Internet hookups. $220.

Holiday Inn Georgetown 2101 Wisconsin Ave NW ☎202/338-4600 or 1-800/465-4329, ✆www.holiday-inn.com. The only relative cheapie in Georgetown – a bit far up Wisconsin Avenue (on the way toward Upper Northwest), though buses and cabs get you down to M Street pretty quickly. Parking, outdoor pool, and fitness room, too. $120.

Latham 3000 M St NW ☎202/726-5000 or 1-800/368-5922, ✆www.thelatham .com. Well-sited hotel with rooftop pool, sundeck, and one of the city's finest dining experiences, *Citronelle* (see p.156). Some rooms have canal and river views. There are also some superb split-level executive suites with business facilities such as high-speed Internet access and fax/copy machines. A suite may run $100 more; rooms $220.

Monticello 1075 Thomas Jefferson St NW ☎202/337-0900 or 1-800/388-2410, ✆www.hotelmonticello.com. All-suite hotel nicely located off M Street, near the canal towpath, with spacious standard suites and some two-level penthouses that sleep up to six; all units have a wet bar, microwave, and fridge. Free Internet access in the business center. Summers see a small saving, as do some weekends. $180.

New Downtown and Dupont Circle

Carlyle Suites 1731 New Hampshire Ave NW ☎202/234-3200 or 1-866/468-3532, ✆www.carlylesuites.com. An Art Deco-styled structure whose furnishings have been upgraded, though the rooms are more functional than fancy. Still, with high-speed Internet hookups, kitchenettes with fridges and microwaves, and an on-site café and laundry, it's a good choice for the area. $130.

Hay-Adams 800 16th St NW ☎202/638-6600 or 1-800/424-5054, ✆www .hayadams.com. One of DC's finest hotels (see p.92), from the gold-leaf and walnut lobby to the sleekly modern rooms and the suites with fireplaces and original cornices, marble bathrooms, balconies, and high ceilings (which can cost thousands per night). Upper floors have great views of the White House across the square. Breakfast is served in one of the District's better spots for early-morning power dining. $385.

Helix 1430 Rhode Island Ave NW, near Logan Circle ☏202/462-9001, ⌨www .hotelhelix.com. A prime choice if you're into a young, convivial atmosphere and bright, festive design – multicolored furniture, boomerang shapes, and other eye-popping decor. Rooms come in three flavors – the chill-out "Zone," chic "East," and kid-friendly "Bunk." Save $70 or so on weekends, otherwise $190.

Jefferson 1200 16th St NW ☏202/347-2200 or 1-800/365-5966, ⌨www .thejeffersonhotel.com. Patrician landmark on 16th Street, a bit away from the main action, but still a favorite since the 1920s for its antique-strewn interior, with busts, oils, and porcelain at every turn, fine restaurant, and nicely stylish rooms. Weekend rates can fall to less than $200 a night. $340.

Mayflower 1127 Connecticut Ave NW ☏202/347-3000 or 1-800/228-7697, ⌨www.renaissancehotels.com/WASSH. Beautiful and sumptuous Washington classic, with a Promenade – a vast, imperial hall – that seems endless from the lobby; smart rooms with subtle, tasteful furnishings; and the terrific *Café Promenade* restaurant (see p.127) that's much in demand by power diners. If there's one spot in DC where the national and international political elite come to roost, this is it. $320.

Rouge 1315 16th St NW ☏202/232-8000, ⌨www.rougehotel.com. Dupont's Circle hippest hotel (though it's actually on nearby Thomas Circle), where the 137 sleek rooms are outfitted with crimson velvet drapes, red leatherette headboards, swanky art and decor, and minibars stuffed with the likes of Redi-Whip and condoms. The ground-floor bar-lounge is a definite highlight (and a real weekend scene) where you can also indulge in a complimentary cold pizza and Bloody Marys – for breakfast. $220.

St Regis Washington 923 16th St NW ☏202/638-2626 or 1-800/562-5661, ⌨www.starwood.com/stregis. President Calvin Coolidge cut the ribbon opening this 1920s Italian Renaissance classic, located

a few blocks north of the White House and rich with antiques, chandeliers, and a carved wooden ceiling in the lobby that looks right out of a European palace. As one of the cozier of DC's top-shelf luxury items, it features elegant rooms with stylish appointments, plus on-site gym and business center. $315.

Tabard Inn 1739 N St NW ☏202/785-1277, ⌨www.tabardinn.com. Three converted Victorian townhouses, two blocks from Dupont Circle, with forty unique, antique-stocked rooms, with an odd mix of modern and old-fashioned decor. Laid-back staff, comfortable lounges with romantic fireplaces, courtyard, and an excellent restaurant. Rates include breakfast and a pass to the nearby YMCA. Save at least $40, if you share a bath; otherwise $140.

Topaz 1733 N St NW ☏202/393-3000, ⌨www.topazhotel.com. Boutique hotel brings West Coast flash to quiet N Street. Padded headboards with polka dots, lime-green striped wallpaper, and funky furniture add even more spice to the vibrant rooms, several of which also have space for yoga – complete with workout gear and videos – or treadmills, stationary bikes, and elliptical machines. Weekend rates save $20–30, otherwise $230.

Westin Embassy Row 2100 Massachusetts Ave NW ☏202/293-2100 or 1-800/ WESTIN-1, ⌨www.starwood.com/westin. Formerly the *Ritz-Carlton* and then the *Fairfax*, this hotel still caters to clubby politicos, media types, and business people who frequent its *Jockey Club* restaurant. Anglo-French country-house chic, with on-site gym and nice rooms with high-speed Web access. Weekend rates drop to $250, otherwise around $300.

Old Downtown

Grand Hyatt 1000 H St NW ☏202/582-1234 or 1-800/233-1234, ⌨grandwashington.hyatt.com. Nearly 900 rooms, but its location opposite the Convention Center keeps it busy during the week. The twelve-story atrium, lagoon, waterfalls, and glass elevators are a definite highlight, but rooms have also been newly renovated and upgraded and are now properly stylish and modern. Also an on-site deli-café, restaurant, and sports bar. Rate can drop by half on weekends; otherwise $275.

Harrington 1100 E St NW ☎202/628-8140 or 1-800/424-8532, @www .hotel-harrington.com. One of the classic old, clean-and-basic downtown hotels, of which few remain these days, with a prime location near Pennsylvania Ave – though the rooms (singles to quads) are a bit worn around the edges. Still, the prices are tough to beat for the area, plus there's cheap parking. $95.

JW Marriott 1331 Pennsylvania Ave NW ☎202/393-2000 or 1-800/228-9290, @www.marriott.com. Flagship Marriott property in one of the best locations in the city, overlooking Freedom Plaza (ask for a room facing the avenue). Rooms are a notch or two above the standard, plus there are several restaurants, a sports bar, and a health club with indoor pool. $330.

Monaco 700 F St NW ☎202/628-7177, @www.monaco-dc.com. Perhaps the most architecturally significant hotel in the area, opened in 2002 in what was once a grand Neoclassical post office designed by Robert Mills (see p.100). The old offices have been remodeled into ultra-chic accommodation, complete with sleek modern rooms (with busts of Jefferson above the armoires), minimalist contemporary decor, and public spaces with marble floors and columns and grand spiral stairways. Weekend rates can drop to $170; otherwise $250.

Morrison-Clark Inn 1015 L St NW ☎202/898-1200 or 1-800/332-7898, @www.morrisonclark.com. Antique-and-lace accommodation in a historic Victorian mansion complete with veranda, located one block from the new convention center and two from the Metro. Fifty-odd rooms in Victorian and other old-fashioned styles, balconies overlooking a courtyard, a comfortable lounge and a good restaurant. Although the area can get dicey at night, this is still one of Old Downtown's better deals. $150.

Washington 515 15th St NW ☎202/638-5900 or 1-800/424-9540, @www .hotelwashington.com. Good value, historic hotel next to the *Willard* and across from the Treasury Building, with a popular rooftop restaurant-bar, the *Sky Terrace* (see p.114), which boasts one of the city's best views, and heavily decorated Edwardian rooms. It rarely needs to offer discount rates, but off-season weekends when Congress isn't in session can reduce costs by $20 or more. $150.

Willard InterContinental 1401 Pennsylvania Ave NW ☎202/628-9100 or 1-800/327-0200, @www.washington .intercontinental.com. A signature, truly iconic Washington hotel that dominates Pershing Park near the Treasury Building. In business on and off since the 1850s, it's a Beaux Arts marvel with acres of marble, mosaics, and glass; stunning lobby and Promenade; finely furnished rooms; and top-drawer clientele thick with politicos, lobbyists, and other honchos. Weekends around $250, weekdays $450.

Upper Northwest

Days Inn 4400 Connecticut Ave NW ☎202/244-5600 or 1-800/329-7466, @www.daysinn.com. Near the University of DC and a Metro stop, and in reasonable vicinity of Rock Creek Park. Has a colorless, bunker-like exterior, but does offer reasonable, if smallish, rooms with all the usual chain-hotel conveniences. $80.

Marriott Wardman Park 2660 Woodley Rd NW ☎202/328-2000 or 1-800/228-9290, @www.marriott.com. Woodley Park's monumentally historic, celebrity-filled hotel-palace (see p.140) that manages to be the largest hotel in DC (and frequent site of political fund-raisers), with two pools, health club, and restaurants bristling with attentive staff. Very good weekend and off-season discounts (down to $160) make this more affordable than you might think, though convention business keeps rooms full most of the year. $330.

Omni Shoreham 2500 Calvert St NW ☎202/234-0700 or 1-800/843-6664, @www.omnihotels.com. Plush, grand Washington institution (see p.140) bursting with history and overlooking the south chasm of Rock Creek Park. Features include swank, comfortable rooms – which have been recently renovated – many with a view of the park, outdoor pool and tennis courts, and the foliage-filled Garden Court for drinks. $250.

Waterfront

Channel Inn 650 Water St SW ☎202/554-2400 or 1-800/368-5668, @www.channelinn.com. The city's first (and, thus far, only) hotel right on the waterfront, a 1970s development at the Washington Channel, with some rooms looking across to East Potomac Park. There's free parking, an outdoor pool, lounge, and sundeck, plus a choice of serviceable seafood restaurants nearby. $140.

Loews L'Enfant Plaza 480 L'Enfant Plaza SW ☎202/484-1000 or 1-800/235-6397,

🌐www.loewshotels.com. Chic modern hotel, a couple of blocks south of the Mall (and north of the waterfront itself) and with direct access to the Metro. Spacious rooms in nineteenth-century French style (but not retro-tacky), most with river or city views, plus health club and rooftop pool. Special winter and weekend rates apply – inquire ahead. Pet-friendly. $160.

B&Bs

Although Washington DC isn't quite the prime bed-and-breakfast territory you might expect – you'd have to search the hills of Maryland or northern Virginia for that – it does offer a handful of affordable, reasonably elegant spots that provide a relaxing respite for visitors who like to mix with other, historic-minded tourists. No, you won't be able to decamp in Aaron Burr's parlor, but you may be able to grab a bed in a centuries-old house in a classic section of town – just make sure you're not allergic to chintz.

Adams Inn 1744 Lanier Place NW, Adams-Morgan ☎202/745-3600 or 1-800/578-6807, 🌐www.adamsinn.com. Clean, simple rooms in three adjoining Victorian townhouses on a quiet residential street. No TVs, but free breakfast, garden patio, and laundry. Sharing a bath saves you $10; otherwise $95.
Arlington Guesthouse 739 S 22nd St, Arlington, VA ☎703/768-0335, 🌐www .americanguesthouse.com/Arlington.htm. Bare-bones lodging, but some of the cheapest in the area (down to $55 off-season), and near the Pentagon City Metro. Four rooms have single and double beds, with some dorm units – add $10–20 per extra adult. $75.
Bull Moose B&B 101 Fifth St NE, Capitol Hill ☎202/547-1050 or 1-800/261-2768, 🌐www.bullmoose-b-and-b.com. Turreted brick Victorian evokes environmental and

political themes from legendary US president and Bull Moose Party founder Teddy Roosevelt – from tropical Panama to the charge up San Juan Hill. The ten guest rooms (some en suite) lack phones, but phone, fax, and Internet access are all available. Other extras include free continental breakfast, evening sherry, and use of a kitchen. $110.
Dupont at the Circle 1604 19th St NW, Dupont Circle ☎202/332-5251 or 1-888/412-0100, 🌐www .dupontatthecircle.com. Eight handsome rooms – high ceilings, kitchenettes, marble bathrooms – in a Victorian townhouse near the circle (at Q St). Free continental breakfast included; offers higher-priced packages (for $100–400 over room rate) with wine, chocolates, and facials, and names like the "Metrosexual Special." $140.
Hereford House 604 South Carolina Ave SE, Capitol Hill ☎202/543-0102, 🌐www .bbonline.com/dc/hereford. Century-old white, brick townhouse with hardwood floors, small garden, and bright, reasonably sized rooms (no TVs) in residential Capitol Hill, just a block from the Metro. Just four, somewhat cramped rooms (sharing two bathrooms), plus three more (with no breakfast) in a separate house five minutes away (also shared bath). $74.
Kalorama Guest House at Woodley Park 2700 Cathedral Ave NW, Upper Northwest ☎202/328-0860. Agreeable and friendly Victorian charm not far from the Metro in Woodley Park. Two houses (19 rooms, 12 en suite) provide good service and facilities – comfortable brass beds,

free continental breakfast, aperitifs, papers, and coffee. Book well in advance. Rooms with shared bathrooms go for $60, private bathrooms tack on another $20, and suites go for another $30 over that.

Swann House 1808 New Hampshire Ave NW, Dupont Circle ☏202/265-4414, ⊛www.swannhouse.com. Elegant B&B in an 1883 Romanesque Revival mansion with striking red-brick arches, gables, and turrets, a ten-minute walk from both Dupont Circle and Adams-Morgan. There are nine individually decorated rooms – some with working fireplaces – as well as porches and decks for reclining, and a private garden with fountain. Free continental breakfast, afternoon refreshments, and an early-evening sherry to round out the day. $140.

William Lewis House 1309 R St NW, Logan Circle ☏202/462-7574 or 1-800/465-7574, ⊛www.wlewishous.com. Elegantly decorated, gay-friendly B&B set in two century-old townhouses north of Logan Circle (and within blocks of Shaw), with ten antique-filled rooms, all with shared bath. Out

back there's a roomy porch and a hot tub set in a garden. Rates include continental breakfast on weekdays and a full American breakfast on weekends. It's ultra-cheap for what you get, so reservations are essential. $80.

Windsor Inn 1842 16th St NW, Dupont Circle ☏202/667-0300 or 1-800/423-9111. Not too far from the Dupont Circle Metro, with units in twin brick 1920s houses and spacious suites. Ground-floor rooms look onto a terrace; some rooms have fridges. Free continental breakfast, served in the attractive lobby. No on-site parking. $90.

Woodley Park Guest House 2647 Woodley Rd NW, Upper Northwest ☏202/667-0218 or 1-866/667-0218, ⊛www.woodleyparkguesthouse.com. Pleasant guest house on residential Woodley Park side street (opposite the *Marriott*) offering a quiet refuge, with 16 rooms (most en suite), ample parking, and free continental breakfast. It's well located near the Metro, the zoo, and a swath of good restaurants along Connecticut Avenue. Reservations essential. $100.

Hostels

For true budget-seekers DC has a few cheapie options – either actual or de facto hostels – scattered around if you know where to look.

HI-Washington DC 1009 11th St NW, Old Downtown ☏202/737-2333, ⊛www.hiwashingtondc.org. Well-sited main DC hostel near the new Convention Center, with free continental breakfast, high-speed Web access, renovated dorm rooms (male and female), and shared bathrooms. Also offers internships and volunteer opportunities. Members save $3 on daily room rate. $29.

Washington International Student Center 2451 18th St NW, Adams-Morgan ☏202/667-7681 or 1-800/567-4150, ⊛www.washingtondchostel.com. Back-

packers' accommodation in plain multi-bedded dorm rooms, with Internet access, lockers for personal belongings, cable TV, and free pickup from bus and train stations. Downtown DC's cheapest bed, but you may find the cramped surroundings, shared bathrooms, and "traveling" crowd tiresome after a while. Book at least two weeks in advance. $22.

William Penn House 515 E Capitol St SE, Capitol Hill ☏202/543-5560, ⊛www.quaker.org/penn-house. One of the least expensive spots in town, in a prime location just blocks from the Capitol – which is the whole idea. This Quaker-run hostel doesn't require religious observance, but does prefer that guests be active in progressive causes. Dorm rooms hold 4–10 people, breakfast is included; there's no curfew, but also no drugs or booze allowed. Morning services available, if you're interested. $35.

Essentials

Arrival

Those traveling to Washington DC by train or bus arrive at the most central locations: Union Station and the downtown Greyhound terminal, respectively. Union Station is linked by Metro to the city center, as is Reagan National Airport if you're arriving by plane. For Dulles and BWI airports, you can't count on being downtown much within the hour, though the various transfers are smooth enough.

By air

The most convenient destination for domestic arrivals is **National Airport** (DCA; ☎ 703/417-8000, ⓦ www.mwaa .com/national) – officially, Ronald Reagan Washington National Airport – four miles south of downtown in Virginia. It takes thirty minutes to an hour to reach downtown DC by road, though National Airport has its own Metro station, making the subway the clear choice for transit. A taxi downtown costs about $14–17 (including airport surcharge). Another option is SuperShuttle (24hr service; one-way $14; ☎ 1-800/BLUE-VAN), which will drop you wherever you like.

The area's major airport is **Dulles International** (IAD; ☎ 703/572-2700, ⓦ www.mwaa.com/dulles), 26 miles west in northern Virginia. Taxis downtown run $45–55, while SuperShuttle costs $22. It's cheaper to take the Washington Flyer Express bus (every 30min, Mon–Fri 5.45am–10.15pm, Sat & Sun 7.45am–10.15pm; one-way $8, round-trip $14; ⓦ www.washfly.com) to the West Falls Church Metro station, a thirty-minute ride, from where the train ride into DC takes twenty minutes. The most inexpensive option is to take public transit all the way into town: catch Metrobus #5A from the airport, which connects with the Metrorail at the Rosslyn and L'Enfant Plaza Metro stations.

The area's third main airport, **Baltimore-Washington International Airport** (BWI; ☎ 301/261-1000, ⓦ www.bwiairport .com), lies 25 miles northeast of DC. From here, taxis to the city cost about $55, while SuperShuttle vans charge $30–32. It's cheaper to take commuter rail from BWI. (A free shuttle connects the airport with the BWI rail terminal, a 10–15min ride.) The southbound Penn Line of the MARC transit system (every 20–60min, Mon–Fri 4.45am–9.25pm; one-way $6) takes 45 minutes to reach DC's Union Station. Amtrak trains (half-hourly 6.20am–midnight; one-way $13) make the trip in thirty minutes with regular service and a mere twenty with Acela Express ($36).

By train and bus

Union Station, 50 Massachusetts Ave NE, three blocks north of the Capitol, sees **rail arrivals** from all over the country. Trains are operated either by Amtrak (☎ 1-800/872-7245, ⓦ www.amtrak.com) or the Maryland Rail Commuter Service (MARC; ☎ 1-800/325-7245, ⓦ www .mtamaryland.com), which connects DC to Baltimore, BWI Airport, and suburban Maryland. Union Station has a Metro station, a taxi rank, and car rental desks.

Greyhound (☎ 1-800/229-9424 or ☎ 202/289-5154, ⓦ www.greyhound .com) and Peter Pan (☎ 1-800/343-9999, ⓦ www.peterpanbus.com) **buses** stop at the terminal at 1005 1st St NE at L Street, in a fairly unsavory part of town, five long blocks north of Union Station. Take a cab at least as far as Union Station Metro (around $6), or head a block north to the new Metro station at New York Avenue, with an entrance at M Street.

By car

The Capital Beltway encircles the city at a ten-mile radius from the center. It's made up of two separate highways: I-495 on the western half and I-95/I-495 in the east. Approaching the city from the northeast, you need I-95, before turning west on Route 50; that will take you to New York Avenue. From Baltimore there's the direct Baltimore–Washington Parkway, which also joins Route 50. From the south, take I-95 to I-395, which deposits you south of the mall near the waterfront. From the northwest, come in on I-270 until you hit the Beltway, then follow I-495 (east) for Connecticut Avenue south. From the west (Virginia) use I-66, which runs to Constitution Avenue.

City transportation

City transportation in Washington DC is typically excellent: most places downtown are within walking distance of each other, while a good public transit system connects downtown to outlying sights and neighborhoods. The Washington Metropolitan Area Transit Authority (WMATA; ⦿ www.wmata.com) operates a subway system (Metrorail) and a bus network (Metrobus); other options include using taxis or even renting a bike.

The Metro

Washington's Metrorail, or simply "**the Metro**," is quick, cheap, and easy to use (a map of the system appears on the front cover flap of this guide). It runs on five lines that cover most of the downtown areas and suburbs, with the notable exception of Georgetown. Each line is color-coded and studded with various interchange stations. Stations are identified on the surface by name and the letter "M" on top of a brown pylon. Keep in mind that while the system itself may be substantially safe, a few stations are in fearsome neighborhoods, away from the tourist zones.

Operating hours are Monday through Thursday 5.30am to midnight, Friday 5.30am to 3am, Saturday 7am to 3am, and Sunday 7am to midnight. Trains run every five to seven minutes on most lines during rush hours, and every ten to twelve minutes at other times. Pick up a copy of the useful Metro guide (free, available in most stations, or see ⦿ www.wmata.com/metrorail/systemmap.cfm).

Each passenger needs a **farecard**, which must be bought from a machine before you pass through the turnstiles. Fares are based on when and how far you travel, though are usually just $1.20 (one-way, peak or off-peak) if you're traveling around downtown, the Mall, and the Capitol. One-way fares range from $1.20 (base rate) to $3.60; the higher, peak-rate fares are charged Mon–Fri 5.30–9.30am and 3–7pm, otherwise the top fare is $2.20. Children under five ride free, and seniors are admitted for half price.

Farecards work like debit cards – you "put in" an amount of money when you purchase the card, and then the fare is subtracted from your total after each ride. Feed the card through any turnstile marked with a green arrow and then retrieve it; when you do the same thing at the end of your journey, the machine prints out on the card how much fare remains. Passes are also available for one-day ($6) and one-week ($20–30) periods. All passes are available at Metro Center station, many area supermarkets, and online through the WMATA website.

Buses

DC's **buses** operate largely the same hours as the Metro. The base fare for most bus journeys is $1.20, payable to the driver, though surcharges and zone crossings can increase this and express routes will cost you $2.50. The same peak-hour rates apply as on the Metro; rail transfers cover 85¢ of your bus fare. Two good passes to consider are the Daily Pass ($3), which covers all regular routes and reduces express trips by $1.20, and the Weekly Pass ($11), which has the same express-trip reduction and buys seven days' unlimited base-fare trips.

Taxis

Taxis are a useful adjunct to the public transit system, especially in outposts like Georgetown and Adams-Morgan, which aren't on the Metro. Unlike cabs in most American cities, taxis in DC charge fares on a concentric zone basis. Standard rates are posted in each cab; a ride at the **basic rate** within one zone costs $5.50. Most **crosstown fares** run from $5 to $17.20. During rush hours there's a $1 surcharge, and groups may be asked to pay up to $2 for each extra passenger (in addition to the first one).

You can either flag cabs down on the street or use the ranks at hotels and transport terminals. If you call a taxi in advance there's a $2 surcharge. See the Directory under "Taxis" for a list of the most reliable companies. For more information, call the DC Taxicab Commission at ☎202/645-6005.

Driving

It's not worth **driving** in the capital unless you really have to. Traffic jams can be nightmarish, the DC street layout is a grid overlaid with unnerving diagonal boulevards, and without a map it's easy to get lost.

Parking lots and garages charge from $5 per hour to $18 a day and hotels $15–30 per night. Looking for free on-street parking is not likely to pay for itself in terms of time and energy. Should your car get towed, call the DMV at ☎202/727-5000 and expect to pay $100 or more to get it back.

Bikes

True **bicycling** fans will doubtless want to use their two-wheelers more for sport than transit while in the city, and these opportunities are detailed in chapters concerning bike-friendly locales such as Rock Creek Park, the C&O Canal, and along the Potomac. Given the traffic, few visitors will want to brave the DC streets on a bike simply to get around. Bike rental costs a $25–50 a day, or $100–120 a week (depending on the model and company). Bikes are permitted on Metrorail except on weekdays during rush hour and on some holidays.

Bike rental companies

Better Bikes ☎202/293-2080, ⊛www .betterbikesinc.com. 24-hour service that will deliver anywhere in DC and has information on bike trails.
Big Wheel Bikes 1034 33rd St NW, Georgetown ☎202/337-0254; 2 Prince St, Old Town Alexandria, VA ☎703/739-2300; 3119 Lee Hwy, Arlington, VA ☎703/522-1110, ⊛www.bigwheelbikes.com. The Georgetown location is convenient to the C&O Canal and Capital Crescent trails, while the Alexandria location is near the Mount Vernon Trail.
Blazing Saddles 445 11th St NW, Old Down town ☎202/544-0055. Closed Nov–March.

Information and maps

At airports, Union Station, and most hotels, the most useful item to pick up is the free *Washington DC Visitors Guide*, with listings, reviews, and contact numbers. Once in the city, your first stop should be at the **DC Visitor Information Center** (see p.190).

In your travels, you'll likely come across National Park Service rangers – in kiosks on the Mall and at the major memorials – who can field general queries.

One of the most conveniently located ranger sites is the Ellipse Visitor Pavilion (daily 8am–3pm), in front of the White House. National Park Service Headquarters runs an information office (Mon–Fri 9am–5pm, ☎202/208-4747) inside the Department of the Interior, 1849 C St NW, that has information about the city's monuments and memorials.

As far as local **newspapers and magazines** go, look for the weekly *CityPaper* (available in stores, bars, and restaurants), which has listings of entertainment and cultural events; the free monthly *Where: Washington* magazine (from major hotels and terminals); the glossy *Washingtonian* magazine ($3.95 at newsstands and bookstores); and Friday's *Washington Post*.

Tourism offices

Alexandria in the Ramsay House, 221 King St, Alexandria, VA ☎703/838-4200 or 1-800/388-9119, @www.funside.com. Daily 9am–5pm.
Arlington 735 S 18th St, Arlington,

VA ☎703/228-5720 or 1-800/677-6267, @arlingtonvirginiausa.com. Daily 9am–5pm.
DC Visitor Information Center in the Ronald Reagan Building, 1300 Pennsylvania Ave NW ☎1-866/DC-IS-FUN, @www.dcvisit.com. Mon–Fri 8am–5.30pm, Sat & Sun 9am–4pm.
Georgetown 3242 M St NW ☎202/303-1600, @www.georgetowndc.com. Wed–Fri 9am–4.30pm, Sat & Sun 10am–4pm.
White House Visitor Center 1450 Pennsylvania Ave NW ☎202/208-1631, @www.nps.gov/whho/WHVC. Daily 7.30am–4pm.

Maps

The maps in this guide (and on the cover flaps) should suffice for getting around the city and immediate region, but for a more detailed street plan, your best bet is the untearable, weatherproof *Rough Guide to Washington DC Map* ($8.95/Can$13.50/£4.99), which marks on its street plans all the key city sights as well as numerous listings in this guide.

City tours

There are any number of tour operators eager to show you DC's many sights, though with just a little preparation, it's easy to see most things on your own. Still, specialist tours can show you a side of Washington you may not otherwise see, highlighting historic buildings, cultural touchstones, and famous peoples' homes.

Bicycling

Bike the Sites Inc ☎202/842-BIKE, @www.bikethesites.com. Guided bike tours of the city's major sights ($40 and up, including bike and helmet), plus tours of Mount Vernon. Reservations required.

Buses and trolleys

Gold Line/Gray Line ☎1-800/862-1400 or 301/386-8300, @www.martzgroup

.com/GoldLine. Tours in and around DC, including a two-day tour of downtown sights and Mount Vernon ($80), an evening tour ($56), and trips to Colonial Williamsburg and Monticello ($70 each).
Old Town Trolley Tours ☎202/832-9800, @www.historictours.com
/washington. Motorized, board-at-will trolleys covering the main sights ($26 a day), as well as a "Monuments by Moonlight" tour covering the Mall's presidential and war memorials after dark ($28). Tickets available at trolley stops and downtown hotels.
Tourmobile ☎202/554-5100 or 888/868-7707, @www.tourmobile.com. Narrated, open-sided buses allowing unlimited stops at numerous locations (daily 9.30am–4.30pm), with tours of downtown and Arlington Cemetery ($20–30), Mount Vernon ($25), and the Mall by night ($20). Tickets available at the office on the Ellipse, kiosks on the Mall, and on the bus.

Cruises and river trips

Atlantic Kayak Tours ☎703/838-9072 or 1-800/297-0066, ✉www .atlantickayak.com. Kayak tours along the Potomac, including sunset tours exploring the monuments and bridges of Georgetown ($44–54). April–Oct.

Capitol River Cruises ☎1-800/405-5511 or 301/460-7447, ✉www .capitolrivercruises.com. Forty-five-minute sightseeing cruises leaving hourly throughout the day (April–Oct noon–9pm) from Georgetown's Washington Harbor, end of 31st St NW; $10 per person, reservations not necessary.

DC Ducks ☎202/966-3825, ✉www .historictours.com/washington. Converted amphibious carriers cruise the Mall and then splash into the Potomac (90min; $28). Hourly departures from Union Station (March–Oct daily 10am–4pm).

Specialist tours

Duke Ellington's Neighborhood ☎202/636-9203, ✉cestours@aol. com. Four-hour bus tour of the historic U Street/Shaw neighborhood, boyhood home of the jazz legend ($20). Departures monthly May–Aug.

Goodwill Embassy Tour ☎202/636-4225, ✉www.dcgoodwill.org. The second Saturday in May, some of DC's finest embassy buildings throw open their doors (pre-booked $30; $35 on the day). Reserve well in advance.

Kalorama House and Embassy Tour ☎202/387-4062, ext.18. Various ambassadors' residences and private homes open to the public for five hours (often noon-5pm) one day every September;

reserve in advance for $18, or pay $20 day of tour.

SpyDrive ☎866/SPY-TREK, ✉www .spydrive.com. Two-hour tours ($55–60) of spook sites in the "spy capital of the world," led by retired FBI, CIA, and KGB officers.

Walking tours

Anthony S. Pitch ☎301/294-9514, ✉www.dcsightseeing.com. Historical walking tours of Lafayette Square, Georgetown, and Lincoln assassination-related sites, led by the amiable Mr Pitch on Sunday mornings at 11am May–Aug ($15).

Lantern Lights ☎703/548-0100. Old Town in Alexandria, VA, is the setting for this "Ghost and Graveyard Tour," led by guides in costume. Tours ($6; April–Sept Wed, Thurs, & Sun 7.30pm; Fri & Sat 7.30pm & 9pm) depart from the Ramsay House Visitors Center at 221 King St.

Old Town Walking Tour ☎703/838-4200. Tour focusing on the history and architecture of Alexandria's historic district ($10; daily Mon–Sat 10.30am, Sun 2.30pm), departing from the Ramsay House Visitors Center at 221 King St.

Tour DC ☎301/588-8999, ✉www .tourdc.com. Walking tours covering various aspects of life among the elite, including important women at Tudor Place, the haunts of the Kennedys, World War II subterfuge on Embassy Row, and Georgetown history and cemetery tours. Saturday tours $15–17 per person; reserve in advance.

Washington Walks ☎202/484-1565, ✉www.washingtonwalks.com. Two-hour walks through downtown DC, with colorful themes such as "Washington Sleeps Here," "Best Addresses," "Most Haunted Houses," and so on (all tours $10 for adults, $5 kids).

Phones, mail, and email

Washington DC is served by the 202 **area code**; you do not need to dial the area code when calling within the District. Calls within the greater DC metropolitan area are counted as local even if they require a different code (703 for northern Virginia, or 301 for parts of Maryland, for example).

To **call internationally**: dial 011 + country code + number, minus the initial 0. Country codes are as follows: Australia (61), Canada (1), Ireland (353), New Zealand (64), and the UK and Northern Ireland (44).

As for **mail,** international mail between the US and Europe generally takes about a week. Airmail letters weighing up to an ounce cost 80¢; postcards and aerogrammes 70¢.

Email addicts will realize shortly after arrival that the city lacks any real cybercafé culture. Options include Kinko's/FedEx branches or one of the handful of other spots offering Internet service – see "Directory," p.193.

Festivals and holidays

Washington has a huge variety of annual festivals and events, many of them national in scope: America's Christmas Tree is lit each December on the Ellipse, and the grandest Fourth of July Parade in the country takes place along the Mall.

George Washington's Birthday

February 22 ☎703/838-9350. Spectacular parade as well as other events in Old Town Alexandria, VA. Also, events, concerts and wreath-laying at Mount Vernon (☎703/780-2000).

St Patrick's Day

March 17. St Patrick's Day sees a big parade down Constitution Avenue NW on the Sunday before the 17th (call ☎202/637-2474 for grandstand seats) and another through Old Town Alexandria on the first Saturday of the month (☎703/237-2199).

Cherry Blossom Festival

Late March/early April ⊛www .nationalcherryblossomfestival.org. The famous trees around the Tidal Basin (see p.52), which bloom each spring, are celebrated by a massive parade down Constitution Avenue NW, the crowning of a festival queen, free concerts, lantern-lighting, dances, and races. (Parade ticket information ☎202/728-1137; other events ☎202/547-1500.)

Easter

Early April. On Easter Sunday, a sunrise service is held at Arlington National Cemetery (☎703/695-3250 or 202/685-2851), while on Easter Monday the White House hosts its Easter Egg Roll, with entertainment and egg rolling on the South Lawn. Call well in advance (☎202/456-2200, ⊛www.whitehouse.gov).

Smithsonian Festival of American Folklife

Late June to early July ☎202/357-2700. One of the country's biggest festivals: American music, crafts, food, and folk heritage events on the Mall.

Independence Day

July 4 ☎202/619-7222. A host of events, including a reading of the Declaration of Independence at the National Archives, a parade along Constitution Avenue NW, free concerts at the Sylvan Theatre near the Washington Monument, a performance by the National Symphony Orchestra on the west steps of the Capitol, and finishing with a superb fireworks display.

Adams-Morgan Day

First Sun after Labor Day (early Sept) ☎202/789-7000, ⊛www .adamsmorganday.org. One of the best of the neighborhood festivals, with live music, crafts, and cuisine along 18th Street NW – always packed and great fun.

Halloween

October 31. Unofficial block parties, costumed antics, and fright-nights in Georgetown, Dupont Circle, and other neighborhoods.

Christmas

Events throughout December. Separate early December ceremonies for the lighting of the Capitol and National (Ellipse) Christmas trees – the latter lit by the president (☎202/619-7222). Services are held all month at Washington National Cathedral, with carols, pageants, choral performances, and bell-ringing. (☎202/537-6200, ⊛www .cathedral.org/cathedral). Rounding out the holiday, the White House hosts its candlelight tours, usually held December 26–28. (Call well in advance for reservations ☎202/456-2200 or 619-7222, ⊛www.whitehouse.gov).

Directory

Addresses The US Capitol – which itself doesn't have an address – is the center of the District's street-numbering system, and the four quadrants of the city (NW, SW, SE, NE) relate to their position respective of the building. North and South Capitol Street divide the city by east and west, and the National Mall and East Capitol Street divide it by north and south.

Doctors and dentists For a doctor referral service call Washington Hospital Center ☎202/877-3627 or George Washington University Hospital ☎1-888/449-3627. Contact the DC Dental Society ☎202/547-7615 for dentist referral.

Electricity 110 volts AC. Plugs are standard two-pins – foreign visitors will need an adaptor and voltage converter for their own appliances.

Embassies and consulates Australia: 1601 Massachusetts Ave NW ☎202/797-3000, ⊛www.austemb.org; Canada: 501 Pennsylvania Ave NW ☎202/682-1740, ⊛www.canadianembassy.org; Ireland: 2234 Massachusetts Ave NW ☎202/462-3939, ⊛www.irelandemb.org; New Zealand: 37 Observatory Circle NW ☎202/328-4800, ⊛www.nzembassy.com; United Kingdom: 3100 Massachusetts Ave NW ☎202/588-6500, ⊛www.britainusa.com.

Emergencies ☎911.

Hospital George Washington University Hospital, 901 23rd St NW (☎202/715-4000, general patient information), has a 24hr emergency department (☎202/715-4911).

Internet access Available at *Cyberlaptops.com*, 1636 R St NW, Dupont Circle ☎202/462-7195, ⊛www.cyberlaptops.com; *Cyberstop Café*, 1513 17th St NW, Dupont Circle (closes midnight) ☎202/234-2470, ⊛www.cyberstopcafe.com; FedEx Kinko's, 325 7th St, Old Downtown (24hr) ☎202/544-4796, ⊛www.kinkos.com; 715 D St SE, Capitol Hill (24hr) ☎202/547-0421; 1612 K St NW, New Downtown ☎202/466-

3777; 3329 M St NW, Georgetown ☎202/965-1415; and The Newsroom, 1803 Connecticut Ave NW, Dupont Circle ☎202/332-1489.

Pharmacies 24hr CVS stores at 1199 Vermont Ave NW, New Downtown ☎202/737-3962; 7 Dupont Circle ☎202/833-5704; and 4555 Wisconsin Ave, Upper Northwest ☎202/537-1459.

Police In an emergency call ☎911. For non-emergency help, information, and the location of police stations call ☎202/727-1010. The Metro Transit Police can be contacted at ☎202/962-2121.

Post offices and mail services DC's main downtown post office is across from Union Station at 2 Massachusetts Ave NE, 20002 (Mon–Fri 7am–midnight, Sat & Sun 7am–8pm; ☎202/523-2368). There are also convenient branches at 1800 M St NW, New Downtown, 20036 (Mon–Fri 9am–5pm; ☎202/523-2506), and 1200 Pennsylvania Ave NW, 20004 (Mon–Fri 7.30am–5.30pm, Sat 8am–12.30pm; ☎202/842-1444).

Tax DC sales tax is 5.75 percent; restaurant tax, 10 percent; hotel tax, 14.5 percent.

Taxis Capitol Cab ☎202/546-2400, Diamond Cab ☎202/387-6200, Yellow Cab ☎202/544-1212. Information at ⊛dctaxi.dc.gov.

Time Washington DC is on Eastern Standard Time, five hours behind Greenwich Mean Time. Daylight saving time, when clocks are turned forward an hour, operates between April and October.

Travelers aid society Useful help, emergency, and information desks run by a voluntary, nonprofit agency (⊛www.travelersaid.org). Main office is at Union Station (Mon–Sat 9.30am–5.30pm, Sun 12.30–5.30pm; ☎202/371-1937); other offices at National Airport (Mon–Fri 9am–9pm, Sat & Sun 9am–6pm; ☎703/417-3972) and Dulles Airport (Mon–Fri 8am–9pm, Sat & Sun 8am–7pm; ☎703/572-8296).

ROUGH GUIDES TRAVEL...

Rough Guides are available from good bookstores worldwide. New titles are published every month. Check www.roughguides.com for the latest news.

...MUSIC & REFERENCE

Also! More than 120 Rough Guide music CDs are available from all good book and record stores. Listen in at www.worldmusic.net

ROUGH GUIDE MAPS

Printed on waterproof and rip-proof Polyart™
paper, offering an unbeatable combination of
practicality, clarity of design and amazing value.

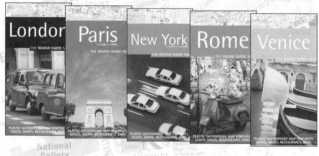

ROUGH GUIDES
REFERENCE SERIES

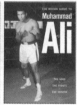

DON'T JUST TRAVEL!

Index & small print

A Rough Guide to Rough Guides

Washington DC DIRECTIONS is published by Rough Guides. The first *Rough Guide to Greece*, published in 1982, was a student scheme that became a publishing phenomenon. The immediate success of the book – with numerous reprints and a Thomas Cook Prize short-listing – spawned a series that rapidly covered dozens of destinations. Rough Guides had a ready market among low-budget backpackers, but soon also acquired a much broader and older readership that relished Rough Guides' wit and inquisitiveness as much as their enthusiastic, critical approach. Everyone wants value for money, but not at any price. Rough Guides soon began supplementing the "rougher" information about hostels and low-budget listings with the kind of detail on restaurants and quality hotels that independent-minded visitors on any budget might expect, whether on business in New York or trekking in Thailand. These days the guides offer recommendations from shoestring to luxury and cover a large number of destinations around the globe, including almost every country in the Americas and Europe, more than half of Africa and most of Asia and Australasia. Rough Guides now publish:

- Travel guides to more than 200 worldwide destinations
- Dictionary phrasebooks to 22 major languages
- Maps printed on rip-proof and waterproof Polyart™ paper
- Music guides running the gamut from Opera to Elvis
- Reference books on topics as diverse as the Weather and Shakespeare
- World Music CDs in association with World Music Network

Publishing information

This 1st edition published April 2005 by
Rough Guides Ltd, 80 Strand, London WC2R 0RL.
345 Hudson St, 4th Floor, New York, NY 10014, USA.

Distributed by the Penguin Group

Penguin Books Ltd, 80 Strand, London WC2R 0RL
Penguin Group (USA), 375 Hudson Street, NY 10014, USA
Penguin Group (Australia), 250 Camberwell Road, Camberwell, Victoria 3124, Australia
Penguin Group (Canada), 10 Alcorn Avenue, Toronto, ON M4V 1E4, Canada
Penguin Group (New Zealand), Cnr Rosedale and Airborne Roads, Albany, Auckland, New Zealand
Typeset in Bembo and Helvetica to an original design by Henry Iles.
Printed and bound in China by Leo

© Jules Brown and JD Dickey April 2005

No part of this book may be reproduced in any form without permission from the publisher except for the quotation of brief passages in reviews.
208pp includes index

A catalogue record for this book is available from the British Library

ISBN 1-84353-394-4

The publishers and authors have done their best to ensure the accuracy and currency of all the information in **Washington DC DIRECTIONS**, however, they can accept no responsibility for any loss, injury, or inconvenience sustained by any traveller as a result of information or advice contained in the guide.

1   3   5   7   9   8   6   4   2

Help us update

We've gone to a lot of effort to ensure that the first edition of **Washington DC DIRECTIONS** is accurate and up-to-date. However, things change – places get "discovered," opening hours are notoriously fickle, restaurants and rooms raise prices or lower standards. If you feel we've got it wrong or left something out, we'd like to know, and if you can remember the address, price, the phone number, so much the better.
We'll credit all contributions, and send a copy of the next edition (or any other DIRECTIONS guide or Rough Guide if you prefer) for the best letters.

Everyone who writes to us and isn't already a subscriber will receive a copy of our full-color thrice-yearly newsletter. Please mark letters:
"**Washington DC DIRECTIONS Update**" and send to: Rough Guides, 80 Strand, London WC2R 0RL, or Rough Guides, 4th Floor, 345 Hudson St, New York, NY 10014. Or send an email to
mail@roughguides.com
Have your questions answered and tell others about your trip at **www.roughguides.atinfopop.com**

SMALL PRINT

Rough Guide credits

Text editors: Jeff Cranmer, Hunter Slaton
Layout: Dan May
Photography: Angus Oborn
Cartography: Jai Prakash Mishra, Miles Irving
Picture editor: Jj Luck, Harriet Mills

Proofreader: Margaret Doyle
Production: Julia Bovis
Design: Henry Iles
Cover design: Chloë Roberts

The authors

JD Dickey has contributed to eight different Rough Guides, including Washington DC, Los Angeles, Seattle, the Pacific Northwest, and California. He makes his home on the West Coast, but enjoys traveling with much vigor and gusto, and is a rabid consumer of news, culture, history, and folly.

Jules Brown has written and researched Rough Guides to Sicily, Barcelona, England's Lake District, and numerous other titles.

Acknowledgments

JD would foremost like to thank his editor Jeff Cranmer, who contributed much skill, energy, and panache to this book, and Andrew Rosenberg, who oversaw the Washington DC project with steely eyes and a velvet touch. Thanks also are due to JD's wife and family, his travel contacts and coordinators in Washington, Jj Luck and Harriet Mills for photo research, Dan May for typesetting, Margaret Doyle for proofreading, all the cartographers in London and Delhi who contributed to making the maps, and Hunter Slaton for first rolling the mighty Neoclassical stones of this volume.

Photo credits

All images © Rough Guides except the following:

p.1 Bird perched on sign © James Leynse/Corbis
p.2 Supreme Court © Dennis Degan/Corbis
p.5 Cherry blossoms near Jefferson Memorial © Marc Nomura/Reuters/Corbis
p.5 National Museum of the American Indian © Molly Riley/Reuters/Corbis
p.6 Francis Scott Key Memorial Bridge © Joel W. Rogers/Corbis
p.7 View down the Mall © Charles O'Rear/Corbis
p.7 Dupont Circle © Dcstockphoto.com/Alamy
p.7 Capitol Building rotunda © Royalty-free/Corbis
p.8 Row Houses in Georgetown © Bruce Burkhardt/Corbis
p.8 Adams-Morgan © Kelly-Mooney Photography/Corbis
p.16 Rock Creek Park © Richard T. Nowitz/Corbis
p.32 Celebration of George Washington's Birthday © Richard T. Nowitz/Corbis
p.33 Smithsonian Folklife Festival © Richard T. Nowitz/Corbis

p.33 Easter egg race on the White House Lawn © Bettmann/Corbis
p.42 Clyde's © Ron Blunt Photography
p.45 Jogger with cherry blossoms © David Brooks/Corbis
p.45 Buffalo Sabres in game against Washington Capitals © Wally McNamee/Corbis
p.48 East garden of the White House © Jason Reed/Reuters/Corbis
p.71 National Statuary Hall © Michael Freeman/Corbis
p.98 Kinkead's © C.W. Kelly III of Kinkead's
p.104 Close-up of the United States Constitution © Joe Sohm/Alamy
p.126 Kramerbook's Afterwords Bookstore © James Leynse/Corbis
p.144 Peirce Mill, Rock Creek Park © Giles Stokoe/Dorling Kindersley
p.165 Old Town Alexandria © Walter Bibikow/Alamy

Index

Maps are marked in **color**

INDEX

206

INDEX